BREVIG

MISSION

PLAGUE

BREVIG MISSION PLAGUE

FRANK SIMON

BARBOUR
PUBLISHING

Published by Barbour Publishing, Inc., P.O. Box 719, Uhrichsville, OH 44683, www.barbourpublishing.com

Our mission is to publish and distribute inspirational products offering exceptional value and biblical encouragement to the masses.

 Member of the
Evangelical Christian
Publishers Association

Printed in the United States of America.
5 4 3 2 1

For Bill Plate

ACKNOWLEDGMENTS

I want to thank the people who helped make this book possible:

My wife, LaVerne, first editor and my sweet helpmeet;
James Cain for his editorial assistance;
Dr. Richard Voet for his help in understanding
the pathology of viruses and vaccines;
Bill Crouse for his help in researching the varying faces
of radical Islamic terrorism;
Carl Hammert and Tom McCullough for sharing
their knowledge of things aeronautical;
My friend and agent, Les Stobbe.

PROLOGUE

Large raindrops thumped against the umbrella's taut, black fabric, ran down the sodden panels, then dropped to the slick sidewalk, where they splashed up on a pair of shoes and cuffs. The tall man huddled beneath this feeble shelter frowned, and an involuntary shiver passed over him. He wasn't drenched yet, only thoroughly damp and chilled, which reflected his mood on this gray and dreary September day. The man had a wiry build and obviously believed in exercising. Behind him the dull rumble of distant traffic carried clearly from the main road leading into Cambridge, England, from the north; but the side street the man hurried along was almost deserted, exactly as he had hoped.

He crossed over and passed between two cars parked close together, dropping his newspaper as he did. A quick flick of his eyes reassured him that no one had observed this act of littering. He chided himself on the unnecessary risk, but he was anxious to be rid of the paper, purchased to pass the time during the long bus ride. It seemed every page carried a story about the recent wedding of Prince Charles and the oh-so-photogenic Lady Diana Spencer, now Her Royal Highness, the Princess of Wales. He gritted his teeth as sullen anger simmered deep inside him. After all, the world *didn't* revolve around the royals, or Britain, or the West for that matter, and *someday* the infidels would come to realize that.

The man turned the corner and tilted his umbrella up so he could see his destination. Cars lined each side of the narrow street, taking up every available parking space. Two long rows of identical apartment blocks marched along, coming right up to the sidewalks. The only hint of green came from the tiny park where the street ended. The man spotted the building he was looking for and smiled. His face twinged a little, even though the plastic surgeon had assured him it was completely healed. A sudden gust jerked at the umbrella, nearly turning it inside out. The man gripped the handle harder and dipped the flimsy canopy into the wind.

Almost there.

He rushed up the steps and collapsed the umbrella then pulled open the outside door and stomped inside. He looked all around to make sure he was alone. The wind moaned, and the rain pecked at the dirty foyer windows, but there was no sign of life. He exhaled slowly then walked up to a door that was just like the other three on the ground floor except that behind this one was his enemy; only the man inside did not realize it.

The visitor raised a brown hand, hesitated, then rapped on the door with measured force. He waited as the moments slipped slowly by. Something rattled inside, then the deadbolt retracted with a solid, metallic *thump*. The door swung open, revealing a man whose expression shifted quickly from query to puzzled amazement. The visitor looked into the dark brown eyes and smiled as he wondered how it felt to be facing one's anonymous double, complete down to the shaggy brown hair and wide mustache.

"Who are you?" the man finally managed to murmur, barely above a whisper.

The visitor didn't reply, savoring the moment he had waited years for. It had been a long, long wait, but now it was finally over.

The man's puzzled expression melted into fear. "What is the meaning of this?" He tried to shut the door, but the intruder prevented that with his shoe. "Go away! I'll call the police!"

The intruder shoved his way inside and carefully shut the door. "No, you won't," he said, his voice low and menacing.

The man's eyes grew round and stood out. "Wait a minute! You're. . ."

But he never got to finish. The assailant jerked a 9mm silenced automatic out of his shoulder holster and fired two quick shots. One drilled a neat hole in the center of the victim's forehead, and the other passed through his heart. He was dead before his relaxing muscles dropped him to the carpeted floor in a heap.

The assailant holstered his gun and dragged the body into the tiled kitchen. He stood there a few moments, his eyes tracing the broad trail of blood. He sighed. Cleaning this up would be difficult, but it had to be done. Then there was the disposal of the body. But all these tasks had been carefully worked out over the last few years, and the man had no doubts that his plans would succeed.

He began opening cabinets, looking for cleaning supplies, but he was in no hurry. The apartment was his now, and there was much yet to accomplish. And accomplish these tasks he would.

CHAPTER 1

Gary Nesbitt's smile said it all, although his blue eyes, hidden behind his sunglasses, were all but invisible. His sandy blond hair streamed along behind him as he cruised down Devonshire in his red Mustang convertible, his speed a little above the limit, but he was far from the fastest driver out today. An early morning shower had swept away the smog, and the gentle breeze wafting over the Santa Monica Mountains was keeping the San Fernando Valley clear, at least so far. Under a deep blue, cloudless sky, the tawny mountains, which surrounded the valley on three sides, were clearly visible for a change. Gary sighed. Up ahead he spotted the entrance to the run-down office park, which marked the end of this extraordinary Monday commute and the start of his business week at Security-Check, Inc., the company that he and John Mason owned. September 13 was about to get under way.

Gary glanced in his rearview mirror, whipped into the right lane, and flicked on his turn signals. He downshifted to third gear and finally to second, kicking the V8's muted rumble up to a healthy reverberating roar. He cranked the wheel over, zipped through the drive, and maneuvered the nimble car around all the speed bumps he could and endured the jounces from the ones he couldn't. Reaching the last office block, he pulled in beside John's gray Toyota Camry, set the emergency brake, and turned off the ignition. He sat motionless for a few moments, savoring the unusually clean air. Then, unable to delay any longer, he put up the top, grabbed his briefcase, and stepped out. He stretched his long legs and twisted his slim torso, trying to relieve the stiffness. He had skipped his morning workout, and it felt like it. He thumbed the car remote. The door locks thumped, and a short whistle announced the arming of the alarm system.

Gary walked across the parking lot and along the sidewalk. He paused at the door to admire the sign, which proclaimed SECURITY-CHECK, INC. in flowing, futuristic white letters on a blue background. He and John had considered moving to new quarters after the company's involvement in what the media had dubbed "the Crown Jewels Heist." Almost a year and a half ago, they had audited the Tower of London's security systems for MI5 only to become embroiled in a caper involving the theft of the queen consort's crown. Although that operation had been the most profitable to date, the two men had decided their improved circumstances did not warrant a change of venue. In this, Gary mused, they had been wise, since their subsequent projects, while keeping them busy, had not covered expenses, and the drain on the company bank account was beginning to get critical.

Gary finally opened the door and walked inside. He removed his sunglasses, stuffed them in his shirt pocket, and started across the compact reception area. "Morning, Rose," he said as he neared her desk. "How was your weekend?"

Rose Gibson looked up from her computer monitor. With her short, stocky figure, she made a formidable impression on visitors. At forty-five, she was the oldest employee by over ten years but didn't look it because she used her cosmetics to best advantage. She smiled at Gary, but the way she grabbed a file folder let him know that escaping to his office was out of the question.

"Okay, I guess," she said. "I spent most of my Saturday here, trying to catch up on all our accounting entries." She nodded toward the monitor and frowned. "The new HR programs keep saying the employee records are out of balance, but I can't figure out how to fix them. Listen, the old system worked just fine. I don't see why we had to change."

Gary laughed nervously, since he was well aware of her dissatisfaction. "The short answer is: The new system is better, plus it makes our California and federal reporting easier."

"Gary. What about all these problems?" She absentmindedly smoothed her bright red hair.

"Call the customer support number."

Her brown eyes flashed. "They always talk in gobbledygook. Makes me feel like a *complete* idiot."

The front door opened, but Gary didn't dare look around. He shrugged. "Well, why not have Ann call them? They sure can't snow her."

"What exactly are you volunteering me for?" a voice behind him asked.

Gary turned and saw it was Ann O'Brien, SecurityCheck's resident hacker. Moderately tall with a willowy figure, she constrasted sharply with Rose. Ann smiled, and her blue eyes twinkled. She tucked an errant strand of long brunette hair behind her ear.

"The accounting and HR system is giving Rose fits," Gary explained. "Looks like a job for Cyberwoman, that is, if you can work it into your busy schedule."

Ann laughed. "I think I can manage." She turned to Rose. "Let me grab some coffee, and I'll be right back."

Rose smiled in obvious relief. "Thanks, I appreciate it."

Ann hurried down the corridor to her office and disappeared inside.

"May I go now?" Gary asked.

Rose swatted at him with the file folder, but he dodged. "Yes, but don't disappear on me. I need you to sign some proposals so I can put them in the mail."

Gary's grin faded on the short walk back to his office. He knew the proposals she was referring to, but even if they *all* went through, it wouldn't do much more than put a dent in the company's over-head. What SecurityCheck *really* needed was a big, juicy contract.

He tried to ignore the shabbiness all around him, but somehow it seemed to echo the company's less than robust finances. Gary's eyes took in the dingy beige walls, the water-stained ceiling tiles, and the well-worn and faded carpet that had once been dark blue. The only semi-recent renovation was the white vinyl tile floor in the back workshop, now a little more than two years old. Gary con-soled himself with the knowledge that the company payroll came before routine maintenance. But still, he was concerned about the impression it could make on potential clients.

A smiling black face with close-cropped black hair and lively brown eyes popped out of the workshop's doorway. "Brother Gary," John Mason said, making a show of looking at his watch. "Nice of you to drop in. I hope our work schedule isn't a burden on you." Besides being the co-owners, John and his wife, Sarah, attended the same church as Gary.

His friend's cheerfulness lifted Gary's spirits. "Good morning to *you*, Brother John. In early to play with your gadgets?"

"Just doing my job."

A wry smile came to Gary's face. "Meaning I'm not." He held up his hand to stop John's reply. "If you're not too busy, we need to talk."

John's expression became serious. "Sure. Want some coffee?"

"Yeah. I'll grab my mug."

Gary entered his office and placed his briefcase on the corner of his desk. Then he looked all around but didn't see his mug. He frowned then hurried to the break room across from the workshop. John was holding the coffeepot.

"Where's your mug?" he asked.

Gary walked to the dishwasher, opened the door, and pulled out the upper rack. "*Aha*," he said, grabbing a blue mug that displayed the company name in white lettering. "The sanitation police made a raid over the weekend."

When they returned to Gary's office, John picked a chair at the round conference table and settled his large, athletic frame into it. Gary sat next to him, leaned back in his chair, and took a long sip of coffee. It was hot and had plenty of authority. "That ought to keep the eyes open," he said.

"Yes, indeed." John's expression became serious. "So what's the problem, as if I didn't know?"

"Yeah, it's kinda obvious, isn't it?" Gary paused. "I've been going over the books, and it isn't a pretty picture."

"How bad is it?"

Gary shrugged. "We're not covering overhead, so our cash reserve is leaking out slowly but surely."

"What can we do about it?"

"Beat the bushes for new business, and we *have* to be more careful in our bidding. We've been *way* too optimistic, so most of these dinky little jobs end up being leeches." He paused and absentmindedly played with his coffee mug. "You know, it would help a lot if we could land a big project. That's what we *really* need."

"What's the bottom line?"

"We lost over ten thousand last year, despite the Tower of London job, and year-to-date, we're minus six thou' or so. The home team's not looking too good."

"How long can this go on?"

Gary took a long sip of coffee as he thought that over then set the mug down deliberately. "A little more than a year, assuming we pay more attention to our expenses, which is one of the reasons I wanted to have this talk. You and Dan need to cut back on equipment purchases. Next to payroll, that's our heaviest expense."

John frowned. "But we *have* to have security equipment to do our work. I mean, it's our stock-in-trade."

"Take it easy. Just try to be more frugal; that's all I ask. I'll be talking to Dan about it, too."

"He won't like it, either."

"I know. Since we're talking about it, what *are* we looking at in hardware purchases?"

"Oh, couple a hundred dollars or so. We're almost done with the Cal State Northridge project, and I have most of what I need for the rest of our jobs."

"That's good news, I guess." Gary settled back in his chair and stared off into space as he thought of the proposals he would sign today. They would go out in the afternoon mail and probably all be rejected, and if one *did* come through, it would probably turn out unprofitable.

Gary heard a sound in the corridor and looked around. Ann was standing at the door.

"Excuse me," she said, holding up a sheet of paper. "I jotted down Rose's questions. Some of the problems I can fix, but I'll have to call tech support for the rest. Rose said you have our customer number."

"Oh, yeah," Gary said. "Come on in and sit down while I look for it." He got up, walked around his desk, and opened a file drawer in the credenza. He thumbed through the folders until he found the right one. He pulled it out and returned to the table. "Here," he said as he sat down. "Give it to Rose when you're done. It needs to be in with her vendor files."

"Will do." She started to get up.

Gary hesitated then said, "Don't go. There's something you need to know. John and I were discussing current business, or rather the lack thereof." He paused. "We haven't exactly been swimming in profit since our one and only international project. And that job, and the survival of SecurityCheck to this point, is thanks to you."

She blushed. "I'm glad it worked out, but I'm sorry about all we had to go through. Look, I don't mean to be nosy, but I know you guys are having a hard time. I'm praying for the business."

"Thanks," John said. "Please keep it up."

Ann pushed back from the table and picked up the folder. "I will. Now for my tête-à-tête with tech support."

Gary grinned. "Be nice."

"Oh, I will, as long as they give me what I want." She hurried out.

The sound of the front door opening drifted in. A few moments later, a tall man with a medium build and slicked-down brown hair walked past, obviously in no hurry.

"Dan!" Gary called out.

Dan Thompson appeared in the doorway. His brown eyes seemed to hide behind the thick lenses of his heavy glasses. He pushed them up on the bridge of his nose, but they immediately slid back down. "Yes?" he said.

"Got a few minutes?" Gary asked.

"Sure." He came over to the table and sat down.

"John and I were going over current projects. What's the status on your Cal State Northridge work?"

"I have all the data I need. Their communications network is about average for a state institution; moderately secure, however they do have a few glaring holes. A serious hacker could do some *real* damage. I'm working on my recommendations now."

"Good. Any more expenses?"

He shook his head. "Not for them and not much overall. Why?"

"We're trying to watch expenses. Our work for the past year or so hasn't been profitable."

"I figured as much. I only buy what's necessary, you know."

Gary noted the hint of defensiveness. "I know, and John and I appreciate all your good work. SecurityCheck couldn't survive without you."

Dan nodded, and a tentative smile appeared. "Thanks. It's nice to be appreciated. Anything else?"

"No, that's it."

Dan pushed back from the table, got up, and walked out.

"What do you have on tap for today?" Gary asked John.

He shrugged. "Nothing much. I'll probably spend the day checking things. You know, replace batteries, empty out the bit buckets, stuff like that."

"Sounds exciting. Call me if you need any help."

John laughed as he got up. "You'll be the first to know."

As he had promised, Gary signed the three proposals around eleven while Rose waited impatiently to scoop them up. After that came a quiet lunch with John and Ann at a Pizza Inn on Reseda Boulevard. He had invited Dan, but the communications expert had begged off, saying he had to double-check a microwave link at the college. Rose, as usual, assumed command of Security-Check until their return.

When they returned around one o'clock, Gary led the way through the front door. He walked up to Rose's desk and handed her a paper bag while John and Ann continued to the back.

"Any calls?" Gary asked.

"Only telepests." She reached into the sack and pulled out a square plastic container and a large paper cup with a lid on it.

"Chicken salad and Diet Coke, right?"

19

She looked down and smiled. "Right. Thanks, Gary."

"You're welcome. If you need me, I'll be in my office."

"I know how to find you," she replied without looking up. She opened the salad container, applied a liberal amount of honey mustard dressing, and mixed it with the plastic fork.

Gary hurried off to his office. Rose *was* quite adept at finding people. She had been with SecurityCheck for over three years now, at first part-time as their bookkeeper then coming on full-time after the Tower of London job.

Gary sat in his executive swivel chair and turned away from his desk to face his computer monitor and keyboard, which sat on the top of his credenza. He activated his Outlook program and saw he had no e-mails, not even spam, thanks to Ann's spambot, which lurked on the network server. Gary smiled in spite of his business worries. The spambot and a few dozen other security applications provided extra income for the company; not enough to staunch the red ink, but every little bit helped.

Gary jumped at a sudden electronic warble. He turned around and looked at his speakerphone as if he couldn't believe he was actually getting a call. He knew from the flashing light that Rose had taken it because it wasn't his direct line. He hesitated then reached over and picked up the handset.

"Yes, Rose?" he said.

"You have a call from a Thomas Brooks; says he's with the department of the army in Washington, D.C., and you'd know what it was about. Says it's *very* urgent."

Gary took a deep breath. "Thanks, Rose. Put him on."

The line clicked. "Hello, Thomas, this is Gary. How are you?"

"Busy as a bureaucrat with a fresh roll of red tape. How are things in sunny California?"

"Oh, same as always, I guess. Hollywood keeps churning out dreams while the rest of us are stuck with reality."

Thomas laughed. "Washington is guilty of that sometimes; dealing in dreams, that is. By the way, that was *some* caper you guys pulled off in England."

Gary's mind flitted over what had been almost unbearable at the time. "It was the worst experience I have ever had."

"But it worked out all right. I'm really impressed."

"Thanks, but it was God's answer to our prayers that brought us through it. Without that, we'd be in some prison in England or worse."

The line remained silent for a moment. "Well, whatever floats your boat, as the saying goes." Again he paused. "Are you guys real busy right now?"

Gary felt a sudden jolt of anticipation. "Talk to me," he said.

"Remember the Fort Knox security audit that GAO yanked out from under us and gave to the army?"

"How could I forget?"

"Right. Well, the army flunked—big-time—big fat zero. So GAO says to get someone else to do it, like right now. You guys interested?"

Gary sent up an arrow prayer. "I'll have to check with John— John Mason—but I'm sure the answer will be 'yes.'" He grabbed a pad and started making notes. "Listen, we'll get our heads together, and I'll e-mail you a proposal sometime tomorrow."

"Would it be any different from what we discussed last year?"

"Uh, no, I'm sure it would be essentially the same."

"Good. Now I have to move fast on this. I'm meeting with my boss tomorrow morning, so can you e-mail me the proposal today?"

Gary hesitated only a moment because he was positive John would agree. "Sure, I'll do it right after we hang up."

"Great, and I'll e-mail you the contract. The only changes will be adjustments for inflation. Are we agreed?"

"Sure, and thank you for remembering us."

"No, I thank you. Hey, I felt real bad about what happened. I always believed that SecurityCheck should have done the audit, and what you guys did in England proved it, as far as I'm concerned. I'll give you a call tomorrow to confirm everything, and we can work out the schedule then."

"Okay. I'll look forward to your call, Thomas."

"Right. Bye."

Gary slowly replaced the telephone handset. Then he picked it up again and punched in John's extension. John answered on the second ring.

Gary smiled. "Brother John. Get yourself in here. We have some serious things to discuss."

CHAPTER 2

It was a little after three in the afternoon when John took the Cahuenga Boulevard exit off the Hollywood Freeway. Gary sat beside him, still aggravated because he hadn't been able to reach Sean Sullivan. Sully usually wasn't hard to find, but Gary had tried his mobile phone and apartment, reaching his voice mail and answering machine, respectively. In desperation Gary had Dan query Sully's custom pager, which had a GPS repeater, but all that revealed was that Sully had left it in his apartment. It wasn't until Ann performed an Internet power search that Sully's whereabouts were at last discovered: He was a stuntman on an independent film. A quick call to the producer's office revealed that the film crew would be shooting at the Rancho La Brea tar pits that day.

Gary saw Hollywood Boulevard sweep past out of the corner of his eye as he turned to face Ann. "You're *sure* they're at pit ninety-one?" he asked. "I don't want to be driving all over L.A."

"I got it directly from the producer's executive assistant."

Dan, seated beside Ann, looked up from his portable communications analyzer. "What's the movie about?" he asked.

Ann rolled her eyes. "You don't want to know."

"Yeah, we do," John said. "We have to keep up with Sully's career, don't we?"

"Okay, if you insist. According to their Web site, it's a sci-fi flick titled *Time Release*. Scientists digging in the La Brea tar pits uncover a spaceship buried thousands of years ago, and inside they find the mummified remains of the alien crew and a cargo of what looks like large coconuts. Naturally the scientists remove one and take it to a secret lab, and guess what happens next?"

"It morphs into a monster, returns to the ship for its slimy buddies, and wipes out L.A.," John said.

"Very good. Maybe you should take up screenwriting."

John laughed.

Despite his overriding concern about finding Sully, Gary couldn't help being drawn in. "They wipe out L.A.? The entire city?"

"No," Ann replied, "just a large chunk of West Hollywood, due to a limited special effects budget, no doubt."

"Pity. It would have gotten rid of the smog."

John turned right on Wilshire Boulevard. A few blocks later, Gary leaned forward. "What's going on up there?"

"Looks like the street's blocked off," John said. "Guess it's for the shoot."

Gary eyed the blue-clad policemen standing in front of orange sawhorses. The street beyond looked like a disaster scene, with cars, SUVs, and trucks parked facing in every direction. A tall camera crane hovered high above the open tar pit, flanked on either side by banks of reflectors.

"Rats!" Gary said with feeling.

"We'll have to park and walk," John said.

"No, see if you can talk our way in."

John looked doubtful as he stopped the car. "I'll try."

One of the cops began striding toward the car. John's window buzzed down, allowing the acrid smell of ozone inside. The officer's eyes were impossible to see, hidden behind his mirrored sunglasses, but his displeasure was only too apparent.

"Street's closed," he said, pointing. "You have to go around."

"We're here to see one of the cast," John began.

The officer put his hands on his hips. "Yeah, I'll bet. Now clear out, or I'll write you up."

"Officer, we really do have business here," Gary said, leaning over so the cop could see him.

The man turned his head slightly. "Is that so? Mind showing me your pass?"

"Uh, we don't have one."

"Then I can't let you in."

Gary gritted his teeth, sat upright, and looked through the windshield at the director and cameraman atop the crane. Then he spotted a familiar face standing beside an immaculate dirt bike. John rolled his window up and started backing up.

"Wait!" Gary shouted.

John stepped on the brake, and the car lurched to a stop. "What?" he asked.

"I see Sully."

Gary threw open his door and jumped out.

The cop reached for his ticket pad and started around the car. "Okay, I warned you. Let me see some identification."

Gary looked past him and waved. "Hey, Sully!" he shouted. Sully looked around but didn't immediately see who was calling him. Gary kept waving. "Sully! Over here."

"Sir, I want your ID *now*, or I'll take you in," the policeman said. "What'll it be?"

Gary glanced at him then back toward Sully. He breathed a sigh of relief. SecurityCheck's part-timer was on his way over.

Gary pointed. "Officer, he'll vouch for us."

Sully finally made it through the maze of vehicles and walked up to the barricades. He was a young Hispanic of medium height with a wiry build. He had long black hair and a thin mustache, but what really stood out were his intense brown eyes. "Hey, dude! You guys lost or something?" He and Gary traded high fives.

"Or something," Gary replied, smiling with relief. "Would you *please* tell this officer we have business with you?"

"You do?"

Gary gritted his teeth. "Yes, Sully, we do. Now tell him."

Sully turned to the cop. "He does." Then he stooped and glanced inside the car. "Whoa. You brought the whole office."

"Are you on this film shoot?" the policeman asked, obviously suspicious.

"Yeah, wanna see my union card?"

"Don't get smart with me. So are you one of the crew?"

"Naw, I'm the stuntman. Brum-brum." He gripped his right hand and twisted it like he was riding a motorcycle. "Now how about letting these dudes inside?"

The policeman glared at Sully for a few moments, glanced at Gary, then turned to his partner. "Gimme a hand, here," he said.

Gary followed Sully through the barrier and waited while John drove inside and parked. Three doors popped open, and Ann, John, and Dan got out. Sully's sharp eyes took them all in then focused on Gary.

"So did John get lost, or did you come to see Sully-man do his thing?"

Gary laughed. "Actually, neither, but I never have seen you perform, and I'd like to."

Sully seemed surprised and touched. "Well, thanks, man. I'm serious about my career."

"I know you are. Are you doing a stunt today?"

"You bet, and it's my big scene. Know anything about the plot?"

"Yeah. Ann found the film's Web site. That's how we located you."

"Okay, so you know that the head slime monster oozes back to the mother ship and revives its playmates, and after that West Hollywood gets slimed big-time."

"That's roughly what Ann said."

Sully eyed her before turning back to Gary. "Uh-huh. Well, just before the ending, the scientist's son—I'm his stunt double—figures out where the slimeball is going, so he races back to the pit on his dirt bike, see? He loses control, crashes through that plywood barrier over there, and goes splat in the tar."

Gary looked where Sully was pointing. The special effects "damage" stood out clearly. "How big a drop is it?"

"About fifteen feet. I landed on a big air bag. Shot turned out terrific."

"Glad you didn't get injured."

"Hey, man, I know what I'm doing. Anyhow, the kid does his best, but he's too late to stop the slimesters. His only hope is to jump on his bike and escape by riding up the scaffolding."

"How can he do that?"

"He pops a wheelie to get up on the lowest level; it's only a foot or so above the tar. Then there's this long, sloping plank that reaches a little over halfway to the street."

Gary nodded. "I see. So you do a ramp jump up and over the barrier."

Sully grinned. "That's what the script says, and that's what I'm going to do in about fifteen minutes, right after the crew lowers my bike into the pit." He pointed to two grips rolling the bright red cycle to a gap in the barrier. "Excuse me, I gotta go get ready."

"Gary, remember why we're here?" Ann asked quickly.

Sully looked at her then back at Gary, a puzzled expression on his face.

"Oh, yes," Gary said. "Sully, we just landed a hot project; the same one we lost last year."

"The Fort Knox gig?"

"That's the one, and it has a *real* short fuse."

"How short?"

"It kicks off on Wednesday. Are you available?"

He paused for only a moment. "Yeah, don't see why not. I don't have anything lined up after this shoot wraps up. Assuming my stunt comes off, I'll be all done."

"I'll pray that it does."

Sully's grin was hard to read. "Thanks, man. I'll take all the help I can get."

"Sully!" The bullhorn's hollow echo drew Gary's attention to the camera crane. The director was waving toward the now-disappearing dirt bike. "You're on!"

Sully waved. "Got to go," he told Gary.

"I understand. We'll wait here until you're done."

Sully's expression grew very animated. "No way; you guys *gotta* see this. Listen. See that scaffold beside the camera crane?"

"Yes."

"One of the cameramen is going to take handheld shots from there. It's lined up with the ramp so you can look right down it, clear to the spaceship. Climb on up, and you'll have a great view."

"Won't the cameraman object?"

"I doubt it, but if he does, tell him you're scouting me."

Gary smiled. "Which we are, in a way." He glanced at the director, who was waving. "You better go now."

Sully looked around. "Yeah. Catch you after we wrap."

Gary watched as he loped off and disappeared over the barricade. "Shall we?" he said, waving toward the scaffold. He led the way over to the rickety-looking tubular steel structure and grabbed one of the vertical supports.

"I don't know about that," John said, lowering his voice.

"We've been through worse," Gary said.

"Yeah, but we were being paid for it."

Gary turned to the others. "Ann?"

"Can't see anything from down here." She started up.

"Dan? How about you?"

His expression turned sour, but he grabbed the steel tubing and began climbing.

"See you up there," Gary told John.

The top of the scaffold was covered by a sheet of heavy plywood, the long side perpendicular to the black pit some thirty feet below. The cameraman took his eye away from the viewfinder, looked the newcomers over, then returned to his work.

Gary stepped cautiously to the opposite side of the platform and looked down. The black, gooey surface seemed to suck all the light out of the hazy afternoon sun. The excavation, which covered the entire block, had provided many of the skeletons displayed in the nearby Page Museum. Small squares marked off the pit floor, which was littered with buckets, picks, shovels, and other archaeological detritus.

Gary sighted down the ramp and saw that the jump would pass almost directly over their heads. Down in the pit, Sully pushed his dirt bike along a narrow trail that blended almost perfectly into the surrounding asphalt. The spaceship set hunkered down in the mire some hundred feet beyond, constructed so that it looked half-buried. A large gray object that resembled a giant, slimy puffer fish with tentacles sat in front of the spaceship's open hatch. Sully laid the motorcycle on its side, facing away from the ship, and moved a tentacle out of the way.

"Guess that's one of the aliens," Ann said.

"Doesn't look very menacing to me," Dan said.

The cameraman turned his head, gave him a scathing look, then busied himself checking the camera's settings.

"Sorry," Dan said.

"Places, everyone," the director announced through the bullhorn. "Ready, Sully?" The cinematographer had his eye pressed into the viewfinder. Sully took his position next to the flaccid alien and waved.

"Okay, roll cameras." A few seconds later, "Cue Waldo." The alien sprang to life, and its tentacles began waving. Sully dodged, raced to his motorcycle, and jumped on all in one smooth streak of action. He cranked the engine and revved it. Blue smoke billowed up when he popped the clutch, lifting the front wheel high in the air as the bike roared across the pit with the alien in hot pursuit. Sully dropped the front wheel onto the scaffolding. The frame screeched across the wooden plank until the rear tire bounded up, nearly throwing the rider, or so it appeared.

Gary's eyes grew round in anticipation. The motorcycle hit the narrow, wooden ramp and streaked upward, moving ever faster. It flew past the end, and time seemed to stand still as Sully stood on the foot pegs. Bike and rider soared higher and higher in a grand arc directly over the platform, so close that Gary could see the pattern on the soles of Sully's boots. The jump reached its apex then started down. The bike landed on the street with a loud clatter. Sully brought the bike around in a broad, sliding turn, popped a wheelie, and roared back, riding on the rear wheel, then dropped down and slid to a stop. He jumped off, pulled the bike onto its stand, and removed his helmet. He looked up at the director with a big grin on his face.

"Great, Sully," the bullhorn announced. "Now how about a protection shot?"

Sully waved. "Sure thing."

"He's really in his element," Ann whispered to Gary.

"Don't you know it," he replied.

Two grips rolled the dirt bike over to the barricade, lifted it over, and maneuvered it down the ramp. Sully followed them and took over at the bottom near the limp and lifeless alien. After getting an okay from the second cameraman, the director brought the bullhorn up once more.

"Roll cameras," his amplified voice said. "And, cue Waldo." Once more Sully dodged the flailing alien, jumped on his motorcycle, and thundered up the ramp. The jump was even higher than the first. After landing, Sully rode the bike back on its rear wheel and stopped beside the camera crane without dropping back down. He killed the engine, remained balanced for several more seconds, then finally dropped the front wheel to the pavement.

"That was cool, Sully," the director said with a smile. Then he turned to the crew and lifted the bullhorn to his lips. "That's a wrap."

Gary waited for the cameraman to climb down and out of hearing. "That was fantastic," he said.

"I don't know how he does it," John said. "It would scare me senseless just thinking about it."

"I know, but that's why we hire him. He can drive anything."

"Plus he's a nice guy," Ann said.

"That, too," Gary agreed. "Let's catch him before he gets away."

They found him supervising the loading of the dirt bike into the back of a pickup truck.

"Thanks for getting us in," Gary said. "It was a blast seeing you do your thing."

Sully grinned. "Glad you liked it." His eyes drifted over the set. "I got to do a lot of cool stunts that'll look good on my demo reel."

"One thing I didn't understand," Ann said.

Sully turned to her. "What was that?"

"I thought all the aliens were supposed to chase you out of the pit."

"Oh, they will, once the editor does his magic. The actors filmed the close-up scenes a few weeks ago. The editor will cut my jump in with those shots, and it'll look like one continuous scene. At least that's the idea."

"If I could change the subject," Gary said.

"Speak," Sully said, still grinning.

"Since you're done here, can you come back with us and help plan the Fort Knox job?"

The young Hispanic maintained his grin, but a serious glint came to his eyes. "Naw, man. I'm going to the cast party. I'll come by tomorrow."

"Sully, the kickoff is this week. You and Dan are flying out to Louisville on Wednesday."

"Sorry, I'm not missing this party for anything."

"We can spare him one day," John said.

Gary decided John was right. "Okay, Sully man. See you tomorrow then."

"I'll be there."

"Sully," a voice called out.

Gary turned to see a short, heavyset man striding toward them. The man had thinning brown hair and was wearing the loudest Hawaiian shirt Gary had ever seen over blue Bermuda shorts. His sandals made insistent slapping sounds that underscored his obvious rush.

"Glad I caught you," the man said.

"What's up, Paul?" Sully asked.

The man hesitated as he looked around at Sully's companions. "Are these friends of yours?"

"Oh, yeah. These are the guys I work for on my day job." Sully nodded toward Gary and John. "Guys, this is Paul Wilson, the producer. Paul—Gary Nesbitt and John Mason own SecurityCheck."

"Pleased to meet you." Paul's face creased into a dubious smile as he shook their hands.

"Gary and John show people how to hold their cards so the bad guys can't see 'em," Sully continued.

"Thanks, Sully," Gary said.

"No problem."

Sully turned. "And Dan Thompson is the communications guru."

Dan and Paul shook hands.

Sully winked at Ann. "I saved Ann O'Brien for last because *we're* the Irish gang."

Paul shook her hand. "Pleased to meet you, Ms. O'Brien."

Ann murmured a quiet response, but she was obviously distracted by what Sully had said.

Paul turned back to Sully. "I always wondered about your name."

"Hey, what can I say? My grandfather was New York Irish, and after he moved to San Diego, he married a Mexican woman. When my dad came along, they named him Seamus, although he looked more Hispanic than Irish. He moved to L.A., where he met my mother. So I'm only one-quarter Irish and thoroughly Hispanic but named for my grandfather. Mystery solved."

"I see."

"But there's more. Ann's real name is Anastasia."

She flushed. "Irish father and Russian mother," she explained. "And I prefer 'Ann' to 'Anastasia,' " she added.

"Ann's the resident hacker," Sully continued. "She's never met a computer she didn't like or one she couldn't break into. She's the one who tracked me down today."

"I checked out your Web site," Ann said. "Very nice."

Paul smiled in sudden appreciation. "Well, thank you. You must come to the sneak preview as my guests. I'll send an invitation through Sully."

"Thanks, that's very kind of you."

"Not at all." He glanced at his watch. "Whoa, gotta run. My jet's waiting at Van Nuys to fly me to New York." He turned back to Sully. "Oh, almost forgot. Remember the car crash in the opening credits?"

"You kidding? My harness came loose, and I almost got thrown out!"

Paul waved his hand impatiently. "I know, I know. Won't happen again. Listen, we may have to reshoot it."

"No way, man! That stunt was perfect!"

"Take it easy; that's not the problem. We can't find the camera original, and without it, the editor can't conform the opening sequence."

"How did *that* happen?"

Paul waved his hands impatiently. "Who knows? Look, it just happened, okay? We're still looking, but I don't think we'll find it. Probably got thrown out by mistake."

"Uh, Paul?" Gary interrupted. "We need Sully for this hot project. He's due to leave midweek."

Paul put his hands on his hips. "Look, Sully's under contract to me to do these stunts, and that includes reshoots if necessary."

"Now, hold on. . ."

John stepped quickly around Gary. "Paul, we know how important Sully's stunt work is to him, and we've always worked around his schedule. Now when do you want to reshoot the stunt?"

Paul dropped his hands but didn't reply immediately. "Uh, I'm not sure. I'll have to check with my editor. Sometime in the next few weeks I would guess."

"Sully is flying to Louisville on Wednesday. Could he do the stunt tomorrow?"

"Yeah, I guess so," Paul said after a moment's hesitation. "We allowed for two takes, so we have all the stunt gear we need." He nodded. "Okay, I'll have my assistant set it up. Thanks." He sounded grateful.

"Don't mention it," John said.

Paul turned to Sully. "Well, I'm off. Enjoy the party."

"Oh, I intend to."

Paul turned and hurried off toward a large trailer.

Gary closed his eyes briefly as all the worries associated with the Fort Knox project exploded in his head and swirled about in seeming chaos. And on top of that, John had given away a valuable day of Sully's time. His agitated glare took them both in.

"Okay, guys, how are we going to make this work?" he demanded.

"We can do it," John insisted. "Sully goes to the party while we return to the office, dig out all our documentation, and start reviewing. Look, we were ready to go a year and a half ago. All we have to do is come back up to speed."

Gary snapped his fingers. "Right, just like that," he grumbled.

"So we're in for a few long days, but we can hack it. All Sully has to do is review his tasks and rent the vehicles, right?"

"And take care of the disguises."

John looked at Sully. "Can you work in a trip to Costumes for U tomorrow?"

"Sure, no problem."

John broke into one of his trademark grins. "See, everything's under control."

"We'll see," Gary said, only a little mollified. But his irritation quickly drained away when he recognized that he was being overbearing. That wasn't right, and he wasn't being fair to Sully. He turned to the stuntman. "John's right. Sorry, dude." He smiled. "Hope you enjoy the party." Then he thought about tomorrow. "And I'll pray that your stunt goes okay."

Sully grinned. "Meaning I shouldn't break a leg."

Gary laughed. "Or anything else."

"Don't worry. What disguises do you want?"

"Army uniforms, FedEx, and so on. I'll e-mail a list to you."

"Right. I'll check in with you tomorrow."

CHAPTER 3

Lieutenant Colonel Dick Edwards was a big man, but his orange Racal field biological suit made him look even bigger. He stood on the edge of the pit and looked down into the deep shadows, his heart pounding so hard, he imagined he could hear it above the blowers that pressurized his suit with filtered air. He took a cautious breath. The filters were designed to keep out viruses; at least that was the theory. He ran a gloved hand over the flimsy plastic fabric and examined the suit's seals once again. They seemed secure, which meant he had no valid excuse to delay any longer. He exhaled, fogging up the helmet's faceplate. He cursed and pressed the flexible plastic against his face to clear it. That produced a few clear spots amid his condensed breath, the best he could hope for. Even though he had worked in field biological suits many times, he never forgot what could happen if he were careless or a suit failed.

Edwards looked down at his yellow rubber boots, turned, and began backing down into the hole. He stepped into the shallow niches cut into the side and soon entered the permafrost layer, where the Alaskan tundra never thawed. The frosty air sucked the warmth out of his body, despite the layers of plastic and his thermal underwear. Finally he reached the bottom and looked up. The early morning sun bathed the top of the pit in anemic light, but very little reached the bottom. A Racal-clad soldier was lowering a large nylon bag. Edwards waited until the bag touched down then untied the rope and waited while it was withdrawn. Only then did he pick up the bag and turn around.

Edwards scanned the dense shadows, pulled out a large flashlight, and punched it on. He squinted in the sudden glare and aimed the beam at the far end of the pit. Edwards stopped breathing for a moment, and a chill colder than the permafrost ran down his spine. He was looking into the frozen face of a native Alaskan woman who had last taken breath over eighty years ago before dying in agony. The body, thanks to the permafrost, was perfectly preserved except for a few gouges caused by careless shovel work.

I doubt if she minds, the army microbiologist thought as he straddled the body with his feet and shuffled forward so he could shine the light on her face. Her eyes were closed, he was glad to note, although why this should make a difference he couldn't say. He set the bag down, pulled out a heavy rubber mat, and placed it beside the body at waist level. Edwards kneeled on this, taking great care not to tear his suit on the frozen rocks. He exhaled and fogged his faceplate again, only then realizing he had been holding his breath. Again he mashed the clear plastic against his face to clear it.

Can't put it off any longer.

Edwards reached into the bag and grabbed an ordinary garden trowel and began chipping away at the ice and dirt that covered the body's chest, taking great care, fearful that a slip might rupture a wrist seal or tear his plastic cocoon. A heavy skin garment began to appear. Edwards stopped when he had a hand-sized area cleared and traded the trowel for a utility knife. He felt sweat pop up under his armpits. He lowered the cutter, pushed the thumb slide to extend the razor blade, drew the knife slowly toward himself, then used the blade tip to lift a flap. Edwards retracted the blade and dropped the knife into the bag. Only then did he pull the fabric aside, revealing the body's frozen chest.

Glad that's done.

Edwards took out what looked like a carpenter's brace except it was smaller and made of stainless steel. He set the flashlight on the corpse, aiming the beam toward the head. Only then did he retrieve the most important instrument of all. It resembled a drill bit but was actually a custom-made stainless steel auger with razor-sharp cutting edges and hollow passages inside to hold tissue samples. Edwards attached the bit, lifted the auger, and set the tip on the frozen chest. He began turning the handle and felt the bit digging through the skin, ribs, fat, and finally the all-important lung tissue, the whole reason for this gruesome task.

Edwards stopped when the bit reached full penetration then backed it out, leaving a dark, smooth hole in the body. He removed the bit and set it carefully in front of the flashlight. Breathing a sigh of relief, he removed an oblong plastic box, opened it, and placed the bit, with its precious sample, inside. Only then did he struggle to his feet, wincing at the sharp pains that shot through his knees. He looked up, and moments later the soldier lowered a plastic bag with red bio-hazard trefoils emblazoned on its sides. Edwards placed the box containing the sample inside and watched as the bag made its leisurely journey to the surface. He returned the flashlight and tools to the nylon bag, and again the soldier lowered the rope. Edwards tied it to the bag, and up it went.

His job done, he climbed up the steps and back onto the barren landscape. About a hundred feet away, the decontamination team waited for him. He walked up to the Racal-suited soldiers, held his arms out, and spread his legs to prepare for what the army called "nuking." A fog of laundry bleach, applied by a hand sprayer, enveloped him, ensuring that nothing living remained on his suit, the tools, or the outside of the sample box. However, whatever lived within the sample was spared by the box's airtight closure.

The decon drill done, Edwards shook the excess liquid from his suit and waited impatiently while the soldiers packed up their gear. Then would come the relief of peeling out of the suit and the short trip back to the lab. And after that, Edwards would prepare the tissue sample for culture. He had no doubt that this would produce a viable virus.

Gary stood up and reached across the conference room table. Sully slid the laptop over to him. The team driver had just finished describing the vehicles he would rent in Louisville and his role in the operation. They would have a car, but their primary transportation would be a large truck. Sully, with Dan's help, would load the equipment and modify the interior, transforming it into a state-of-the-art mobile surveillance unit. Gary smiled. As he expected, Sully's presentation had been thorough and colorful and spiced with his usual disdain for authority and convention.

"Thank you, Mr. Sullivan, for that scintillating performance. I see 'the kid' hasn't lost his edge."

Sully grinned, and his dark brown eyes twinkled. "Hey, man, I'm good at what I do."

"And modest to boot."

Gary returned the PowerPoint presentation to the opening slide, an aerial shot of a tan, square building surrounded by a perimeter fence, the entrance to the Fort Knox Bullion Depository vault. The headline read OPERATION GO FOR THE GOLD in gold, drop-shadow lettering; but that was misleading because the team wouldn't be going anywhere near the gold bullion since it was administered by the U.S. Mint. Gary's gaze lingered on the picture as he marveled at the gorgeous detail and vivid hues on the ViewSonic fifty-inch Plasma HDTV. The pricy display had been an impulse purchase. It had cost over eight grand, and many times he had wished the funds were back in the company account. He sighed.

"That's it, guys," Gary said. "Any questions, comments?" His eyes made a circuit of the table.

"I have one," John said. "Do you want a backup hang glider?"

Gary's immediate thought was to say "yes," although he wasn't sure they would need the one already on John's list.

"Do you have time?"

John flashed a broad grin. "You ask this of the gadget meister? Say the word, and it'll be in tomorrow's shipment."

"In that case, do it, since the contract covers all expenses."

"Consider it done. One other question."

"Shoot."

"Do you want to take the UAV?"

Gary visualized the unmanned aerial vehicle, a delta-winged craft that John had demonstrated a few weeks ago. It had reminded Gary of a cross between a remote control model airplane and Sherlock with wings. The thought of John's diminutive robot flitting through the air tickled him.

"What's so funny?" John asked.

Gary shook his head. "Nothing. Are you *sure* that contraption is ready for prime time?"

"Absolutely."

"Then by all means bring it along." Gary looked over at Sully. "When will the disguises be ready?"

"Oh, yeah, forgot about that. The dude at Costumes for U said sometime this afternoon."

"Did they have everything?"

Sully nodded. "Yeah, army uniforms, officer and enlisted, including a large assortment of ribbons and rank insignia. UPS and

FedEx uniforms, plus uniforms for sanitation workers, telephone, and cable, you name it."

"How about the beards and cosmetics?"

"Those, too. You're good to go."

"Excellent. I'll pick everything up after I take you and Dan to LAX."

"What time do we blast off?"

"The itinerary says 3:10 p.m., and our travel agent recommends you be at the airport two hours before flight time." He glanced at Ann.

"I printed your boarding passes," she said, holding up a folder.

"You change flights at Dallas/Fort Worth," Gary continued, "and arrive in Louisville at 11:58."

Dan pushed his glasses up on his nose. "At least we'll be in before midnight," he said without changing his somber expression.

Gary snickered. "I'm so glad you're pleased." His eyes made another round of the table. "Anything else? Going once, going twice. . ."

"I have something," John said. "I want to hear how Sully's stunt went."

"So do I, now that you mention it." Gary turned to their driver. "So, dude, did you do it in one take?"

"Had to; like they only had the one stunt car left. Blow the shot, and my reputation is toast."

"Well, I'm certainly glad you came through for them. Wish I could have seen it."

"Your wish is my command." He held up a DVD and waved it. "Got an iMovie of it right here."

"Sorry, we don't speak Apple in this shop."

"I do," Ann said. "I converted it to Windows Media Player format. Shall I play it?"

"Sure."

He pushed the laptop over to her. She grabbed it eagerly, and her fingers flew over the keyboard. Moments later, the plasma screen flickered then steadied on a panoramic shot of Hollywood from an overlooking hill, which then panned a sylvan park, past the Hollywood sign, finally stopping on a winding road in Griffith Park. In the distance, two cars raced toward the camera then roared past inches away. The video cut to a reverse angle of the cars entering a curve.

Sully leaned forward, his eyes wide. "Whoa, here it comes! Keep an eye on the red car."

The black racer skidded sideways and smashed into its opponent. The red car rolled to the right, tumbled down the hill, and exploded in a towering ball of fire. The shot continued for several more seconds then ended in a freeze-frame.

"Cool, huh?" Sully said.

"Way cool," Gary said, "but what does it have to do with the La Brea slime monsters wiping out Hollywood?"

"Hey, the stunts will get the young dudes to buy tickets. It's all about box office."

Gary laughed. "I figured as much."

"But seriously, there *is* a tie-in, sort of. See, the guy in the red car gets thrown clear. He's banged up some, but nothing serious, until the cops haul him in for drag racing. His dad is the mad scientist, and by the time he gets to the jail, he's *really* mad. It's sturm und drang, big-time. So the cops release the kid to Pops, and so the dude has to spend his whole summer at the pit ninety-one dig. The rest you know. Now, wouldn't you pay to see a flick like that?"

"I plead the fifth, but it's a moot point since Paul Wilson invited us to the sneak preview."

"Well, at least you'll get to see the kid do his thing on the big screen."

"I'm looking forward to it."

This seemed to please him. "Thanks."

Gary again looked around the table. "If there's nothing else, let's get back to work."

Sully snapped his fingers. "Hey, one more thing."

"What's that?"

"Are we supposed to swipe a tank like last time?"

"I haven't had time to review the contract, but Thomas said there were no changes. So, yes, it's a bonus item if you can steal an M1A1 Abrams."

Sully rubbed his hands together rapidly. "Cool."

"I certainly hope you can pull it off. That it?"

No one said anything.

Gary took the laptop back from Ann and shut it down. The others pushed back from the table and began filing out of the room. "You heading back to your gadget shop?" he asked John.

John's eyebrows went up a notch. "I was. Do we need to talk?"

"Yeah, but we can do it back there." He smiled at John's serious expression. "Don't worry, it's nothing drastic."

He looked relieved. "Good. Time's getting short."

"Let me grab my coffee mug. My eyes need a wake-up call."

"Mine, too. See you in the break room."

Gary followed John out and glanced in Rose's direction. She was staring intently into her monitor and didn't look up as he walked past. *That is probably a good sign,* Gary thought. Apparently Ann's session with tech support had been effective. Gary entered his office, grabbed his mug, and hurried back to the break room. John glanced up as he finished filling his mug. Gary joined him and held his mug out for John to fill; then they crossed the hall into the workshop.

Gary looked all around. The shelves and worktables looked bare. Almost every piece of equipment was packed into the boxes stacked neatly on the floor, awaiting shipment. Gary spotted a familiar piece of gear on the nearest table.

"You leaving Sherlock behind?" he asked in surprise.

"No way." John patted the miniature wheeled robot. "One of

the drive motors fritzed out on me. Won't take long to get it changed out."

"Glad to hear it. I'd hate to leave your buddy behind, especially since we're bound to need surveillance in tight places."

"Don't you know it." John paused. "So what's up?"

"My FAA biennial flight review was due the first of September, and until I take care of it, I can't fly a plane. It won't keep me from flying hang gliders since those don't require a license, but if we need to rent a plane, we'll be out of luck."

John's expression grew serious. "I see. Do you think we'll need a plane?"

Gary shrugged. "Probably not, but if we do, it's not likely I'd have time to find a flight instructor and get the review done."

"How much time are we talking about?"

"A minimum of one hour ground instruction plus an hour in the air with an instructor, assuming I can schedule it, which isn't a sure thing since the instructors at Van Nuys Aviation stay pretty busy. But the real question is: Can I spare the time? We're out of here on Friday, and I still have a lot of research to do."

A wry smile came to John's lips. "So you're wanting *me* to make the decision."

"Well, you *are* half owner of SecurityCheck."

"But aviation is *your* thing. Look, if you really want my opinion, I'd feel better if you were qualified to fly a plane, but do as you think best."

Gary opened his mouth to say something but closed it just as quickly. All the things he had to do, real and imaginary, whirled about in his head, but a clear leading on what he should do eluded him.

John reached into a pocket and pulled out a quarter. "Would this help?" he asked.

Gary smiled in spite of his concern. "I'd like something a *little* more scientific."

John put the quarter back. "Maybe 'scientific' is the wrong approach. Do you feel led one way or the other?"

This only added to Gary's confusion. "Maybe. I was surprised I remembered the review, with all we have going on. The requirement only comes up every two years, so it's easy to overlook. Two years ago I didn't realize I was due until I scanned my log book before checking out a plane for a cross-country flight."

"What happened?"

"I had to cancel. Fortunately one of the instructors had some free time, so we did the ground stuff and then went up for the check ride."

"Very interesting."

"What?"

"That this should come up right now. If you really want my opinion, I think you should go do it."

"But all my work. . ."

"Don't sweat it. Just do the best you can and play catch-up when we get to Louisville." John grinned. "Hey, that's what we end up doing most of the time anyway."

"Yeah, you're sure right about that. Okay, I'll see if an instructor can work me in tomorrow."

"See. That wasn't so hard, was it?"

Gary laughed. "I'll tell you after the flight review."

CHAPTER 4

Gary looked out through the windows at Van Nuys Aviation, still holding his pilot's log book, whose last entry recorded his biennial flight review. It had been a grueling hour and fifteen minutes of intense dual instruction, but the certified flight instructor's signature made it official: Gary now had the FAA's permission to fly an airplane as pilot-in-command.

And the Fort Knox preparations were proceeding better than expected. Gary had seen Dan and Sully off yesterday and run by Costumes for U afterward to pick up the disguises. Their equipment would be going out airfreight—Gary glanced at his watch—right about now, so, after grabbing something to eat, he would be back in the office by around one o'clock.

Gary started to turn away but stopped when he caught a glimpse of a plane nearing touchdown on runway one-six right. It was a Lear-jet, and it looked new: sleek with a glossy white paint job and cobalt blue trim. Twin puffs of smoke marked the landing spot. The aircraft slowed rapidly and turned off the runway and onto the taxiway. The whine from the twin fan-jets increased in volume as the plane approached.

"Very nice," a nearby voice said.

Gary glanced to his right and saw an instructor he knew by sight. "Sure is. Love to fly one of those."

The instructor laughed. "You and everyone else in here."

The plane taxied up to the Van Nuys Aviation flight line. Gary looked on with what pilots call "turbine envy."

"Wonder what one of those rents for?" Gary mused.

"If you have to ask. . . ," the instructor said.

Gary laughed. "Yeah, you can't afford it." He sighed. "But I can dream."

The plane rolled to a stop. A few seconds later, the whine dropped off as the turbines spooled down.

"Must not be any passengers. Don't see any of our guys hustling out with a red carpet."

"So it would seem," Gary said.

The air-stair door opened outward like a clamshell, the lower segment providing steps down to the tarmac. The blue-clad co-pilot, surprisingly short, descended first, followed by the pilot-in-command, a tall, thin man whose coat sleeves carried four gold stripes. To Gary's surprise, he recognized him.

Gary hurried to the door and out to the chain-link fence that marked the edge of the flight line. The copilot hurried past on his way to the cool interior of Van Nuys Aviation's flight planning room. The pilot stooped down to examine the tires on the left main landing gear then stood up and started walking toward the fence.

"Mike," Gary called out.

Mike Jacobs spotted him and smiled. "Hey, Gary. How are you?" he said as he walked up.

"Fine. Been a long time."

Mike removed his cap, ran a hand through his medium-length black hair, and carefully set his cap back in place. "Yes, it has. Let's see, I guess it's been something like four years since we went through ground school here."

"Uh-huh. *And* flight instruction." Gary paused. "And then we chose different careers."

"Yeah." Mike nodded toward the Learjet. "I fly guys around who can buy and sell me a hundred times."

"At least it's doing something you love."

"Got that right. Say, I never did hear what you went into."

"I'm part-owner of SecurityCheck with a guy by the name of John Mason. We're security consultants. We do break-ins to show our clients what needs fixing."

"Sounds exciting."

"It can be." Gary's eyes traced the sleek lines of the Learjet. "So who do you fly for, some Fortune 500 company?"

"More like Fortune 500 wannabes. I fly for GalaxyBizJet. They're an aircraft fractional ownership company. Their clients buy a percentage of a business jet fleet that allows them to fly just about anywhere without having the expense and hassle of owning and maintaining a jet. And with a light jet like the Lear, we can fly into smaller airports, which saves our customers time on the ground."

"Is that part of the PR spiel?"

"Sure, but it happens to be true. We have an interesting clientele: a lot of medium-sized corporations but also movie stars, professional athletes, and so on."

"Where do you fly to?"

"All over. In the winter, we log a lot of flights to ski resorts and Florida, but our most frequent destinations are New York, Washington, D.C., Los Angeles, Chicago, and, of course, Las Vegas."

Gary was listening, but most of his attention was lavished on the Learjet, so it took him awhile to notice his friend had stopped talking. Gary turned his head and saw the pilot's broad grin.

"Like to see the inside?" Mike asked.

"Thought you'd never ask."

"Follow me." He led the way to the steps in the air-stair door. "No drooling," he said over his shoulder.

"No promises," Gary muttered as he stepped up into the compact cabin. He had to duck to clear the ceiling, but the seats were large, and the club seating offered generous legroom.

"The 45XR carries eight passengers and two pilots. It has a galley, closet, and a complete lav, but I imagine what *you* want to see is up front."

"How did you guess?"

Mike grinned.

Gary followed him into the cockpit and stood there in silence as his eyes searched out every instrument and control. He shook his head slowly. "Oh, that is simply magnificent."

"A complete Honeywell avionics suite with four flat-panels; primary flight displays, ILS, GPS moving map, flight planning, engine management, weather radar; you name it."

"All that and twin turbines to boot."

"You bet. Two Honeywell TFE731s producing thirty-five hundred pounds of thrust each."

"What do you cruise at?"

"About .79 mach; 450 knots at 43,000 feet. It has nice range for a super-light business jet. We can fly around 2,000 nautical miles, with IFR reserves." Mike crossed over to the right and sat down. He waved toward the left side. "Like to try out the captain's seat?" Gary eased into the contoured seat and relaxed in its generous size and comfort. He followed Mike's hand as the pilot pointed out each control, switch, and knob. In his mind's eye, Gary could see himself taxiing out then pushing the power levers forward and feeling the brisk acceleration. He continued to look over the controls after Mike finished talking.

"Do you wish you had gone into commercial aviation?" Mike asked at last.

Gary shook his head. "Sometimes I daydream about it, but no, I'm happy where I am." He sighed. "So are they keeping you busy?"

"I'll say," he said as he began counting on his fingers. "We flew a film producer to New York on Monday. Then it was a corporate CEO making a grand tour of his company's divisions: Chicago, Atlanta, Dallas, and finally San Francisco. That took care of Tuesday and Wednesday. Then we flew down here today to pick up four banking bigwigs. We'll take them to San Francisco for a meeting then back here tonight. Tomorrow we fly to New York to bring back the producer we flew there on Monday."

"Busy week. Is that typical?"

"Pretty much."

A thought popped up in Gary's mind. "I'm curious. Can you tell me the producer's name?"

"Don't see why not. Guy by the name of Paul Wilson. Why do you ask?"

"Just wondered. I met Paul on Monday, and I remember him saying he was flying to New York." Gary grinned. "Now I know who flew him there."

"Interesting coincidence."

"Yeah, isn't it? I'm flying out to Louisville tomorrow with two others from my company. Actually, the whole company will be there except for our receptionist/bookkeeper."

A thoughtful expression came to Mike's face. "What's happening in Louisville, or is it a secret?"

Gary laughed. "It's not classified, at least not yet. We're doing a security audit on Fort Knox for the department of the army."

"Ah, making sure the gold's safe."

"Nope, the depository is actually part of the U.S. Mint. We'll be checking out the army stuff: the armor school, training facilities, and command units."

For a few moments, Mike said nothing. He looked at Gary as

if weighing what he should say. "You want to hear something interesting?"

"Sure."

"We'll be stopping at Louisville tomorrow for fuel."

Gary felt an electric tingle in his spine. "Oh?"

"Yeah. How would you guys like to come with us? It's just us pilots since the company wasn't able to schedule any passengers going to New York."

"Is that a trick question? We'd love to!"

"Great. We'll enjoy the company."

"Where and when?"

"Right here, but now comes the bad part. We leave at 4:30 a.m. sharp in order to make our arrival time in New York."

"Listen! I'd be here at *midnight* to hitch a ride on this mean machine."

Mike laughed. "Perhaps your colleagues might not be that enthusiastic."

"Maybe, but we'll be here if I have to drag them." Gary looked over the instrument panel one more time then looked out the windshield. "Nice. Very nice."

Gary sat quietly in the passenger seat of Rose's red Malibu as she drove along Sherman Way in the light, early morning traffic. In the backseat, Ann hadn't said a word since they had picked her up at her apartment. Next they had gone by John's house, and he was being unusually quiet, as well. It was 4:15 a.m., and Gary was in severe need of caffeine. He yawned, making no attempt to stifle it.

John cleared his throat. "Who said this would be so terrific?"

"Hey, it beats flying out of LAX and changing planes in Dallas."

"If you say so."

"What street do we turn on?" Rose asked.

"Left on Hayvenhurst," Gary said, "then take a right at Van Nuys Aviation."

"Thanks," she said, slurring the word in a big yawn.

Gary looked at her out of the sides of his eyes. He wasn't sure how she felt about getting up this early. He and John had discussed taking a cab but had gratefully accepted Rose's offer to see them off.

"We appreciate you doing this," he said.

"You're welcome." There might have been a smile. "We're a team, or so you and John keep telling me."

"You're right about that, and I can't think of anyone I'd rather have holding down the fort."

This time she did smile. "Well, don't you forget it."

"Don't worry, I won't."

Rose pulled into the left turn lane, waited for the light to change, then made her turn. Up ahead a sign marked the entrance to Van Nuys Aviation. Rose slowed then entered the parking lot.

Gary straightened up and pointed. "Park over there near that fence."

"Okay," Rose said.

She pulled into a slot between a Lexus LX SUV and a new Corvette. "You sure they let Malibus park here?"

"No problem this early in the morning."

She put the car in park, shut off the engine, and pushed the button to open the trunk. A muted *thump* sounded behind them, and the trunk lid raised partway up. Gary got out, stretched his legs, and stepped to the rear of the car. He lifted out Ann's bag and then his own. John grabbed his, and Rose closed the trunk.

"If you need us for anything, call Dan's mobile number," Gary told Rose. "He'll be monitoring it twenty-four-seven."

"I'm counting on it, but I especially want to be able to reach Ann in case those HR programs give me any more trouble."

"Don't worry," Ann said. "I'll keep in touch."

"Thanks." Rose turned to Gary. "Now be careful. Don't be doing anything foolish."

Gary laughed. "Why are you looking at me?"

"Because you're the main troublemaker."

Gary glanced over at John.

"Don't be pulling me into this," John said. "Sounds like she has your number."

Gary stood on his tiptoes and looked over the fence. Light from the mercury vapor lights reflected off the Learjet's glossy paint. The open air-stair door looked like a narrow mouth. Two men in dark suits stood behind the wing near the baggage compartment.

"Come on, they're waiting for us," Gary said. Then he looked back at Rose. "Bye, Rose."

"See you," she said.

Gary led the way through the gate and out onto the tarmac, his shoes making a grinding sound on the rough surface. Mike turned and waved.

"Right on time," he said.

"Didn't want to hold you guys up."

"Thanks. Our paying customers aren't always that considerate, but then, they're the ones that pay the bill."

"I hear that."

Mike nodded toward the man beside him. "Gary, I'd like you to meet Chuck Allen. Chuck's my regular copilot."

The man had brown eyes and close-cropped brown hair, and he was a good head shorter than Mike. Gary shook hands with him.

"Pleased to meet you, Chuck. I'm Gary Nesbitt, and these are my colleagues, Ann O'Brien and John Mason."

Chuck murmured his greetings and shook their hands. He was obviously in a hurry to get under way, and that suited Gary.

Chuck waved toward the cargo hatch. "Please step over here, and I'll load your baggage."

Gary handed him his suitcase and watched as Chuck stowed it, followed by Ann's two bags and one for John. After securing the baggage, the copilot closed the hatch and made sure it was secure.

"We're good to go," he told Mike.

Mike waved his hand toward the cabin door and grinned. "You heard the man. We're boarding all rows."

Ann went up first, followed by John. Gary entered the cabin and saw Ann settling into the first forward-facing seat on the left-hand side while John, with a Cheshire cat smile, stood beside the one on the right.

"You weren't wanting this seat, were you?" he asked. Before Gary could answer, John laughed and moved over to the opposite, rear-facing club seat. "Sit down. I know you want to see what's going on up front."

"Thanks," Gary said sheepishly.

Mike and Chuck clambered aboard. The pilot pushed aside the curtain and slipped his lanky frame into the left seat while Chuck retracted the air stair, pulled the door shut, and latched it. That done, he hurried forward, sat down, and began reading the checklist. Mike answered each item as he checked or set each control, his hands darting about like a symphony conductor. Gary's eyes roved about the narrow view he had of the flight deck. Soon a whine sounded and quickly ascended in pitch and volume, followed by the other engine. They spooled up quickly, and moments later the cabin lights flickered.

Mike's assured voice drifted back from the flight deck. "This is one-seven-four-niner Golf Bravo at Van Nuys Aviation for taxi instructions."

Gary couldn't hear the tower's reply since Mike and Chuck were wearing radio headsets with boom mikes. But a few moments later, the whine of the engines increased, and the Learjet rolled onto the taxiway and turned north.

"Looks like we'll be taking off from runway one-six right," Gary said.

John grinned. "Wish you were up front driving?"

"I cannot tell a lie," Gary replied. "You *bet* I do."

"Our line of work not interesting enough for you?"

Gary shook his head. "No, it's not that. I just love flying."

"I could hardly tell."

"Right, and who is it that gets all wrapped up in making gadgets?"

"I prefer 'custom electronic equipment,' but that's related to our business."

"So is flying, at least on occasion."

John's eyebrows shot up. "One occasion in particular."

"Yeah."

Gary sat back in his seat, alternating looking out his window at the runway and out a narrow slice of the windshield. There were no aircraft in front of them, so he expected a quick departure. He listened to the pilots continuing their checklist litany. The aircraft reached the end of the taxiway, turned right, and stopped.

"This is one-seven-four-niner Golf Bravo, ready for takeoff," Mike said. He listened to the controller's response then said, "Four-niner Golf Bravo, roger." He glanced back into the cabin and announced over the intercom, "Hold on to your breakfast; we're cleared for immediate departure."

Mike pushed the power levers forward and steered the Learjet onto the runway then continued applying power. The powerful fan-jets pushed Gary back in his seat, and the runway markers began streaking past. About halfway down the strip, Mike eased back on the control wheel, and the plane leapt into the air and entered a steep climb. After a sharp left turn, they held an easterly course for several minutes then made several gentle turns while continuing to climb.

About twenty minutes later, they leveled off. Mike turned his head and pushed one of his earphones back so he could hear.

"Anyone want coffee?" he asked.

"Thought you'd never ask," Gary said.

"I hear that. I'll send Chuck back after we get caught up on our chores."

"I think I can manage it."

"Okay. The dispensers are back near the lav."

"You guys want regular or decaf?"

"We both take the real thing," Mike said.

Gary released his seat belt, got up, and promptly bumped his head on the ceiling. He hunched and walked down the narrow aisle. He spotted the two spigots then located a plastic tray, some foam cups, and next to them a bowl containing sugar, nondairy creamer packets, and stirrers. He filled two cups from the regular spigot.

"I better take care of our pilots first," Gary said as he passed Ann. "Wouldn't want them going to sleep on us."

"By all means," Ann said.

Gary reached the flight deck and looked out the windshield. Most of the urban ocean of lights was behind them now, and ahead lay desert blackness stretching out to the unseen horizon. The sky directly ahead was beginning to turn gray, the first sign of the approaching sunrise.

"Here it is," Gary said, lowering the tray.

Mike took one of the cups. The copilot dumped two sugars and one creamer into his coffee. Gary put in a stirrer. Chuck took the cup and began mixing.

"Thanks," Mike said. "Our clients would *never* think of serving us coffee."

"Hey, it's the least I could do."

Gary returned to the cabin, filled two more cups, served Ann and John, then put away the tray and supplies, filled his cup, and returned to his seat. He took an eager sip and smiled. It was exactly the way he liked it, hot and strong. He settled down and looked out through the flight deck. The eastern horizon gradually turned light gray then pink until the sun's blazing orange disk finally made its appearance. Morning progressed quite rapidly, sped along by the plane's eastern movement. It wasn't long before the sun's brilliant glare turned the flight deck into a greenhouse.

About an hour later, Chuck appeared in the aisle and looked at Gary. "Mike wants to know if you'd like to join him in the cockpit."

Gary looked up and grinned. "That isn't a trick question, is it?"

Chuck smiled, but it was strained. He obviously didn't want to give up his seat even for a little while. "Nope. Go on up. I gotta make a trip to the lav anyway." He hurried past.

Gary got up, stepped through to the flight deck, and stood behind the center pedestal.

"Sit down," Mike said.

Gary eased himself into the comfortable contour seat but had to bend his knees at an uncomfortable angle.

"Move it back," Mike said, pointing to the controls. "You're quite a bit taller than Chuck."

Gary adjusted the seat to his liking then looked all around the instrument panel, marveling at the wealth of information presented on the large screens. Then he looked up and out through the large, curved windshield. The sky was an inverted bowl of deepest blue except where the sun turned it white. Fluffy white clouds lay ahead and below them.

"Nice, very nice," Gary said finally.

"The plane or the view?"

"Both."

"The Lear is a sweet plane to fly, and you couldn't ask for better avionics."

"I'll say. Makes the Piper Arrow look like a toy."

"*Any* plane beats driving."

"Yeah, except when the weather's lousy."

"That can be a problem even for a jet, but not today. Ceiling and visibility unlimited all the way to New York, at least according to the FAA Flight Service Station guys." Mike scanned the instruments then looked over at Gary. "Like to take the controls for a bit?"

"You don't have to ask me twice."

"As you probably know, we usually stay on autopilot while we're cruising, but what's the fun in that? I have it." He reached down and flipped a switch. "Autopilot is now off. See the altimeter and heading displays?"

Gary did a quick scan of the integrated screen in front of him. "Got 'em."

"Okay, keep our altitude at plus or minus a hundred feet, and don't wander too far off course."

"Will do. Anything else?"

"Try not to upset the passengers."

"I think I can manage that."

"Very good. You have it." Mike took his hands off the control wheel and eased back in his seat a little.

Gary grasped the wheel, well aware that his grin was probably as close to ear-to-ear as it would ever get. He pulled back on the control yoke gently, and the altitude shot up by ninety feet. He used a gentler touch and eased back down to the assigned flight level.

"It's quite responsive," Gary said.

"Isn't it, though?"

Gary turned the wheel left and pressed the left rudder pedal. The Learjet obediently entered a left bank with the altimeter indicating a slight descent. Gary pulled back on the yoke to stop that then leveled out and turned right, this time a little steeper.

"How's it feel?" Mike asked.

"Great. I'd love to learn to fly one of these."

"Well, once you're rich and famous. . ."

"Yeah, right."

Gary turned his head at a sound and saw Chuck standing behind him. "You have it," he said to Mike.

Mike took the controls, made a minor course correction, and flipped on the autopilot.

"Thanks," Gary said.

"You're welcome."

Gary got up, slipped past the copilot, and returned to the cabin. He sighed as he sat down across from John.

"So how was it?" John asked.

"Great. It handles like a dream."

John grinned. "Wondered if that was you driving. Made me wish I had bought flight insurance."

"Very funny."

John glanced at his watch. "Pretty soon we'll be punching the time clock."

Gary took a deep breath. "Yeah. I hope Dan and Sully are ready for us. I'm looking forward to getting to work."

CHAPTER 5

The intercom speaker crackled. "This is your captain speaking," Mike announced. "On behalf of myself and the entire crew, thank you for choosing Air Jacobs, and we hope that next time you travel, you'll take the bus. Now be sure to check for any items you may have brought on board 'cause we get to keep anything you leave behind."

"Very funny," Gary said, raising his voice.

The Learjet rolled to a stop at Bluegrass Aviation, a fixed base operator at Louisville International Airport. Mike finished the shutdown procedure and entered the cabin. Chuck squeezed by him, opened the door, and stepped down onto the tarmac.

"Hey, I never get to joke with paying customers," Mike said. He hurried out the door and into the midmorning sun.

Gary, John, and Ann followed him around to the baggage compartment. Chuck stood beside the door and began pulling out the suitcases.

"I'll finish here," Mike told Chuck. "How about getting the pump jockey started on refueling?"

"Right." Chuck turned and did a quick scan of the faces

surrounding him. "Nice to meet all of you," he said quickly then turned and headed for the fuel truck.

Mike lowered his voice. "Chuck's kinda task oriented." He pulled out the last bag and shut the compartment door.

"We understand," Gary said. "Listen, we sure appreciate the ride. Thanks."

"You're welcome. Glad it worked out this way." He shook each of their hands in turn.

"And I know you're busy, so we'll get out of your way."

Mike looked toward the fuel truck then back at Gary. "We *do* have a tight schedule today. Hope I see you soon back at Van Nuys."

"Me, too. Take care."

Mike turned, walked around the wing, and entered the aircraft.

Gary led the way toward the modest terminal. Sully and Dan waited at the fence that guarded the flight line.

Sully waved. "Hey, dude," he said. "Cool way to travel."

"Sure is," Gary said. "Are we ready to roll?"

"Don't know about the spook shop, but the kid is."

Dan frowned and pushed his glasses up on his nose. "We're ready."

Gary saw a large white truck in the parking lot. "Let's do it. Is Thomas expecting us?"

"He is."

Dan led the way across the asphalt parking lot to the rear of the truck and opened the large double doors. Gary's sharp eyes couldn't spot the exterior video cameras, but he knew they were there. He looked inside. The auxiliary power unit hummed away in a corner, supplying power for the air-conditioning and the electronics. A worktable ran along the front and wrapped around the right side. Up above, a row of monitors provided views of outside and the truck cab's interior. On the left, the costume locker occupied the front corner, followed by storage cabinets with shelves above and below.

"Where's the telescoping mast?" Gary asked.

"Ran out of time," Dan said. He handed out three, tiny flesh-colored objects. "Here are your earphone radios."

"I'll help you with the mast after the meeting," John said.

"Let's get this show on the road," Gary said.

Sully dashed forward to the cab and jumped inside. Dan stepped up into the cargo box and walked forward to his communications console. Ann and John followed. Gary climbed up and closed the doors then grabbed a chair and joined the others around the communications expert.

Dan flipped a switch and spoke into a mike. "We're all set," he said.

"Roger," Sully said over the intercom.

Sully wasted no time in exiting the airport and pulling up onto westbound Interstate 264. Several miles later he turned south on U.S. 31 for the long drive that merged with the Ohio River. Gary watched the busy traffic in the forward monitor.

"So how did the preliminary work go?" he asked.

"The truck took most of our time, but we managed to map some of the communications lines. Most are secure, but a surprising number are unprotected. Ann should have a field day hacking into that mess."

"Can't wait," Ann said.

"What's your overall impression of Fort Knox?" John asked.

Dan brought up PowerPoint on his laptop and directed the display to an overhead monitor. A series of slides began cycling. "First of all, it's huge; the reservation is nearly as big as Louisville. It's an open post, which means it doesn't have a secured perimeter, however, about half of the reservation is divided into training areas and army commands, and those *are* guarded. Fort Knox is a Kentucky town as well as an army facility, with civilians living and working throughout. Also, the town of Radcliff is inside the reservation while Muldraugh is completely surrounded by it."

Ann grinned when she spotted a familiar picture. "What about the gold vault?" she asked.

"The bullion depository is inside the reservation, but since it's part of the mint, we're not concerned with it. It's a good thing, too, because the physical security goes *way* beyond paranoid."

"I bet we could find a way in," Sully said over the intercom.

"Pay attention to your driving," Gary said.

"I am."

"Where are we meeting Thomas?" Gary asked Dan.

Dan punched up a GPS moving map display. "In an unused classroom that belongs to the armor school."

"Speaking of armor. . . ," Sully said.

Gary grinned. "What about armor, Mr. Sullivan?"

"I think I know a way we can swipe a tank."

That surprised Gary, despite his experience with Sully's resourcefulness. "You're kidding."

"Nope."

Gary glanced at Dan, who shrugged.

"Let's talk about it after the meeting," Gary said.

"Can't wait."

Neither can I, Gary thought as he mulled over the size of the bonus.

The road made an arcing turn to the south and entered the Fort Knox Reservation. Several miles later, Sully took the Chaffee Avenue exit and drove through the main gate. A few minutes later, he held up a temporary pass for a guard and drove into a compound.

"We're here," Sully announced as he turned into a parking lot beside a drab, two-story building.

Dan grabbed a joystick, slued the forward camera around, and zoomed in on a man standing in a doorway. "There's Thomas," he said.

Gary eyed the close-up picture. Thomas looked about five ten and was stocky without being fat. Gary guessed him to be in his early thirties. Thomas's brown eyes, behind wire-rimmed glasses, watched the truck approach with obvious interest. His fringe of black hair and prominent bald spot reminded Gary of a monk's tonsure.

"He's wearing a suit, I see," Gary said.

"And us in California casual," John said.

Gary laughed. "So much for matching the client's dress code. Oh, well, the army's paying for performance not appearance."

Sully brought the truck to a smooth stop. Thomas started walking toward the parking lot.

"Here we go, ready or not," Gary said. He led the way to the back, opened the doors, and stepped down, squinting in the sudden glare.

Sully joined the team as Thomas made his way through the parked cars.

Gary stepped forward. "We meet at last," he said. "I'm Gary." They shook hands. "And this is John Mason and our computer expert, Ann O'Brien, Dan Thompson, communications, and our driver, Sean Sullivan."

Ann, John, Sully, and Dan exchanged hurried greetings with Thomas, who was obviously preoccupied.

"Are you ready to start the audit?" Thomas asked.

"After we complete the paperwork," Gary said.

"Then let's go inside."

Thomas turned and led the way, taking long strides. Upon reaching the door, he opened it and waited while the team filed inside. Gary's eyes took in the classroom's well-worn student desks and noted a faint, musty smell. The front row of desks was pushed aside to make room for a long table and six folding chairs. Thomas sat at the head of the table. Gary and John took the chairs nearest him. Ann sat beside Gary while Dan and Sully took the chairs next to John.

"I hope you'll forgive the rush, but I want this audit under way ASAP." Thomas looked at Gary. "I know you remember what happened last time, and I don't want to borrow trouble, but it could happen again because this contract also has a termination clause."

Gary felt a pang of concern. "Do you think it's likely?"

"Probably not, since the GAO is known for capriciousness but not speed." A wry smile came to his face. "That is *not* on the record."

Gary smiled. "Understood."

"Now, here's the contract, one copy for you, one for me." He pushed two thick binders over to Gary and an unsealed envelope. "I've already signed them, and the envelope contains the addendum you requested. SecurityCheck personnel are absolved of responsibility for reasonable collateral damage resulting from the execution of this contract, etcetera, and so on and so forth."

Gary gave John one copy of the contract then pulled out the addendum and read it over quickly. Once he was sure it offered them the protection they needed, he turned to the contract and began skimming it.

"It's exactly what I e-mailed you," Thomas said.

Gary could see that it was and saw no reason for delay. He luxuriated in the weight of the document, which seemed to represent the amount of revenue they would earn from it. He looked up at John.

"Shall we?" Gary asked.

"Let's do it," John said. He turned to the last page and signed his name, and Gary did likewise with his copy. Then they traded and completed the signatures. Thomas took the binder John held. Gary slipped the addendum into the company's copy.

Thomas handed Gary a check. "And here's your advance check, the balance to be paid on completion."

Gary took it, scanned the amount, and smiled. "Our creditors thank you." He folded the check and stuck it in his wallet.

"Now, let's review the ground rules. Once you leave this classroom, you're on your own. The contract allows you a month to complete the report, but I believe you estimated two or three weeks?"

Gary nodded. "That should be enough."

"Good. You have my mobile number. Call when you're done—or if there's an emergency."

"We'll try to avoid that."

"I certainly hope so. Anything else?"

Gary stood up, and the rest of the team did, as well. "I don't think so," he said. "Thanks. I'll be in contact." He led the way to the door and outside.

"Take us off the post," Gary said to Sully. "We have some planning to do."

"Right, boss," Sully said. He loped to the truck and climbed into the driver's seat.

Gary hurried to the back of the truck, opened the doors, and waited for the others to climb in. Then he stepped up and closed the doors. The truck started backing up.

Lieutenant Colonel Dick Edwards leaned over his keyboard and reread the e-mail, this time more carefully. His brown eyes flashed as he digested this latest status request from Hamid Momeni, the Iranian expatriate who had somehow wormed his way into the CIA as an infectious disease expert. Ever since the project's inception, he had been resentful that Hamid was, in effect, Dick's boss because of the CIA's direct involvement through the department of homeland security. That wasn't what the army's chain of command said, but that's the way it actually worked out.

Dick sat back in his chair and pondered what he should put in his report. Icy pangs shot through his entire system as he thought about his findings so far. His lab had indeed managed to culture the frozen virus locked within the tissue samples, and chances were good they would be able to culture a vaccine, which was fortunate because the original outbreak had killed 85 percent of the people in Teller Mission, now called Brevig Mission. Whatever this virus was, it had been highly infectious and extremely lethal. *What if it got out again?* Dick wondered. A shiver ran down his spine. If that happened, it wouldn't be an epidemic or even a pandemic. It would be the end of civilization.

John climbed up into the truck and closed the doors. "That should do it," he said.

Dan pressed a button, and a high-pitched whine came from outside. Gary looked up at the center monitor. The microcam's view opened up as the telescoping mast shot up high into the air. Dan panned the camera around, providing a bird's-eye panorama of Otter Park. To the north, a bend in the Ohio River separated the park from southern Indiana while the Fort Knox Reservation surrounded them on the other sides except for a narrow gap in the west.

"Nice," Gary said. "How about the parabolic antenna?"

Dan flipped some switches and checked the various meter readings on his PC. "Performing like a champ," he said. "Our Internet connection is up, and I'm picking up just about every flavor of radio transmission there is. We're not hurting for communications."

Gary rubbed his hands together. "Okay. Looks like we're good to go, and that includes a fully stocked larder, thanks to our chief nutritionist."

Ann put her hands on her hips. "Listen, Gary, if I left it to *you* guys, all we'd have would be chips and soft drinks."

Gary grinned. "And your point is?"

"Very funny."

"Seriously, thank you."

"You're welcome."

Gary looked at Dan. "So what have you and Sully scoped out so far?"

Dan pushed his glasses up his nose. "About what I expected. We mapped out a lot of their comm lines, both landline and microwave. Most are secure or encrypted, but a few aren't. I expect Ann will be able to wreak a lot of havoc. We videoed all the secured perimeters and recorded a lot of their comm signals. Physical security looks pretty good, but you and John are the experts on that."

"Okay, then we'll review all the data and start sniffing out the weak spots." Gary suppressed a grin as he noted Sully's growing excitement. "Does Mr. Sullivan have something to add?"

"Hey, dude, you want a good deal on a clean, low-mileage tank?"

"You got one to sell?"

"Naw, but I know where we can swipe one."

"I presume you mean an army M1A1 Abrams main battle tank, which our contract mentions as a bonus item."

"Aw, you got it on the first try."

Gary settled back in his chair. "Tell me about it."

Sully leaned forward and a bright animation came into his eyes. "It started when Dan snagged this e-mail. . . ." He looked at Dan. "Help me, dude."

"I located an unsecure microwave link, part of the post intranet. It was an e-mail to the armor school command reporting an M1A1 Abrams tank stranded on a boulder in one of the training areas."

"Wait," Gary interrupted. "This e-mail wasn't encrypted?"

"It was. But thanks to Ann's hacker suite, I was able to crack it."

Gary looked down the table at Ann. "Way to go."

She flushed. "That's what I'm paid for."

Gary turned back to Sully. "Go on."

"Right. So while Dan was slurping up all the net traffic, he came across the reply. They're sending an M88 tank retriever at 4:00 p.m. to pull the tank off."

"Sixteen hundred hours," Dan said.

"Whatever. Anyhow, I figure if we get there first, the kid gets to drive a for-real army tank while the cash register goes *ka-ching*."

"Sully! That's no plan. What about security? How do we get the tank off the rock?"

"Hey, dude, I'm just the driver."

Gary was tempted to throw the idea away since it would take at least some planning, and they didn't have much time. He glanced at his watch and saw it was almost twelve thirty. Almost *no* time. Still, taking the tank would certainly help the company's bottom line, and they might not have another chance. His mind began exploring the obstacles that stood in their way.

"We have less than four hours," John said. "We can't do it—period. We need to—"

"Hold on," Gary interrupted. "Why don't we brainstorm it? The least that can happen is we run out of time. For starters, how would we get the tank free? Tow it?"

"That's how the army plans to do it," Dan said.

"Yeah, but we don't have a tank retriever. Give me something else."

"Well, I guess we could pulverize the boulder with shaped charges," John said.

"Okay, that sounds promising," Gary said. "How would we place them? Is there enough room under there?"

"I have seen Abrams blueprints," Ann said. "There is ample clearance."

"What about entry?" Gary asked. "The training area *is* guarded, isn't it?"

"Oh, yes," Dan said. "Perimeter fence, gates, and guards."

"What about going disguised as soldiers?" Ann asked. "You could tell the guards the armor school sent you over, I don't know, for something or other."

Gary thought that over. "Maybe. But we sure can't drive up in the spy-mobile."

"What about our rental car?"

Gary looked at Sully. "What did you get us?"

"Like you said, boss, a nice family car," Sully said. "It's a Windstar minivan complete with a child seat."

"How thoughtful."

"Glad you like it."

"Did you fix it up with post decals?" Gary asked Dan.

"Sure did, for an armor school officer; exact replicas. Made 'em on the plastic film printer."

"That tank training area is probably rugged, and a minivan isn't exactly a Hummer. What happens if we get stuck?"

"We have a couple of sheets of plywood," John said. "How about I cut us some planks, just in case?"

"Yeah, that should do it. I like what I'm hearing so far. We get in, John and I blast that boulder, then Sully drives the tank out."

"Say we pull this off," Ann said. "Where do we stash it? Don't we have to have possession for a certain length of time?"

"That's right. A day, I think." He looked at John.

John nodded. "That's a roger. Twenty-four whole hours."

"When we discussed this possibility back home, we assumed we'd be able to rent a transport truck. But we don't have time for that." He looked at each team member in turn. "Listen. Sully has a *good* idea, and we've worked out most of the obstacles. Come on now. Where can we hide that tank?"

"What about behind an embankment?" John said. "Abandoned rail line, old overpass, something like that?"

Gary shook his head. "Not gonna work. The army's going to be *all over* the place looking for their lost toy. Now I know this thing is huge, but there must be *some* way we can hide it."

Sully turned in his chair and looked at Gary, his dark eyes glinting. "Hey, the best place to hide that thing is out in the open."

"What?" John asked, raising his voice.

Gary started to object, as well, but stopped when he saw Sully's intent expression. "Please explain," he said instead.

"Any of you dudes ever seen a tank in a park?"

Gary only hesitated a moment as his mind took the idea and

ran with it. "Yes, I'm sure we all have. But they've all been old World War Two tanks."

"Yeah, man, but we're in Tankland. I bet some of the local parks have modern stuff. Like, even the new ones wear out sometime."

"That won't work," John said. "The army's bound to spot it, and when they check it out, there goes our bonus."

"Hold on; this has possibilities," Gary said. "We have everything we need to disguise a tank: change the serial numbers, make it look beat-up and old. And I bet we can find a handy park."

"Won't we need a dedication plaque or something?" Ann asked.

"Probably." Gary smiled and rubbed his hands together. "How about searching for a suitable National Guard donor?" He turned to Dan. "Can you and Ann work out a suitable dedication?"

"As long as she does the artwork."

"Be glad to," Ann said.

Gary shifted in his chair and looked up at the ceiling. The auxiliary power unit and air-conditioner hums mingled with the various cooling fans inside the communications and computing hardware. The prospect was certainly enticing, and the plan seemed to be taking shape. There was a lot to do and not much time, but then, that was the way most of their operations went. He smiled as he reflected on the fact that they had had very few failures. There was no substitute for quick, decisive action, of that he was quite sure.

Gary stood up. "Okay, let's do it!"

Everyone except Dan got up. He pulled his laptop over and began checking his communications circuits.

"Sully," Gary said.

"Yes, boss?"

"Drive us to the minivan, then get back in here and I'll help you with your disguise."

"I'm gone." He jumped up and ran for the back doors.

CHAPTER 6

Gary glanced at the clock on the Windstar's dash and felt an icy jolt in his stomach. It read 2:49, and they had a little over an hour to snatch the tank. Tight, very tight, but he was convinced they could do it. He shifted his gaze to the laptop computer displaying the GPS moving map and saw they were nearing the gate. He returned his eyes to the road.

"This is Armor Base, radio check," his earphone radio announced. Dan's voice was crystal clear over the encrypted radio link.

"Armor One," Gary said in a normal voice.

"Armor Two," John replied.

Gary waited, but the only sound he heard was road noise. "Hey, Sully, answer the man."

"Oh, yeah, sorry. Armor Three, locked and loaded."

Gary rolled his eyes but said nothing.

"This is Armor Base, all systems are go. Hacker reports destination downloaded."

Gary looked at the map again and saw a flashing red tank icon.

"Roger, Armor Base. We have it."

"Armor Base out."

"Cool," Sully said.

"Glad you approve," Gary said.

The team's truck was parked several miles away, where Dan could monitor the operation while linked into the post's intranet. Gary rounded a curve and spotted the gate leading to an armor training area. Two armed soldiers stood guard outside.

"Here we go," he said. "Remember your military bearing."

"Roger that, boss," Sully said.

"That's 'Captain' to you, Corporal."

"Yes, sir."

"That's better."

Gary slowed down and lowered his window as he neared the gate. The guard on the driver's side of the van snapped to attention and saluted. Gary returned it.

"May I see your ID, sir?" the private asked.

Gary pulled out his wallet and showed the guard the ID Ann had produced after a brief search on the post intranet. The seconds dragged on, and Gary began to worry.

"Thank you, sir," the soldier finally said. His alert eyes made a quick circuit inside the van, taking in John and Sully before returning to Gary. "Sir, the only authorized entry is for an M88 team at 1600 to retrieve a tank."

"I'm aware of that, but the command duty officer wants us to look the situation over. If we can drive the tank off, it will save a lot of time and expense."

The man frowned and shifted his feet. "I don't know, sir. This isn't covered in my orders. I'll have to radio for instructions."

Gary felt an almost irresistible urge to whisper a warning, but he knew Dan would be on the job.

"This is guard post—" The man stopped suddenly when his radio speaker erupted in static. "This is guard post Foxtrot, radio check!" Nothing but static came from the speaker. The man glared at his shoulder-mounted mike in disgust then looked up at Gary.

"Private," Gary said, "I don't know why command failed to notify you, but we have our orders to check out that tank. Now, since you can't get through to your command post, I suggest you let us get on with our work."

Still the man hesitated then finally stepped back and motioned for his companion to open the gate. The chain-link barrier topped with razor wire swung open, and the guard saluted. Gary returned it and drove through the gap and onto a rolling expanse of grass and dirt tracks.

In the distance, dark green trees and dense brush broke up the undulating terrain that seemed almost pastoral except for the dark shell holes, rutted trails, and wrecked wooden buildings. The van bounced and lurched along an uneven dirt road. Off to the left, a line of trees blocked their view of the parallel trail that led to the tank. A few hundred yards farther, the road degenerated into a barely passable trail. Gary slowed and angled to the right and through a rocky gully toward smoother ground.

"Stop immediately, Armor One!" Dan's voice shouted in Gary's ear.

Gary stomped on the brake. The van slid to a stop on the soft shoulder of what looked like a dirt road.

"What's wrong, Armor Base?" Gary replied.

"You're right on the edge of a tank trap. Hacker just found it."

Now Gary understood. What looked like a road was actually a deep trench covered by lightweight planking and a thin covering of dirt. A tank plunging through that would be trapped until retrieved by an M88. That the pit would be equally effective on a minivan went without saying. Sweat popped up under Gary's armpits.

"That was close," he said. John looked over at him, his expression a mixture of fear and relief.

"Roger that," Dan said in Gary's ear. "Go back to the trail you were on."

"Roger. Armor One out." Gary turned the wheel sharply left, turned away from the trap, then angled back toward the rutted track. He looked down at the laptop's moving map display and saw they were about a thousand yards from their first turn, a trail that crossed at right angles. He tried increasing his speed several times, but each time he had to back off to avoid wrecking the van. Several minutes later Gary made a broad, lurching left turn. He tried to steer along the new trail's outer edge, which was slightly smoother than the deep ruts in the center, but still had to slow to a crawl.

"Want me to drive?" Sully asked.

That made sense to Gary, now that they were past the guards, but still, they didn't have that far to go.

"I think I can handle it," Gary said.

Up ahead he saw their next turn, another left that would bring them around parallel to the entrance road. Gary slowed down, dodged a deep hole, and made the turn. The van started up a steep hill. A few moments later, the screening line of trees blocked their view of the way they came in. Several hundred yards away on the right, a dense forest cut off their view in that direction. Gary worked the wheel constantly, wincing each time the van bottomed out. Finally they reached the hill's crest, and a shallow valley opened up below. The forest on the right wrapped around until it joined with the tree line, forming an elongated U. Gary's eyes followed the track down to a large, squat shape right in the middle of the trail.

"There's the tank," he said.

"Watch it!" Sully shouted.

The van lurched and slid to a grinding stop.

"You fell in a hole," he added.

Gary pressed the accelerator. The left front wheel whined, throwing grit and rocks up against the wheel well. Gary let up on the gas and turned his head. "Thanks for that live update," he grumbled. "Sully?"

"Yes, boss?"

"Drive."

"I'm on it."

Sully threw open the side door, jumped out, and came around to the front. Gary got out, and together they looked down at the wheel. John hurried to the back and opened the rear doors.

"Could we jam something against it?" Gary asked.

Sully shook his head. "Naw, gotta put something under it. I'll get the jack."

"Hurry it up."

Sully pulled out the jack, set it under the frame, and started pumping the handle. "Yo, John. I need something about five or six inches high to put under the wheel."

"How about a toolbox?"

"That should do it."

Sully worked frantically jacking the van. Less than a minute later, he stopped and looked into the hole. "See if that's high enough."

John lowered the box into the hole and pushed it under the tire.

"Perfect," Sully said.

He let down the jack, pulled it out, and jumped into the driver's seat, holding the door open so he could see. He cranked the engine, drove out of the hole, and stopped. He jumped out and threw the jack into the back while John retrieved his toolbox.

"Pile in, dudes," Sully said as he got back in.

Gary dashed around to the other side, held the door for John, and got in beside him. Sully yanked the gearshift into drive and started out. He worked the throttle and wheel constantly, and although the ride was far from smooth, he made better time. When they reached the bottom of the hill, Gary glanced at the dash clock. They now had less than forty-five minutes. As they neared the back of the tank, he saw it was tilted up in the front. Sully brought the van to a sliding stop a car length away and jumped out.

Gary opened his door and got out. He looked over at the line of trees on the left and saw they were hidden from the entrance road and gate.

John opened a side door, grabbed two plastic cases, and pulled them out. He nodded toward the other side. "How about grabbing some flashlights."

"Right," Gary said. "Sully, hop in the tank, and start checking it out."

"I'm on it." Sully took a running leap and landed on the tank's left fender. He clambered up on the hull, onto the turret, opened the hatch, and disappeared inside.

Gary reached into the van, grabbed two flashlights, and joined John at the back of the tank. They dropped to their knees then down on their stomachs. Gary looked into the dark cave formed by the underside of the hull and clicked on a flashlight.

"Look at the size of that rock," he said. "Must be three or four feet across."

"Yeah, but we can take that top right off. Looks like about six inches ought to do it. I'll set the charges in the front while you take care of the back." He pushed one of the boxes toward Gary and grabbed one of the flashlights.

"You're sure these are safe?" Gary was kidding, for the most part.

John laughed. "Guaranteed or your money back." He stood up and hurried around to the front of the tank.

Gary crawled under, pushing the box of explosives and his flashlight ahead of him. After reaching the boulder, he positioned the light so he could see, opened the box, and pulled out the first charge. He heard John scrabbling around on the other side but couldn't see him.

"Where do I place them?" Gary asked.

"About six inches down from the top. I'll place one on the side to guide you."

Gary crawled around and watched as John pulled the protective tape off and pressed the explosive block firmly against the rock.

"See how the angle of the rock varies?" John asked.

"Yeah. Some places are straight up and down but others slope at an angle."

"Right. Your box has a divider in it. The blocks marked '90' are for the vertical places, and the ones marked '45' are for the angles. Leave about an inch between blocks."

"Are these things already fused?"

"Yes. Now, how about some action over there? Time's wasting."

Gary pulled out a block marked "90" and gingerly pulled the protective tape away. He inched closer and stuck the explosive near the one John had placed. Gary worked his way along quickly until the line of blocks went all the way around the rock like a belt and he met up with John on the other side.

"Okay," John said. "Back the van away while I set up the detonator."

"I'm outta here."

Gary grabbed his flashlight, squirmed around, and pushed the explosives box out ahead of him. He emerged into the bright afternoon sunlight and stood up. John came around from the front of the tank and pulled out a small electronic device that resembled a telephone keypad.

"Where to?" Gary asked.

John looked around and pointed. "Drive off to the side. The blast effect should be minimal since the shaped charges direct all the force into the rock."

"Famous last words."

John grinned. "Remember the guarantee."

"Where are you going to be?"

"On top of the tank."

"Okay. Take care, now."

Gary gathered up the explosives boxes and flashlights and returned them to the van then drove around to the left of the tank, about fifty feet away. John scrambled up onto the tank's hull and walked forward until he was next to the turret. Then he held up the detonator.

"This is Armor Two, stand by."

"Armor One, roger."

"Armor Base, roger."

Gary waited for Sully's acknowledgment, but the seconds ticked on in silence.

"Armor Three, this is Armor One. Acknowledge."

"Oh, yeah. Sorry, dudes. This is Armor Three. Blow that thing."

Some things never change, Gary thought. He considered ducking down in the seat but decided he trusted John's expertise. Besides, he wanted to see what happened. He tensed up and riveted his eyes on the wheels within the tank's left track. A bright flash briefly illuminated the undercarriage, accompanied by a muted *whump*. The tank dropped down with a loud mechanical crash and rocked on its suspension. Fine, white dust billowed out and slowly settled.

Gary opened his door and stepped out of the van. John jumped down and ran over. He opened the passenger door and got in.

"Nice job," Gary said.

"I aim to please."

A high-pitched whine sounded and quickly increased in pitch and volume. The tank's turbine was running, and the air behind shimmered in the hot exhaust.

"Armor Three, ready to roll."

"Roger," Gary replied. He looked down at the GPS map then scanned the surrounding trees. The only way out was the way they had come in. "Armor Base, Armor One is coming out."

"Copy, Armor One."

"Armor Three, move out."

"Roger that."

The massive M1A1 Abrams lurched into motion and made a sharp 180 to the right. Gary waited until it roared past then turned the van and pulled in behind. He smiled. Up this trail, across, and back down the entrance road. They were within minutes of making off with their bonus item.

"Armor One, we have trouble."

Gary felt an icy jolt in the pit of his stomach. "Go ahead, Armor Base."

"The tank retriever and a transport truck just passed us."

"Any chance we can beat them to the gate?"

"Negative."

Gary stepped on the brake. "Armor Three, stop immediately."

The heavy tank ground to a halt in a cloud of dust.

Gary eyed the map. "Armor Base, we need another way out."

"Wait one."

Gary glanced at the dash clock. It was now 3:41. He looked over at John.

"They're early," John said.

"Sit tight."

"Hey, dudes, what do we do?" Sully asked.

Gary gritted his teeth. "Armor Three, this is Armor One. Armor Base said wait. Out."

If they got caught, which now seemed likely, the procedure for getting released was straightforward, but it was also embarrassing, and it meant forfeiting the bonus. And this Gary wasn't willing to accept, at least not without a fight.

"Armor One, this is Armor Base. We may have something for you. Hacker found an old map showing an abandoned trail. Check your map. Hacker just transmitted the coordinates."

Gary glanced at the blinking red X then looked out his window, his eyes following the forest back a little beyond the truncated boulder. There he saw a gap, almost invisible amid the dense weeds and brush.

"I see it. Where does it go?"

"It curves to the left then runs parallel to the trail you're on and turns right when it reaches the fence. Here's the approximate location."

Another red X appeared on the fence around a bend from the gate they came in. Gary saw they would be hidden from the guards, but that left the problem of getting through the fence. Gary grinned. He knew how they would handle that.

"Armor Three, do you copy?" Gary said.

"I heard that," Sully replied.

"Armor Three, turn around. I'll guide you in."

"Roger."

Sully pivoted the tank and roared past the van. Gary turned around and followed. His eyes flicked back and forth between the GPS map and their bumpy progress down the trail.

"Armor Three, stand by. On my mark, turn 45 degrees right."

"Roger."

Gary mentally marked a point about fifty feet from the truncated boulder and waited until the tank crossed it.

"Mark," Gary said.

The tank pivoted to the right and trundled out over a rolling meadow in the general direction of the gap. Gary knew Sully probably couldn't see the trail because of the restricted view in the driver's periscope. He turned into the tank's wake and waited while the distance to the gap dwindled.

"Armor Three, check your eleven o'clock. See that gap?"

The seconds ticked on.

"Got it," Sully finally said.

"Make us a road."

"Roger that."

The Abrams angled to the left and lurched along, its hull and turret bobbing up and down like a boat cutting across waves. Gary followed the ruts made by the tank's wide treads. Grass, weeds, and brush scraped along the bottom of the van while rocks rattled and banged against the wheel wells. The tank plunged through the gap between two trees with only inches to spare then began a gentle turn to the left.

"This is Armor Three. I can see the trail now. Keep up."

"Roger." Gary steered the van into the forest in a controlled swerve, dodging the scraggly bushes that survived the tank's passing. Once inside, the trail through the trees was easy to see, and scattered saplings showed how long ago it had been abandoned. Sully mowed down most of this new growth, but many of the young trees were merely bent over. Gary had to drive around these, and he gradually fell behind the tank's relentless pace. He soon lost sight of the lumbering Abrams, but its course was impossible to miss. Several minutes later he heard Sully's cheerful voice in his ear.

"Armor Three at the fence."

"This is Armor One, roger. We're still slogging our way through the brush."

"Want me to hammer the fence?"

"Negative. Wait for us."

"Roger."

Gary squeezed the van through a gap between a bent sapling and good-sized oak then sprinted across a clearing. Up ahead he spotted the idling tank, and his eyes jumped to the razor wire that formed a concertina atop the chain-link fence. The Abrams, Gary knew, would have no trouble rolling over it, but the van would never make it without help. Gary's mind raced beyond that problem to the next major hurdle.

"Armor Base, we need an alternate escape route once we're out."

"Understand. Hacker is sending you one now."

Gary pulled in behind the tank and stopped. John looked over and wiped his hands on his pants. Gary watched the progress bar on the download. A yellow overlay appeared on the GPS map marking a loop around the gate that connected with the route to a park several miles away.

"Armor Base, this is Armor One. I have it."

"Armor Base, copy. Be advised, M88 and transport entering gate now. Armor Base, out."

"Armor Three, flatten the fence, turn right, and hold short of the road," Gary said.

"Roger that."

The Abrams lurched into motion and shoved the fence over in what seemed like slow motion. The treads ground their way over the steel mesh, posts, and razor wire. Sully pivoted to the right, rolled forward fifty feet, and stopped. Gary drove the van up onto the chain link and stopped just short of the razor wire.

"Help me with the plywood," Gary said.

They both jumped out and ran around to the rear doors. John threw them open, and Gary grabbed several plywood planks and hurried back to the razor wire. He wedged a board against the front wheel and centered it across part of the sharp metal spiral. The second plank completed the bridge. Gary looked over and saw John had his section in place.

"Drive across," John said. "I'll pick up the boards."

Gary jumped into the driver's seat, yanked the gearshift into drive, and began inching his way along. The mesh and wire twanged as the boards mashed them into the soft turf. With creaks and groans, the front wheels rolled across the planks and down on the grass beyond. The rear wheels followed just as smoothly. Gary turned the van in behind the tank and stopped. He started to get out but saw that John already had the plywood up. The pieces thumped into the open back, and John slammed the doors, raced around, and got in. Gary pulled around the idling tank.

"Armor Three, this is Armor One. Follow me."

"Roger that."

Gary watched in his rearview mirror as the Abrams lumbered out of the ditch and onto the road.

"Armor Base, we're on our way."

"Copy, Armor One."

The trip to their destination turned a few heads, but it didn't attract as much attention as Gary thought it might. Army tanks were a common sight around Fort Knox and not all that rare on civilian streets, according to Ann's research. It was a new park and still under construction, so the team wasn't bothered by onlookers. Gary parked the van behind their truck and hurried over to where Ann was waiting. The Abrams idled in the street, its turbine whining.

"This is Armor Three. Where do you want this thing?" Sully asked.

"Armor Three, wait one."

Gary flicked off his radio earphone.

"Is the plaque ready?" he asked.

"Right over there." Ann pointed toward what looked like a low cement pedestal with an angled brass plate. He took the time to read it.

M1A1 ABRAMS MAIN BATTLE TANK
PRESENTED BY KENTUCKY ARMY NATIONAL GUARD,
149TH ARMOR BRIGADE

"Very nice. Looks real."

Ann laughed. "It's supposed to. The pedestal is foam concrete over cinder block, and the plaque is molded plastic with a matte metallic paint job."

"Excellent. Where should we place the tank?"

She eyed the dedication. "Centered on the plaque, about two feet back."

"Yeah, that should look good." Gary turned on his radio. "Armor Three, this is Armor One. Bring it on."

"One M1A1 Abrams, loaded, coming right up."

Sully pivoted the tank and inched up to the curb. The wide treads climbed up, clattered across the sidewalk, and out onto the grass. Gary guided Sully in with hand signals until the tank was precisely centered.

"Armor Three, shut it down."

"Roger."

The tank's turbine whine quickly tapered off. Moments later a hatch popped open, and Sully clambered out and jumped down to the ground.

"Man, that is one cool machine," he said.

Gary turned off his radio. "Glad you like it, but I'm even happier the army's going to have to pay to get it back." He snapped his fingers. "Almost forgot; is there any ammo inside?"

"Naw. I checked."

"Good." He turned to Ann. "Got all the disguise gear?"

"Right over there." She pointed to two large boxes.

"Okay," Gary said. "Let's make this thing ugly."

An hour and a half later, Gary stood back and admired the team's handiwork. In place of the immaculate army tank sat a rusty, dented National Guard machine, complete with new serial numbers and unit markings. The aging was applied using body shop fillers and spray paint. Sully and Ann handled the more artistic touches, such as the simulated rust patina. It was a good job, and Gary couldn't detect any imperfections.

He turned to the team. "Excellent work, everyone. By this time tomorrow, the bonus is ours."

"I can go for that," John said.

"Now, how about some dinner? I'm starving."

"Don't have to ask me twice. Haul out the company credit card."

CHAPTER 7

It was a little after eleven, and Gary was about ready to call it a night. His bleary eyes scanned the open document on his laptop screen as he finished reviewing the latest version of the security audit notes, as updated by Dan's communications intercepts and Ann's penetrations into the Fort Knox intranet. They were making good progress, and the more the team uncovered, the more new leads turned up. It looked like the final report would be one thick document. There was no doubt in Gary's mind: The army *needed* SecurityCheck's services—big-time.

Dan's face popped up in the screen's lower right corner. "Gary? Are you there?" his barely audible voice asked.

Gary clicked up the volume and turned on his own camera. "Yeah, what's up?"

"Ann's pattern-matching software found something in the broadcast signals we're recording. I think you need to see it. It's a segment from the ten o'clock news on WAVE, Louisville's NBC affiliate."

"Okay, put it on."

Gary maximized the video window. The news logo for WAVE

appeared for a moment, then the video went into fast-forward through the newscast. After the first segment and three commercials, something familiar flashed on the screen. The window went into freeze-frame, reversed to the start, then began playing. The anchorman looked into the camera, a serious expression on his face.

"The break-in at the Fort Knox armor training area was discovered around 5:00 p.m. today."

The video cut to a handheld shot of a flattened chain-link fence topped with razor wire. The camera dropped down low and followed along the deep tread marks leading to the fence and into the dense undergrowth beyond.

"When questioned about the incident, an army spokesperson at first admitted that an M1A1 Abrams tank had been stranded inside the training area, however, she terminated the interview when asked about the vandalized fence, and all subsequent calls have gone unanswered."

The video returned to the anchor.

"So that leaves a very disturbing question: Is the army missing a main battle tank, and if so, who has it now?"

The anchor thumped the papers he was holding against the desktop and allowed his grave expression to relax a little.

"Weather is next after these messages."

Dan's grainy image replaced the opening scene of a dietary fiber commercial.

Gary managed a nervous laugh. "That sounded a little ominous and confusing. Do you have more?"

"A little. We intercepted a few e-mails, plus there was an earlier segment on the six o'clock news. I can play it for you if you like."

"No thanks; put it together for me."

"Okay, but it's not much. First, a WAVE news team was covering an awards ceremony at the Fort Knox Armor School, and they apparently spotted the flattened fence on their way back to the station.

Then they called the school's public affairs office."

Gary nodded. "Uh-huh. So rather than ask about the fence, they probably asked if anything interesting was going on in the training area."

"That's my guess, and if the missing tank report hadn't made it down to public affairs, the spokesperson probably told the reporter about the tank getting stranded. No big deal."

"Until the reporter called back."

"Yeah. Ann has deciphered several e-mails from the armor school to the Fort Knox command duty officer. They describe what happened to the boulder, the tracks made by the tank and our minivan, and what happened to the fence."

"Anything else?"

Dan shook his head. "That's about it."

"Thanks."

Gary closed the window and found himself staring at the audit notes again. He saved the document and shut down his laptop, deciding that he had had enough fun for one night.

Just before seven on Saturday morning, Gary pulled into the Waffle Fort's parking lot. He had selected the restaurant by the scientific method of noting the number of cars parked outside and the fact that he was fond of waffles. He parked the minivan and led the way to the door. Spotting a newspaper rack, he froze when he saw the headline on the Louisville *Courier-Journal*: ARMY TANK MISSING: TERROR TIE-IN?

Gary inserted quarters into the rack, opened the door, and pulled out a copy. He held it up and scanned the first few paragraphs.

"What does it say?" John asked.

Gary shook his head in amazement. "Great. The TV report was picked up by the department of homeland security. Listen to this:

'While there is no credible terrorist threat for the Louisville area, the disappearance of this army tank is being taken very seriously.' Then it goes on to say that the CIA and FBI have been called into the investigation."

"Wow. What should we do?"

Gary folded the paper. "Nothing. We're operating within the scope of our contract. The ball's in Thomas's court."

"Glad I'm not in his shoes," Dan said.

Gary forced a laugh. "Me, too."

He held the door while the others filed inside. A waitress led them through the crowded restaurant and pushed two tables together. Gary sat at one end. Dan and Sully sat on his left, Ann on his right, and John on the opposite end.

The waitress handed out menus. "Coffee?" she asked.

Getting no refusals, she left and came back moments later with five steaming mugs. Gary's mouth watered when he smelled the rich aroma.

"Everyone decided?" the woman asked.

Gary took a sip of coffee and found it rich and with exactly the caffeine kick he needed. The orders went around the table and ended up with him.

"I'll have the macadamia waffles," he said.

"Very good," the waitress said. "I'll be right back."

Gary could tell by John's anxious expression that he wanted to talk about the media blitz, but they couldn't chance it in this crowd. Besides, they deserved some peace and quiet during mealtimes.

Gary's mobile phone gave an electronic trill. He yanked it off his belt clip and waited for the caller ID to appear, then he punched a button to silence the ringer. He looked up at John.

"That was Thomas," Gary said.

"He's not supposed to call us," John said.

"I know, and that's why he gets to talk to voice mail."

"Maybe it's an emergency," Dan said.

Gary shook his head. "There *is* no emergency. Per the contract, *all* communications are supposed to originate from us. And whatever it is, we're not ruining our breakfast over it."

Having said that, Gary resisted the urge to open the newspaper to read the front-page article. The waitress came out with a large tray and placed the steaming platters before her customers. Next came the pitchers of syrup and several bowls of butter. Then she refilled the coffee cups and left.

Gary's phone rang again. Frowning, he grabbed it, and when he saw it was Thomas, turned it off. What Gary had hoped would be a pleasant, peaceful breakfast with the team was turning out to be anything but. He sighed and looked down at his heaping plate. The mouth-watering aroma of the waffles made his stomach growl. The food looked delicious, and he was grateful for it. He bowed his head and gave his silent thanks.

After the team returned to the motel, Sully drove them out into the country and along a remote road as Dan monitored the signals being intercepted by the partially raised antenna. The various meters jittered to life and slowly increased in strength. Finally they peaked.

"Here," he said.

The truck stopped with a lurch.

Dan checked to make sure the signals were being recorded on the hard disk. "Looks good," he said.

"Ready for me?" Ann asked.

"Have at it," Dan said.

Ann pulled her PC over and started sifting through the recordings, looking for the needles within the vast army haystacks.

Sully came inside and closed the doors.

Gary looked down at the *Courier-Journal*'s front page. The

headline seemed like typical media hype, but what if things were getting out of hand? He turned to Dan. "Do you have *The Today Show* on disk?"

"Sure. I'm recording everything on the local TV and radio stations."

"Punch it up."

Dan accessed the WAVE broadcast recording and punched in a time code. A stock shot of an Abrams tank flashed up on the overhead monitor. Dan adjusted the volume.

"The department of homeland security announced early this morning that Fort Knox, near Louisville, Kentucky, is missing an M1A1 Abrams tank. Who stole it or why is not known, but a government source told NBC News that a terrorist tie-in cannot be ruled out."

"That's enough," Gary said. "Now how about a national squawk show?"

"This is live," Dan said. He clicked his mouse.

". . .what's going on with those guys? The army loses a tank out of a heavily guarded area, and homeland security says we're supposed to remain calm? Yeah, right. Terrorists could level half of Louisville with that thing. I wanna know what the government's doing about it."

"Point well taken," the host said quickly, cutting the man off. "Today's question: 'Have terrorists infiltrated the army?' We'll take the next caller after this break."

Gary drew his finger across his throat. Dan clicked his mouse.

"Guess we know what Thomas wants," Gary said. He plucked the phone off his belt and turned it on. "Whoa. Four messages." He punched up the first one and held it to his ear.

"Gary, this is Thomas Brooks. Please call me ASAP. Bye."

Gary deleted the message.

"Gary, this is *really* important. I *must* speak with you immediately."

Gary felt his anger rising. He deleted that message, also.

"*Gary*, I'm sitting on an emergency here. Look, I *know* what the contract says, but we have to talk *now*. Either call me back within the hour, or I'll invoke the termination clause."

Gary's eyes grew wide at that. He checked his watch and saw the deadline was fast approaching. He deleted the third message and started the fourth. Since it, too, was from Thomas, he deleted it without hearing it out.

"What does he want?" John asked.

"He says it's an emergency; he has to talk to me *immediately*, or he'll terminate the contract."

"Whoa, that dude plays dirty," Sully said.

"Play with the feds, and you play by their rules. Dan. . ."

"Coming right up," Dan said. He started flipping switches and checking signal strengths. "Okay, I've found a tower I can spoof."

He punched in a number. The first ring cut off abruptly.

"This is Thomas Brooks," came the agitated voice on the speaker.

"Thomas, this is Gary, returning your messages."

"It's about time! Do you have that tank?"

"I can't answer that. If we did, hypothetically speaking, you're supposed to wait until we call you, after the twenty-four hours are up."

"Listen. The armor school has been looking all over for it, and homeland security is going ballistic. Washington's in an uproar, and they're all coming down hard on the Fort Knox commanding officer. They *all* want answers, and they want them now. So *do you have that tank?*"

"No comment."

"Look, Gary, I *know* you have it."

"Say we did, and I'm not saying we do. You'd be getting it back around four this afternoon, so what's the big deal?"

"The big deal is the secretary of homeland security will have a bunch of heads by then, and mine will be one of them. Gary, I want this thing shut down *now*."

"What about our bonus?"

"That's above my pay grade."

"Well, that's just lousy. We're only doing our job here, and our contract says if we can make off with a tank and keep it for twenty-four hours, you owe us."

"You'd be on your way to California by then. So what'll it be?"

"Just a minute."

There was a brief pause. "Okay, but please hurry."

Dan muted the call without being told.

Gary turned to John. "We *have* to do it," he said. "We'll probably lose the bonus, but it's still a lucrative contract."

John's frown changed to sullen acceptance. "Yeah, I know. Let's get it over with."

"Hey, dudes, that's *my* tank you're talking about."

"Sorry," Gary said. He pointed to the speaker, and Dan released the mute.

"Okay, we'll turn it over."

"Great," Thomas said, obviously relieved. "Where is it?"

Gary watched the army personnel take possession of their errant tank. The rescue team consisted of an armor major, four armed guards, a tank driver, and two crews, one for an M88 tank retriever, which was not needed, the other for a tank transporter. Military police trucks blocked the street on either end of the park, and four MPs detoured the traffic onto the side streets.

John nudged Gary. "We swipe that thing with three people, and it takes a whole company to drive it off."

"Very funny," Gary said, but he wasn't smiling.

Moments after the tank driver disappeared through a hatch, a whine came from the tank's turbine and increased rapidly. The tank backed up then pivoted and clattered away toward the street. Two men guided the tank up onto the transporter's trailer and secured it. A few minutes later, the convoy was on its way.

"Well, that's that," Gary said.

"Bummer," Sully said.

"Couldn't agree with you more, but it's time to move on."

"Speaking of. . . ," John said, pointing. "Here comes Thomas."

Gary forced a smile and waited until Thomas was within earshot. "If you're done with us, we'll get back to work. We still have a lot on our plate."

"Ah, yes," Thomas began, obviously flustered. "Well, there's something else we have to talk about; just came up."

"Oh? What's that?"

"Is there someplace we could talk in private?"

That seemed almost paranoid to Gary, but Thomas was the customer. "Okay, how about our spy-mobile?" He waved toward the truck waiting at the curb.

As Gary led the way over to their truck, his mind raced ahead. What had come up now? Had the flap over the tank brought about the cancellation of the contract? That was a very real possibility, he knew, and it would certainly add insult to injury. He sent up an arrow prayer: *We need this, Lord.* But even as he prayed, he knew he had to be prepared to accept the Lord's decision, something not at all easy to do.

Sully opened the back doors. Ann looked out. Dan glanced around then returned to monitoring his communications equipment.

"Hide all our secret stuff," Gary said, trying for a light tone.

Thomas climbed up inside, and Gary, John, and Sully followed. Gary grabbed an extra folding chair and made a place for their client. When they were all seated, Gary asked, "Okay, what's up?"

Thomas was clearly uncomfortable. "Uh, it's rather complicated."

"How about giving us the CliffsNotes version?"

"Very well. The department of homeland security has taken charge of the project."

"What?"

"Secretary Foster met with the secretary of defense, and they agreed it was necessary, especially with the terrorist tie-in."

Gary gritted his teeth. "There *is* no terrorist tie-in."

"No, but there could have been, and terrorists in possession of an M1A1 Abrams is serious business."

"Cut to the chase, Thomas. Are you telling me the contract is cancelled?"

"Gary, I said it was complicated."

"Come on. Out with it."

"Well, yes, the Fort Knox contract *is* cancelled."

"I *knew* it!" Gary said, making no attempt to keep his voice down.

"Now wait, Gary. Reason is Secretary Foster wants you to do a security audit on another government facility. Same basic terms, with a cost-plus extension for any additional work that might be required." Thomas paused. "Secretary Foster has been briefed on your company, and he's quite impressed. He wants the best team he can get."

"Oh, I see. Sorry, didn't mean to jump down your throat."

"I understand. So do you accept?"

Gary glanced over at John but knew there was no need for a conference. SecurityCheck needed the work, and working for a different government facility would make no difference. Gary looked Thomas in the eye. "We accept. What does homeland security want done?"

Thomas looked relieved. "You'll be briefed in Washington."

"Can you at least tell us the facility?"

"It's the United States Army Medical Research Institute of Infectious Diseases at Fort Detrick, Maryland."

CHAPTER 8

Gary followed Thomas Brooks into the large conference room, trailed by the rest of the SecurityCheck team. Gary was still in awe of how fast the federal bureaucracy could move when prodded by a cabinet secretary. Department of homeland security personnel had taken complete charge of the team's logistics, from turning in the rental vehicles to transporting their equipment. Then had come the trip to the Louisville airport followed by a short flight to Andrews Air Force Base on a VIP C-20, the military version of a Gulfstream G-4 business jet.

A tall, solidly built man strode into the room, instantly recognizable from his frequent appearances before the media. Secretary Brad Foster seemed about fifty and had brown eyes and neatly trimmed black hair. His gray suit fit him well and echoed the quiet authority the man projected. A tall, thin man trailed along a respectful distance behind. Gary thought he looked Middle Eastern. The man wore an ill-fitting black suit that was in dire need of pressing.

Thomas stepped forward. "Secretary Foster, these are our outside security auditors. This is Gary Nesbitt, one of the owners of SecurityCheck."

"Pleased to meet you," Foster said.

Gary nodded and shook his hand. "Mr. Secretary."

Thomas continued with the introductions, ending with Sully. Then all eyes turned to the middle-aged man in the black suit.

"This is Hamid Momeni," Foster said. "He's a CIA special agent on assignment to Fort Detrick."

Gary shook Hamid's hand, noting the firm grip and the man's intense gaze. Thomas was the last to greet the man, after which Foster led the group over to the long, heavy table.

"Please be seated," the secretary said. He took the chair at the head of the table in front of a large whiteboard. A wide-screen monitor hulked in the corner, perched on its cart. Foster looked at Gary. "Did Mr. Brooks tell you what I want?"

"Yes, a security audit on the United States Army Medical Research Institute of Infectious Diseases," Gary said.

Foster smiled. "That's correct. Quite a mouthful, isn't it? It's also called 'you-SAM-rid,' for U-S-A-M-R-I-I-D, or simply 'the Institute.' The Institute is located at Fort Detrick in Frederick, Maryland. It and the Centers for Disease Control and Prevention in Atlanta are our premier facilities for studying the most lethal biological agents known; nasty stuff like Ebola, Marburg, and anthrax. As you can imagine, I'm quite concerned that the Institute's security be absolutely airtight, and that's where you come in."

"Is the audit limited to USAMRIID?" Gary asked.

Foster hesitated then said, "No, you'll also be auditing a satellite facility in Alaska. Mr. Momeni will cover that aspect in his briefing. But before we go any further, do you accept the job?"

Gary cleared his throat. "As I told Thomas, yes, John and I are ready to sign on as soon as we've read the contract. But there is one thing I'd like to ask."

"Oh, what's that?"

Gary saw a pleading look come to Thomas's face but decided to go ahead anyway. "I understand your concerns, and there's no question in my mind that we're the company to do this job."

Foster nodded. "My sources agree with you, or you wouldn't be here. And your question is?"

"Taking that tank was a bonus item on the Fort Knox contract. Since we succeeded, I'd like that bonus."

"Mr. Secretary, I *told* Gary we can't do that," Thomas said with obvious irritation. "That contract is history."

Gary felt heat rising in his face. "But we *earned* it," he said, sharper than he intended.

"Sir—" Thomas began.

"Just a minute," Foster interrupted him. He turned to Gary. "Taking that tank was a test of the Fort Knox security?"

"Yes, it was." He said it in a softer tone. He could recognize defeat when he saw it, since being powerful means never having to say you're sorry.

Foster leaned back in his chair. "Sounds like you're saying the secretary of homeland security did you dirty."

Gary picked his words carefully. "I know it wasn't your fault. Given the circumstances and all the media hype, I'd have been worried about a missing tank, also."

"Well, thank you." A wry smile came to his lips. "Most of my critics don't cut me that much slack." He looked at Thomas. "Am I correct that the department of the army has transferred you to this new project?"

"Yes, sir."

"Does the new contract have a contingency clause, you know, something to cover unforeseen expenses?"

"Yes, sir. It's in the cost-plus section."

"Good. I want you to make that bonus a line item. These folks deserve to be paid for what they did."

Thomas smiled. "I'll take care of it."

"Thank you, Mr. Secretary," Gary said.

Foster nodded. "You earned it. Now, Mr. Momeni will handle the next part of the briefing. He holds a master's degree in bioscience enterprise from the Cambridge Graduate School of Biological, Medical, and Veterinary Sciences. After graduation, the CIA recruited him as an expert in biohazards. Presently I've assigned him to work with USAMRIID and placed him in charge of a lab at the Institute and a research facility in Brevig Mission, Alaska. While the army is in charge of the facilities and security, Mr. Momeni directs the researchers and reports to the CIA."

"Thank you, Secretary Foster," Hamid began. He had a slight accent, part British and part something else. "First of all, as a veteran CIA agent, I am confident that our security is quite good, however, it never hurts to make sure.

"All my labs are designated biosafety level four, which means the hot agents we work with are extremely deadly and have no known cures. As you know, the government is quite concerned with bioterrorism, the threat of anthrax and smallpox to name just two. However, we've recently become aware of a threat from the past that could be far more serious. Anyone care to take a guess?"

Gary shrugged. "The plague?"

"Bubonic plague *is* a concern, but the agent we're most worried about makes the plague look like a skin rash. In 1918, the world experienced its first pandemic, so-called because it was worldwide. It was called Spanish flu because the Spanish press initially reported it. The newspapers in the United States, Britain, and France censored the outbreak since the Allies were still at war with Germany, and the effect of the pandemic on the armies was devastating."

"How bad was it?" Ann asked.

"Most estimates place the worldwide death toll at between 20 and 50 million worldwide, but it could easily have been as high as 100 million, since the reports from places like India and China were highly inaccurate. Around 675,000 Americans died."

"Wow, I had no idea," Gary said.

Hamid smiled. "The national memory, unfortunately, *is* rather short. Here's how bad it was: The virus was spreading like a global wildfire, convincing the health professionals they were looking at doomsday. Then as quickly as the outbreak started, it died out, and no one knows why. And when that generation passed into history, so did the dread of the disease."

"I notice you haven't called it flu," Gary said.

Hamid's dark brown eyes glinted. "How very perceptive of you. In plain fact, we *don't* know what the pathogen was. It was called influenza because of the symptoms, and research on preserved tissue samples shows a similar RNA structure to modern flu strains. Some scientists believe that it was an early strain of H1N1-subtype influenza A, similar to classic swine flu. However, many researchers, myself included, disagree. First, RNA similarity does not prove relationship, and the 1918 virus produced disturbing symptoms modern flu does not. In some cases, victims died within two days of massive pulmonary edema."

"You're saying they bled out," Gary said.

Hamid nodded. "Yes, that's the common term for it. In other words, combine flu with Ebola, and that's the effect of this pathogen, whatever it is."

Gary felt a sudden chill that had nothing to do with the room's temperature. "You say, 'is.' "

"Yes. The mysterious virus lives again. We know of at least two sites where virus victims were buried in permafrost, and thus their bodies have been preserved. One site is in Brevig Mission, Alaska, called Teller Mission at the time, where 85 percent of the Inuit villagers died of the disease. The other site is Longyearbyen on the island of Spits Bergen, in the Norwegian Arctic archipelago of Svalbard. Seven Norwegian miners died there between September and October of 1918."

"Could there be other sites?" Ann asked.

"Good question," Hamid said with a nod. "In all likelihood there are; the permafrost regions of Siberia come to mind."

"You say the virus lives," Gary said. "Are you saying you've cultured it?"

"Yes, at my Brevig Mission facility. The administration, as you can imagine, is quite concerned that America be prepared in case terrorists somehow manage the same thing."

"I can believe that."

"Good, but do you really understand how bad it could be? If this virus got loose—if it *only* duplicated what happened in 1918—it would kill over 2.2 million Americans and 330 million worldwide."

Gary shifted uneasily. "Are you suggesting it could be even worse?"

"I am indeed. One, the 1918 outbreak died out unexpectedly. A new outbreak might continue, especially if terrorists keep spreading it. Two, I believe the 1918 virus was actually several strains, varying greatly in lethality. The average mortality rate worldwide was 2.5 percent of those infected, whereas at Brevig Mission, it reached 85 percent."

"But wasn't that because the villagers were isolated, sort of like the early Hawaiians and measles?" John asked.

Hamid shook his head. "Not the same thing at all. Influenza, like the common cold, affects all ethnic groups. That this virus managed to kill *85 percent* of the sturdy Inuits is of extreme concern."

"You said it's like Ebola," Gary said.

"Yes, some of the victims died from 'bleeding-out,' as you put it, which makes it very much like Ebola and, obviously, far more lethal than ordinary flu." Hamid paused. "Now can you see why we are so concerned?"

"Yes, if a virus like that got loose, it would overwhelm the world's health-care systems."

"Indeed it would. And if the terrorists were the only ones with a vaccine, they would be able to keep spreading the virus until all their enemies were annihilated."

"That would devastate them, also, since it would destroy the entire world economy."

Hamid's expression was hard to read. "You obviously do not understand the terrorist mind, Mr. Nesbitt."

"Thank you," Secretary Foster said. "I believe that gives the necessary background for the security audit." He looked right at Gary. "That, in a nutshell, is why I want the USAMRIID security to be the very best it can be."

"I understand," Gary said. "Uh, do you have reason to believe that terrorists are trying to get their hands on this virus?"

"That's classified, and you don't have the need to know. But I will say this: It should be obvious why we need to know as much about this virus as we possibly can."

"To develop a vaccine."

"That's a safe assumption, and that's really all I can say." Foster turned to Thomas. "As I mentioned, Mr. Brooks will continue to administer the contract for the army, and Mr. Momeni will be your primary technical contact at Fort Detrick."

Gary locked eyes with Hamid for a few moments and wondered at what he saw. The man was obviously reserved, and his body language seemed defensive. Well, Gary couldn't really blame the man. The audit might pose a professional threat if it turned up glaring deficiencies. Gary almost smiled. No one likes an auditor.

"Mr. Brooks," Foster said.

"Yes, sir?"

"I want status reports forwarded to my office on a weekly basis."

"I'll see that you have them."

"Very good." The secretary looked all around the table. "Meeting adjourned."

Secretary Foster stood up. "I need to see you in my office," he said to Hamid.

"Yes, sir," the agent said. He got up and followed Foster out.

Gary turned to Thomas. "So what's next on the agenda?"

"Execute the contract, then start doing your thing," Thomas said with a smile as he handed Gary a thick binder.

Gary took it. "John and I want to look this over first."

"I understand. How about I meet you for breakfast?"

"Let's do it on Monday. We'll be standing down on Sunday."

Thomas looked a little surprised. "Oh, yeah, I'm sure that'll be okay. Probably suit the USAMRIID honchos better, too."

"Good. Now how do we get out of here?"

"Secretary Foster has a limo waiting for you at the main entrance; take you anywhere you want to go. I live in Reston, Virginia, so I'll be taking a cab home."

"No living out of a suitcase?"

"Not this time. Now if you'll follow me, I'll escort you outside."

"Yeah, wouldn't want to get lost."

Thomas led them out into the corridor.

"Where do you want to stay?" John asked.

"Someplace close to Fort Detrick," Gary said.

"I booked us five rooms at a Days Inn in south Frederick," Ann said. "It's off the Eisenhower Highway about five miles from the base."

"Excellent. When—"

"I did it on the Internet on the way over here. The local motels were filling up, so I thought I better grab us a place before it was too late."

Gary smiled. "Glad you're on our side."

"Thanks."

"When do you want me to get the vehicles?" Sully asked.

"Monday after breakfast," Gary said.

"I saved you a file of all the rental companies," Ann said.

"Cool," Sully said.

They reached the elevators. Thomas pressed the DOWN button.

"Where's our equipment?" Gary asked.

"In a hanger at Andrews. I'll give you a contact on Monday."

Gary waited until they were safely inside the limo and on the way to their motel. "Did you get all the mobile phone IDs?" he asked.

"Surely you jest," Dan said, patting the compact recorder in his shirt pocket.

Gary sat back in the luxurious seat and relaxed. That was one detail out of the way.

Lieutenant Colonel Dick Edwards tried to relax inside his blue Chemturion biological "space suit," but that was impossible for two reasons. One, the suit, which made him look like a frostbitten Pillsbury Doughboy, was uncomfortable, and the hissing air coming in through the coiled hose made it hard to hear. Second, he was watching Major Francine Ingram die by agonizing inches, and there wasn't a thing he could do about it. He frowned. He could have added a third reason: What was killing one of his best researchers could also hammer him if any of the elaborate safety precautions failed.

Edwards had company inside the emergency clinic, which the army scientists had dubbed "Slammer Junior." Major Larry Canton, the facility's doctor, and his nurse, Major Helen Baker, were in attendance, not that they could do anything except monitor Ingram's last agonizing moments this side of eternity. Francine was bleeding-out despite massive transfusions of whole blood and plasma. All her internal organs had dissolved into a puree of blood and nuked cell parts. The heavy rubber sheet underneath her channeled the red tide to one corner of the stainless steel table, where it drained into a large plastic bottle. Bright red trefoils on a yellow background left no doubt as to the danger posed by these bodily fluids.

Edwards looked up at the monitors. Ingram's temperature was high, extremely high. Her pulse was rapid and fluttery, and her blood pressure was almost nonexistent. It wouldn't be long now. Her chest heaved in a feeble spasm.

Edwards cursed under his breath. This shouldn't have happened. The research facility had been built to the highest specifications, and the elaborate containment features were tested on a daily basis. All the scientists knew what they were doing and carefully followed the safety precautions. You didn't take chances with biosafety level-four hot agents unless you had a death wish. But even with the greatest care, accidents can happen. Ingram had been working with the exposed virus when a weld broke on a defective bracket. The shelf had come crashing down, slicing through the arm of her heavy space suit like a knife through butter.

Edwards sighed in appreciation of Ingram's calm professionalism. Rather than come out, she had called for assistance, which had probably saved the lives of the others inside the building. The responders had done all that they could. Another researcher had brought in a spare space suit and helped Ingram to change. Then both had been decontaminated in the chemical shower. From there, Ingram had been taken directly into Slammer Junior while a decon team nuked her lab. With those actions, containment had been complete.

A buzzer went off, loud enough to be heard over the rush of air in Edwards's suit. He looked up and saw that the life monitors were flatlined: no pulse, no blood pressure, flat EEG. The patient was dead, although the virus inside her body was very much alive. Larry Canton began removing the sensor leads. After he finished, Helen Baker pulled a sheet up over the corpse's face.

Edwards took a deep but cautious breath. Now all that remained was to decontaminate the body, slip it into two body bags, decontaminating everything after each step. Finally the encapsulated body would be placed inside a hermetically sealed steel casket that would be shipped back to Washington, D.C., for cremation. They would take *absolutely* no chances. Meanwhile, the search for a vaccine would continue.

CHAPTER 9

Gary felt relaxed after a day of rest on Sunday and what John referred to as recharging the spiritual batteries. But now it was Monday, and Gary had exercised his prerogative as co-owner of SecurityCheck to pick where they ate breakfast. Since he loved pancakes and waffles, he had selected the Waffle House in south Frederick, not far from their motel. He mopped up maple syrup with a large chunk of waffle and stuffed it in his mouth. A thin ribbon of syrup dripped down his chin. He wiped it away with his napkin.

He looked around and spotted Thomas standing in the crowded waiting area. Gary waved. Thomas nodded and hurried through the tables, dodging servers and guests like a running back.

"Have a seat," Gary said, pointing to the empty chair beside John. "Like something to eat? We're on an expense account." He speared his last piece of waffle, sopped up the remnants of the maple syrup, and savored the bite.

A wry smile came to Thomas's face. "Be my own guest, huh?" He sat down and placed two thick binders on the table.

Gary chewed fast, swallowed, and took a sip of coffee. "Actually the army's guest, that is, after we sign the contract."

Thomas shook his head. "No, thanks. I had breakfast at home. I will take some coffee, though."

John took the thermos and filled a spare cup.

"Thanks." Thomas took a sip. "Ready?"

"Pass 'em down," Gary said.

"I've already signed for the army. Sign both copies and keep one for your records. Per Secretary Foster's instructions, I've added the bonus for the tank. The advance check I gave you for the Fort Knox job is still valid."

"And the collateral damage addendum?"

"That, too. And here's something else you might find useful." Thomas handed him a sealed envelope. "Go ahead, take a look."

Gary opened the envelope and pulled out a letter. Before his eyes reached the last line, they were very wide indeed. "Whoa." He looked up at Thomas. "VIP military transportation by order of the secretary himself. I'm impressed."

Thomas nodded. "You should be. In the Washington area, your contact is the operations officer of the Eighty-ninth Airlift Wing at Andrews Air Force Base, but the letter's valid anywhere. You have cabinet-level authority to military transportation."

"Speaking of Andrews, we need to pick up our equipment so we can get started on our new spy-mobile."

"May I make a suggestion?"

"Sure."

Thomas pointed. "Do what you think best, but the troops at the Eighty-ninth will help you fit out your truck. Remember, Secretary Foster wants you on-site ASAP. Here's the ops boss's direct number." He handed Gary a sticky note.

"Thanks. I'll do it."

"Great. Give me a call when you're done, and I'll introduce you to the USAMRIID commander."

"Will do."

Gary looked all around the compact command center that was shoe-horned into the back of the rental truck. John, Dan, and Sully had done some of the work, but the bulk had been performed by the men and women who normally worked on *Air Force One*. That the work was absolutely first rate went without saying. The team even had a complete set of *Air Force One* coffee mugs as a parting gift.

It was late afternoon when Sully pulled up at Fort Detrick's main gate and stopped. Gary scanned the monitors arrayed above Dan's workstation. Ann was right behind them in their minivan. Thomas hurried over to the guard who was trying to give Sully the third degree. Dan aimed a side camera and zoomed in then turned up the volume.

"They're with me," Thomas told the guard.

The soldier scowled. "And who are you?"

"If you will take a look at this." Thomas handed him a piece of paper.

It took the guard a few moments to get to the meat of the document, but when he finally did, his eyebrows shot up. He looked up at Thomas, and for a moment, it looked like he was going to salute.

"Uh, yes, sir. How can I help you?"

"I want temporary passes for this vehicle and the one behind it."

"Yes, sir, but you'll have to sign for them."

"Fine. Just do it."

The soldier hurried back into his guardhouse and returned with two cardboard placards and a metal clipboard. Thomas dashed off his signature twice. The guard took back the clipboard then handed Sully and Ann the passes and waved them through. Thomas trotted back to his car and led them past the parade grounds and into a parking lot beside a massive, yellow brick building. Tall vents pierced the roof in a way that looked unnatural. Sully and Ann pulled into parking spaces on either side of Thomas's car.

"Okay, dudes, it's time for our dog and pony show," Gary said over the team's secure radio net.

"Are we working for Secretary Foster or USAMRIID?" Ann asked.

"Both. Let's look sharp, everyone, like we know what we're doing."

"Roger that, boss dude," Sully said.

"Glad you agree, Mr. Sullivan."

Gary moved to the back, opened the rear doors, and stepped down into the bright September day. Fluffy white clouds dotted the bright blue sky. John and Dan followed him out, and Sully and Ann joined them. Thomas walked over a few moments later.

"Before we go inside, I want to review the ground rules," Thomas said.

"Okay," Gary said.

"Once you leave this building, you're on your own. Per Secretary Foster's e-mail to me, you will retain the temporary passes, which give you access to the base, but that's all. As you know, your task will then be to wring out the Institute's security systems."

"Including the facility in Alaska."

"That's correct. Now, are you ready?"

"Lead on."

Thomas took them in the back entrance and stopped at the security desk. He handed the guard his department of the army ID and the same letter he had shown at the main gate then waited for the startled reaction. He was not disappointed.

"How can I help you, sir?" the man asked.

"I need visitor badges for myself and my guests." Thomas waved his hand around to include the team.

The guard opened a drawer, and six badges appeared so quickly it reminded Gary of a card shark dealing, or at least his mental image of one. Thomas dashed off his signature six times then handed out the plastic rectangles.

The man snatched up his phone and summoned another guard to escort the visitors. An earnest young woman guided them to the commanding officer's office. The escort stopped before an imposing door and knocked. The sound was barely audible.

"Come," said a diminished voice on the other side.

The guard opened the door and stood to the side.

Gary looked into the large, well-appointed office. A tall man, well over six feet, stood behind a massive desk. He had to be over two hundred pounds, but not a pound of it was flab. He had neatly trimmed brown hair and inquisitive brown eyes. Large silver eagles rested on the shoulders of his dress uniform, and four rows of ribbons adorned his chest.

Standing off to the side was another officer, this one with silver oak leaves on his uniform. He, too, had several rows of ribbons, but not as many as the colonel.

"Colonel Roberts, I'm Thomas Brooks."

"Come in," Colonel Roberts said. "I've been expecting you and our visitors." The man seemed open and friendly. "I am Colonel Zack Roberts, commanding officer of. . ." He glanced at Thomas. "Has Mr. Brooks told you what we call ourselves?"

"I believe it's 'you-SAM-rid,' " Gary said.

"That's right. We never use the formal title; takes too long. We're also called the Institute. I believe you've been briefed on what we do here."

"Yes, Colonel."

"Please call me Zack." He waved toward the officer beside him. "This is Lieutenant Colonel Nate Young. He's head of security for the Institute."

Young nodded. Gary could tell he was more reserved than his boss and seemed a little tense. He was much shorter, around five eight; but he, too, seemed in good physical shape. He had thinning black hair and brown eyes that seemed to have a permanent squint.

"Shall we gather around the conference table?" Zack asked.

Thomas led the way. He and the team sat around the long table, leaving the head and the seat beside it for the commander and his security chief. Nate opened a thin file folder and pulled out a single sheet of paper. He pulled out a pair of wire-rimmed glasses, put them on, and scanned the document. He looked up and removed his glasses.

"To save time, let me just say that I've been briefed on the security audit," Zack said. He paused and looked at Gary and shook his head. "As for SecurityCheck, your fame, like Napoleon's, has preceded you." He chuckled. "You tied our armor school up in knots, not to mention the department of homeland security. Amazing. Simply amazing."

Gary forced a smile. "Believe it or not, we try for a low profile. Security experts are not supposed to be seen *or* heard."

"Well, how about we try for a quiet approach this time around?"

"We'll do our best."

"I appreciate it. Now, in times past, security audits were pretty much internal functions conducted by the army, augmented by the FBI, but nine-eleven changed all that. Now we're subject to scrutiny by the department of homeland security, as well." He frowned. "I won't insult your intelligence by saying we're pleased about that."

"Please remember we're just hired to do a job. I think you're better off with us finding your security breaches—"

"There aren't any," Nate said, his face quite red. "Security at the Institute is airtight."

Gary stared at Nate a few moments then turned his focus back to Zack. The commanding officer seemed uneasy. "With all due respect," Gary began carefully, "in our experience, *all* organizations have security breaches. Hopefully they are few and of little consequence, but no security system is perfect. And that, gentlemen, you can take to the bank."

Zack nodded. "I agree. Nate takes his job quite seriously, so I'm sure he only meant to say that our security issues are not serious."

"I hope that's the case, since we have no desire to cause the Institute grief. What we will provide is a thorough and accurate audit, with special emphasis on Mr. Momeni's lab here and the facility in Brevig Mission, per our instructions."

"Understood." Zack and Nate traded glances. "I planned on having Hamid describe the facilities under his supervision, however, he was called away unexpectedly. Instead, I've asked Lieutenant Colonel Ken Underwood and Major Carol Underwood to fill you in. They'll provide background information, data any diligent researcher would have access to." A strained smile appeared on Zack's face. "But no security details. That's for *you* to find out."

With that he stood.

"Thank you, Zack," Gary said. "We'll try not to make pests of ourselves."

"I would appreciate it."

Thomas led the team out into the colonel's reception area. Gary's eyes immediately fell on two black officers dressed in working uniforms.

"You must be the Underwoods," Thomas said.

The two officers stood. The man's smile was friendly and open. He was tall and thin, and his hair was neatly trimmed and short. The woman was short and petite. Her smile outdid her husband's.

"That's us," the man said. "I'm Ken Underwood, and this is my wife, Carol."

"Pleased to meet you," Thomas said.

Gary introduced himself. He shook Ken's hand then Carol's and introduced them to the rest of the SecurityCheck team.

"Colonel Roberts gave us a heads-up this morning," Ken said with a broad grin. "Said homeland security was sending over some folks to make our lives miserable."

Carol elbowed her husband. "He did *not* say that," she said, but her scowl quickly turned to a smile.

Ken arched his eyebrows, and furrows appeared on his forehead. "It seems I stand corrected." He looked at his wife then turned back to Gary. "Well, now that we're all such good friends, why don't we go down to a break room? It'll be a lot more comfortable there than trying to cram us all inside my office."

"Sounds good to me," Gary said.

They took the elevator down, and Ken led them through a maze of corridors to a large room with banks of vending machines. He went right to the coffeemaker and, when no one refused, poured foam cups for everyone.

"If anyone's hungry, there're snack machines," he said, "but can't say as I recommend it. I think the surgeon general ought to put warnings on 'em, but nobody asked me."

"For good reason," Carol said.

Gary nudged Sully and pointed to a machine loaded with fried pies and pastries. "Could be another stunt for your résumé."

Sully grinned. "Naw, man. Way too dangerous."

"Stunt?" Ken asked.

"Yeah, I'm a Hollywood stuntman," Sully said. "My day job is driving these dudes around while they break into things, high-speed chases as required."

"I see," Ken said.

"We're rather an eclectic group, even by Southern California standards," Gary said.

"I'll take your word for it," Ken said. He pointed toward a long table in a corner of the room. "Why don't we sit over there so we'll have some privacy?"

The team split roughly in half. Gary, John, and Ann followed Ken along one side of the table while Sully, Dan, and Thomas joined Carol on the other. After everyone was seated, Ken leaned forward and placed his forearms on the table.

"As I'm sure you gathered, Colonel Roberts is a little nervous about all this," Ken began in a low voice. "See, we're used to the army chain of command, but with homeland security in the picture, knowing who's really in charge gets dicey. It can't be helped, of course, but it still complicates our mission."

"I imagine it would," Gary said.

"Take my word for it. And it's not just this audit. We're also seeing outside managers inserted into our organization, Hamid Momeni being a perfect example. Although he's a CIA agent, he manages a lab here at USAMRIID plus the facility at Brevig Mission, but he doesn't appear *anywhere* in the army chain of command. Hamid reports to the CIA and ultimately the secretary of homeland security, while Colonel Roberts is responsible for military matters, and that includes security."

"Divided responsibility."

"Yeah. Now don't quote me, but if something goes wrong, I can tell you for *sure* which organization gets whacked."

"Your observation is noted."

Ken nodded. "Now don't misunderstand: Hamid's a good scientist. I've seen his résumé, and it's absolutely first rate. Bachelor of science in microbiology from the University of Texas, then a master of philosophy in bioscience enterprise from Cambridge. He can't do cutting-edge research without a doctorate, but he's well qualified to manage labs."

"I'm curious. How did you two choose this kind of career?" Ann asked.

Ken shot a glance at his wife. "Oh, I've wanted to do research since I was a kid. Carol just followed me."

"I did not," Carol said. "Now you tell it right." She said it with some fire, but Gary saw the loving glint in her eyes.

Ken chuckled. "You got me." Then he turned serious. "Actually, to tell the gospel truth, I followed her."

"How's that?" Ann asked.

Ken's expression became serious. "We both grew up in Tuscumbia, Alabama. After high school, I went to the University of Alabama but didn't know what I wanted to study. Then, after my sophomore year, Carol enrolled and talked me into microbiology. We fell in love and got married the day she graduated. By that time, I was two years into a master's in molecular and cellular biology at Harvard. Somehow we both made it through, earning our PhDs by hard work and student loans. And prayer."

"How did you decide on the army?" Gary asked.

"While Ken was working on his thesis," Carol said, "I decided I wanted to do research on Zaire Ebola and Sudan Ebola after I graduated. As I'm sure you know, there have been serious outbreaks of Ebola in Africa, and the Zaire strain, the worst of the worst, has a mortality rate of 90 percent."

"Wow," Ann said.

"Uh-huh. Nasty stuff. Well, the leading research labs for bio-safety level-four hot agents are USAMRIID and the Centers for Disease Control and Prevention. Ken and I decided the Institute would probably be on the leading edge."

"Or bleeding edge," Gary said without thinking.

Carol nodded solemnly. "If you're not careful, that's exactly what happens. These viruses kill by destroying internal organs, which results in massive hemorrhages, commonly called 'bleeding-out.'"

"Sorry."

"That's okay," Ken said. "Believe it or not, we indulge in gallows humor around here; otherwise, we'd probably all go crazy."

"I can believe that."

"Now, Colonel Roberts said to tell you how we operate. Well, here goes. This building we're in is divided into biosafety levels zero, two, three, and four. Most of the building is level zero, meaning no hazardous biological agents are present. There is no level one, and why that is, no one knows. Levels two, three, and four are biocontainment areas of increasing danger, with four reserved for such deadly agents as Ebola and Marburg—hot agents for which there is no cure.

"Containment is maintained by airtight seals and negative air pressure. Each succeeding level has a lower pressure, so if there *is* a leak, the air would flow toward the hot areas, preventing virus escape. Access is via air locks. The researchers wear surgical scrubs, latex gloves, and Chemturion biological suits, also called space suits, pressurized by coiled air hoses. On the way out, we go through decontamination showers to nuke any bugs trying to hitch a ride outside."

Gary shifted uneasily. "What about building ventilation?"

"Did you see all our roof vents?"

"Yes, I wondered about that."

"Well, obviously the hot areas require ventilation. The exhaust air goes through elaborate mechanical and chemical filters and finally up those vents. Believe me. There isn't *any* biological agent that can survive treatment like that."

"That's good to know. Is Hamid Momeni's lab classified level four?"

Ken nodded. "Yes, because at the present time, the virus he's researching has no vaccine."

"So you don't think it's flu, either."

"That's outside my area of expertise, but from what I've heard, we really don't know what it is, except it's extremely deadly."

"Nearly as deadly as Zaire Ebola, but far more infectious," Carol added. "That virus, whatever it is, has the proven ability to spread like wildfire."

"Nasty," Ann said.

"In the extreme," Carol said.

"What about the facility in Brevig Mission?" Gary asked.

"Carol and I were part of the design team, along with Hamid," Ken said. "It consists of four buildings and a helipad inside a perimeter fence that's guarded twenty-four-seven. The largest building is a combination dormitory, recreation room, and dining hall. The lab building is divided into a series of biosafety level-four suites plus the supporting changing rooms, air locks, and decon showers. Ventilation is through filtering systems identical to the ones here. Then there's the maintenance and storage building, which also houses the diesel generators. The last building is the guardhouse and communications center."

"Does it have on-site medical facilities?" Ann asked.

Ken hesitated a moment, as if deciding what to say. "Yes, there's a four-bed clinic plus a level-four emergency clinic called 'Slammer Junior.' "

"Why is it called that?"

"It's a scaled-down version of our level-four hospital, which we call 'the Slammer' because victims of hot agents are confined there until they're no longer contagious." He paused. "Of course, many of those who go in never come out, except as corpses."

"Does that happen often?"

"That's classified."

Gary had been expecting they would run afoul of security eventually, and he felt sure Ann had just made an entry in her mental to-do list. Then another question arose in his mind, something he had wondered about ever since their meeting with Secretary Foster.

"Ken, can you tell us how Hamid Momeni got involved in this research?" Gary asked.

Ken sighed. "Hamid has an interesting and tragic background. He's Iranian, the son of a longtime U.S. embassy employee. His father was captured when the embassy fell, and Khomeini's thugs summarily executed him as a traitor. At the time, Hamid was an undergrad at the University of Texas. A few years later, he became a naturalized citizen then continued his education at Cambridge. Upon graduation, the CIA snapped him up, first as an Iran expert, then they decided to make use of his microbiology studies."

"What about the rest of his family?" Ann asked.

"Hamid never talked about them, but I rather suspect they were executed, as well."

"How sad."

"Yes, it is," Carol said. "It's an ugly, evil world we live in."

"Got that right," Sully said.

"Yeah, well, anything else you want to know?" Ken asked Gary.

"Is Hamid the only spook working here?"

"No, there's one other. Homeland security sent over another microbiology expert, a man by the name of Saeed Alsaadoun. He works for Hamid in his lab here."

"Another Iranian?"

"No, Saeed is a Saudi."

"Why would Hamid pick him rather than one of the army researchers?"

Ken shrugged. "Don't know. Maybe he feels more at home with a fellow spook."

"Know anything else about him?"

"Not a whole lot. He got his PhD from Harvard, same degree program we went through." He nodded toward Carol. "I think his dad is the manager for a furniture factory near Riyadh. Saeed is quiet and competent, but then that's what you'd expect from a Harvard grad."

Gary grinned. "Well, we've taken up enough of your time. Thanks for all the info." He found himself liking Ken and Carol.

"You're welcome."

Thomas escorted them to the back entrance and through the ritual of surrendering the badges and signing out. They walked out to the parking lot.

"Here we are again," Thomas said. "You know the drill. As of now, you're on your own."

"Understood," Gary said.

"The only exception is that in the event of a major security breach, Colonel Roberts or Hamid Momeni can call a status meeting."

"What constitutes a serious breach?"

Thomas laughed. "You'll know it if it happens." He got into his car and drove off.

Colonel Zack Roberts set his coffee mug on his desk and tilted back in his executive swivel chair. "What do you make of the accident at Brevig?" he asked.

Lieutenant Colonel Nate Young shifted in his chair. "It was unfortunate but unavoidable; a simple manufacturing defect. Hamid's report said that Colonel Edwards ordered a complete inspection of all the shelving units and found no other problems. These things happen."

Zack frowned. "Yeah, I guess so, but that defect cost a life. And now we have these consultants snooping around while Hamid's up in Alaska."

"I understand your concern, but I think he made the right call. If it were me, I'd sure want to check it out personally. Too bad Dick's people haven't come up with a vaccine yet. We might have saved Major Ingram."

"That's what makes it even more tragic. Dick thinks they're on the verge of creating a vaccine; a week or two, perhaps." Zack toyed with his coffee mug. "But all this aside, what *really* worries me is the whole reason why we're doing all this."

Nate shrugged. "We don't have any choice. CIA intelligence reports a Saudi sleeper cell working on the same virus somewhere on the East Coast. If that's true, we had better beat their time or we're in deep trouble."

"But is it a credible threat?"

"The CIA sure thinks so, and it makes sense. The 1918 outbreak is well known among researchers, and it's the most lethal virus there's ever been."

"Do you have any concerns about Saeed Alsaadoun?"

"You mean the fact that he grew up in Saudi Arabia?"

"Yes."

"He's been vetted by the CIA, and you know how thorough they are. He's a naturalized citizen, and I believe Hamid checked him out, as well. And personally, I'd give more weight to Hamid's opinion."

"Glad to hear you say that. We have enough going on without adding to our troubles."

CHAPTER 10

The hum of the auxiliary power unit provided a gentle background sound as Sully drove the truck along a road almost a mile from the USAMRIID building. John had taken the minivan into town to purchase gasoline for the UAV in anticipation of aerial surveillance at some point. Gary slipped into the chair beside Dan. Ann sat on the other side, her head low and eyes focused on her laptop's screen.

It was late afternoon on Friday, and the team had worked long hours since Tuesday, sniffing out the Institute's unsecured communications lines. They had found some but not as many as Gary had anticipated, which was a pleasant surprise from the client's point of view. They had not yet attacked USAMRIID's physical security. That would come later, but right now they needed a way into the Institute's intranet so Ann could do her magic. But so far, Dan had not been able to find a way in.

"Okay, what do you have?" Gary asked.

Dan punched up a video recording taken the previous night under a half moon, using the low-light camera atop the telescoping mast. He hit FAST-FORWARD then shifted to FREEZE-FRAME, showing the

Institute's roofline. He selected a small rectangle and blew up the image. The video disintegrated into a mush of grainy black and white pixels.

"Didn't know you were into abstract art," Gary said.

"Very funny. Watch what happens when I call up other frames of the same area and clean them up with Ann's image merge program."

Four more images moved into place over the blurry shot, and the indistinct pixels began to coalesce and sharpen. A few moments later, a surprisingly distinct blowup of a section of the roof appeared. Dan adjusted the brightness and contrast.

"See anything odd?" he asked.

Gary leaned forward. "Looks like a box on its side with something circular inside." He turned to Dan. "What is it?"

"Don't know for sure, but it might be a microwave antenna."

"Why put it inside a box?"

"Only two reasons I can think of. Either to protect it, which I doubt, or to hide it from prying eyes."

"A microwave link? Why not use a landline?"

"Good question."

"The other end has to be close, right?"

"Oh, it's short haul, all right."

"So what are you suggesting?"

"For starters, find the other end, then figure out what they're using it for, assuming it's active."

"Sounds good to me. Add it to the task list."

"Okay. Wanted to check with you first since it may take awhile. Our night ops schedule is pretty full." Much of the research had to be done after dark, especially the tasks requiring the telescoping mast.

"I know. Any idea where the other end might be?"

Dan pointed to the freeze-frame. "That only gives an approximate direction, and close doesn't count for much in microwave communications."

Ann's fingers stopped their clattering, and she looked over at Dan's PC. "Where is that?" she asked.

Dan brought up the Fort Detrick map and marked the approximate location on the Institute's building. Ann accessed the map on her laptop.

"Hmm, that's interesting," she said.

"What?" Dan asked.

Ann studied the map for a few moments then opened another window and searched down a long Word document. She took her mouse and entered a pair of coordinates and updated the map.

"You might take a peek there," she said.

Dan looked at her with a puzzled expression. "Why?"

"That's Nate Young's post quarters. His house is in the general direction the antenna is pointing, and somehow I suspect that's not a coincidence."

Gary grinned. "Somehow I suspect you're right." He turned back to Dan. "Let's check it out."

"Okay," Dan said. He clicked on the target and turned it red. He flipped the intercom switch to the truck's cab.

Gary grabbed the mike. "Sully, drive us by Nate Young's house. Dan's marked it for you."

"Roger, boss dude."

They made two leisurely passes using the exterior cameras hidden around the truck's roof. The house looked typical of the post quarters Gary had seen at Fort Detrick—plain but well maintained with a small, neat yard. It was the second house from the corner and shared a common back fence with the house on the next street over. The backyards were all fenced. A small sign in front announced the occupant's name and rank. But what really drew Gary's attention was the tall, steel tower in the backyard, which supported a horizontal, three-element antenna.

"What is that thing?" Gary asked.

"It's an amateur radio beam antenna," Dan said. "Apparently our friend is a ham radio operator."

"A what?"

"That's what they call themselves," Dan said with a smile. "Don't ask me why."

"That's not in his bio."

Dan shrugged. "Maybe the antenna belonged to a previous occupant."

"Maybe." Gary turned to Ann. "Could you check it out?"

"Sure."

"Did you see a microwave dish?" Gary asked Dan.

"I'll need to analyze the video recordings to be sure, but I didn't see it on the house," Dan said. "I think it's more likely we'll find it up on that tower. There's a platform near the top, where the beam antenna's mast is attached, but I can't see what's on it from this angle."

"Well, we can check it out tonight with the mast camera while you're snooping around for the microwave link."

Zack was on his way out of his office for the weekend when his phone rang. Irritated, he hesitated, not sure if he wanted to answer it or let his voice mail take charge of it until Monday. Duty won out. He returned to his desk, sat down, and picked up the handset.

"Colonel Roberts," he said.

"Zack, this is Dick," Dick Edwards said. "I have wonderful news."

The USAMRIID commanding officer felt a jolt of excitement because he thought he knew what was coming. "Tell me about it."

"We have a breakthrough on the vaccine. We've cultured a batch, and it works."

"That's terrific. Now you're sure about this, right?"

"Absolutely. It's completely effective as long as it's administered before exposure."

"What about production?"

"I don't foresee any problems. We should have the vaccine into small-scale production within a few weeks."

"Wonderful. Have you notified Hamid?"

"Not yet. I wanted to give you a heads-up first."

"Thanks. You certainly made *my* day." Zack was well aware of Dick's game of passive resistance with Hamid but didn't feel like interfering unless he had to. As long as homeland security was happy, Zack was happy.

"I won't keep you," Dick said. "Have a nice weekend."

"Thanks. You, too."

"Bye."

Zack smiled as he hung up. That was good news indeed.

Gary yawned. He had not yet adjusted his internal clock to the team's new operational schedule, which called for a late-morning start with operations extending well into the night to avoid detection. The team had enjoyed a late evening meal at Lamplighter Restaurant in Frederick. Now it was nearing midnight, and they had at least several more hours of surveillance before returning to the motel.

Ann looked up from her laptop. "Guess what? Nate *is* an amateur radio operator. I found him on the ARRL Web site."

"What's that stand for?" John asked.

"Don't know. The site says it's for the National Association for Amateur Radio."

"It stands for 'American Radio Relay League,'" Dan said. "It's an organization of folks who are really serious about radio, but they also provide emergency communications in times of natural disasters like hurricanes and tornadoes."

"Okay, I guess that explains the antenna," Gary said. "But I'm a little surprised the post housing people would let him have it."

"Well, he *is* a senior officer," John said.

"Yeah, but still. . ."

"You ready to start looking for the microwave link?" Dan asked.

"Are you sure we're by ourselves?" Gary asked.

"That last pass looked good," Dan said. "Didn't see anyone out, and I'm not picking up any unusual radio signals."

"Okay, let's check it out. Cut in the intercom." Dan flipped a switch. "Sully, turn around and take us by real slow," Gary said into the mike.

"Roger that."

Sully made a tight U-turn at the next intersection and slowed to a crawl. Dan eyed the forward monitor to make sure they were clear of obstacles then started the telescoping mast up. Gary watched the monitor above Dan as the view of the corner house and Nate's quarters opened up, showing the surrounding houses and yards. Dan zoomed the low-light camera in on the elusive platform. He glanced down at the GPS map displayed on his laptop. The truck's position was almost on the line between the Institute and Nate's tower.

"Almost there," Dan warned Sully. "Stop," he said a few moments later.

The image shivered and shook a little. Gary's eyes zeroed in on an open box mounted in the center of a metal shelf, and nestled inside was a circular object.

"Is that what I think it is?" he asked.

"Looks like a microwave antenna to me," Dan said. "Now let's see if we can locate the beam."

Dan rotated the parabolic antenna atop the mast until it faced toward the Institute. He raised the mast another ten feet then started it on a slow descent, watching a bank of signal-strength meters. One of the bar readouts moved slightly. Dan stopped the mast and raised it a little.

"Sully, move us forward an inch," Dan said.

"I left my measuring tape in the back," Sully said.

"Humor us, Mr. Sullivan," Gary said.

"An inch it is."

Gary barely felt the truck's movement. The meter's ghostly reading disappeared.

"Back up two inches."

"Hey, dude, make up your mind."

The meter reading rose a little higher than before. Dan played with the mast height, and the bar went higher still. Dan pressed a button and started recording.

"Not a very strong signal," Gary said.

"Doesn't have to be," Dan said. "Besides, my antenna isn't optimum for the frequency they're using."

"What do you think it's used for?"

"Why guess?" Dan said. He pressed two switches and pointed to Ann. "It's on router two."

Ann ran a network cable over to an empty port on the router and started a network analysis program. Complex grids of numbers and letters flashed on the screen, changing rapidly. Ann's eyes flitted about the screen. A few seconds later, she looked around at Gary.

"It's a network connection."

"Into their intranet?"

"Sure looks like it, and it's not encrypted."

Gary sat back in his chair. "Very interesting. Is it being used right now?"

Ann shook her head. "Nope, just the normal network chitchat between nodes when they don't have anything better to do. You know, the digital version of 'Yes, we have no bananas.'"

Gary chuckled. "Very funny." A puzzled expression came to his face. "So Nate has his own personal connection at home. I can understand that, but why not run a landline connection instead?"

"I bet that's what he wanted, but the army bean counters

wouldn't let him have it," John said. "The military strictly limits the equipment allocated to various personnel."

"So this was all his troops could cobble together for him?" Gary asked.

"That would be my guess. The cost of a few microwave parts would sure be easier to hide than the monthly charge for a broadband connection to his house."

"I think I see," Gary said. "Nate wants the connection at his house, and his boss backs him up. The amateur radio license is a subterfuge to install a tower that can support the microwave antenna."

"That's what it looks like to me," Dan said. "And hiding the antennas inside those boxes means they're at least somewhat concerned about security."

"Yeah, but they're still getting written up for it."

"Sure would be nice if we could use it in the meantime," Ann said.

Gary stared at the distant box. "Yeah, it would, but I don't know how we'd do it."

"We've done harder," John said.

Gary's mind drifted back to a very unpleasant job they had done over a year ago. "You got that right." He looked around at John. "You got any ideas?"

"The equipment's no problem. Dan and I can slap an antenna and transceiver together in a day, no sweat. But placing it where it can intercept the beam is the hard part."

"How close does it need to be?"

"A couple of inches would be best," Dan said.

"I don't suppose there's another place between Nate's house and the Institute," Gary said.

"That's a roger on your last," Dan said. "The only possible place is on top of that box."

"Well, how about the direct approach? Jump over the fence, climb the tower, and pop John's black box on top."

"I don't think so." Dan tilted the camera down. The image was shaky but clear enough to show a large German shepherd sprawled on the ground near the house.

"Whoa, I guess not."

"What about the dart gun?"

"Nope, there's no way we could approach without him kicking up a ruckus and probably the rest of the dogs in the neighborhood, as well. Plus he's a pet, not a guard dog. I wouldn't feel right doing it even if I thought it would work."

"Tilt the camera back up," John said. The image of the box atop the tower came into view. "What if we rigged a span wire from here to the tower and used it to install our antenna?"

Gary turned and looked at him. "I suppose you have a way of doing that?"

"Yeah, with a little help from you."

Gary glanced at his watch and saw it was nearly 2:00 a.m. Sunday. The team, except for John, had spent most of Saturday searching for additional unsecured communications lines without success. Gary filled his mug from the coffeemaker the team had chipped in to buy in order to make the nighttime schedule more bearable. He took a sip. John had spent the day checking out the UAV and working on the equipment for the operation. Now he was hunkered down on the truck's floor installing a monofilament spool on the underside of the delta wing craft. Something that looked like a giant fishing lure was attached to the end of the husky line. Actually it was a small stabilizer that would keep the three hooks from spinning.

"You sure that contraption will work?" Gary asked.

John looked up and grinned. "Hey, my gadgets *always* work. It's the pilot I'm worried about."

131

"Then it's in the bag." Gary looked around at Dan. "Ready for our final check?"

He nodded and keyed the intercom mike. "Okay, Sully. Take us by real slow."

"Roger the pokey pass. Hold tight, dudes."

Dan started the mast up. A few seconds later, the whining sound stopped, and he shifted his gaze to a signal-strength meter. The bar display nudged off the bottom then settled down. "Did you get it?" he asked.

"Yes," Ann answered. "The link's up but unused at the moment."

"Looks like Nate's not in the habit of working late," Gary said.

Dan nodded and started the mast down. He leaned forward and spoke into the mike. "Take us around the block."

"Roger," Sully said.

"Show me the tower one more time," Gary said.

Dan punched up a recording and started it in slow motion. It was a close-up they had taken earlier, showing the top of the tower's three legs with the sheet metal shelf near the top below the mast that supported the radio antenna. The box containing the microwave antenna rested on the platform. Gary pointed to where the mast base attached to the tower's legs.

"That's where we want the hook, right?" Gary asked.

John took a quick look. "Yeah, as high up as you can get it."

Gary eyed the tiny target and wiped his hands on his jeans. "Okay, let's do it."

Sully turned left, drove a block, and turned left again. At the end of this block was the street that ran by the front of Nate's quarters. Gary looked down at the UAV. In less than a minute, he would be alone with it under the early morning skies while the rest of the team awaited his success—or failure. Sully slowed as the truck reached the corner.

"Ready or not," John said with a smile.

"Yeah," Gary said.

"Don't forget your radio," Dan said, handing Gary a small, flesh-colored object.

Gary inserted it in his right ear and turned it on.

John stooped down and picked up the unwieldy aircraft. "Bring the controller and starter, will you?"

Gary grabbed the radio-control transmitter and the electric drill, which held a rubber cup.

"Good luck," Ann said.

"Thanks," Gary said.

Gary followed John out and closed the truck's rear doors. It was a clear night, and the half moon provided adequate light, eliminating the need for night-vision goggles. A gentle breeze, so faint it could scarcely be felt, blew from the east. John set the UAV down, kneeled, and looked it over one last time. The small aircraft faced back down the street, soon to be its runway. John held out his hand, and Gary gave him the starter.

"Better check the flight controls," John whispered.

Gary flipped on the master switch and checked the transmitter's signal strength. The meter was well into the green range. He moved the joystick around. The tiny servos whined, and the elevons, combination elevators and ailerons, and twin rudders worked smoothly.

"Set the throttle," John added.

Gary pressed and held a switch until the throttle servo reached the full forward position. He had taken almost as much interest as John when they had decided to add a UAV to their surveillance equipment. Gary had been a radio-control model airplane enthusiast in high school and college, and back then most planes had been powered by glow plug engines that used fuel containing nitromethane and castor oil. But for the UAV, John had selected a gasoline-powered engine with an electronic ignition and miniature spark plug. It was smoother, quieter, but most important, it had more endurance.

"Apply the brakes," John said.

Gary activated the servo.

John pulled the propeller through by hand a few times then turned on the ignition and set the choke. Holding the UAV down with one hand, he brought the drill up, pressed the rubber cup against the engine's spinner, and switched it on. The propeller spun a few times then became a blur. Gary could barely hear the engine's muffled exhaust over the propeller's gentle thrumming as he brought the throttle back to idle. John waited a few moments then turned off the choke and stood up.

"You're good to go," he whispered.

"Thanks."

Gary watched John hurry over to the truck and disappear through the back doors. Sully drove off, turned the corner, and continued toward the side street nearest Nate's quarters. Gary checked the controller's backlit LCD screen and noted that he would have no problem seeing where the UAV was going. He took a deep breath, ran the throttle all the way forward, and released the brakes. The plane raced down the street like it had been shot from a catapult. Gary pulled back on the joystick, and the UAV leapt into the air. Gary watched it climb for a few moments then looked down at the LCD screen. From now on he would fly the plane using it's low-light TV camera.

"Skyhook is airborne, Home Plate," Gary whispered. "Are you in position?"

"Roger, Home Plate is on station," Dan said.

Gary felt himself relax a little. The UAV was well above the trees, and there were no obstacles within a several-block radius. Since he had plenty of time, he brought the throttle back to cruise and made a large, looping turn to come in from the west. The moon, nearly overhead, provided stark white lighting. Objects below stood out in sharp relief, punctuated by inky shadows. Gary lined up on the lofty radio antenna and made a high-speed descent, level with the top of the tower. Three guy wires braced the structure, but they were below the UAV's flight path.

Gary made a close pass, just above the level of the box enclosure and verified with his eyes what he had seen on the video. The tower's three legs formed a triangle, with the imaginary base of one side parallel with the front of the box, giving the microwave antenna an unimpeded path to the Institute's roof. What Gary had to do was snag one of legs that formed the base then unreel the monofilament line, creating a span wire to the truck.

Gary moved the joystick to the right then pulled back slightly. The UAV streaked around in a tight 180-degree turn that would have been impossible for a manned aircraft. He toggled the switch to pay out the triple hook and about six feet of line and ran the throttle up to full power. After passing the tower, Gary waited ten long seconds and brought the plane around in a broad right-hand turn, rolling out over the street that ran by the front of the house.

The tower was now off to the right. Gary watched it closely, and when it was nearly off the display, he banked the plane sharply to the right until the target was nearly centered. The box's image, a little to the left, grew rapidly. Gary forced himself to wait, then he rolled the UAV into a left vertical bank and pulled back on the stick. The plane pivoted around the tower, dragging the unseen line past the target support. After a 90-degree turn, Gary rolled the craft level. A moment later, the display jiggled; he had hooked something.

"The line's playing out," Dan said over the radio.

Gary poised his finger above the button that would jettison the spool. The boxy shape of the team's command center truck grew rapidly in the display. Gary waited two seconds after the UAV flew past then dropped the spool.

"That's it," Dan said. "Skyhook is cleared to land."

Gary grinned. "Roger that. Tell John to get the crash trucks out."

"You better get it down without a scratch," John said.

"I'll do my best."

Gary brought the throttle back to idle and initiated a gentle bank to the left to bring the UAV around in a broad circle. The ground below continued to turn in his display until he spotted the truck ahead. He lined up on the street and pressed forward on the stick. The plane came down rapidly. Two figures stood beside the truck. Gary flared out about a hundred feet from the truck, touched down, and flipped on the brakes. Now all he had to do was go down one block and turn left and he would be back with the team.

He watched the display as he walked. John ran toward the UAV, loomed large, then reached down like a giant and picked it up. A minute later, Gary rounded the corner and spotted the truck in time to see John come back out. Gary broke into a jog and soon reached the rear doors. John took the controller.

"Any problems?" he asked.

"Nope. It handles like a dream. The pylon maneuver around the tower had me worried, but when the time came, the controls were smooth and positive all the way through. The UAV is *definitely* a keeper."

"Glad to hear it."

Gary looked up. Sully was kneeling down on top of the truck. "Sully working on the span wire?" he asked.

"Yeah."

"Did I get the hook in the right place?"

"Won't know for sure until we run the microwave assembly out to the tower."

"This I gotta see."

"Come on up."

John climbed up the ladder, and Gary followed him onto the truck's roof. Sully finished tying the monofilament line to a clamp and looked around.

"Hey, boss dudes," he said. "You sure this thing will work?"

"You better believe it," John said.

"If you say so. Guess that makes it the opposite of a special-effects prop."

John hesitated but finally asked: "I know I'll regret it, but why is that?"

Sully laughed. "Special-effects props look like they work but don't."

"I suggest you fade to black," Gary said.

"Yes, boss."

Gary looked closely at what could only be called a serious gadget. Even by John's standards of ingenuity, it looked strange and improbable, however much of the design Gary understood. It was a lightweight box housing a microwave antenna, transmitter, and battery. Mounted above it was a grooved wheel and friction roller to pull it along the line. Beside this, retracted to keep it out of the way, was a sturdy articulated arm that ended in a set of jaws. A tiny camera with a wide-angle lens provided eyes for the contraption.

"Man, I know that took a bunch of work," Gary said.

"It sure did," John said. "How about putting it on the line?"

Gary lifted the box, placed the grooved wheel over the line, and pressed the button to engage the friction roller. John pulled over a laptop attached to a jury-rigged controller. He pressed a button, and the box started up the long span wire. Gary brought his head close so he could watch the trolley's long ascent. For several minutes there was nothing to do but watch the top of the tower slowly increase in size. Several minutes later John stopped the box near where the monofilament was tied to the treble hook. The gadget was suspended in midair, a little to the left and above the existing microwave box.

"How—" Gary began.

"Watch," John said. "Sully, get ready to slack off on the line."

"Gotcha covered," Sully said.

John flipped a switch and began moving two joysticks in smooth coordination. The hinged arm pivoted up and extended horizontally toward the tower leg behind the microwave platform. As it inched closer, John opened the jaws and clamped onto one side of the U-shaped leg.

"Give me some slack," he said.

"Here it comes." Sully laid the line out slowly.

Again John moved the joysticks; only this time the arm pulled the gadget in over the target box. He pivoted the camera, and when the assembly reached the center, he lowered it. The image on the laptop screen jittered.

"It's in place," John said. "Try it out, Dan."

"Wait one," Dan replied. "Solid, guys," he said a few moments later. "We're in."

John looked at Gary and grinned.

"I didn't have a doubt in the world," Gary said.

"Yeah, right," John said. "Now to make sure it stays put." He pressed a button on the controller.

"What's that?"

"Glue dispenser. It's like superglue only better. That thing's there forever."

"What about the span wire?" Gary asked.

John looked at Sully. "Is the high-speed winch ready?"

"Sure thing," Sully said. He handed John a push button on a cable.

John shifted into a cross-legged sitting position and placed the cable over one leg within easy reach. When he released the friction roller, the line dropped free and hung from the hook in a lazy arc. John unclamped the articulated jaws, pivoted the arm, and extended it again. The jaws reached the treble hook and closed on one of the free hooks. Then they retracted, pulling the hook free from the tower leg.

"Is the winch set on slow speed?" John asked.

"Roger," Sully said.

John took up the slack until the line was taut once more. "Okay, flip the switch to high."

"Ready."

John jabbed the winch button and opened the arm's jaws a fraction of a second later. The winch emitted a muted scream as the spool reeled in the stretched line faster than it could fall. Moments later the hook ferule hit the guide, snapping the line instantly. John released the button, and the geared drive whined to a stop. Gary watched the laptop display as John retracted the arm and parked it on top of the box.

"Any chance of Nate spotting that?"

John shook his head. "Almost impossible. The box underneath hides our antenna. The only thing we have to avoid is using the link at the same time as Nate."

That would be up to Ann and Dan, Gary knew. He took the laptop and began climbing down from the truck roof. John and Sully gathered the rest of the equipment and followed.

CHAPTER 11

After standing down on Sunday, Gary decided to start Monday's workday a little earlier since they could expect to have access to Nate's intranet connection while he was at work. Dan had patched in the link through the broadband server he had established in his motel room, which made it accessible to the team through the Internet. Sully had found them a parking spot on a quiet street several blocks from the security boss's quarters. The entire team was gathered about Ann in the command center. Gary watched her as she worked away, but if the kibitzing bothered her, she gave no sign. The minutes slipped by and turned into hours. Soon it would be time for lunch, assuming Ann would be willing to take a break.

Ann sat up straight. "There," she said without any particular inflection. She continued looking at her laptop screen for a few more seconds then turned to Gary.

Gary was curious and tickled at the same time. "Uh, that could mean many things," he said with a self-conscious grin. "Perhaps you might point your remark a little more."

"I have installed a backdoor into the Institute's network operating system."

"You mean. . . ," Gary began.

"We have access to just about everything on their intranet, and that includes a link to the Brevig, Alaska, lab."

"That's great. Any chance the network honchos might detect us?"

"Possible but not likely. The files I altered are the same size as before, and I reset the date/time stamps, as well."

"Can't they track our activity?"

"Nope. I made us a special ID that's exempt from normal network logging. We're invisible, guys. The only thing we have to be careful about is using the microwave link when Nate's home. I have a program running on the server that alerts me if Nate logs off at the Institute."

"That'll help, but he could leave the building without logging off."

"True, but he can't get out of the building without us knowing it. Among other things, I'm capturing all the security access records."

"You mean when they swipe their ID cards?"

"Exactly. Everyone entering or leaving the building or the labs, for that matter. All saved on disk. I have a filter that alerts us when Nate goes out."

"Excellent," John said, "but it would be nice if we could spot him approaching his house. He might not go straight home."

Gary snapped his fingers. "The camera on top of our microwave transmitter. Can we use that?"

"I think so. I'll dig out the controller for Dan."

A few minutes later, Dan had the box tucked among his other communications gear. He punched up the video and placed it on the monitor closest to Ann's workstation.

"That about what you want?" John asked.

"Great view of the side street," Ann said. "How about centering it on the street that runs by the front of his house?"

John reached up and tweaked the controller.

"That's good," Ann said. "Now I can hack away without fear of getting caught."

Gary looked around. "We haven't had a status meeting since last Thursday. I have to get caught up on our report draft, so what about your project notes? Everyone up to date?"

"I am," Sully said.

"You're exempt," Gary said.

John shook his head. "Nope, I've been kinda busy."

"I'm pretty much current," Ann said.

"Guilty," Dan said. "I'll do it by this afternoon."

"And I'm behind, also," Gary said. "Let's have the status meeting at 4:00 p.m. I'll keep it short. We're doing a pretty good job on their communications, and finding this microwave link is a *whopping* discrepancy."

"Big-time," Sully said.

"I'll make a note of that, Mr. Sullivan. Now we're fast approaching the next phase of our audit."

"Checking out the physical security?" Ann asked.

"Right. So be thinking of ways we might break in. We have fairly good drawings and diagrams of both the Institute and the Brevig lab, so it's time we started putting them to good use."

"Do you have any preference which one we attack first?" Ann asked.

"Not particularly, but the Institute *is* a little more convenient."

"Clarify that for me," John said. "Is a physical break-in at Brevig really on the to-do list?"

"If we can manage it, yes."

Then one more task came to Gary's mind, one that would put him even further behind.

"Sully," Gary said.

"Yes, boss?" Sully replied.

"Sometime after lunch, you're going to drive John and me out in the country. The UAV needs additional flight testing."

Sully grinned. "You want someone to pick up the pieces?"

Gary caught John's stricken look and had to laugh. "For John's sake, I hope not."

Gary looked down at the controller. It was large and rectangular because it had to accommodate two LCD displays but thin since the electronics and controls didn't take up much space. The displays could be configured several different ways, but at present, one gave a wide-angle view of the sky in front of the UAV. The other panel presented a high-resolution picture of the ground below using a powerful, image-stabilized zoom lens.

Gary switched that display to the GPS map and studied it while the UAV autopilot handled the flying chores. The altimeter read exactly five thousand feet, and the plane was northeast of the Frederick Municipal Airport. The map currently displayed nine aircraft contacts whose locations and altitudes were provided by their transponders. None was close. Seven were either landing at or departing from the airport, while the other two were airliners flying over. The UAV had no transponder because it was supposed to be invisible.

"Can you see it?" Gary asked Sully.

John pointed him in the UAV's general direction. Sully swept the skies with his powerful binoculars. "Naw, man. That thing is, like, way stealthy."

"That's the general idea," John said. "Bring it down to twenty-five hundred feet," he said to Gary.

Gary thumbed a switch to bring the throttle back to idle and put the plane into a steep dive. "The new flight display is a great improvement," he said. "The wider view makes the UAV easier to control."

"Yeah, nothing like being able to see where you're going," John said. "What about the infrared view?"

About a minute later, Gary leveled out and began running the payload camera through its paces. First came the high-resolution color picture. Gary zoomed in and had no trouble seeing small objects on the ground. Then he flipped to the infrared view designed to cut through darkness, fog, haze, smoke, or rain. Even though it was a clear day, the infrared depiction emphasized the details on the ground below. Gary had no trouble picking out the monochrome depictions of the golf course, airport, and the town of Frederick.

"This is great," he said. He flipped the payload display back to the color camera. "See anything, Sully?"

"Nada," Sully said.

"That's good enough for me. If the kid can't see it with binoculars, then it's pretty near invisible."

"Yeah," John said. "That variegated gray/blue paint job blends in with the sky, and with a near-zero radar cross-section, air traffic control won't be picking us up, either."

"I'm satisfied," Gary said. "Are we done?"

"Try the emergency recovery system."

Gary hesitated then said, "It's your toy."

"Unmanned aerial vehicle."

"Whatever." Gary lifted a safety cover and flipped off the controller's master switch. The two displays went black, and the transmitter's signal-strength meter dropped to zero.

All three men looked in the general direction of where they thought the UAV was but saw nothing. According to John, the plane was supposed to return to the takeoff point upon loss of signal, but would it? Gary tried to figure how long the maneuver would take but quickly gave up. The UAV would either come back, or they were out a very expensive piece of equipment. Minutes passed. Just when Gary began to worry, a white object blossomed almost directly overhead. It was the UAV's parachute.

John ran out into the field and retrieved the plane when it touched down. He wrapped the parachute around it and came striding back with the unwieldy package, beaming every step of the way.

The three men walked back to the minivan.

It was a little after three, and lunch was an unlamented, high-fat memory. Ann had updated her project notes over an hour ago, and since then she had been doing what she called data mining, snooping around the digital nooks and crannies of the Institute's intranet. Most of what she had found she simply copied onto Dan's capacious server to be examined in detail later. Ann smiled at the thought. She had special programs to handle the grunt work, leaving the mother lode files for her.

Most recently, Ann had concentrated on e-mails and documents concerning the Brevig lab. There were a lot of both, and they highlighted how difficult the facility was to operate. There was the sensitivity of the research itself, but they also told of the long, thin supply line between Fort Detrick and Alaska. She hovered over her laptop, oblivious of what was going on around her.

At 4:10 p.m., Gary opened the truck's rear doors. Sully jumped inside, and John hurried in carrying the UAV. Gary stepped up, closed the doors, and handed John the controller after he returned from stowing his new pride and joy.

Gary grinned. "Better take care. Sherlock might get jealous."

"Not a chance," John said. "They're both great."

Gary looked around, and his expression grew serious. He knew they were waiting for the status meeting he had called, but after telling everyone to get caught up, the UAV's test flight had preempted *his* documentation.

"Would it hurt anyone's feelings to postpone the status meeting?" he asked finally.

Ann snickered. "Meaning *you* aren't ready," she said.

"*I'm* ready, but I'm not so sure about John."

"Wait a minute," John said.

"At ease, everyone. I think our time is better spent on exploiting our link into the Institute's intranet because we could lose it at any time. But I do suggest strongly that we get caught up on our notes."

"Okay by me," John said.

"Dig out any new nuggets while we were gone?" Gary asked Ann.

"Quite a bit, but one really caught my eye."

"Shoot."

A grin came to her face. "Would you be interested in breaking into the Brevig lab?"

"You mean right now?"

"Yes. Because of logistics, it's either now or wait at least a week."

"Tell me about it."

"I was digging around in an archived e-mail file and came across one dated over a month ago from Hamid Momeni to Dick Edwards. Subject line said: 'classified equipment,' but what really grabbed my attention was that Hamid told Edwards he had to pick up the device from an army courier at the Nome airport."

"Interesting. Anything else?" Gary asked.

"Routine stuff. Edwards said he would pick it up. Later he griped big-time to Colonel Roberts about the agent bossing him around."

"Don't blame him for that. What did Roberts say?"

"Essentially, live with it."

"That's very interesting," he said when she finished. "So what are you suggesting?"

"What if we sent Edwards an e-mail saying he's receiving another classified something or other? Then when he comes to pick it up, we lead him on a wild goose chase while you impersonate him and do the break-in."

"Whoa." Even though the idea was sketchy, Gary saw it had merit, providing the details could be worked out. "What kind of timeline are we looking at?"

"We'd have to leave tomorrow morning."

Gary was tempted to say they would have to put it off a week, but in his experience, such a delay might mean missing the opportunity entirely. Then it occurred to him that Ann wouldn't have brought it up if she thought it was impossible.

"You really think we can do this?" Gary asked.

She smiled. "If we hustle."

"Ms. O'Brien, hustle is what we do best. Now have you, perhaps, been busy working out any of the details?"

"A few."

"Tell me about it."

"Transportation is the most critical part, assuming we can't use government planes."

"You assume correctly. Terrorists aren't exactly welcome on military bases."

She giggled. "Yeah. If we leave tomorrow morning, we can be in Nome around 7:00 p.m. local time. We break in on Wednesday, depart Nome Thursday morning, and get into D.C. around 6:00 a.m. on Friday."

"And flat worn-out."

"I'm sure. But if it works. . ."

"Yeah, that would *really* be something. I take it Hamid is back at the Institute."

"He is."

"Do we have enough on Edwards for me to come up with a disguise?"

"I think so. I have his vital stats." She handed over a folder.

Gary opened it and saw a large color print of Edwards in a dress uniform. Behind it he found a page giving his physical description.

"Hmm. I'll need brown contacts and a black wig; no problem, but he's three inches taller than me and fifty pounds heavier. I have some special shoes that will make up about two inches of that. The other inch probably won't matter. The extra beef I can make up with padding." He looked up. "I think I can do this."

"So is it a go?" Ann asked.

"Absolutely." Gary looked all around, making eye contact with each team member. He was pleased to note their looks of confident expectation. "First, let's get our flight reservations then get cracking on the plan."

"I've already taken care of the tickets."

"Okay, so now we need the e-mail that kicks the operation off."

"Right. I have a draft, but I don't know anything about their equipment. What can we say the Institute's sending him?"

"Something we're familiar with. They're bound to have security cameras, so have John fill in the blank. But what about Edwards's e-mails? If Hamid or Zack gets wind of this, we're dead."

"I have that covered. I'll program my mailbot program to intercept any messages related to the operation to a special file. Hamid and Roberts will never see it. But speaking of e-mail, we better fire off Hamid's message in the next few minutes so we can see his response before we leave."

"John, we need your assistance," Gary said.

"Okay. Let's make it a new digital recorder for their surveillance cameras. Open up the draft, and I'll help you."

Gary looked at Dan. "What time is it in Brevig?"

"Minus four hours from here," Dan said. "A little after noon. What about personal surveillance equipment? Do you want cameras and data recorders?" Dan asked.

Gary thought that over. "Let's do data recorders only," he said finally. "Ann already has what we need on the visual end."

"I'll include them in my bag of tricks."

Gary turned back to Ann. "When are we ordering Edwards to pick up his magic box?"

"Nine in the morning on Wednesday."

CHAPTER 12

Gary felt like he was standing on stilts even though his special army dress shoes added only two inches to his height. He looked down at them as if to verify this fact and saw that they looked normal, the extra altitude cleverly hidden in the upper portion of the shoes. His black wig looked natural; however, it certainly didn't match his blue eyes. Gary opened a tiny beige box and inserted brown contacts. He blinked until his eyelids became accustomed.

Gary turned and examined the dress uniform coat of an army lieutenant colonel that was lying on his bed. It was accurate down to the rows of ribbons Sully had carefully assembled from Edwards's picture that Ann had found on the Institute's intranet. Whether the officer would come to the Nome airport wearing a dress uniform Gary had no idea, but it seemed likely. But just in case, he would take a working uniform along and make a quick change if necessary.

Despite yesterday's long trip on Alaska Airlines, including a two-hour layover in Anchorage, Gary felt fresh, mostly due to the excitement of the impending operation. He believed they would succeed today, given the skill of each team member.

Gary picked up the bag containing the working uniform and left his room in Nome's Aurora Inn. One by one, other doors opened, beginning with John's and ending with Sully's. Gary seemed to be surrounded by his own personal army. John and Ann wore dress uniforms with gold oak leaves designating them as majors, while Dan wore the stripes of a sergeant first class. Sully's service jacket displayed the two chevrons of a corporal.

"Looking good, people," Gary said. "Anything new?" he asked Ann.

"Nothing today," Ann said. "He sent an acknowledgment on Monday saying he'd be at Nome Aviation Services at 9:00 a.m." Dan had accessed the Internet for Ann via a specially modified satellite phone hookup. While not as fast as the team's broadband server in Frederick, it had given the team the information they needed.

"Man, that dude hates the rock ol' Momeni crawled out from under," Sully said. " 'Next time you want equipment installed, come do it yourself.' Talk about flail mail."

"I believe you've captured the feeling," Gary said. "But Edwards's anger gives me the excuse to keep my mouth shut."

"And we'll be running interference for you," Ann said.

Gary chuckled. "I'm sure I'll need it." He turned to Dan. "Can you stop Edwards if he tries to call while we're inside?"

"No problem. I'll install a trap in their equipment room. If he calls, he'll get an 'all circuits are busy' message."

"Don't they watch their phone traffic?"

"Big-time, and e-mail, as well. All calls are routed through the Institute's comm center, so they have complete control. Got you covered."

Gary glanced at his watch. They had a little less than a half hour to get to the airport, which would be no problem since it was only a mile away. "Need some help with that?" he asked, pointing to the two bags Ann was carrying.

"I have them. Remember, you're senior."

Whether she was referring to his status as an ersatz lieutenant colonel or the fact that he was co-owner of SecurityCheck, he wasn't sure. "Hmm, carry on, I guess."

"Yes, sir." She gave a fairly credible salute.

"Oh, and here we are without a red carpet," Sully said.

"Get a move on, Corporal," Gary said.

"Yes, boss sir."

Gary led the way outside to their rental car, a Ford Expedition. The sun, halfway to its zenith, blazed down with rays that seemed devoid of heat. Gary's breath came in white puffs since the temperature was hovering near the freezing point. The brilliant blue sky merged with the deeper blue of Norton Sound less than a mile away. Gary opened the back of the SUV. Ann hoisted her bags inside, and Dan lifted up his toolbox and the digital recorder. Sully slid into the driver's seat while Gary sat beside him. Ann, John, and Dan crowded into the back.

Nome wasn't what Gary had imagined. It was called a city, but downtown consisted of a tightly packed cluster of houses and businesses, few taller than two stories and arranged on a grid of less than ten short streets parallel to the sound. A white church with a tall steeple graced the center of town. Nome was located by itself on the south coast of the Seward Peninsula. Its primary contact with the outside world was by air, 457 nautical miles to Fairbanks and 488 to Anchorage. The airport west of town took up as much space as downtown did.

There were only three highways: the Nome Council Highway, which ran along the coast to the east; the Nome Taylor Highway, which ran north into the interior for about one hundred miles; and the Nome Teller Road, the northwest coast road, which ended at the old Teller Mission, about six miles from Brevig Mission.

Sully turned right on West F Street then left on West Third

Avenue. This street wended around to the north until it merged with Seppala Drive, which led to the Nome airport main terminal and Nome Aviation Services, a fixed base operator (FBO). The FBO provided fuel, maintenance, and flight information for general aviation aircraft and crews. It was also the jumping-off point for passengers or freight destined for the Institute's satellite lab at Brevig. Sully parked along the east side of a large hanger near the only door in the long steel wall.

"That'll hide us from the helicopter," John said. "We'll bring Edwards inside the hanger and through that door."

"Right," Gary said. He wondered how fast he could change uniforms if it came to that. "Warn me if he's wearing a working uniform."

"Don't worry. We'll stall him if he is."

John and Sully got out and walked around to the front of the hanger to await the army helicopter.

Gary turned on his earphone radio.

Lieutenant Colonel Dick Edwards looked out the side window of the UH-60 Blackhawk as it clattered over the desolate green tundra between Brevig Mission and Nome. The Blackhawk was a true utility workhorse used by the army, air force, and navy for such varied tasks as transporting combat-loaded troops, performing medical evacuations, and carrying out search-and-rescue operations. Edwards frowned. The UH-60 could also be used for useless trips at the whim of a certain CIA special agent, with his boss's blessing. He gritted his teeth, seething inside.

"ETA Nome in five minutes, Colonel," the pilot said over the intercom.

Edwards ignored him. After a few moments, the man glanced back and, after one look, immediately returned to his flight duties.

Edwards almost smiled at the pilot's startled reaction. Then gloom settled over him again. There was nothing at all funny about the intolerable situation the department of homeland security had forced on the Institute.

Edwards listened halfheartedly to the pilot's communications with the tower controller. With less than eighty takeoffs and landings a day, getting into Nome Airport was not a problem; however, the proper procedures had to be followed. The pilot descended rapidly and made a straight-in approach to Nome Aviation Services. The Blackhawk's nose came up, and the turbine whine increased as the helicopter transitioned into a hover twenty feet above the tarmac. The pilot eased the squat aircraft in over the helipad's white circle and allowed it to settle on its stubby landing gear.

Neither pilot turned his head, Edwards noted, not that he blamed them. The crewman jumped up, pulled open the sliding side door, and jumped down onto the tarmac. Edwards got out and, as an afterthought, returned the man's salute. Now all he had to do was find Major Kane and get on with Hamid's ridiculous interference. Edwards was grateful for one thing: At least he would be dealing with army personnel rather than CIA spooks; and after they were gone, he would be able to get back to his research. He walked out from under the slowing rotor blades and toward the open hanger doors.

"He's wearing a dress uniform," John said over the radio. "You're good to go."

"Roger," Gary said. He turned to Dan. "Hide this."

Dan took the bag holding the working uniform, stuck it under the third-row seats, and folded them down. Gary got out and led his two assistants to the back of the hanger, turned the corner, and stood with his back to the metal wall. Ann and Dan went around him and set their burdens down.

"Colonel Edwards, I'm Major Isaiah Kane," Gary heard John say over the radio. "And this is Corporal Perez. We're here to install the new digital recorder."

"Yeah, great, *just* great," an indistinct voice said, hard to hear over the background sounds. "How about we grab your gear and get out of here? This is eating into my research."

"Sorry, Colonel," Sully said, "but there's a problem."

"And what would that be, Corporal?" Edwards asked in obvious irritation.

"Let me handle this, Perez," John said.

"Yes, sir," Sully said.

"Colonel, the recorder requires a special power supply, an off-the-shelf unit that's not classified."

"What does that have to do with anything, Major?" Edwards said in a rising voice.

"Sir, the power supply was supposed to be on an Alaska Airlines flight this morning, only the cargo people said it missed a connecting flight. They said it should be on the 12:05 flight."

"Well, that's simply terrific. Here you guys have already taken a *huge* chunk out of my day and now this." In the pause Gary could hear faint background noises. "I'm going back to Brevig, Major. You and. . ."

"Perez," Sully said.

". . .Perez can come if you want or wait here."

"No, dude, you can't do that," Sully said.

"What did you say, Corporal?" Edwards said in almost a shout.

"Forgive him, Colonel," John said quickly. "Perez is extremely task oriented. He puts getting the job done above almost everything else. Good man, though."

"Well, he certainly needs to learn proper respect for officers if he expects to advance in rank."

Gary almost laughed as he imagined what must be going through

155

Sully's mind after hearing *that* observation.

"I'll see to it, Colonel," John said smoothly. "Now if I might make a suggestion?"

"Yeah, yeah. Go ahead. My day's ruined anyway."

"Why don't we go into town? The trip to Brevig and back would chew up roughly an hour, wouldn't it?"

"Near enough."

"I know your work's important, but you'd barely get started before we had to come back. I have a rental car, and I'm on per diem. How about I treat you to lunch? What do you say?"

After a brief pause, Edwards said, "Might as well, I guess. I'll go tell my crew."

A few moments later, John whispered, "Think fast, Gary. You'll have to come up with some excuse why you've changed your mind."

"Roger," Gary said. "We'll handle it." He pointed to Ann. She looked surprised and pointed to herself with a silent question. Gary smiled and nodded.

"Okay," John mumbled. "He's on his way back now. Stand by for your cue."

"Roger that," Gary whispered.

"Perez, take us into town," John said in a louder voice.

"Yes, sir," Sully said.

Gary peered around the corner, along the side of the hanger. The side door opened, and three men came out. Gary pulled back and waited. Doors opened and closed, then a car started. Gary waited until the engine sounds tapered off then took a look. Their Expedition was partway down Seppala Drive.

"What are we going to do?" Dan asked.

Gary looked at Ann. "When we get around front, go tell the pilot that the power supply *did* make the earlier flight, but the baggage handlers misplaced it. Say I'll be along shortly."

"What about me?" Dan asked.

"You go with Ann. I'll be out when she's had a chance to tell the crew what I want."

"Got it," Ann said.

She picked up her two bags while Dan hefted his heavy toolkit and the recorder.

"Showtime," Gary said.

He followed them into the hanger through the side door and waited inside as if he were examining the aircraft parked inside. Ann and Dan continued through the hanger's open front and out under the bright blue sky. One man, the pilot Gary guessed, broke away from the other two crewmen. The men saluted, and Ann returned the honor.

"Change of plans," Ann said over the radio. "We found the missing shipment. Colonel Edwards says he wants to be back at Brevig ASAP."

"Yes, ma'am," Gary heard the pilot reply.

Gary set his face in a stern expression and walked out of the hanger. The distance to the Blackhawk dwindled quickly. Now would come the first test of his disguise.

"We're ready to go, Colonel," the pilot said. He saluted, as did the copilot and crewman.

Gary returned their salutes then raised his right index finger and whirled it around.

The pilot and copilot scrambled around and clambered into the cockpit.

The crewman waited beside the open door. A turbine began to whine, and the pitch increased rapidly. Another whine joined it, and the massive four-bladed rotor began to turn and quickly became a blur. Gary took a seat near the flight deck and strapped in. Ann and Dan sat beside him. The crewman jumped in and slid the door shut. He pulled on his helmet then looked at Gary and pointed to a spare helmet. Gary shook his head. He had no intention of getting on the intercom, where his voice might give him away.

The pilot looked back and, when he saw Gary's expression, faced forward and continued the checklist litany with the copilot. Soon they were airborne and flying northwest toward Brevig Mission. Gary looked down at the green, rolling tundra and, off in the distance, the dark blue of the Bering Strait. He could tell by the screaming turbines that the pilot wasn't wasting any time, which meant they would be on the ground in a little more than a half hour. With Edwards out of the way until around noon, that gave the team plenty of time to establish a security breach, but they had to evade the lab personnel to succeed. Gary was determined they would not get caught.

All too soon the Blackhawk thundered over the Teller Mission airport, out over an inlet of the Bering Sea, and finally past Brevig Mission and its airport. From there it was fourteen nautical miles northwest to the lab. Several minutes later, Gary looked between the pilots and spotted a compact group of buildings inside a perimeter fence. The helicopter began slowing, descending into the wind toward the white circle inside the fence that marked the helipad. Gary made sure his angry expression was firmly in place before they touched down. The Blackhawk settled on its landing gear, and the turbines began spooling down. The crewman opened the door, stepped down, and waited for his passengers.

CHAPTER 13

John glanced at his watch. It was 9:50 a.m., and he knew the team was probably on the ground by now. He struggled to maintain a cheerful disposition; however, Edwards's perpetual scowl made that difficult. Edwards and John sat across from each other with Sully on the side. The three sipped coffee at a small table in Fat Freddie's, a popular restaurant on Front Street. John's gaze drifted out the window and across the deep blue expanse of Norton Sound. A fishing boat traced a leisurely course about a half mile out, parallel to the shore.

"You know, if that dude out there would turn south and hang ten for about three thousand miles, he'd end up at Malibu," Sully said.

John jumped and looked at him in surprised amusement.

"Corporal, I don't recall asking for a geography lesson," Edwards grumbled.

John felt his jaws tighten. "With all due respect, Colonel, Corporal Perez is my responsibility."

"I understand that, Major, but it's clear to me he needs instruction in military etiquette."

"I'll take care of it, sir." John ransacked his mind for something to stimulate the conversation, but everything he had tried so far had turned out more like a monologue. The colonel was obviously interested in medical research, but John was neither equipped nor interested in tackling that gambit. "When would you like to eat?" he finally asked.

Edwards looked at his watch. "What time did you say that plane is due in?"

"Twelve-oh-five."

Edwards sighed. "Let's make it around ten forty-five, then. That'll give us plenty of time to get back to the airport."

Gary took his time walking out from under the slowing rotor blades. The team was, for the time being, in the clear. The flight crew was occupied with their postflight duties. Gary would have to call them back when it was time to leave, but he would worry about that later. Right now he had to get Ann and Dan in where they could do their damage.

A rectangular fence, at least fifteen feet tall and topped with razor wire, ran all the way around the facility, its long sides facing east and west. A large steel building anchored the northeast corner for about half the length of the east fence. This, Gary knew, housed the diesel generators and storeroom. Twin black spumes rose into the air, visible evidence that went with the rumble of the diesel engines. The helipad came next, followed by an open courtyard and parking area that wrapped around the compound's southern side. A Jeep Grand Cherokee and two Humvees were parked next to the guardhouse. A heavy gate on rollers breached the south corner of the eastern fence.

The middle building housed a small clinic, the biosafety level-four labs, and, at the north end, Slammer Junior. It extended from the parking area to the north fence. Gary looked up at the roof and noted the tall vents that discharged the lab's thoroughly nuked exhaust air. He felt a chill that had nothing to do with the cold wind.

Gary heard a crunching sound coming from somewhere behind him. He turned and saw a single sentry walking past the fence with a slung M-16. He wondered if the man carried a loaded weapon and if he knew how to use it but was grateful the team didn't have to find out.

Gary finally reached the parking area. A compact building housing the guardhouse and equipment room occupied the southwest corner. Next to it, taking up the rest of the west side, was the facility's largest building, divided internally into a dormitory and a combination recreation room and dining hall, with primitive kitchen.

The compound was tightly packed, with only narrow walkways between buildings. The facility was, in short, an efficient military establishment.

"There's the target," Gary whispered, even though he knew no one else could hear. "Do your stuff." This was for Ann, since she would be running interference for the verbally challenged "Colonel Edwards."

"Roger that," Ann said with a grin.

She led the way over to the guardhouse. She reached up, opened the door, and stepped inside. Gary followed, and Dan came next.

A young sergeant jumped to his feet when he spotted the female major and, behind her, his commanding officer.

"Good morning, Colonel," he stammered.

Ann looked at his name tag. "At ease, Sergeant Davis," Ann said. "We're here to install some special security equipment for Colonel Edwards. Carry on with your work."

"Yes, ma'am." Eddie Davis looked back at Gary. "Anything you need, Colonel, just let me know."

Gary nodded. Davis returned to his security and communications equipment. Monitors lined the wall above the wraparound work space dominated by a large display right in the center at eye level. Gary took a close look and recognized the long corridor inside the lab building, taken from a camera mounted above the entrance. Windows at the end looked in on Slammer Junior. The smaller monitors provided views of outside and selected shots of the dining hall and the lab building, but he didn't see any inside the generator room or storeroom. However, since there were more cameras than monitors, those rooms might not be selected.

"Major, okay if I start working?" Dan asked.

Ann set her bags down. "Yes," she said. "Where do you want to put it?"

"In the equipment room." Dan pointed to the wall that divided the building into two unequal portions. He opened the door and walked into the smaller room where all the cables terminated into patch panels and a jumble of electronic equipment, some on shelves but much scattered across the floor. He set the recorder and his toolbox down and returned for the bags Ann had carried in. Dan took them into the room, picked a spot next to the computer server, and placed the recorder next to it. He looked all around then glanced at Gary. Gary closed the door.

"Sergeant, how many cameras do you have?" Ann asked.

Davis looked around for confirmation. Gary nodded.

"We have four outside cameras mounted on a pole attached to the guardhouse. They're low-light units with built-in infrared capability. They face north, east, south, and west and give us a view over the entire compound and all the approaches."

"How high up?" Ann asked.

"Oh, I'd say about twenty feet. With the rolling tundra, no way anyone's going to be able to sneak up on us, even at night."

"Okay. How about the interior cameras?"

Davis thought for a moment. "Uh, there are seventeen in all. Two in the dining hall, and the rest are all in the lab building.

That's what we're most concerned about."

"I imagine so. Now, can you cycle through all the cameras for me? I need to verify that the coverage we have is adequate."

"Yes, ma'am. I'll start with the outside cameras."

Dan looked around the equipment room carefully and finally sighed in relief. There were no security cameras, confirming Ann's earlier research, which meant he was free to do as he pleased. He pulled a phone intercept box out of one of the bags and attached the leads to the lab's trunk lines. After making sure it was working, he kneeled down and installed the new digital recorder with its internal receiver and transmitter. Next he removed the back from the existing recorder and attached the new unit's video feeds. He carefully probed around inside, tucked a transmitter behind an untidy mass of ribbon cables, and connected it to the video inputs, as well. He verified that everything was working and replaced the back.

One by one, Sergeant Davis punched up each camera on the large monitor. The first one pointed north across the rolling green tundra. The image backed up the sergeant's claim that sneaking up on the facility overland would be nearly impossible. The next camera pointed east toward the interior of Seward Peninsula, and the south camera showed Brevig Lagoon and beyond that the Bering Sea. The west camera revealed several small lakes, with the sea off to the left. The guard switched between cameras quickly since there wasn't much to see. Gary noted there were blind spots between the closely spaced buildings and in front of the dormitory building because it was so close to the guardhouse.

"That's it for the outside cameras," Davis said. "Here are the interior ones."

Dan scooted over to the computer server and removed its case. He pulled the CD-ROM drive and substituted a unit that looked just like it except it also contained a miniature digital video recorder. He connected the cables and slipped the old drive into a bag. After replacing the server's cover and front panel, he verified that the hidden recorder was receiving the video signals.

The first camera Sergeant Davis brought up gave a view of the dining hall taken from the southwest corner, followed by the southeast camera. Ann spotted the helicopter crew seated at one of the tables and drinking coffee. Two men wearing white lab coats sat at another table talking. A woman stood at a long counter pouring coffee into a mug.

Davis continued with the lab cameras, describing each image with a terseness that came with intimate knowledge.

"Whoa, slow down there," Ann said.

"Sorry, ma'am."

He started over at a more sedate rate. Gary watched over their shoulders as the shots progressed in precise order. Following the dining hall were views of every room in the lab building, starting with the corridor camera and ending with shots of the slammer. When he was done, Davis reselected the lab building's corridor camera. Evidently Edwards considered this the most important one, which made perfect sense to Gary. If trouble broke out, that camera provided the best overall view. There were no cameras in the dormitory, guardhouse, or the building housing the generators and the storeroom. The first omission Gary understood, but not the other two. He made a mental note to include this in the deficiency report. Ann glanced his way. Gary nodded.

"I see there are no cameras in here," Ann said. "Why is that?"

"Don't know, ma'am," Davis said. "Guess it's because the

guardhouse is manned twenty-four-seven." He looked over at Gary. "Is that right, sir?"

Gary nodded and said, "Uh-huh." The man seemed satisfied with that.

"Sergeant, if we could stay focused," Ann said.

The young man looked embarrassed. "Yes, ma'am."

"Thank you. Now review for me your security duties. I presume you have a manual."

"Yes, ma'am. Right there." He pointed to a thick binder on a bookshelf. "I'll get it down."

Dan stood up and breathed a sigh of relief. Only two more tasks remained. One would be a snap, but the other would depend on circumstances. He set up a stepladder under the fluorescent light fixture nearest the door and picked up a tiny cylindrical device and his cordless drill. He climbed up and drilled a hole in the acoustical tile next to a smoke detector then pushed the slab up and to the side. He attached the combination video camera and transmitter to the light's wiring and fitted the lens into the hole. He lifted the tile back into place. The hole looked like it was part of the smoke detector's installation.

Dan descended and saw it was 10:20. He regretted the time it was taking, but he was moving as fast as he could. He moved the ladder close to the door, climbed up, and pushed a tile aside. He stuck his head up through the hole and looked toward the guardroom. As he expected, there were several places where light shined up from below, marking holes in the tiles, and one was within reach.

"Be back in a minute," Edwards said.

"Yes, sir," John said. He watched the man cross the room and head for the rest rooms.

"Wonder how the team is doing," Sully whispered.

"I'm sure everything's under control," John said. "This is easy compared to some of the things we've done."

"Got that right."

A few minutes later, Edwards came out and approached the waiter. The man pointed to a phone on the wall. Edwards walked over, picked up the receiver, and punched in a number.

"Hope Dan's on his toes," Sully said.

"Don't worry."

Dan had just come down off the ladder when he heard a muted electronic chirp. He hurried over and saw that the intercept device had captured an incoming call. A red LED indicated that the caller was hearing an "all lines are busy" recording. Outside calls wouldn't be getting through to the army lab until Dan removed his black box.

Dan grabbed an LCD screen with attached camera probe and went back up. Watching the screen, he slowly unreeled the cable until the camera was over the nearest hole, which turned out to be a corner missing out of a tile. He maneuvered the camera partway into the hole and saw that the position was excellent. The wide-angle lens would be able to see most of the room.

Dan pulled the video probe back a little, stepped down from the ladder, and picked up the miniature camera and transmitter. Once back in place, he used padded jaws on the end of a slender pole to position the device near the hole. With the aid of the LCD screen, Dan prodded the camera's lens into the hole. Then he hooked the device to power and brought down all his tools. After stowing them, he set the ceiling tile back in place. He pulled out an LCD monitor with built-in receiver and checked both cameras. The pictures were average for black-and-white surveillance units.

Dan replaced the ladder. He looked at the call interceptor for a few moments and decided he would come back for it later. He packed up the rest of his gear and checked the room over carefully. Satisfied, he reached for the doorknob.

The door to the equipment room opened, and Dan walked out carrying his toolbox and both bags. "New recorder's working like a champ, Major," he said as he closed the door.

"Excellent. Then we're just about done." Ann turned to Gary. "Colonel, I'd like to take a walk around the grounds, and then we'll be ready to go."

Gary walked to the door.

"What did you do with the old recorder?" Sergeant Davis asked Dan.

"It's still hooked up," Dan said. "The new recorder is running parallel to it, and I'd leave 'em that way for a couple of weeks. Then you can take the old one out."

"Sounds good to me," the man replied. "I'll inform our maintenance geek when I see him."

"Let's go," Ann said. "I want to be on our way before eleven."

"Yes, ma'am," Dan said.

Gary led the way outside. They walked quickly across the parking area toward the east fence. The sentry was halfway down the south fence heading toward the guardhouse. Gary waited until they neared the far corner of the lab building.

"Couldn't ask for better timing," he said. "Let's check out the generator room."

"Do we have time?" Dan asked.

"If we hustle."

Gary hurried down the side of the windowless lab. Off to the right, the Blackhawk sat, its massive rotor rocking gently in the wind. The thudding sounds from the diesels increased rapidly. The generator room had a single steel door on the west side near the fence. Gary tried the door and, as he expected, found it locked.

"Not much of a lock," he said. "I think I can pick it."

"Gary," Dan said.

"What?"

"Look at the hinges."

Gary blinked his eyes in surprise. The door opened out, so the hinges were on the outside. Dan opened his toolbox and pulled out a large screwdriver and a hammer. Less than a minute later, he popped the last hinge pin out. Using a small crowbar, he levered the back of the door out, and he and Gary lifted it clear. The diesel sounds increased in volume but not as much as Gary feared. After he unlocked the inside knob, he and Dan shoved the door back into its frame, and Dan hammered in the pins.

"Hurry," Gary said.

Ann and Dan jumped inside, and Gary followed them into the brightly lit room. Gary closed the door and looked around. Two massive diesels drove electric generators, providing power for the facility. Gary noted the pungent ozone smell.

"Think the sentry heard us?" Ann asked.

"Maybe, but he'll probably assume it's a maintenance man," Gary said. He grinned. "And if not, you have Colonel Edwards with you."

"Yeah, but you can't say anything."

"Details, details."

Gary turned and held out his hand. Dan rummaged around inside one of the bags and pulled out a clear plastic–laminated sign. It said: THIS COULD HAVE BEEN A BOMB! Gary placed it on the nearest diesel engine.

"Let's go," he said.

"Wait," Dan said.

He pulled out a large PDA, plugged it into a receiver, and turned both on. A few moments later, the display showed the long corridor inside the lab building. Dan cycled quickly around to the outside camera that faced north. The sentry was walking along the north fence almost to the generator room. As soon as he walked past, Gary opened the door and stepped out. Ann and Dan came out and started walking toward the helipad. Gary locked the knob, closed the door, and hurried to catch up.

"Ann, go find the helicopter crew, and tell them you're ready to return to Nome," Gary said.

She nodded and hurried down the narrow gap between the generator room and the lab building. Ahead lay the helipad and the facility entrance.

"My call interceptor is still in the equipment room," Dan said.

"Go get it. Hurry."

Dan dropped off his toolbox and the bags on the helipad and disappeared around the corner of the lab building moments after Ann. Gary went over to the helicopter and waited beside the bags. After a few minutes, Dan came loping back with his call interceptor, which he stuffed into one of the bags. Ann rounded the side of the lab building in step with the pilots. The crewman hurried along behind. The men saluted, and Gary returned the honor. Apparently Ann had been quite explicit, because the pilots went about their preflight checks without saying anything to their querulous commanding officer.

The crewman opened the side door. Gary boarded first, followed by Ann and Dan. Within minutes they were in the air and racing toward Nome at low altitude. Gary found the ride fascinating, and he considered getting up and standing behind the pilots but decided it would belie his grumpy persona. It was 11:40 when the pilot received clearance to land. He brought the Blackhawk in hot, pulled back on the stick briskly to enter a hover, then settled quickly on the helipad. Gary barely felt the wheels touch down. The whine of the turbines attenuated rapidly. The pilot looked back.

"Wait here," Gary said softly, knowing the engine sounds would mask what he said.

The pilot nodded.

The crewman opened the door. Gary stepped down and started walking toward the Nome Aviation Services hanger. Dan grabbed his toolkit and one bag while Ann took the other. They hurried across the tarmac until they caught up with Gary. Once inside the hanger, Gary and Dan went into the men's rest room and locked the door. They stripped out of their uniforms and shoes, stowed them in the bag, and dressed in warm, casual clothes. Gary removed his wig, handed it to Dan, and removed his contact lenses. These he placed in their case and slipped it into his pocket. They beat Ann outside but not by much. She came out of the women's room dressed in slacks, a blouse, and a sweater.

"Can we watch the show?" Dan asked.

"Yeah, but stay inside the hanger. I don't want the helicopter crew to see us."

"Roger that," Ann said.

They walked up the right side of the hanger, near the tall sliding doors. The huge opening gave them an excellent view of the airfield and Seppala Drive. A few minutes later, a familiar Ford Expedition entered the airport and drove by the side of the hanger. Gary looked toward the passenger terminal and soon saw John, Sully, and Edwards walking toward it.

"Flight's early," Ann said.

Gary looked up and saw an Alaska Airlines 737 on short final. The plane touched down and taxied to the terminal. To Gary, the wait seemed like forever, but it was only 12:35 when he spotted Edwards striding toward his helicopter with an expression that seemed lethal.

"Apparently it didn't go well," Dan said without batting an eye.

Gary looked at him and burst out laughing.

CHAPTER 14

"Still nothing?" Gary asked with a yawn. They had departed Nome on Thursday and arrived at Dulles at 6:45 a.m. on Friday. After returning to Frederick and a quick breakfast at the Waffle House, Gary had convened a meeting in the truck's command center.

"Not a thing," Ann said. "I've deactivated the mailbot that was intercepting messages about the operation."

"Did it catch any?"

"Just the nastygram Edwards sent Hamid on Monday. Apparently he's given up on complaining to Colonel Roberts."

"I'm surprised Edwards hasn't found out you broke into his lab," John said.

"I am, too," Gary said. "I guess he was in too much of a funk, and his troops were scared to talk to him."

"Don't blame 'em," Sully said. "Thought he was gonna have my head for lunch."

"We ought to give him some slack," John said. "He's doing a hard job under difficult circumstances."

"Agreed," Gary said. "Dan, anything interesting on the recordings we made inside the lab?"

Dan shook his head. "Nothing to write home about. Just standard stuff. No deficiencies there."

"Good." Gary looked around at the others. "Listen up, we need to have a face-to-face with Zack."

"You mean now?" John asked.

"I mean as soon as Thomas can set it up. This is too important to let slide. They need to take immediate action on what we got away with."

"Yeah, I guess you're right. Are we going to tell them everything?"

Gary thought that over. He certainly wasn't going to reveal their link into the Institute's intranet; however, most of what had happened at Brevig Mission they needed to be aware of. "No, not everything," he said finally. "I'm mainly concerned that they take care of the critical stuff." He turned to Dan. "Make the call."

"Coming right up," Dan said. He punched in a number and gave Gary a handset.

Gary tried to relax as he waited for the meeting to begin. The team sat on one side of the table in a conference room near Colonel Zack Roberts's office. Thomas was on Gary's left while Nate and Hamid faced them. Zack occupied the head of the table, and a large TV monitor at the other end represented the final member of the meeting. A very disgruntled Lieutenant Colonel Edwards glared alternately at Gary and Hamid. He looked tired, Gary noted, which wasn't surprising. While it was 10:05 a.m. in Fort Detrick, it was a little after six in the morning in Alaska.

"Gentlemen," Zack began, "and lady," he added, looking at Ann. Then his eyes bored into Gary. "We're here to discuss security deficiencies at the Brevig Mission lab, is that right, Gary?"

"That's correct," Gary said.

"Would you care to brief us, then?" Zack said, sitting back in his chair.

Gary gave them a bullet list summary, beginning with a description of John and Sully sidetracking Edwards while the rest of the team carried out the operation. As Gary expected, Nate and Edwards took the news hardest. Zack seemed concerned, but it was hard to read Hamid's expression.

"What were you doing up at Brevig Mission?" Nate demanded as soon as Gary finished speaking. His angry gaze shifted from Gary to Thomas. "I thought they were hired to check out the Institute."

"That's right," Gary answered before Thomas could speak. "And the security audit specifically includes the lab at Brevig Mission."

"But. . ."

"He's right," Zack said, interrupting Nate. He shifted his gaze to the camera atop the monitor. "Dick, I suggest you have someone verify what Gary's just told us. We'll wait."

"Yes, sir," Edwards said with a crestfallen expression. He turned to someone off camera and relayed the order. He then turned back and waited. About ten minutes later, he again looked away and took a piece of paper and a laminated placard. His face flushed as his anger flared again. He held the placard up for the camera. THIS COULD HAVE BEEN A BOMB! it said. "Whose idea of a joke is this?" he demanded.

"It's no joke," Gary replied. "We penetrated your facility, and real terrorists could have blown up everything, not just the generators."

"By impersonating me? I think not."

"It's a mistake to underestimate the resourcefulness of terrorists."

"People," Zack said. "We're all on the same side here. Our goal is to make our security as tight as it can be, not squabble among ourselves." He returned his gaze to Edwards. "Dick, did you verify the recorder?"

"Yes, sir. It's hooked in parallel to the old one. We found hidden transmitters in both the new recorder and the old one." He glared at Gary. "What were they supposed to do?" he demanded.

"Simulated transmission of the recordings to Brevig Mission."

"Why two?"

"Backup."

"And *how* would the terrorists pick up the signals in a native village? Huh?"

"Nate, that's the easy part," Gary said with a touch of irritation. "But since you asked, one way would be to come up from Nome disguised as a Native Housing Authority employee and install a receiver at the mission washeteria."

"Let's stay on track," Zack said. "Now we obviously have some security issues here, Nate. What are you going to do about this?"

"I'll be reviewing the Brevig Mission lab's entire security setup of course, but—"

"I would think so," Hamid interrupted.

"Let him finish, please," Zack said with an edge to his voice.

Nate glared at the CIA agent. "As I was *about* to say, my first order of business will be to require ID checks of all personnel entering the facility." He glanced at Gary. "And I agree that the guardroom, equipment room, generator room, and storeroom all need security cameras."

"Does Brevig have the equipment?" Zack asked.

"Not all of it, sir. They have enough cable, but I'll have to ship them the cameras. Take a few days, but we'll get these holes plugged."

"Do you have the cameras here?" Hamid asked Nate.

"Well, yes," Nate said. "Why do you ask?"

"I have had a trip to the lab planned for some time now. I'll move it up to today so I can check out the security situation for myself. I might as well take the cameras with me."

"Is that really necessary?" Nate asked, his voice rising. "I have a handle on this."

"I agree with Nate," Zack said. "I believe this is his responsibility."

"With all due respect, Zack, this is a homeland security issue. I'm sure the secretary will want these breaches fixed as soon as possible. As you know, the Brevig Mission lab is under my administrative control."

Gary could tell from Zack's acid glare that the colonel was well aware of this and didn't appreciate having it pointed out. Edwards's video image glowered at the CIA agent, but he apparently knew better than to start bailing out a sinking ship.

"Very well," Zack said. "Do as you think best."

"Thank you."

"That's all we have," Gary said to Zack.

"Thank you," Zack said. "Any idea how much longer your audit will take?"

"I really don't know. We've made a lot of progress, but the end date will depend largely on what else we find."

"I see. Well, I won't keep you from your work any longer. This meeting is adjourned."

Gary closed the truck's rear doors and joined the team around Dan's command center. Although it was almost time for lunch, he wanted to check on something first. He pulled a chair beside Ann and scooted over to where he could see her laptop screen.

"Prowling around the Institute's intranet?" Gary asked.

She nodded.

"Have Nate's dudes spotted our link?"

She looked at him. "Not yet."

"Man, ol' Nate's getting whacked big-time today," Sully said.

"That he is," Gary said. "How about the video recorder Dan installed on the CD-ROM drive?" he asked Ann.

"They haven't found that, either. That's zero for two."

"Can you access it?"

"Sure can. All it takes is the IP address, which Dan gave me."

"You're welcome," Dan said without looking over.

Ann grinned and glanced at him. "I *could* have found it for myself, but you saved me the trouble." She turned back to Gary. "Take a look."

She cycled through the Brevig Mission lab's cameras, starting with the outside ones. The views were dark since it was an overcast day and still quite early in the morning. A handful of scientists sat about the dining hall tables eating breakfast or drinking coffee. Some read newspapers while others talked to friends or wore earphones. Gary spotted Edwards walking into the dining hall from the dormitory. Ann shifted to the lab building. A few scientists were already at work.

"Now watch this," Ann said. "They finally found the ceiling cameras."

She brought up a recording and played it in a separate window. A technician entered the equipment room and looked all around. His eyes took in everything, ending their search with a slow scan of the ceiling. Gary saw the man blink while he was looking right at the hidden camera's lens.

"Uh-oh, Dan," Gary said. "He's on to you."

"Tut, tut," Dan said in a monotone. "How careless of me."

"Looks like the sacrifice worked," Gary said.

"So far," Ann said. "Let's hope they think they've found everything."

The man pulled over a ladder and climbed up. His face blossomed into a gigantic misshapen blob as he took a good look. The image jiggled and the angle changed; the ceiling tile had been pushed up and to the side. The image flashed and went dark.

"The other unit died the same way about five minutes later," Ann said. "Want to see that?"

"No thanks. Do you think the minirecorder is safe?"

"Yes."

"Dan?"

"I doubt they'll check the server, but even if they do, the CD-ROM drive looks exactly like the one I took out. I think we're home free."

"Hope so. We can sure use it."

"What's on the top of our to-do list?" John asked.

"A credible break-in at the Institute's main building."

"We've worked on quite a few scenarios. Which one do you want to execute?"

Gary gave it a few moments' thought. The top ideas all had merit, but one in particular stood out. "Posing as a heating and air-conditioning company. It has the edge for one very good reason."

John smiled. "And what would that be, if I might inquire?"

"I know it'll work."

"That's fortunate, because we're pretty far along on the props we'll need: uniforms, badges, driver's licenses, truck signage. I've even bought the tools and a utility cart. We still have to rent the truck, but that's about it. You *do* have your disguise ready, don't you?"

"Of course. What's the name of the company that has the USAMRIID maintenance contract?"

"Valley Heating and Air-Conditioning."

"Good," he said. "Now let's get to work on all the niggling details."

"When do we go for it?"

Gary thought over the remaining tasks. "Let's shoot for Monday morning, before they've had time for their coffee. Sully, I want you to get our maintenance truck first thing tomorrow. Check with Ann to find out what kind Valley uses."

"Right, boss," Sully said.

"Ann, have you picked out a suitable emergency for us?" Gary asked.

"I think so," she said. "I've hacked into the building's energy management system. There are several possibilities, but our best bet is to force an alarm indicating the cooling tower water pumps have failed. That will force the air-conditioning system to shut down."

A look of concern came to Gary's face. "What about ventilation to the labs?"

"Oh, no problem. Ventilation is a separate system with battery and emergency generator backup, so the labs will be okay. However, the air won't be cooled, which would eventually force evacuation of the building if the air-conditioning remains down for a long time."

"Not to worry. Valley Heating and Air-Conditioning will have everything back up and running in no time."

The UH-60 Blackhawk helicopter touched down a little after eight thirty in the evening, since Hamid Momeni's departure from Andrews Air Force Base had been delayed until late afternoon. The VIP C-37, the military version of the Gulfstream G-5 business jet, had gotten him and Saeed Alsaadoun to Nome quicker than any commercial flight could have, but the great-circle distance of almost thirty-three hundred nautical miles still took hours to span. The minus four hours time difference helped a little but not much. Hamid was bone-tired, but he and Saeed still had things to do that evening.

The helicopter's twin turbines began spooling down, the high-pitched whine descending the audible scale as the rotor slowed. The crewman opened the door. Hamid ducked his head and stepped out. Saeed followed him.

"Welcome," Lieutenant Colonel Edwards said. The man's expression didn't seem to match his greeting.

"Thank you, Colonel Edwards. We appreciate your hospitality."

"Sir, where do you want your gear?" the crewman asked.

"In my quarters," Hamid replied. "All those are mine." He pointed. "The other bag is Saeed's."

The crewman and two other soldiers grabbed the bags and boxes and led the way around the lab building and down to the dormitory.

"I imagine you and Saeed are ready to pack it in after your long trip," Edwards said.

"Not quite yet," Hamid said. "As you probably know, I've had this trip planned for some time, but the, ah, security problem made it necessary for me to come early."

"I see." The way Edwards said it told Hamid it was still a *very* sore subject. "Well, what's on tap for tonight, then?"

"I want to see the labs where the virus and vaccine are being produced."

"You're the boss."

Hamid smiled. That was something he was well aware of.

"Sorry to call so late," Dick Edwards said. It was a little after eleven, which made it three in the morning in Frederick. But Nate's e-mail had made it clear he wanted an immediate report.

"That's okay," Nate said in a groggy voice. "So, has Secretary Foster's *wunderkind* got us all straightened out?"

Dick felt a surge of anger. "He's making an absolute pest of himself, if that's what you mean."

"What all did he do?"

"He said he would review our security procedures tomorrow, including *personally* supervising the installation of five more security cameras."

"What, he didn't take care of it tonight?" Nate grumbled.

"No. He wanted a lab tour for himself and Saeed. Said it was a visit he had planned some time ago."

"I know. He told us the same thing. What did he want to see?"

"The production labs."

"Virus or vaccine?"

"Both. I had to bring the scientists on duty out so there'd be enough suit air hoses for him, Saeed, and me. What a zoo. I don't think he knows how much an inspection like this upsets our routine."

"He probably knows but doesn't care. I'm curious, how *is* production going?"

Dick hesitated since Nate didn't have a need to know. However, Nate was well aware of what the lab was working on, and he knew the facility's physical layout intimately. Besides, he was a sympathetic ear, something he had lost with Colonel Roberts. "It's going quite well, despite Hamid and everything else. We have plenty of virus now, and it's nastier than we could have possibly imagined."

"I remember what happened to Major Ingram."

"Yeah, that was a real tragedy. I'm very sorry about what happened to her. But the good news is, we finally have the vaccine production line going."

"How effective is the vaccine?"

"Almost a hundred percent," Dick said. "And believe me, we'll need it if terrorists ever get hold of the virus. Any news on the threat?"

"Not that I've heard of, but intel on that is CIA private property."

"Right, and they aren't saying."

"You got that right. All lips zipped and full speed ahead."

Dick sighed. "I don't know what bothers me most: Hamid butting into our business or the 1918 virus."

"I know what you mean. We have the same situation with his lab here. Keep me posted. How about giving me a call after Hamid leaves and bringing me up to date?"

"Don't worry, I will."

CHAPTER 15

"Sully's back," Dan announced.

Gary looked up at the monitor and saw a plain white van pull into a parking spot beside the command center. The team's Saturday was well under way after a solemn breakfast at the nearby Golden Corral.

"So he is," Gary said. "That truck should do the job nicely."

Sully came inside and closed the rear doors. "Got your wheels, boss," he said to Gary. "When do you want to put the signs on?"

"Monday morning, just before we leave." Gary turned to Ann. "How's it coming?"

"Almost done," she said. "Faking an alarm is easy. The hard part is wiping out my tracks so they won't know I was there. We wouldn't want our back door taken away."

"Not after all the trouble we went through to get it."

"How are we going to make sure we get the call?" John asked.

"I'll make an update to their vendor file changing the contact number," Ann said.

"Then change it back afterward," Gary said.

"Yes, and anything else I mess with. Once I execute the cover-up routine, everything will be the way it was, and those helpful technicians from Valley Heating and Air-Conditioning will be a fading memory."

"More like a nightmare." He smiled. "I like it. Now make sure you take care of all those jots and tittles."

Ann grinned. "You know I will."

"Yeah, and I appreciate it. Where are the blueprints and drawings of the building?"

"John's got them. I included the cooling tower and chiller schematics."

"Good." He looked over at John. "You and Sully need to get cracking on how you're going to slip the guards."

"That's the next item on my to-do list," John said.

"We gonna use blue smoke or mirrors?" Sully asked.

"Come here, and I'll show you."

Hamid yawned as he watched the maintenance technician work. They were inside the generator room, the next to last stop on their rounds to install the new security cameras. The camera mounts were the hardest part. Running the cable would go quickly, no more difficult than a cable television installation; however, that would be done after he and Saeed left. The technician finished, and Hamid handed him the camera. The man attached it to the bracket and came down off the ladder.

"Where does the last one go?" he asked.

"The dormitory corridor," Hamid replied. "Now hurry up. I have to get back to Washington."

"Yes, sir."

The technician stuck the power screwdriver back in its holster, grabbed the ladder, and went outside. Hamid picked up the box containing the remaining camera and followed him. Saeed came last and closed the door. They passed the Blackhawk crew on the way. Both pilots were performing a thorough preflight inspection, Hamid noted. Clearly Colonel Edwards was as anxious to be rid of his two guests as Hamid was to return to USAMRIID.

Hamid entered the dining hall, where scientists and army support personnel were still busy with their breakfast routines. A few looked up at the visitors, but most ignored them. Hamid and Saeed followed the technician through the door leading to the dormitory. A shower was running, and somewhere a door closed. The technician set his ladder against the wall.

"Where do you want it?" he asked.

"Over the door pointing down the corridor," Hamid replied.

The technician propped open the door and set the ladder in place. In fifteen minutes, he had the camera mount in position. He checked his work over and stepped back down. Hamid opened the cardboard box and slipped the camera out. He handed it to the man, who bobbled it before he got a good grip.

"Be careful with that!" Hamid said. "It's delicate."

"Sorry, sir." Then the technician grinned. "Thought for a moment we were going to have to order another one."

"That's *not* funny. I want these security breaches taken care of today, not in a week."

"I'll try to be more careful, sir."

"See that you do."

The man attached the camera, aimed it down the corridor, and came down off the ladder. "That takes care of the cameras," he said. "We'll have the cables laid by this afternoon and everything up and running by evening. Is there anything else you want me to do?"

"No, that's all."

The man grabbed his ladder and hurried out.

"Are you packed?" Hamid asked his assistant.

"Yes, I did it before breakfast," Saeed replied.

"Good. Go find Colonel Edwards, and tell him I'll be ready to leave in fifteen minutes."

The man nodded and left the room.

Dick held his service cap tightly as the Blackhawk lifted off the helipad, transitioned to forward flight, and turned southeast toward Nome. The glimpse he caught of Hamid and Saeed through a window added to his mixed feelings. He felt an intense relief that the CIA special agent was on his way back to Washington, but the distance failed to remove Hamid's administrative control. Dick longed for conditions to return to the way they were before September 11, 2001. But, of course, that could never be. Although Dick understood the need for increased national vigilance, how that worked out for him had turned into a never-ending pain.

The maintenance technician approached and saluted. Dick returned it absentmindedly.

"Colonel, I'm scheduled to pull preventive maintenance on the diesel generators today. You want me to do that before I run the cables for the new cameras?"

Dick gritted his teeth. "You heard the CIA spook. Those cameras are to be up and running ASAP."

"Yes, sir. Just thought I'd check." He hurried off.

Dick watched the dwindling speck of the helicopter for a few more moments then began walking around the end of the lab building, taking his time so he could think. Reaching the dining hall, he went inside. One scientist was standing by the coffeemaker waiting for it to brew a new pot. The man waved. Dick nodded and pushed through the door into the dormitory, glancing up at the new camera as he did. Once inside his private room, he picked up his phone and punched in Nate's number at the Institute.

"Switchboard," the operator at the Institute's communications center replied.

"This is Colonel Edwards," Dick said. "Put me through to Colonel Young."

"Yes, sir."

The line clicked, and Dick heard two rings.

"Colonel Young," the voice on the other end said.

"Hello, Nate, this is Dick."

"Hi. How is everything in Alaska, or should I ask?"

"It's a mixed bag. Just calling to bring you up to date. Spook one and spook two are on their way back to Nome as I speak."

"So how did it go?"

"It was a repeat of the heads-up you sent me. We're to check IDs on everyone and install new cameras, which his majesty kindly brought along. The cameras are up and will be hooked up by the end of the day."

"Well, he can't fault our cooperation. How is the research going?"

"Excellent, actually, *despite* the interference. The production labs are cranking out both virus and vaccine. If a Saudi sleeper cell really *is* working on the 1918 bug, we're within a few months of being able to counter it. All we have to do is transfer the vaccine production to commercial labs."

"*That's* certainly good news."

"Don't you know it. Then maybe we can pack up and come home to the Institute."

"Yeah, and say good-bye to Mr. Momeni."

Dick laughed. "Wouldn't *that* be nice?"

By late afternoon, Gary was satisfied with the planned break-in of the USAMRIID main building. It depended on Ann sabotaging the energy management system plus the substitution of a new phone number for Valley Heating and Air-Conditioning. Gary's part would be to provide a suitable decoy while John and Sully penetrated as deep into the secure areas as they could. The rest would depend on the team's resourcefulness.

"Do you and Sully have your game plan?" Gary asked.

"We've come up with quite a few scenarios," John said. "What we end up doing will depend on how the security honchos react to the mayhem we stir up."

"Ann, how about you?" Gary asked.

"Ready," she said. "I just finished the program that'll erase all my tracks, assuming I haven't forgot something."

"I haven't a doubt in the world."

She smiled. "Thanks."

Gary looked at his watch. It was almost six and time to be thinking of dinner.

"Okay, people," he said. "Let's call it quits. Whose turn is it to pick the greasy spoon?"

"Mine," Sully said.

"And what's the kid's choice?"

"Papa John's Pizza."

"I can live with that."

"Why does that not surprise me?" Ann said.

"I'm going to ignore that," Gary said. He looked around at them all. "We stand down tomorrow, then on Monday, we see if the team still has it."

CHAPTER 16

Gary yawned. "How do I look?" he asked. His Monday morning was having a little trouble getting started.

Ann studied Zack Roberts's photo then carefully examined Gary's disguise. This time it was a brown wig with the same brown contact lenses he had used in Alaska. Zack was five inches taller and sixty pounds heavier.

"Hair and eyes are fine," Ann said. "And the facial disguise is dead-on." She looked into his brown eyes. "You look just like him."

He grinned. "That's the general idea."

"You don't sound like him, though."

"Fortunately that won't matter."

"Right. Now stand up."

"Yes, ma'am."

"You're not any six foot four even with those special shoes."

"The guards probably won't notice in all the confusion."

"The padding is about right." Ann checked the rows of ribbons against the photo.

"That *better* be correct," Gary said. "Sully and I worked hard enough on it."

She looked up and smiled. "You're good to go except as otherwise noted."

"Thanks." Gary checked the alignment of all the insignia.

"Cool duds, dude," Sully said.

"You and John ready?" Gary asked.

"All except the signs. You said to save them for last."

"Where is John?"

"Outside waiting on me."

"How about a status check on the Institute?" Gary said to Ann. She sat down at her PC and began cycling rapidly through multiple windows. "Everything looks normal," she said several minutes later.

"Is Zack in yet?"

Ann selected a window and scrolled down it. "Yes. He swiped his badge at seven fifty-nine and thirteen seconds, according to the Institute's system clock."

"Good, then seeing me should cause quite a stir."

"We can only hope."

"Sully. Get those signs on the truck, and wait for Dan's call."

"You got it, boss."

Ann parked the command center truck in the Institute's parking lot and ran around to the back. Gary let her in and closed the doors. Ann hurried over to her PC and again checked the Institute's primary security systems. Gary inserted his earphone radio and turned it on.

"How's my video?" he asked.

"Turn toward Ann," Dan said.

Gary did so and looked down at the large button on his dress uniform coat. The lens was tiny, almost invisible.

"It's not broadcast quality, but it'll do," Dan said.

Gary glanced at the main monitor. The grainy, color picture

showed Ann cycling through a series of windows on her PC.

"Not bad," he said. "Everything okay?"

"Waiting for your command," Ann said.

"Bring up the radio net," Gary told Dan.

Dan flipped a series of switches. "Radio net is live."

Gary felt momentarily self-conscious, but he knew that would soon be blown away once the operation got under way. "Valley Dudes, this is Colonel Bogey," he said. "Stand by for Operation Bold Venture."

"Valley Dudes standing by," John said over the radio.

Gary glanced at Ann. She nodded.

"Execute," Gary said.

"Valley Dudes, roger."

Gary pointed to the radio indicators for John and Sully and drew a finger across his throat. Dan cut their transmission links.

Ann's fingers clattered across the keyboard. She watched the screen for a few seconds then glanced at Gary. "The energy management system has just shut down all air-conditioning compressors and cooling tower equipment, and the alarm has been reported to building security. The contact number for Valley Heating and Air-Conditioning has been updated."

"Roger that," Gary said. "Has security placed the call yet?"

"Negative," Ann said. "Apparently it's taking them some time to decide what to do."

"Don't they have a manual?"

"I'm sure they do, but maybe they haven't read it."

"Make a mental note."

"Ah, here we go. Get ready, Dan. They're making the call."

"I can't wait," Dan said with a deadpan expression.

The phone at Dan's right hand rang once, then twice, then a third time.

Lieutenant Colonel Nate Young picked up his phone after the first ring. "Colonel Young," he said.

"Colonel, this is security. We have an engineering casualty in the building," the man reported. "The cooling tower water pumps have failed, and that's shut down the air-conditioning compressors."

Nate sat bolt upright. A pain stabbed his stomach. "What about the ventilation system?"

"Didn't affect that. We have airflow to the labs, and negative air pressure is being maintained. The only thing we've lost is cooling."

"Have you called for maintenance?"

"My assistant is doing that as we speak. Valley Heating and Air-Conditioning is quite reliable. They should be on-site within the hour."

"They better be. But review your emergency procedures. If the inside temperature gets too high, we'll have to evacuate the building. Keep me posted."

"Will do, Colonel."

Nate punched a button to disconnect and then placed a call to his boss.

"Colonel Roberts," Zack said.

"This is Nate. We have a situation in the building."

Dan picked up the handset. "Valley Heating and Air-Conditioning, may I help you?" He did not feed the caller into the speakers for fear of feedback. "One moment, please." Dan paused for a few seconds but didn't do anything. "Yes, I have you on our database. What seems to be the problem?"

Dan took his time leading the caller through the cumbersome customer service routine. He doodled on a line pad and from time to time glanced at Gary as if he were bored out of his skull.

"Yes, I have the information," Dan said finally. "I'll dispatch a crew at once." He listened to the response. "Yes, I'll inform them that it's an emergency. Good-bye." He hung up the handset. "Sounded rather excited about it," he said to Gary.

"After what Ann did to them, I'm not surprised," Gary said.

Dan reached up and cut John and Sully back into the radio net. "Valley Dudes, this is Central Command. Give it five then come in the gate. Report when you are inbound."

"This is Valley Dudes, roger," John said.

Gary looked at his watch repeatedly as if this would make the time go faster, but the minutes ticked off more like hours. The five-minute mark came and went.

"Central Command, this is Valley Dudes," John said. "We're inbound with an ETA of one minute."

"Roger that," Gary replied. "Colonel Bogey will be right behind you."

Dan cut the transmissions from the command center to allow private conversations until it came time for Gary to leave.

Gary kept watching the main monitor and soon saw a white van pull into the parking lot and drive directly to a parking spot reserved for maintenance vehicles. Two men got out, walked around to the back, and opened the rear doors. John set a ramp in place, and Sully brought down the first work cart. John unloaded the second one and together they approached the building.

Dan reached up and flipped a switch. An unsteady picture of the rear entrance appeared on the main monitor, replacing the video from Gary's hidden camera. The doors into the Institute grew ever closer. The image of a cart occupied the very bottom of the screen.

"Signal from John's camera is good and strong," Dan said. "Shouldn't have any trouble receiving his camera inside the building."

Gary wiped his sweaty hands on his uniform trousers. "Almost time for Colonel Bogey to do his thing," he said.

"And I'm picking up GPS signals from Sully's pager," Dan said. He brought up a detailed map of the building, which had a tabbed page for each floor. Sully's icon slowly approached the rear entrance.

Gary looked up at the monitor and saw John disappear inside then Sully.

John pushed his cart toward the guard's desk. The cart was light and easy to push. Sully's, however, was quite heavy by design.

"We're from Valley Heating and Air-Conditioning," John said to the guard.

"Right, glad you're here. It's already beginning to warm up. I need to see your driver's licenses."

John pulled out his wallet and gave the man his fake license. Sully did the same. The guard examined both carefully then compared the pictures with the men standing before him.

"Thanks," he said, handing them back. "Now sign in, and your escorts will take you up to the roof." He held out a metal clipboard.

John signed his assumed name and handed the clipboard and pen to Sully. After Sully signed, the guard took back the clipboard.

"Here," the man said to one of the escorts and gave the man a ring of keys.

The escorts led the way to the elevator lobby. One of them eyed the carts and shook his head. "Man, those things are huge. You sure they'll fit in our elevators?"

John smiled because he was positive they would. "Nothing to worry about. We've been here before."

The man gave a self-conscious laugh. "Oh, yeah, I guess you have."

An elevator door opened, and an assortment of white-coated scientists, soldiers, and civilians came out. The man with the keys directed waiting passengers to the other elevators then entered and inserted a key in the car's control panel and turned it.

"I have it," he said.

John turned his cart and slowly backed in on the same side as the man controlling the elevator, stopping when his back was against the wall.

"That thing just barely clears the doors," the man said.

"Yeah, I know," John said.

Sully backed in until he was beside John. The other escort squeezed inside and stood beside Sully's cart. The guard by the panel turned the key and pressed the button for the top floor. The elevator started up smoothly. Each floor indicator lit up in turn accompanied by a clear electronic *ding*. At the top, the doors opened, and the operator locked them open with his key. The other guard stepped out and waited.

"You first," John told Sully.

Sully's cart rolled forward a few inches and stopped. "Man, we gotta get new wheels for this thing. I'll throw my back out if I'm not careful."

"Want some help?" John asked.

"I can get it."

Sully shoved again, and the cart trundled out of the elevator with wheels squealing then stopped with a lurch with one rear wheel bridging the narrow gap between the elevator and the floor. Sully stood back and scowled.

"Bummer," he grumbled.

John glanced at Sully, who gave an almost imperceptible nod. Sully had pressed a hidden button that had locked all four wheels. He shoved again, giving every indication he was pushing as hard as he could.

"Won't budge," Sully said, standing back.

"How about some help?" John said to the guards.

Both men seemed reluctant, but the one out in the lobby grabbed on and pulled while Sully pushed. The cart moved a fraction of an inch but then settled back when the two men slacked off.

John came around and gripped the push bar beside Sully.

"Help your buddy," John told the man controlling the elevator. The man hesitated.

"Go on," John said. "The elevator's not going anywhere."

The man squeezed through the gap and gripped the front.

John took a deep breath. "All together now," he said. "One, two, three."

He pushed on the bar, and the wheels suddenly released. John stepped quickly to the right by the control panel. Sully shoved the cart out and sideways, blocking the elevator's open doors. He pushed the button locking the wheels and jumped back into the elevator. John twisted the key and punched the first-floor button. The elevator started down.

"Valley Dudes have the elevator," John said over the radio.

"Roger that," Dan replied. "Be advised that Colonel Bogey is on his way."

"Roger. We'll take all the help we can get."

Gary took one last look at the monitor, which showed a close-up shot of an elevator control panel. Then, after making sure there was no one outside the truck, he hurried out into the bright sunlight. The sky was deep blue with a few high, wispy clouds. His uniform shoes made an insistent clicking sound as he hurried across the parking lot and up the sidewalk to the back entrance. Two soldiers came out and saluted as they passed. Gary returned the honor.

He pushed through the doors and walked toward the guard desk. The man on duty spotted him, and a look of recognition came to his face but was quickly replaced by one of confusion.

"Colonel Roberts?" the man said.

"Yes?" Gary asked.

The guard made a quick inquiry on his computer. "Sir, I have you already signed in." He sounded unsure.

Gary glared at him.

"Guards," the man said, raising his voice cautiously. He stood and unsnapped his holster. "Sir, may I see your ID?"

Two soldiers rushed up to the desk. They looked at the officer standing there as if not sure what to do.

Gary fumbled around inside his uniform coat, found his wallet, and pulled it out. He pulled out a replica of a military ID and handed it to the guard, who looked at it and handed it back.

"I need to see your USAMRIID ID, sir," the man said in a firm voice.

Gary checked all his pockets then smiled and gave a short, self-conscious laugh. "Funny thing. I must have misplaced it."

"Take this man to detention," the guard said.

The two soldiers escorted Gary away.

The guard sat down and punched in the security command center number.

The command center supervisor reached for the phone. "Security," the man said. He saw from the console it was the guard at the rear entrance.

"We just detained an intruder; claimed he was Colonel Roberts, but he didn't have a USAMRIID badge, and it didn't sound like him."

The supervisor's fingers clattered on his keyboard. "I have Colonel Roberts signed into the building," he said.

"I *know*. I have two guards taking the man to detention. Better notify Colonel Young."

"I'll take care of it. Don't let that guy go anywhere."

The man hit the disconnect button without waiting for an answer. Moments earlier he had received a radio transmission reporting the

Valley technicians commandeering an elevator and now this. He quickly scanned the alarm indicators. Everything registered normal, except the cooling tower pumps. He glanced at the elevator display and saw that car one was on the first floor, locked with the control key.

"Dispatch guards to all first-floor exits and the elevator lobby," the supervisor said. "Force the doors on car number one and arrest the Valley technicians."

"Roger," the assistant sitting next to him replied.

Then the display changed. Car number one was going up again. The supervisor cursed and grabbed his phone. The number he punched in didn't even get past one ring.

"Colonel Young speaking," a strained voice said.

"Colonel, this is security. We have some problems here. We're holding an intruder who *says* he's Colonel Roberts—"

"What?" Nate said, his voice rising.

"Sir, the guy tried to bluff his way through the rear entrance just now."

"Where is he?"

"First-floor detention."

"I'll be right down."

"Wait a minute, Colonel. There's more."

"Hurry it up."

"The Valley technicians have commandeered an elevator. They faked out their escorts and took the elevator down to one. Now they're going back up again."

"Send guards to all floors."

"I don't have enough to do that, Colonel. I have guards on all exits and the first-floor elevator lobby and two with the intruder, plus the regular patrols." He glanced up at the monitors arrayed before him. "I'm monitoring all floors. When they stop again, I'll have guards on them ASAP."

"See that you do." The line clicked dead.

The supervisor scanned the monitors. As his eyes turned to the one for the second-floor elevator lobby, the image flickered then steadied. He watched it for several more seconds, but it remained steady as a rock.

John removed the last screw from the control panel's faceplate.

"This is Central Command," Ann said over the radio. "Third-floor cameras are now patched into the second-floor monitors. You're invisible, guys."

"Valley Dudes, roger that," John said. "Stand by to take control."

"Standing by."

John took down the faceplate and set it on the floor. "Hand me that box," he said.

Sully gave him a small plastic box with color-coded wires all ending in alligator clips. John attached the clips to wires inside the elevator's control circuitry then cut two wires with a pair of nippers.

"Try it," John said.

"Good, strong signal," Ann said. "I have it."

John removed the control key and gave it to Sully. He had been keeping the elevator in constant motion to prevent the guards from breaking in. Now, under Ann's control, it paused at the first floor and started back up.

"Get ready," she said. "Car number two is going up, and it's just ahead of you."

"We're climbing out now," John said.

Sully shoved the cart under the access panel in the car's ceiling and locked the wheels. John opened a drawer, pulled out two bags with long straps, and gave one to Sully. John climbed on the cart. Sully handed him two chemical luminescence sticks. John threw open the panel and crawled out on top of the elevator, holding the sticks in one hand and his bag in the other. When he broke the sticks, a cold blue light flooded the elevator shaft. Sully crawled out on top with his bag.

"We're in place," John said.

The car next to them stopped. John felt his stomach lurch as Ann stopped their car.

"Jump," John said.

He went first with Sully right behind him.

"We're clear," John said.

Their former car started down to the first floor.

"Move it, guys," Ann said. "The computer just summoned car two to the first floor."

Sully threw open the roof's access panel, swung in through the hole, held momentarily, and dropped to the floor. John's technique was not as quick or agile, but he made it. He thumped down just before Sully stopped the car with the purloined key. They were at the second floor and exactly on schedule.

"This is Valley Dudes," John said. "Are we clear to break out?"

"Affirmative," Ann said.

"Roger that." John motioned to Sully. "Open it up."

Sully opened the door and removed the key, returning control of the elevator to its computer. They raced out into the deserted elevator lobby. John led the way deep into the building on a level-zero corridor, rapidly approaching a series of level-four labs where the most lethal viruses on earth lived.

Gary looked around as Nate burst into the detention room one step ahead of the guard in the security chief's wake. Nate slid to a stop. Gary almost smiled. There were three guards in the room now along with the security boss himself, but obviously Gary's appearance still unnerved him.

"Who are you?" he asked tentatively.

If Gary could have mimicked Zack's voice, he would have, but that wasn't possible. Instead he fixed Nate with a stern look he thought appropriate for commanding officers.

"I *asked* you a question," Nate finally said with a little more confidence. "You can knock off the charade. I *know* you're not Colonel Roberts."

Gary's scowl shifted to a smile, but still he remained silent. Nate opened his mouth to speak, but his mobile phone preempted him. The officer snatched it off his belt and punched it on.

"Colonel Young here," he said.

All Gary could hear of the caller was a faint buzzing sound. Nate's face took on an animated expression.

"I'll be right there," he said. He returned the phone to his belt. "The intruders are trapped on one," he said to the guards. "Our guys are forcing the door open." He started to move.

"Leaving so soon, Nate?" Gary asked.

The officer stopped in his tracks and looked closely at his prisoner. "Gary? Gary Nesbitt? Is that really you?"

"What's up, doc?" Gary said.

"You. . ." Nate started; then his confidence seemed to slip. "This is what you did in Brevig. Then those guys on the elevator. . ."

"It's not exactly the same, more like a variation on a theme."

"This is absurd. Now call this thing off."

"Can't do that. The exercise isn't over."

"But this is serious."

"You bet it is. That's why we're doing it."

Nate hesitated for several more seconds as if searching for something else to say; then he rushed out, slamming the door.

John slowed down when he spotted a heavy glass window, all that separated the level-zero corridor from the level-four lab suite on the other side. A scientist in a blue Chemturion biological space suit apparently saw a flash of movement, turned, and stared. John looked through the clear plastic faceplate and saw the startled black face of Ken Underwood. Ken walked over to the window, trailing a coiled yellow air hose behind him. He picked up a telephone handset and held it against the suit and pointed. John looked around and saw a telephone. Reluctantly, he took the receiver off the hook.

"What are you doing out there?" Ken said, his voice hard to hear over the roar of air that inflated his suit.

"I'm afraid we're here on business," John said.

"Is this a security exercise?"

John nodded. "We'll have to talk about it later." He hung up the phone and turned to Sully. "Plant the charge, and let's get out of here."

Sully pulled a rectangular object out of his bag, pulled two tape strips, and stuck the package to the window. He set a timer with a large LED readout to ten minutes and pressed the button to start the countdown. "All set," he said.

John pulled out a digital camera and snapped several pictures. "Let's get out of here," he said.

They ran down the corridor away from the center of the building and down to an exterior wall; however, there was no window. John pulled a series of long, thin bars out of his bag. One by one he pulled off the protective strips and stuck each one to the wall, forming a window shape. When he finished, he documented the work with the camera.

"This is Valley Dudes," John said. "Mission accomplished."

"Roger," Dan said, calm as ever. "You shouldn't have long to wait."

"Time to put your toys away," Dan said.

"I'm working on it," Ann said. She executed the program that would restore the second-floor security cameras, reset the bogus water pump alarm, and set the contact number for Valley Heating and Air-Conditioning to its original value. In seconds it was all done.

"I was never there," she said.

"Now we wait," Dan said.

Ann looked up at the monitors. One showed the guards watching Gary while Sully's smiling face appeared in the feed from John's camera. The young man waved and mugged.

Ann laughed. "He's sure enjoying his audience," she said.

"What is *that*?" the security supervisor said. One of the second-floor corridor cameras suddenly showed two men standing near a wall where moments before there had been no one. A dark rectangle framed a large section of the wall, and each man held a coiled rope. They just stood there as if waiting for something.

"Get some guards up there on the double," the supervisor told his assistant.

The man grabbed his phone and punched in a number.

The supervisor's eyes cycled over the rest of the second-floor monitors. "Hey, that looks like a bomb outside that level-four lab!" he said. He zeroed in on the oblong shape with its bright red indicator. He couldn't read it but knew it had to be a down-counter.

The assistant hung up his phone. "They're on the way," he said. Then he, too, saw the suspicious package. "Is that what I think it is?"

The supervisor wasn't sure, but he decided to err on the side of safety and self-preservation. He reached over, lifted a safety cover, and hit a big red button. Throughout the building the deafening sound of a whooping siren erupted from speakers accompanied by a strident recorded message: "There is an emergency in the building. Proceed to the nearest exit."

The supervisor punched in Nate's mobile number and waited.

Nate answered immediately. "Colonel Young."

"Colonel, this is security. We—"

"Did you activate the emergency evacuation alarm?" Nate interrupted.

"Yes, sir. We have a possible bomb on the second floor. Also, that's where the two intruders are. We've sent guards to arrest them."

"Cancel the alarm," Nate said.

"But, sir."

"Cancel the alarm. This is a security test."

"But we didn't receive any notification—"

"Cancel the alarm."

"Yes, sir."

CHAPTER 17

Gary looked around the table. For the second time within a week, the SecurityCheck team was sitting in a conference room with Zack and Nate, only this time they were missing Hamid Momeni and Dick Edwards because the current incident didn't affect them. Gary had been relieved that Zack had been able to meet immediately after the exercise, since failures needed prompt attention. Thomas sat on Gary's left while Sully was on his right. They were all waiting for Ken Underwood, invited because of his contact with John during the exercise.

"It's déjà vu all over again," Sully whispered to Gary.

Gary smiled. "Thanks, Yogi, I needed that," he whispered back. Then his grin faded when the gravity of the situation came back to him. The deficiencies the team had uncovered *had* to be addressed or USAMRIID might find themselves devastated by a real terrorist attack.

The door opened, and Ken strode into the room.

"Sorry I'm late, Colonel," he said. "It took me awhile to go through decontamination."

"I understand," Zack said. "Please be seated."

Ken went around to the other side of the table and sat down beside Nate. He made eye contact with Gary and nodded. Gary thought he looked uncomfortable.

"Gentlemen and lady," Zack began with a sour expression on his face. "Here we are once again." He paused. "I *know* I should be grateful that it's you guys rather than terrorists, but I do find it a little hard, especially since we take security seriously around here, regardless of how it seems to you."

"I agree entirely, Colonel," Nate said. "The tactics these guys are using are *entirely* unfair."

"At ease, Nate. With all due respect to your efforts, Gary's team is simply doing its job, and what they've uncovered *must* be addressed."

"Thank you, Zack," Gary said. "As you say, we're only doing what homeland security hired us to do. It's our goal as a company to help our clients."

"Yes, I realize that." Zack forced a smile. "Please bear with us while we lick our wounds."

"Believe me, I do understand."

"Good. Now give us a briefing on your latest operation."

Gary spent fifteen minutes providing a summary of what had happened. He took pains to explain that while the charge they placed on the lab window had been real C-4 plastic explosive, there had been no detonator and the timer had been fake. The C-4 charges on the wall had also been real but safe, as well. With actual detonators, they would have blown a hole in the side of the building, allowing egress using ropes.

"You caused the water pump alarm, didn't you?" Nate said as soon as Gary finished talking.

"That will be covered in the final report," Gary said.

"I know you did it, but how? We have a secure system here."

"That's all I can say right now."

"Why?"

"Because we're not done with the audit. As I said: We'll reveal everything in the final report."

"I want to know now."

"Nate, that's enough," Zack said.

"Yes, sir," Nate said in a sullen mumble.

"Ken, I'd like your thoughts on this exercise," Zack said. "In particular, what would have happened if that bomb had been real?"

"Serious badness," Ken said. "It probably would have killed the scientists and technicians in my lab and the surrounding ones. As you know, *all* the labs in that part of the building are biosafety level-four suites. Samples of the Marburg virus are stored in mine, but the adjacent labs contain Zaire Ebola, Sudan Ebola, and anthrax, among others. If these hot agents had gotten out, it might have wiped out Frederick, Washington, D.C., and much of the East Coast."

"And the hole in the outside wall would aid in the spread."

"Oh, yes. No doubt about it."

"Isn't Hamid's lab near yours?"

"Yes, he has the suite next to mine. Saeed does the actual research; Hamid supervises it along with the Brevig facility."

Gary noted the look of irritation that came to Zack's face and Nate's, as well. "I know it's none of our business, but what kind of research does Saeed do?" he asked.

"That's classified," Nate snapped. "You don't have a need to know."

Zack looked steadily at Gary. "Technically that's correct, but I'm going to tell them anyway."

"But, sir—"

"I think they *do* have a need to know," Zack said with a wry smile. "Besides, I imagine Gary has a good idea already, and if he doesn't, he needs to find a different line of work."

Gary returned the smile. "Thanks, Zack."

Zack nodded. "First, the Brevig Mission lab is responsible for culturing the 1918 virus to produce adequate samples for research. Second, they are to produce a vaccine for that virus. They have accomplished both of these objectives. Very soon now we'll close the Brevig facility and bring all samples back here, at which time Saeed will take over research while homeland security decides what to do next."

"Large-scale vaccine production."

"That decision is above my pay grade, but I think that's a safe bet. So are we done here?"

"That's all I have," Gary said.

"Can I assume that was your last break-in?" Nate asked.

Gary looked him in the eye. "No, you *cannot* assume that. As I said, we'll be concentrating on finishing our research and writing the report. But if we come across another weak spot, we'll make every effort to exploit it. My advice to you, Nate, is go plug all those holes before we come jumping through them."

Nate puffed up and looked around at Zack.

"Sounds like good advice to me," Zack said. "Meeting adjourned."

By late Wednesday, Gary became convinced they would be able to wrap up the project by early in the next week, assuming they didn't uncover some gaping security breach. Until he had laid the law down, Ann and Sully had been all in favor of concentrating on holes rather than finishing up the documentation. Gary knew they were motivated by the challenge, but he suspected they also enjoyed needling Nate. Gary had to admit that Nate's attitude inspired *him* in that direction, as well, but that didn't make it the right thing to do.

It was quiet inside the truck's command center. Gary glanced down at his watch and saw it was almost nine—time to pack it in for the evening.

"Everybody at a stopping place?" he asked. Four heads turned toward him.

light dimmed the sea of stars inside the sky's ebony bowl. The frigid air enveloped him like an icy glove, and their boots crunched on the frozen tundra. Davis coughed once, deep and raspy. Dick sprinted ahead to get the door while Larry helped the sergeant along.

Once inside, the doctor ushered Davis into the clinic and had him take off his coat and shirt. Larry removed his coat and pulled on a white coat over his working uniform. He took the man's temperature with an electronic thermometer.

"One-oh-three," Larry said.

He frowned. He grabbed a stethoscope and listened while the sergeant took deep breaths. When Larry finished, he hung the stethoscope around his neck and looked at Davis as if trying to decide what to do.

"You have the flu," he said.

Davis nodded but said nothing.

"How bad is it?" Dick asked.

"It's quite severe, but then flu often is," Larry said. "There's a lot of fluid buildup in his lungs; it could turn into pneumonia."

Dick nodded toward the windows separating the clinic from the four-bed ward in the next room. "So are you going to keep him in there?"

The doctor seemed deep in thought. "Oh, absolutely," he said finally. "I need to keep an eye on him."

Dick turned to the sergeant. "Go on in," he said. "I'll have your things brought over."

"Thank you, sir," Davis said. He held his hand in front of his mouth and coughed.

"I'll be there in a minute," the doctor told him.

Davis nodded and went through the door into the ward. Larry closed the door and returned to where Dick was standing. "I don't like it," Larry said in a whisper. "I'm sure it's the flu, but the onset worries me. It was awfully fast." He paused. "He hasn't been inside any of the labs, has he?"

"Of course not," Dick said in shocked surprise. Then he remembered to lower his voice. "The only reason a guard would come in this building would be to go to your clinic."

"Good, just wanted to be sure."

Dick saw the look of fear in the doctor's eyes. "You don't *really* suspect he's got the 1918 bug, do you?" he whispered.

Larry shook his head. "No, I don't see how that could be possible. Still. . ."

"Still what?" Dick said, biting off each word.

"The symptoms, so far, are similar to what Major Ingram experienced." He gave a nervous laugh. "But that's to be expected since the diagnosis is flu."

Dick glanced through the windows where Davis was getting into one of the ward beds. "Keep a close watch on him."

"Oh, certainly. I think Davis is in for a rough time. I'll call Helen over to help me."

"Okay. Keep me posted."

"I will. I wouldn't be surprised to see more cases in the next week. We're entering the flu season, and we don't know yet how effective our flu shots will be."

"Yeah, I know. Predicting flu strains for the next season never is an exact science."

"That's more in your line than mine."

Dick shrugged and forced a smile. "That's what my degree says. Well, good night, Doc."

"Good night."

Dick left the lab and trudged back to the dormitory deep in thought. The tundra beyond the perimeter fence was swallowed up in blackness punctuated by stars. The floodlights provided a stark light that seemed brilliant in contrast. Dick's breath puffed out in little white clouds as he hurried along. He entered the dining hall and saw the same two technicians, so engrossed in their game they didn't look up. Dick went back to his private room and, deciding he would sleep better after a hot shower, gathered his bathing gear and headed for the bathroom.

Dick Edwards heard something but at first didn't know what it was. Then the sound resolved itself into an insistent electronic trill coming from the phone beside his bed. The last cobwebs of a fitful slumber disappeared when he finally remembered what had happened to Sergeant Davis. Dick turned on his bedside lamp and grabbed his phone.

"Colonel Edwards," he said in a hoarse voice.

"This is Larry over in the clinic," the doctor said. "Sorry to bother you, but I've seen a total of six more flu patients, and I've admitted two to the ward for observation. You said to keep you informed."

Dick glanced at his bedside clock. It was not quite four in the morning. He held a hand over the mouthpiece and coughed. He removed his hand. "I see," he said with a wheeze.

"Are you okay?"

"I have a postnasal drip and the beginnings of a sore throat." He felt his head. "Don't think I have a fever, though."

"Maybe you should come by and see me."

"Later. How is Davis doing?"

"About the same. It's hard to tell since he's sleeping right now."

"And the others?"

"Serious. I think we're in for a *real* nasty outbreak."

There was a question Dick felt he should ask, but he was afraid of what the answer might be. "Are you still convinced this is flu—ordinary flu?"

"That's what it looks like." The line went silent for a few moments. "If I were anywhere else on earth, I'd be positive, but somehow

211

I can't get my mind off what happened to Major Ingram."

Dick felt a combination of fear and anger welling up inside. "But this has *nothing* to do with that." He struggled to regain his composure. "Look, I know how that lab was built, and I've followed the maintenance people around on their safety checks. The scientists and technicians verify the air lock seals every time they go in. We have alarms that will warn us if we lose negative air pressure. I'm telling you, Larry, we do *not* have any containment problems."

"Hey, I'm not saying we do." Larry sounded tired.

"Sorry. I've been under a lot of pressure lately."

"That's okay, I understand. Is there anything else you need right now?"

"No. Thanks for calling."

"Right. Bye."

Dick hung up the phone. He considered going back to sleep, but he was wide awake now, and with Larry's disturbing call, he knew he wouldn't be able to sleep anyway. He got up, and after shaving in the communal bathroom, he dressed, grabbed his coat, and headed for the dining hall door. Somewhere behind him, he heard someone coughing. The dining hall was deserted. He coughed on the way to the door and felt a pain in the back of his throat.

For the second time, he made the frosty trip over to the lab building. He looked up but couldn't see the stars. Then he saw the fine snowflakes swirling about in the light. It seemed the leading edge of the blizzard was early. He drew in an icy breath, and it started a reflexive coughing spasm that took all of his willpower to control. Each cough felt like a knife stabbing his lungs. He forced himself to take shallow breaths.

Dick reached the lab, opened the door, and went inside. Larry spotted him and came out into the corridor.

"I'm glad to see you," the doctor said. "Come in here and let me check you over."

"I'm all right," Dick grumbled.

"And I'm the doc." Larry waved toward the clinic. "Now take off your coat and shirt."

Dick could see there was no getting out of it. He stepped into the clinic, unzipped, and removed the heavy winter coat. Then came the shirt.

Larry stuck an electronic thermometer into his boss's mouth. A few seconds later, he removed it and looked at the LCD readout. "One-oh-two-point-five," he said. He got a tongue depressor and looked in Dick's mouth with an otoscope. "Severe inflammation of the throat," Larry said. "Now turn around and take some deep breaths for me." He listened with his stethoscope, performing the check twice. "Okay, you can put your shirt back on."

Dick slipped it on and started buttoning it. "What's your diagnosis?"

"Classic flu symptoms, however you're not as far along as my other patients."

Dick looked through the clinic windows at the ward beyond. Major Helen Baker, the facility nurse, was standing over Sergeant Davis. There were two other people in adjacent beds, but he couldn't see who they were.

"Who else is in there?" Dick asked.

"Bob Pratt and Corporal Gaines," Larry said.

Captain Pratt was their senior Blackhawk pilot, but all Dick knew of Gaines was that he was a new guy, one of the guards who worked for Sergeant Davis. Dick regretted the loss of the pilot the most because it technically grounded the facility's helicopter. In an emergency their remaining pilot could fly it, but with a blizzard blowing in, that was moot. They would have no contact with the outside world until the weather cleared. Ordinarily Dick wasn't bothered about being isolated since they were well prepared for it. But the prospect of having a large portion of the facility down with the flu did raise the anxiety factor a few notches.

"How are you holding up, Doc?" Dick asked.

"No symptoms so far, knock on wood." Larry glanced at his nurse. "Same for Helen." He laughed, but it sounded strained. "We're not allowed to get sick."

"You two *better* stay well."

Larry forced a smile. "I'll take that as an order. Now you know the drill: You need bed rest and plenty of fluids."

"Yeah, I know, but I have things to do. I have to give Colonel Roberts a heads-up on this." Dick picked up his coat and put it on.

"Just a minute." Larry measured out drugs in individual bags and scribbled notations on them. "Here you go. Tylenol, decongestant tablets, and throat lozenges; take as directed." He held up one of the bags. "These are oselamivir tablets. It's a neuraminidase inhibitor that's moderately effective against influenza A and B. Should help you some. I'll be over later to check on you."

Dick took the bags and zipped up his coat. "Thanks."

He walked out of the clinic and paused at the outside door and listened. The wind was definitely rising. He pushed the door open and started across the tundra. The icy wind seemed to claw at his bare face and sore throat. The snowfall was heavier now, although not nearly as heavy as it would be when the blizzard hit. He hurried across the frozen tundra, leaving clear tracks in the thin white covering. He reached the dormitory and hurried inside.

The dining hall was still deserted, but he could hear muted coughs coming from the dormitory. He passed through the door on the way to his room and heard at least two people hacking away, although no one was up. He coughed and winced at the pain. The urge to keep doing it was strong, but he knew that would be a mistake. He hurried into his room, grabbed a bottle of water, and took the Tylenol, decongestant, and antiviral drug. Then he sat down in a chair and sucked on a lozenge. It was now 4:20 a.m., and since Fort

Detrick was four hours later, he knew Zack would be in his office. Dick punched in the number.

"Switchboard," the Institute's comm center operator said.

"This is Colonel Edwards. Put me through to Colonel Roberts."

"Yes, sir."

The line clicked, and the phone rang once.

"Colonel Roberts."

"Zack, this is Dick." He coughed once and several more times until he could stop the spasm.

"Are you coming down with something?" Zack asked.

"Yeah, Doc says it's the flu. Looks like a good part of the facility could come down with it before it runs its course."

"How many so far?"

"Counting myself, eight. Larry has three of the severe cases under observation in the clinic ward."

"I see." The line went silent for a few moments. "I'm sure you've considered this, but is there any possibility this could be an outbreak?"

Dick's initial irritation was quickly replaced by a sense of ill-defined dread. "No, sir, I really don't see how it could be. From what I know about the lab design and our procedures, I'd have to say it's impossible. And right now Larry says he's seeing classic flu symptoms, exactly what we should expect at this time of year, when the flu vaccine isn't up to snuff."

"Which happens," Zack said.

"Exactly."

"Well, thanks for the info. Let me know how it goes."

"I will. Oh, and one other thing. We're expecting a blizzard, so there won't be any transportation between here and Nome."

"How long?"

"The weather wonks say a couple of days, but it could be longer."

"When it rains, it pours."

"Seems like it. Talk to you later."

"Right. Bye."

Dick hung up. He had one more thing to do, and that was tell Hamid Momeni what was happening. He considered calling because he was quite sure Hamid would be in his office. But instead Dick pulled over his computer keyboard. An e-mail would be plenty good enough for Secretary Foster's protégé. He hammered out a terse report and sent the message on its electronic way.

The team's command center truck was in the Institute's parking lot because there weren't any more operations planned, and the project was now officially in the "grunt phase." Gary checked his Outlook tasks and his calendar and saw nothing special for Thursday. His estimate for finishing the security audit by the end of next week still looked good. Then it would be back to sunny Southern California and beating the bushes for more business. Thomas Brooks would be near the top of his list. Assuming the audit report was well received, surely other government departments could use their services, especially with the ongoing war on terror.

"Hey, Gary," Ann said. "Come look at this."

He scooted his chair over, and she transferred the image to one of Dan's large monitors. It took him a few moments to understand what he was looking at. White specks were flashing toward the screen, but the lower half of the screen was dark.

"Oh, it's snow," Gary said. "That's one of the outside cameras at the Brevig lab."

"Yes. The lens hood is partially blocked by snow."

"I see. You'd think they'd heat those things. You going to note that as an action item?"

"Yes, but what I really want to show you is this."

Ann selected a different camera. Gary recognized the clinic camera. Through the windows he could see a woman in white moving around inside the ward. Men occupied three of the beds, and a man in a white coat was taking the pulse of one of the patients.

"That guy in the first bed looks like Sergeant Davis," Gary said.

Ann pointed. "Yes, and that must be the facility doctor, Major Larry Canton, and his nurse, Major Helen Baker."

Gary looked closely at the screen. They hadn't met the medical staff, but the team had a roster of facility personnel. "Yeah. And isn't that guy one of the Blackhawk pilots?"

"I think so. Captain Bob Pratt."

"So they have three people sick enough to confine in the clinic ward. Any idea what's going on?"

"No, because we don't have sound. But I went back to around nine thirty yesterday evening, local time, and edited together this sequence of videos. Watch."

Gary saw Larry Canton bring Sergeant Eddie Davis to Dick Edwards and the first trek over to the clinic where Davis had remained. Later, Helen Baker had come over to help the doctor. Then had come the parade of three men and two women, which had resulted in two additions to the ward. Around four the next morning, Dick had returned and been examined only to leave shortly thereafter.

"And that's it," Ann said. "That last scene was shot about an hour ago."

Gary frowned. "There's getting to be a lot of sick people in there. What do you think it is?"

"My guess would be the flu. We're getting close to the season."

"Yeah. Dick and the doc seem concerned, but I don't detect any panic."

"So it's not the 1918 plague?"

Gary looked at her. "I certainly hope not."

CHAPTER 18

Although it was 12:30 p.m. and Dick felt he knew what was going on over in the clinic, he had to see for himself. He forced himself up and out of bed and stood there on wobbly legs. This brought on a bout of coughing he found almost impossible to suppress. He felt awful, despite taking the oseltamivir, Tylenol, and the decongestant. He took a step toward the door and almost fell from dizziness. He pulled on his coat and left his room. The sounds of coughing filled the dormitory. One of the technicians trudged past on the way to the bathroom with barely a nod of acknowledgment. Out in the dining hall, three scientists sat huddled together at a table, apparently free of the flu. They looked his way as he walked past, and one gave a tentative wave. Dick couldn't bring himself to respond.

He opened the door and stepped down onto the fresh carpet of snow. It was snowing harder now, and the wind swirled and eddied; but it would get much worse when the full force of the blizzard struck. The icy blasts numbed his face and ears, and with each breath, agony seared his lungs. Several sets of faint tracks traced a dim path to the nearby lab building. Finally he reached the door and went inside.

He stood in the corridor and looked through the windows at the far end. Helen was moving about inside Slammer Junior. Dick went into the clinic and peered through the windows and saw that the ward was full. Larry Canton came out looking very tired.

"Glad you're here," he said. "How are you feeling?"

Dick coughed, wincing at the pain. "Terrible. I've never felt so bad in my life."

Larry scowled. "The antiviral drug didn't help any?"

"No."

"That's discouraging. I haven't had any luck with the other patients, either, which worries me. Well, I'm sorry, but unfortunately there's nothing more we can do."

"What's the count up to now?"

"Six new cases. I've admitted four for observation." He pointed down the hall. "I had to put three in Slammer Junior, and that leaves only one free bed in there. I don't know what I'll do if this keeps up."

"Oh, it's going to keep up, all right."

"Yeah, you're probably right."

"How is Sergeant Davis doing?"

"Worse. He's in very bad shape. I wouldn't be surprised if he slipped into pneumonia."

A sudden concern lodged in Dick's mind. "How are you and Helen holding up? No sign of the flu, I hope."

"Not so far, thank goodness."

"I'll say." He forced a weak smile. "Us sickies wouldn't have anyone to take care of us."

"It would make things difficult, that's for sure. Are you going to keep the labs operating?"

Dick shook his head. "No. At the end of the day, I'm having the supervisors put the automatic procedures into place. We'll pick up production and research after we get past this."

"Sounds like a wise decision."

Dick frowned. "I don't have much choice." He turned away. "I'm going back to my room."

"Okay. I'll be over this afternoon and look in on you."

"Thanks."

Dick left the lab building and hurried across the snow. It was coming down even harder now; his earlier tracks had been completely obliterated. He shivered in misery as a chill took hold of him. All he could think of was getting to his room and crashing.

Gary looked around the truck's command center. It was 5:30 in the afternoon, and his mind was beginning to edge over to something important: where the team would be going for dinner. He, John, and Sully tended toward pizza restaurants, preferably the all-you-can eat variety, but that morning Ann had let it be known that it was *her* turn to pick, and she wanted to go to the Olive Garden. With that already decided, Gary found he was looking forward to it. He glanced at her PC and saw a video of a room. It had four beds in it and three were occupied. A woman in a white uniform was checking a man's blood pressure.

"Is that Slammer Junior?" Gary asked.

She glanced back. "Yes, it is. They're using it for overflow." She switched the video to one of the large monitors. "Take a look." She played a clip she had put together. Most of the shots were of the clinic ward and Slammer Junior, but there were also clips of the dining hall and dormitory corridor.

"I see Dick Edwards is one of the walking wounded," Gary said.

"Yeah, and he really looks bad. The doc examined him earlier this morning, but he's apparently not in bad enough shape to be confined to the clinic."

Gary looked at her. "Do you have a tally on the total cases?"

"Yes. They're up to fourteen total and seven in the clinic and slammer."

"How's the weather up there?"

"Getting nasty." Ann punched up the recordings from the outside cameras. The view from the west was completely dark, and the one from the south was partially obscured. The other two cameras revealed heavy snowfall.

"It's really coming down."

"It'll be even worse in an hour or so." Ann switched back to the camera inside the clinic.

"I don't detect any panic so I guess they're dealing with the ordinary garden variety of flu," Gary said.

"Not that that's anything to sneeze at," Ann said.

Gary forced a deadpan expression and looked at her smiling face. "You know, it's possible to take that more than one way."

"Yes, but I only meant it one way."

Gary grinned. "Uh-huh." He looked around the truck. "How about we go eat?"

There were no dissenting votes.

Even though his sheets were drenched with sweat, Dick pulled his blanket higher to try to ward off the chill that shook his body. He coughed. That started a spasm, each one burning his throat and lungs like acid. The bout finally subsided when he was too exhausted to continue. His head throbbed with an excruciating headache brought on by plugged sinuses.

He levered himself up and looked at the clock on his bedside table. It was nearly seven, and he had slipped into and out of a fevered slumber all afternoon. He vaguely remembered Larry coming in to see him, stocking up his drug supplies, and forcing him to drink water, but nothing seemed to help. Larry had told him that the flu cases were continuing to mount.

Dick remained propped up on his elbows as he tried to decide what to do. What he *really* wanted was to be rid of all his pain and misery, and sleep *did* offer him temporary relief. But a sense of duty would not let him rest. He was responsible for not only what the Brevig lab did but the welfare of all the men and women who worked there, as well. He considered calling the clinic but decided he needed to see it firsthand.

Dick sat up in bed, threw off the wet bedclothes, and stood up. He rocked back and forth, unsteady on his feet. He forced himself to get dressed, pulled on his coat, and stumbled out into the corridor. Hacking coughs sounded all around him; it seemed like everyone had the flu. He made his unsteady way out into the dining hall. Normally, at this time of evening, it would have been full of people either having a late dinner or playing games. But the room was deserted. Dick considered making a cup of soup because he had not eaten since noon, but that would only delay what he had to do.

He reached the outside door and paused to catch his ragged breath and zip up his coat. He opened the door and stepped down into the snow, now higher than his boot tops. Wind whipped the swirling white curtain around, nearly obscuring the nearby lab building. Dick forced himself forward, shuffling his feet in stubborn determination. His vision dimmed, cleared, then dimmed again. He felt himself falling as if in a dream. The snow and his tenuous grip on consciousness softened the impact. The pain in his chest eased, and the intense cold gave way to a warm cocoon of peace.

How long he sprawled there, he didn't know, but there seemed to be a sharp discontinuity between the bliss of unconsciousness and a fresh onslaught of misery and pain. Someone was tugging on his arm, but he didn't know why. Then reality came flooding back. Against his will, he opened his eyes, squinted against the blowing snow, and saw a heavily bundled figure stooped over him. It was Larry Canton.

"Get up!" the doctor yelled to be heard over the wind. "Can you stand up?"

Dick didn't know if he could or not, but he rolled over on his stomach.

"I'll help you," Larry said. He shuffled around, kneeled down, and came up under Dick's left armpit with his shoulder. Larry grabbed Dick around the waist and started to lift. "Come on," he said, "you have to help me."

Dick summoned what little remained of his energy and came up into a crouch. Larry levered him up, and Dick staggered to his feet and stood there swaying. He nearly blacked out, but the doctor grabbed him before he could fall.

"I was on my way over to see you," Dick wheezed.

"We can talk about it in your room," Larry said. "Now let's go."

Dick allowed himself to be steered toward the dormitory building. He stumbled through the snow and followed Larry inside and down to his room. They were surrounded by the sounds of coughing and sneezing. Dick entered his room, sat down gratefully, and allowed the doctor to help him off with his clothes and back into bed.

Larry coughed. "Lucky I found you when I did. You wouldn't have lasted long out there. Now let me check you over." He pulled a thermometer and stethoscope out of his bag and went to work.

"What's the verdict?" Dick asked when the doctor finished.

"You're worse, and I'm *especially* concerned about the way you passed out on your way to the lab. Have you been taking the pills I gave you?"

"Yeah, but they're not doing any good."

"Well, you have a bad case, like a lot of others. I wish we had access to a real hospital, but we don't."

A coughing spasm gripped Dick for a few moments. "What's the count up to now?" he asked finally.

"Twenty total. I'm full up over at the clinic, so I had to send three of the severe cases back over here; that's including you."

Dick felt a momentary twinge of anxiety. "How are you and Helen holding up?"

Larry's look of concern deepened. "We're coming down with it, too."

"That's bad, real bad. We're over the 50-percent mark now. Is it possible we're all going to get it?"

Larry just looked at him but gave no indication he was going to answer.

"Answer me, Larry."

The doctor sat down. It was obvious he was exhausted and not feeling well. "Not with ordinary flu, at least I've never heard of such a thing. I would guess 50 percent is possible in a close environment like we have here, but still not very likely."

"Are you thinking we have an outbreak?"

Larry held up his hands. "I don't honestly know. I sure hope not."

Dick felt a deep chill. "That makes two of us."

"Are you going to notify Colonel Roberts?"

Dick thought that over. He felt a strong urge to make the call but ascribed it to worry. It was late on the East Coast, and he really didn't have anything new to report. There was still no indication of containment failure, none whatsoever; and if he hit the panic button, and a week or so later everyone was on the mend, what then?

"Not yet," Dick said finally. "I'll bring him up to date tomorrow."

Larry was dozing when it happened. One moment he was in the midst of a fevered dream where he was treating an unending line of patients, the next he awoke with a start. For a few moments, he didn't realize where he was. Then the room snapped into focus, and he heard a deep, wracking cough. He looked through the windows into the ward and saw Sergeant Davis flopping around under his sheet and blanket like a huge fish, each flop timed to a cough. Then without warning, Davis vomited a stream of dark, red fluid that reached the foot of the bed and splattered onto the floor. Larry jumped to his feet and rushed into the room.

"Doc!" Davis cried in fear and pain. Then he vomited again, another gory red fountain mixed with black globs.

Eddie Davis began choking. Larry rolled him onto his side and, as he did, saw the sheet underneath was soaked in blood. The sergeant was bleeding out; no doubt about it. That removed the last doubt in Larry's mind; he knew what was making everyone sick and what the ultimate outcome would be. Panic almost overcame him in that instant, but he forced himself to start clearing Davis's air passages. The man coughed a few times, spitting out blood each time. Then he passed out.

Helen rushed in from the corridor. The previous evening they had decided to split up, with Helen watching the patients in Slammer Junior while Larry observed those in the clinic ward. The nurse's eyes fell on the gory mess all around Davis and dripping onto the floor.

"What happened?" she asked in a quiet voice, but it was clear from the fear in her eyes that she knew exactly what it meant. While safely inside a Chemturion biological space suit, she had witnessed Major Ingram's agonizing death. But this time there would be no escape for any of them.

"Get me some morphine," Larry said.

She hesitated a moment then went to a cabinet, unlocked it, and removed a vial. She picked up a disposable syringe and handed it to the doctor. Larry measured out the dose and administered it to his unconscious patient. He considered starting a blood plasma IV but discarded the idea. Davis was at death's door, and there was absolutely no reason to prolong his agony.

During the night, eight brave souls had made the trek through the blizzard to see him: eight new cases, which brought the total to twenty-eight out of a total of thirty-eight men and women at the

Brevig facility; and he suspected there were unreported cases over in the dormitory, people too sick to make the trip to the clinic. He looked down at Davis and shuddered.

"Helen," Larry said.

She was staring at Davis, her eyes wide in shock.

"Helen," he said again, raising his voice. "I need your help."

She turned her head and looked into his eyes. "Oh, yes. Sorry."

Larry positioned the earpieces of his stethoscope, bent over, and listened to Davis's lungs. It was the worse congestion he had ever heard, but the doctor knew he was hearing more than mucus-blocked airways; the man's lung tissue was dissolving. He straightened up and dropped the stethoscope around his neck. He had to call Dick and right now. He glanced at his watch and saw it was a little after six in the morning. He reached for the wall phone.

A distant sound insinuated itself into Dick's uneasy sleep. He ignored it at first, but it wouldn't go away. He had a vague suspicion that the sound meant trouble. He drifted toward consciousness from something deeper than ordinary sleep. Then, at last, he had it. It was his phone. He opened his eyes and threw aside the sheet and blanket, noting absently that they were drenched with sweat. He swung his feet out and onto the floor. He stood up and almost fell as a wave of dizziness came over him. He staggered over and picked up the phone.

"This is Colonel Edwards," he mumbled then broke into a coughing bout.

"Dick, this is Larry. I have terrible news!"

Dick felt a jolt of fear. "What's wrong?" His question was automatic since he knew what was coming.

"The 1918 virus has escaped. Somehow it got out, and that's what we have. Davis crashed a few minutes ago; he's bleeding out now, and there's nothing I can do."

"I see." It was all he could say since he had been expecting this outcome for some time. He had hoped against hope, as long as the symptoms had been the same as for ordinary flu. Now the charade was over, and every man and woman at the facility had a death sentence. Each and every one would die a painful death.

"Dick? Are you there?"

"I'm here." Then his groggy mind reminded him of his duty. "How many cases?"

"At least twenty-eight but probably more. Dick, all of us are going to get it. This place is going to be a morgue in a few days."

"I *know* that, Larry. What can we do?"

"Provide comfort for as long as we can. Narcotics will help. Helen will stay over here, and I'll be over there as soon as I gather up the supplies I'll need."

"Very well. Bring me a status."

"Yes, sir."

Dick replaced the handset, and his feverish mind plodded along as he tried to think of all the things he had to do. Notifying Zack Roberts stood out vividly, however first he had to get the facility's complete status. He decided to let Larry check on the personnel in the dormitory. That left only the man on duty over in the guardhouse, since Dick had pulled the outside sentry when the blizzard came through. He picked up the phone and punched in a number.

"Sergeant Garcia," the man said. "May I help you, sir?"

Dick held his hand over the mouthpiece and waited for a coughing bout to end. "Sergeant, this is Colonel Edwards. I need a status report from you."

"Yes, sir. I'm the only one on duty, since we've secured the perimeter patrol. All security systems are operational except for snow blocking the exterior cameras that are facing west and south. The trunk lines to Nome are functioning, and our data link to the Institute is up." The man paused briefly. "Colonel, how are things. . . ?"

Dick considered putting him off, but his conscience wouldn't let him. The man had a right to know. "Things are bad, very bad. Major Canton and I are convinced the 1918 virus has broken out."

"Then that means. . ." Garcia sounded scared but not surprised. Everyone at Brevig knew what they were working on.

"That means *most* of us are going to die," Dick finished for him. Then he noted a curious thing. Garcia had not coughed or wheezed once. "Sergeant, how are you feeling?"

"Fine."

"No sore throat or fever?"

"No, sir."

That puzzled Dick. Had Garcia somehow avoided contact with the virus, or could he be immune to it? Dick knew that both possibilities were all but impossible. He had probably been infected later than most of the others. But still. . .

"Sergeant, you are to stay in the guardhouse; it's the only chance you have. Do *not* enter either the dormitory building *or* the lab. The storeroom has cases of MREs so you won't starve. Do you understand?"

"Yes, sir."

Dick felt a stinging sensation in his eyes. "Thank you, Sergeant Garcia. I appreciate the job you're doing."

"It's my duty, sir."

"Yes. Well, good-bye."

Dick pressed the button to disconnect. He waited a few moments then dialed Zack Roberts's office number and waited for the comm center operator to answer.

CHAPTER 19

Gary!" Ann said in almost a shout. "Look at this." She transferred the image to a large monitor.

Gary stood, came in behind her chair, and stared at the shot taken by the Brevig clinic camera. He watched in horror as Sergeant Davis went into a spasm that ended in a fountain of blood. Ann fast-forwarded through the treatment that Larry and Helen gave the man. When she resumed normal playback, Larry was on the phone.

"Must be calling Dick Edwards about it," Gary said.

"Has to be," Ann said. "Now one more."

The next scene came from the guardhouse camera. It showed a man talking on the phone.

"Who's that?" Gary asked.

"Don't know. I didn't see him during our visit."

"Probably has something to do with what just happened."

"Yeah."

"How long ago did this happen?" Gary asked.

"A little after 10:00 a.m., our time."

Gary looked around the truck's command center. Everyone was

looking at the monitor in varying states of shock.

"Not much question what's happened," he said. "The 1918 virus is on the loose up there."

"Big-time," Sully said.

"Man, that is grim," John said. "What should we do about it?"

Gary looked him in the eye. "Nothing for the time being, because we have no official knowledge of it. I'm sure Dick's notified Zack and Hamid by now. It's their responsibility."

"I sure hope they know what they're doing. If that virus escapes from Brevig—"

"Don't go anywhere near that."

"I need you in my office," Zack Roberts said. "We have an emergency."

"Be right there, sir," Nate said.

Zack slowly replaced the handset. His face was pale. This would be a Friday he would *never* forget. The magnitude of what had happened was still reverberating inside his head as he tried to come to grips with the horrifying ramifications. Many of his colleagues and friends would soon suffer painful deaths, and there was nothing he could do to prevent it. But the first priority was to make sure the virus didn't spread. Others would have to decide what to do about the research.

Momentary anger flashed through him when he considered homeland security's involvement. Although Zack was responsible for handling the incident, Secretary Foster's people would be nosing around asking questions and pointing fingers. Bringing the secretary into the loop would require precise timing; too soon and Zack would lose all control; too late and he would incur Secretary Foster's wrath, and he could kiss his career good-bye.

A knock sounded at the door.

"Come," Zack said.

Nate hurried in, closed the door, and took a chair in front of

Zack's desk. He gripped the arms so hard, his hands shook. "What's wrong?" he asked.

"The virus has broken out at Brevig. Over half of the personnel there have it."

"What? How could that happen?"

Zack's anger surged. "How in the world would *I* know? Dick has no idea, so *I* sure don't."

Nate's face flushed. "Sorry, sir, but we've been *so* careful: the design, constructions, all the safety procedures."

Zack held up his hand. "I *know* all that, Nate. But right now we *have* to come up with what we're going to do about it, including how we're going to handle the homeland security people."

"Is there any hope for the victims?"

Zack shook his head. "Not much. Ironically, they have the only vaccine in existence, but, of course, it has to be administered before infection."

"Have they *all* come down with it?"

Zack hesitated. "Dick thinks there *might* be one exception. One of the guards, Sergeant Garcia, shows no symptoms as yet. However, he probably *has* been exposed, and if so, he'll probably get it, too."

"What if somehow, someway, he's in the clear?"

"I suppose we can hope. Dick ordered him to stay in the guard-house, just in case."

"Are we going to mount a rescue mission?"

"Of course, as soon as the blizzard clears out. But homeland security will get involved long before then, and who knows what Secretary Foster will want to do."

"When are you going to notify him?"

"After we get done here. But first, review Brevig's communications for me. We still have total control, don't we? I want to be absolutely sure about this."

"Yes, sir, I'm positive. All their telephone lines come directly into our comm center. All incoming and outgoing calls go through our switchboard."

"What about e-mail?"

"Their broadband Internet connection ends up in the comm center, as well. Their e-mails are monitored for sensitive information before they're forwarded. Incoming e-mails are checked, as well."

"Are the personnel allowed mobile phones?"

"No, sir, and that's strictly enforced."

"Good. I want a total clampdown on all communications to and from Brevig. Tell the comm center they are to shut down all e-mail service and Internet traffic. All phone calls are to be routed to either you or me, no exceptions, and tell the operators they're not to give out information. You know the drill."

"I'll take care of it, sir."

"Next, I want you to prepare a brief for me on the Brevig facility: security procedures, construction techniques, and the current status on virus and vaccine production. Ken and Carol Underwood can help you with that. Make *sure* you cover all the bases. I don't want Secretary Foster pulling the rug out from under me, understand?"

"Yes, sir. How long do I have?"

"Don't know, so hop to it. It'll be bad for all of us if the secretary hears about this before I notify him."

"Are you going to tell Hamid?"

"Nope. That'll be up to Secretary Foster. Hamid works for him, not me."

"Hamid won't like that."

"Tough. Now get busy."

Gary rushed down the wide corridor with Ann on one side and John on the other as they all strained to keep up with Thomas Brooks. All Thomas had said on the helicopter ride into Washington was that

Secretary Foster wanted to see them ASAP. They turned a corner, and Gary spotted their destination: the conference room where they had originally met the secretary of homeland security. Thomas opened the door, and the SecurityCheck team filed inside. Six worried faces looked at the newcomers. Gary skipped the chair nearest the head of the table and sat down. John, Ann, Dan, and Sully took the chairs to his right. Secretary Foster sat at the head, and across the table were Hamid Momeni, Zack Roberts, Nate Young, and Ken and Carol Underwood. Thomas hurried over and sat beside Gary.

"Thank you, Gary," Foster said. "I appreciate you and your team coming on such short notice." He paused. "But before we start, I need to be absolutely clear that *everything* we discuss will be classified top secret. Nothing, and *I mean* nothing, is to be discussed outside this room. Understood?"

"Absolutely," Gary said.

"The reason your team is here is to provide advice, if necessary, on a developing situation, something that could easily become a national emergency. Colonel Roberts will brief us on what's happened. Colonel, you're on."

While Zack gathered his notes, Gary considered telling the secretary about the team's inside sources of information but came to the conclusion it would be an unnecessary distraction. Besides, all that they had done would come out in the final audit report.

"Thank you, Mr. Secretary," Zack said. "Well, to bring us *all* up to speed, at approximately 2130 hours on Wednesday, 6 October, Major Larry Canton brought Sergeant Eddie Davis to Colonel Dick Edwards, the Brevig Mission lab's commanding officer. Sergeant Davis had flulike symptoms, but it turns out he has the 1918 virus. Brevig lab has had an outbreak, and after talking it over with Dick, we've tentatively placed the outbreak date sometime Monday or Tuesday of this week."

"Wait!" Foster said, his face suddenly drained of color. He turned to Hamid. "When were you and Saeed Alsaadoun at Brevig?"

"We arrived last Friday and came back the next day," Hamid replied.

Foster glanced at Zack. "Any chance Hamid or Saeed could have been exposed?"

Zack shook his head. "None whatsoever; the incubation period is too short. Besides, if they had been exposed, they'd be infected by now."

"Okay. Proceed, Colonel."

Zack recited the timeline, from Sergeant Eddie Davis's diagnosis through Zack's last conversation with Dick Edwards. He ended by saying: "As you know, the virus we have cultured at the Brevig Mission lab came from samples taken from Native Alaskans buried at what was then Teller Mission. The mortality rate there was 85 percent, and using that as our benchmark, we can expect that more than thirty of the thirty-eight people stationed at Brevig will die."

"Then you're expecting they'll all become infected," Foster said.

"Yes, sir, with the possible exception of Sergeant Garcia. Dick told me that he has twenty-eight confirmed cases so far, but he suspects the actual number is higher."

"What about next of kin. Have they been notified?"

"No, sir, absolutely not," Zack said, shaking his head. "This is a top secret installation, and our men and women know going in that if something like this happens, we impose a security blackout. Families and friends understand this, as well."

"I see. That's a grim picture you paint."

"Yes, it is. Mr. Secretary, this virus is the most dangerous biological agent in all history; that's why our research is so vital. If terrorists manage to culture it—"

"Please stick to the agenda," Foster interrupted quickly.

"Sorry, sir."

"Now, how did this happen? Every report *I've* seen says we're taking every precaution, that a virus outbreak was impossible."

"There's no way to guarantee 100-percent safety, Mr. Secretary. The best you can do is utilize proven containment techniques and thorough decontamination procedures, and that we've done. The Brevig facility was constructed *exactly* like the USAMRIID labs, and they were using identical decon methods. At Fort Detrick, we've never had a hot agent get outside our biosafety level-four areas."

"But the virus obviously *did* escape. What I want to know is how."

"Yes, sir, we all do, but I don't have an answer right now."

Foster looked at Nate Young. "Colonel, do you have anything to add?"

"No, Mr. Secretary. As Colonel Roberts said, we've never had a reason to question the containment safeguards at Brevig."

Foster consulted his notes. "I understand the Underwoods helped design that lab." He glanced up. "Any comments?"

"No, Mr. Secretary," Ken Underwood said. "Carol and I were on the design team, as was Hamid, and I agree with everything Colonel Roberts and Colonel Young related. I'm at a loss to explain how this happened." He looked at his wife.

"I concur, Mr. Secretary," Carol said.

"Mr. Secretary, I've talked with Dick Edwards at length about this," Zack said. "He assures me that all biosafety level-four areas are maintaining negative air pressure, there is no sign of leaks, the air filtration systems are functioning correctly, and proper decontamination procedures were being used. I *know* what he's telling me is true. I'd stake my life on it."

Secretary Foster frowned and tapped on his notepad with his pen. "You people keep telling me it can't get out. Well, it most certainly *did*, and I'll want to know why before this is all over."

"Yes, sir. We all do."

"Is there *any* possibility this could be an act of terrorism?" Foster asked in a very measured tone.

"I suppose it's impossible to rule out, but I'd say the likelihood is remote in the extreme."

"Okay, moving on. How soon will we be able to send a rescue team in?"

"As soon as the blizzard clears out, which should be sometime Saturday or Sunday."

"Do we have any army personnel in Nome who could drive up there?"

"No, sir, and even if we did, they couldn't drive up there in the middle of a blizzard."

"I see. Who do you propose sending?"

"I'll have to prepare a roster, but I know I'll want Nate Young and Ken and Carol Underwood. In addition, I'll send a medical doctor from my staff, plus about a hundred assorted troops and technicians to decontaminate the facility, take care of survivors, if any."

"Will you bring them back?"

"No, sir. Any survivors will have to remain there until we're *sure* they're not contagious."

"Where will you put them?"

"After we thoroughly nuke the site, we'll put them in Slammer Junior."

"I see. Continue."

"We'll secure the area, which includes bagging the bodies and putting them in hermetically sealed caskets."

"Mr. Secretary, I'll have to go along," Hamid said.

"I object," Zack said. "The lab is a satellite of USAMRIID and as such falls under my command."

"The lab and its personnel are under my administrative control, Colonel," Hamid said with a hard gleam in his eye. "The virus research and initial vaccine production are CIA projects. The virus and vaccine samples will be moved back to my lab at Fort Detrick in accordance with the original plan."

"But, sir. . . ," Zack said, looking at Secretary Foster.

"It's his research project," Foster said. "Hamid will be responsible for the virus and vaccine samples, and you will handle everything else."

Zack frowned. "Yes, sir."

"I will need Saeed, as well."

Zack turned his head and glared at Hamid. "Fine. Just *don't* get in the way of my people."

Hamid smiled and interlaced his fingers but didn't say anything.

Foster looked at Gary. "I'd like the SecurityCheck team to go, as well, if they're willing."

"Do you think this is wise?" Hamid asked. "After all, the CIA has the prime interest in this operation. Should we involve civilians in something like that?"

"I understand your concern, but yes, I believe the benefits outweigh the risks. Look. These people are the best in the business when it comes to investigating. We have no idea what happened up there, and I want some answers." He turned back to Gary. "Can we count on you?"

Gary held the secretary's gaze despite the sudden shock. "Speaking for myself, I'll go. I understand how important this is to national security, but let me take a quick poll."

Foster nodded.

Gary looked to his right, his gaze taking in the other team members.

"Count me in," Ann said.

"I'm in, boss," Sully said.

"I go where you go," John said with a conviction that Gary greatly appreciated.

"Me, too," Dan said.

"Thank you," Foster said to Gary. Then he turned back to Zack. "I want them along as extra eyes and ears. We've had some kind of a breakdown here, and I want all the help I can get in finding out what happened."

"I'll include them, as well," Zack said. He hesitated then added, "Mr. Secretary?"

"Yes, Colonel?"

"Since we're asking the SecurityCheck people to come along, I think they need to know why we're doing this research in the first place; background, you know."

Secretary Foster paused then nodded. "I agree. Go ahead."

Zack turned to Gary. "We're not the first to try and revive the 1918 virus, but we're probably the first to succeed. And since we've done it, we know others can, as well. Intelligence sources tell us that a Saudi terrorist sleeper cell somewhere on the East Coast is trying to do it."

"You mean—" Gary began.

"If they succeed, we better have a vaccine in place. See what we're up against?"

Gary took a deep breath and let it out slowly. "Yes, I sure do."

"Again, I appreciate your willingness to help," Foster said. He turned back to Zack. "Will your people be occupying the facility?"

"Only the Slammer, at least initially. The medical personnel, technicians, and guards will live in army field tents a safe distance away and make trips inside as required."

"Okay. What about the samples?"

"We'll pack all the virus and vaccine samples in special biohazard boxes and bring them back here."

"I will handle that personally," Hamid interjected.

Zack frowned at him. "As you wish."

"Weren't we going to close Brevig once the samples were ready?" Foster asked.

"Yes, Mr. Secretary," Zack said. "Ironically, we were within days of bringing them back when this happened."

"I see. What logistics will you need?"

"We'll need air transport for personnel and cargo from D.C. to Nome. We'll have Racal field biological suits for those entering the hot zone, plus decon equipment, and supplies. Then there are the field tents, weapons, and supplies for the troops that we'll leave behind to care for the survivors and guard the site."

"I'll contact the commanding officer of the Eighty-seventh Airlift Wing at Andrews. He'll arrange whatever you need."

"Thank you, sir. That will get us and our gear to Nome. Then we'll need heavy-lift and utility helicopters to get everything to the Brevig lab and perform aerial decon." Zack looked down at his notes. "Fort Wainwright in Fairbanks can supply both. I would like two UH-60 Blackhawks and two CH-47 Chinooks. They can also supply the tents and supplies our troops will need."

Foster made a note on his legal pad. "Consider it done. I'll have the commanding officer call you for the specifics." He glanced at his agenda then back up at Zack. "So is there anything else that needs deciding?"

"No, Mr. Secretary. I'll have all our supplies prepared for shipment to Andrews. Once we get the green light on weather, we'll be ready to roll. And I'll give Colonel Edwards a heads-up when I get back to the Institute."

Foster looked around the table. "Thank you, ladies and gentlemen. We are adjourned. Zack, keep me posted."

"Yes, sir."

Dick awoke from a feverish sleep that was nearly a coma. A wall of pain and mind-numbing weakness washed over him like a tidal wave. His lungs felt full, like he was drowning, but all he could manage was a feeble cough, which only made his agony worse. He tried to turn on his side but couldn't muster the strength. He gritted his teeth, threw his right arm around, and twisted onto his side. Focusing his eyes on the bedside clock, he saw it was a little after eleven. Through a veil of misery, he recognized his duty. It had been hours since he talked with Larry Canton. He *had* to find out how his troops were doing. A sharp thought popped up and lodged in his brain. A stinging sensation came to his eyes when he realized this task would probably be his last.

With an adrenaline rush borne of desperation, he threw aside the drenched covers and stood up. Dizziness swept over him, and for a moment, his vision dimmed. He gripped a chair back to steady himself. Since he had gone to bed fully dressed, all he had to do was pull on his boots and grab his coat. He scooted the boots over to the chair with his feet. He sat down heavily but found it almost impossible to bend over. He tried again, snagged one boot, and pulled it on. Then came the second one. He stared at his feet, helplessly wondering how he would tie his laces, but finally decided it wasn't necessary. He didn't have that far to go. He grabbed his coat and staggered out into the corridor.

He heard someone coughing but didn't know where the sound was coming from. He shuffled his way through the door and into the dining hall. There, almost to the outside door, sprawled a thin man wearing a coat over a rumpled working uniform. A dark brownish-black pool dotted with black clumps spread across the floor around the man's head. As Dick made his way over, he finally recognized Lieutenant Ted Harris, the Blackhawk copilot. Dick kneeled on the floor and felt the man's neck, but there was no pulse, as he expected, since the vomited blood had to be hours old.

With almost the last of his strength, Dick staggered to his feet. A wave of dizziness came over him, but he managed to keep from falling. He shuffled to the door and pushed it open against the howling blizzard. He stepped down into the deep snow and turned toward the lab. He squinted against the blowing snow that all but obscured the nearby building. He took a cautious breath, and the agony in his lungs brought tears to his eyes. The icy wind whipped about him and began leaching the warmth from his body. Dick forced his feet to move, lifting one and then the other in his weary trek. Slowly the distance diminished. Finally he reached the door, opened it, and staggered inside.

Dick stood in the corridor swaying. Men and women, army and civilian personnel he was responsible for, lay all along the hallway under blankets. Through the windows at the far end, he could see Helen moving around inside Slammer Junior. Larry tottered out of the clinic looking gray and drawn.

"What are you doing over here?" the doctor said. "You should be in bed."

"I had to come," Dick said, his words barely audible. "How are you and Helen holding up?"

Larry seemed to sag. "It's hard. We've both come down with it, but we're still better off than most of our patients."

"What's the count up to now?"

"At least thirty-two confirmed cases, including Sergeant Garcia, and five dead."

"Are you counting Ted Harris? I found him dead on the dining hall floor."

"No."

"What do you think the infection rate will be?"

"A hundred percent. It'll be a *miracle* if anyone escapes."

"How many will die?"

"As nasty as this is, I wouldn't be surprised if we *all* die of it. Optimistically, if you can call it that, the mortality rate *may* be as low as 90 percent, say 34 or 45."

"Only three or four survivors?"

"If we're lucky."

"What are your plans?"

"Take care of the people over here for as long as we can. It's been hours since I was over in the dorm building, and I'm sorry about that. But there's just too much to do, and we're getting quite sick ourselves."

"I understand." Dick felt the sting of bitter tears. "You two have already done above and beyond. I appreciate it."

Larry nodded. "It's our duty."

"No, it's more than that." Dick ransacked his fevered brain trying to decide what to do next. Then he slowly turned. "I better get back to the dorm."

"Stay here. I don't think you can make it."

"Got to. I have to report to Colonel Roberts."

"Make the call from here."

"But. . ."

"Doctor's orders. Call him; then I'll make you as comfortable as I can."

Dick didn't have the strength to argue further. He shuffled over to the wall phone, picked up the handset, and punched in Zack's home number. He sat heavily in a chair. The Institute comm center operator answered and routed the call. Dick's boss answered after the third ring.

" 'Lo," said the sleepy voice.

Dick held his hand over the mouthpiece and coughed. "Colonel, this is Dick Edwards."

"Dick. How are you?" Zack said.

"Bad, real bad. This will probably be my last report."

"I'm sorry, Dick. I *wish* there was more that I could do."

"I know, sir. Doc Canton and I figure that at least thirty-two have the virus and at least six deaths; both these figures are probably low since we're in no condition to get an exact count."

"I see. How about Sergeant Garcia? In your earlier report, you said he was symptom free."

"Garcia has it, too. Larry thinks the infection rate will be 100 percent and that we'll be lucky if we end up with three or four survivors." Dick started coughing, and it took all his willpower to bring the bout under control. "Colonel, you should *see* the lab building. It looks like an Ebola outbreak, only worse if you can imagine that."

"No, that's beyond me."

Dick felt an immense sadness welling up inside. "Zack, make *sure* your people are careful. You *have* to contain this agent. If it gets loose. . ."

"*Believe* me, we'll take every precaution."

"Colonel, I doubt we'll talk again." He paused as he struggled for control. "It's been a privilege serving under you."

"Dick, the privilege was mine. Thank you. I'm so sorry."

"Yes, well, good-bye, sir."

"Good-bye."

Dick stood and hung up the phone. He turned back to the doctor and was about to say something when nausea completely overwhelmed him. He felt his knees give way and saw the floor come rushing up. An excruciating pain lanced deep into his brain as a bright red torrent erupted from his mouth. Then everything went black.

CHAPTER 20

Colonel Zack Roberts had spent a long and sleepless night after his talk with Dick Edwards—a talk that would surely be their last. Finally, at 6:00 a.m. Saturday, he had given up, gotten dressed, and driven to the Institute. The rescue plans were well under way now, and he would be receiving status reports at regular intervals. If snags came up, he would deal with them, but he knew that with the secretary of homeland security behind them, there wasn't much that could stand in their way; that and the inertia of the federal behemoth.

Around ten, he had gone for coffee and something to eat and returned to his office to resume his vigil. A quick call to the Fort Detrick weather wonks told him the blizzard in Nome was still raging, but they expected it to clear sometime Monday. Zack leaned back in his chair and took a sip of coffee. It was strong and bitter.

Zack had decided to wait until around noon before calling Brevig, which would be eight in the morning there. He was anxious to find out what was going on, but those dealing with the outbreak had more than enough to contend with without him butting in. Still, he had to know.

His phone rang a little after eleven thirty, causing him to jump. He felt a jolt of adrenaline.

He grabbed up the handset. "Colonel Roberts."

"Colonel, call for you from Major Helen Baker," the operator said.

"Very well. Put her through."

The line clicked. "Colonel, this is Major Baker."

Zack felt his gut tighten. "Good morning, Helen." He winced at how that sounded. It was anything *but* a good morning at Brevig. He heard the muffled sound of coughing that went on for quite a while.

"I have our status report," she finally managed to say. "Major Canton said to call around eight if he wasn't able to. He went into a coma about an hour ago. I don't think he'll last much longer."

"I'm sorry. What about Colonel Edwards?"

"He died shortly after talking to you."

Zack closed his eyes, a cloud of profound sadness settling over him.

"By my count, and it could be off, a total of twenty-six people made it to the lab building, including Major Canton and myself— and Colonel Edwards," Helen continued. "Since our last report, we've had four more deaths. Don't know about the dormitory be-cause I can't get over there. I'm doing the best I can for my patients, but it's not much. I don't know how much longer I can keep going."

"I understand. Do you know anything about Sergeant Garcia?"

"Yes. He calls every few hours. He has it, too. He's staying over at the guardhouse because Colonel Edwards ordered him to."

"I can call and send him over."

"He's probably better off where he is. Doc Canton took him a good supply of meds. Plus, it's a stinking mess over here. He'll prob-ably last longer than the rest of us since he was one of the last to come down with it."

"I imagine you're right."

"Has there been any change on when the rescue team will get here?"

"No. They'll leave when the blizzard clears out; should be sometime Monday."

"I see. Well, how often should I call?"

"I don't want to add to your burdens. If you feel up to it, I'd appreciate updates as you're able."

"Yes, sir. Well, good-bye."

"Good-bye, Helen."

Zack replaced the handset, got up, and walked to a window. He looked down on the Institute's grounds, so peaceful under blue skies with the trees beginning to show their fall colors. He tried to imagine what it was like at the Brevig facility. He thought about the horrible pictures he had seen of Ebola victims in African clinics: poorly constructed buildings with no windows and poor sanitation; patients lying on cots or the floor; overworked doctors and nurses doing their best to care for the dying but lacking adequate medical supplies; the flies, the stench, the sense of hopelessness. His people at Brevig had the very best that medical science could provide, but the result would be the same. And there the analogy broke down. The virus his people were dying from was far more deadly than Ebola. For a long time, all he could do was stand there and stare out the window.

A half hour later, Zack fetched a sandwich and another cup of coffee rather than go out for lunch; he couldn't bring himself to leave the office. He remained firm in his resolve not to bother Helen but decided it couldn't hurt to call Sergeant Garcia since he was better off than the others. However, "better off" was a relative term; death deferred was more honest. He stared at the telephone for a long time and finally reached over and lifted the handset. After a short pause, he punched in the number for the Brevig facility's guardhouse. The comm center operator answered and put the call through.

"Sergeant Garcia," a man answered, his voice low and indistinct.

"Sergeant, this is Colonel Roberts."

The man coughed. "Yes, Colonel. How can I help you?"

Zack felt a brief chill. The Institute ought to be helping Garcia, only it was too late for that. "Just checking to see how you were doing." *And how lame did* that *sound?* Zack wondered.

"I feel terrible, Colonel. I've never been so sick in my life."

"I'm sorry. Is there anything you need?"

"No, sir. Doc Canton fixed me up the best he could, and I have plenty of chow and bottled water. Enough to last me."

"I see." Then Zack remembered that the sergeant could see inside the dormitory building. "Have you been checking on things with the security cameras?"

"I was up until last night. It's horrible, Colonel, what everyone's going through. I couldn't take it anymore."

"I understand, but I need you to do something for me. I *must* have an accurate picture of what's going on. Can you do that for me?"

"Yes, sir, I guess so. What do you want me to look at first? The lab building?"

"No, I think you can skip that. Major Baker told me what's going on over there. Take a look in the dormitory."

"Yes, sir. Wait one." After what seemed like a long time, he again spoke. "Looks bad, Colonel, but *nothing* like the clinic and Slammer. I counted two dead in the dining hall; both bled out. One was Lieutenant Harris. The other was a woman, but I couldn't see who since she was turned away from me. I also punched up the exterior cameras and spotted two bodies, one just outside the dormitory and the other lying across the steps to the lab building. Both are covered with snow."

"Can you tell who they are?"

"No, sir."

Zack integrated all this information with what he already knew. The Brevig facility was fast becoming a morgue, but despite this, duty required that Zack understand all he could about the outbreak and its aftermath. And except for recordings from the security cameras, Sergeant Garcia would soon become the last living witness.

"How long do you think you'll be able to hold out?" Zack asked.

"Don't know, sir. I feel like I'm about ready to crash."

"Well, try to hang in there."

"I'll do my best, sir."

"I know you will. I'll call you again in a few hours."

Garcia started coughing, and it went on for quite a while. "Yes, sir," he finally managed to say.

Zack hung up the phone and sat back in his chair. His thoughts traveled the thousands of miles that separated Frederick from Brevig Mission. What had happened at that lab and to the men and women who worked there was his responsibility. Then he thought of Hamid Momeni and frowned. Part of the responsibility *should* rest with the CIA spook, but Zack knew it wouldn't work out that way. But either way, the personnel at the facility were just as dead.

Gary's shadow preceded him as he walked across the Institute's well-lit parking lot carrying a large white paper bag. Sully followed him holding another. Gary opened the truck's rear doors and climbed inside. Although no one felt hungry, he had insisted on making a food run. The team's demanding work schedule required energy despite the unfolding horror at Brevig.

Sully came in and closed the doors.

Gary emptied his sack on the workbench next to Dan. "Dig in, everyone," he said. The gloom inside the truck's command center seemed to permeate everything. He picked up a sandwich at random and began unwrapping it.

Dan also took one, then John came over. Sully passed out foam cups of coffee along with packets of sugar and creamers. Gary removed the lid from his coffee with one hand, lifted the cup, and took a long sip.

"Anything happen while we were gone?" he asked.

It was after nine, and Gary had intended spending the day working on research and updates to the security audit report rather than sitting around doing nothing. But the team had been unable to concentrate. At frequent intervals, Ann had produced edited videos from the Brevig facility's security cameras. While this interrupted their work, Gary knew it was vital background intelligence. He recognized from Ann's glance that she had another one ready to share, however he decided the update could wait until they finished their break.

Gary pulled a chair over and sat down beside Dan. He took his time eating his sandwich and drinking his coffee as he thought through the team's schedule for the next few days. Despite the impending trip and the lack of progress on the report, he and John had agreed earlier that they would still stand down on Sunday, unless Secretary Foster initiated the mission to Brevig. But according to the latest weather reports, the earliest they could expect clear weather was Monday. Gary finally finished his coffee and tossed the cup into the trash.

"Got another update?" he asked Ann.

"I do," she replied.

He scooted his chair over beside hers, and the others gathered around. Ann called up the video player and transferred the image to the large monitor above Dan.

"What's the timeline?" John asked.

"These shots are almost an hour old," Ann said. "Say a little after four their time."

She clicked the PLAY button. The first scene showed swirling snow with the dim outline of the dormitory building hunkered down in the background with a heavy white blanket covering the roof. Next came the view of the east exterior camera, which revealed the facility vehicles under mounds of snow. A vague shadow was all that could be seen of the lab building.

"Blizzard doesn't show any sign of letting up," Gary said.

"Yeah, looks like the weather forecast was right," Ann said.

Then came scenes from inside the dormitory and lab buildings. While they were gruesome, it was essentially what they had seen before.

"Did anyone spot any signs of movement?" Gary asked.

"Not me, boss," Sully said.

"I didn't see any," Dan said.

John shook his head.

"Not in this scene, but some of the patients have moved since the last time I sampled the recordings," Ann said. She stopped playback and backed up to a freeze-frame. "There's Dick Edwards, obviously dead since he hasn't moved, since late Friday. And there's Dr. Canton. He hasn't moved either, so I assume he's dead, also."

"What about Helen Baker?" Gary asked.

Ann backed up to the Slammer Junior footage. The nurse was flat on her back but without any sign of bloody vomit. "She's moved some since the previous video, but who knows."

"Is that it?"

"One more scene."

Ann clicked the FAST-FORWARD button then selected PLAY a few seconds later. It was the inside of the guardhouse. A soldier sprawled on the floor, face up.

"Who is that guy?" John asked. "He's been in the guardhouse on every clip we've looked at."

"My guess is it's Sergeant Garcia," Gary said. "Zack said there was one soldier who seemed clear of the virus."

"Well, he sure isn't clear of it now," Ann said.

"Is he still alive?"

"I think so. He was sitting at the desk in the last video. Plus, there's no sign of him bleeding out."

"Yeah, but it's for sure he has the virus. Looks like Brevig's infection rate really did reach 100 percent."

Sergeant Garcia felt something intruding on the whirlwind of anxieties that roared around inside his mind, pushing it toward madness, but he didn't recognize what it was. Then it dawned on him. It was pain; pain in every part of his body; his lungs, his stomach, his joints, and his head felt like they would explode. He opened his eyes and saw the guardhouse ceiling. The light sent searing pain lancing through his optic nerve. He closed his eyes and fought down a sudden surge of nausea.

Cautiously Garcia opened his eyes and squinted. It was then that he remembered his duty. Colonel Roberts had been calling him every few hours until everything had gone black. Garcia couldn't remember when that had happened, and he had no idea what time it was now. He really didn't care about any of that, but his sense of duty would not let him rest. He knew he should call Colonel Roberts, but could he do it?

Garcia turned his head and saw his chair lying on its side. He must have fallen, although he couldn't remember doing it. If he was going to call Colonel Roberts, he *had* to reach the desk. He crawled over to the chair and rested for a few moments. Then, with a spurt of energy borne of desperation, he rolled over onto his hands and knees, turned the chair upright, and crawled up into it. As soon as he relaxed, he felt blackness coming over him.

By sheer willpower, Garcia forced it back. He looked at the phone and started to reach for it when he realized something. He opened his mouth and tried to speak, but only a rasping wheeze came out. He couldn't talk. A deep chill raced down his spine, adding to his miseries. He pulled his computer keyboard over, switched over to Outlook, and opened an e-mail message. For the To line, he selected Colonel

Zackary Roberts, left the subject blank, and tabbed down to the message body. But what should he say? He cycled quickly through the security cameras. He saw no one moving. The outside cameras showed it was still snowing hard, but he was surprised to see it was daytime. He glanced at the wall clock and saw it was a little after one in the afternoon.

Garcia turned back to the keyboard, determined to get his e-mail off. After a few moments' thought, his fingers slowly tapped out a one-line message.

I am the last one left. Be careful. Garcia

He clicked the SEND button and saw the e-mail enter his outbox. A few seconds later, it left there and merged with the Internet traffic on its way to the Institute's mail server. His duty done, blackness closed over Sergeant Garcia. As before, he never felt the fall.

The duty meteorologist for the Baltimore/Washington National Weather Service Forecast Office pressed the DISCONNECT button on his hi-tech phone. His office, part of the National Oceanic and Atmospheric Administration, was responsible for weather forecasts and more specifically warnings for the Baltimore/Washington, D.C., area, so why did the secretary of homeland security want weather advisories for Nome, Alaska?

It was 4:13 a.m., Monday, and he had just finished discussing the Nome weather with his counterpart in the Anchorage office. Of course, he already knew Nome's weather because he had been monitoring it ever since his shift began. His Anchorage colleague had simply confirmed it. But just to be safe, the meteorologist ran the satellite and NEXRAD loops again since he wasn't *about* to call Secretary Foster unless he was *absolutely* positive. He watched the trailing edge of the heavy snow clouds sweep past the small town on Seward Peninsula's south coast. He zoomed in and checked carefully. Yes, the weather in Nome was clear and cold.

That settled it. The man sat back in his chair and pondered the second thing that puzzled him. Why was he to call Secretary Foster rather than one of his assistants? But the e-mail had been quite specific. Call the secretary on his mobile phone, no matter what time of day or night. The weatherman leaned forward and punched in the number. He watched the satellite loop playing over and over as the phone rang.

Gary had awakened on the first ring of his phone. Ann's research late on Saturday had predicted clearing weather for Nome sometime early Monday. His bag had been packed since Saturday: two changes of clothing plus personal articles. Thomas had said homeland security and the Institute would provide everything else. John, Ann, and Dan would also have equipment to tote, mostly computers and communications gear. He and Sully would help with that. Looking around to make sure he was ready, he grabbed his bag and went out into the motel corridor. He was the last one out.

"Everyone ready?" he asked.

"I hope they know what they're doing," Dan said before any of the others could reply.

"I believe they do," Gary said. "But if anyone wants to sit this one out, I'll understand."

Dan shook his head, but he still looked worried. That suited Gary, since it was vital that the team members take every precaution. Gary led the way down to the motel office and saw that two Suburbans were already waiting for them. Thomas stood beside the lead vehicle. The drivers had the back doors open.

Gary walked out into the cool, early morning air.

CHAPTER 21

Gary turned all the way around slowly, taking in every detail of the complex military operation arrayed around the SecurityCheck team. Thomas Brooks stood with them on the broad concrete tarmac outside one of the mammoth hangers belonging to the Eighty-ninth Airlift Wing at Andrews Air Force Base. Banks of quartz work lights relieved the predawn darkness with brilliant illumination interspersed with long, black shadows. Gary looked inside the open doors of the closest hanger and saw one of the two Boeing 747s designated *Air Force One* anytime the president was aboard. The huge blue and white aircraft sat with its engine inspection panels open and flaps lowered while maintenance personnel performed their meticulous work oblivious of what was going on outside.

A twin-engine transport sat on the tarmac under glaring work lights while air force men and women continued their loading tasks. The plane, less than fifty feet away, was a C-32A, the air force version of the Boeing 757-200, tricked out for VIP travel. Its blue and white paint scheme and insignia placed it in the same family as the larger *Air Force One*. Behind the blue nose, the words UNITED

STATES OF AMERICA stood out in bold relief against the white of the upper fuselage, and a large American flag adorned the tail.

A chill wind blew across the broad expanse of concrete, a clear warning that fall was the precursor of winter. Gary zipped his jacket all the way up and stuck his hands in his pockets.

An army staff car drove onto the tarmac and swung in close to the SecurityCheck team. The doors opened, and Ken and Carol Underwood and a female major got out, each dressed in working uniforms. Ken and Carol spotted Gary and started toward him.

"Gary, this is Major Kathy Judson," Ken said. "Kathy's one of the doctors on our staff. She'll be heading up our medical team."

Gary shook her hand. "Pleased to meet you, Kathy." He introduced her to the SecurityCheck team. The doctor was short and rather stocky. She had bright red hair and lively gray eyes and a bearing that suggested dedication to her profession.

"I admire your courage," Ken said to Gary after the introductions.

"This is scary business," Gary said. "We're concerned, of course, but we want to help if we can. This virus *has* to be contained."

"In more ways than one," Carol said. "I'm just a researcher, but if terrorists get their hands on it—"

"Doomsday," Dan said.

Gary cocked an eyebrow at him. "Not exactly, but it could turn into a pretty good warm-up."

"Good morning, Ken," Thomas said. "Where's Nate? Isn't he coming?"

"He's riding with Colonel Roberts," Ken said.

"Zack's seeing us off?" Gary asked.

"He'll be here, and so will Secretary Foster."

"Really?" Thomas said. "Well, I guess that's not surprising, considering the circumstances. So who's going to be in charge when we get to Brevig?"

"I'm sure Secretary Foster and Colonel Roberts will cover

that," Ken said. "But it's my understanding that Nate will be in overall command; however, he'll probably have to cater to Hamid Momeni's wishes."

"Because it's Hamid's lab," Ann said.

"Administratively, that's correct." A wry smile came to Ken's face. "But in an emergency like this, control goes up through the chain of command to Colonel Roberts, so that puts Nate right in the middle."

"Weren't we going to take some troops with us?" Gary asked, remembering the previous conference with Secretary Foster.

"They left over an hour ago along with the bulk of our cargo," Nate replied. "A C-130 Hercules isn't as fast as the plane we'll be flying in. We don't want that slow boat holding us up."

"No, I guess not."

Another army staff car drove up. Colonel Zack Roberts and Lieutenant Colonel Nate Young got out and joined the group.

The army officers traded salutes.

"Morning, Colonel," Ken said.

"Morning, Ken, Carol, Kathy," Zack said.

He greeted the SecurityCheck team then turned back to Nate. "Wonder where the secretary is. Did you check with the duty officer before we left?"

"Yes, sir, Secretary Foster should be here any time now. Momeni and Alsaadoun are on the way, as well."

Zack's expression hardened. "Listen, Secretary Foster will lay out our orders, but I'm depending on *you* to take charge of the Institute's tasks. See that everything is done right."

"I will, sir."

"Anything new from Brevig?" Gary asked.

"The secretary will be conducting the briefing," Zack said.

A limousine and a black Suburban drove onto the tarmac and parked near the portable stairs that led up to the C-32's forward door. The limo driver hurried back and opened a rear door. Secretary Brad Foster stepped out and turned toward the Chevy. The Suburban's rear doors popped open, and Hamid and Saeed got out. Together the group approached Colonel Roberts.

"Good morning, Mr. Secretary," Zack said with a deferential nod.

"Good morning, Colonel Roberts," Foster said. He waved toward the stairs. "I think we'll be more comfortable inside the aircraft. Shall we?"

He led the way up the stairs. Gary waited while the various army and CIA personnel sorted out the pecking order. He followed Ken Underwood, with the SecurityCheck contingent right behind him. Gary's eyes grew wide as he entered the passenger cabin. The forward section, just aft of the flight deck, housed the communications center with enough lights, buttons, and displays to rival the spaceship *Enterprise*. He glanced back and saw Dan ogling this excess of electronic finery. This section also contained the galley, a lavatory, and ten business-class seats.

The entourage followed a side corridor past the private stateroom reserved for the primary passenger, usually the vice president or other high government official. Gary suspected this compartment would remain vacant since he doubted Secretary Foster would be accompanying them. The passageway opened up into a full-cabin-width conference area with eight chairs arranged in club seating around two tables. Gary was grateful they would be traveling in this aircraft rather than relegated to the noisy and uncomfortable C-130.

Secretary Foster stood to the side to allow the others to enter. "Sorry about the crowding," he said, "but this is the largest open area on the plane."

Gary immediately saw what he meant. There were only eight seats for fourteen people. Zack and Nate remained with the secretary; and Ken, Carol, and Kathy did so, as well.

Thomas picked one of the chairs on the left side of the cabin.

Gary, John, and Ann took the other three seats. Sully and Dan moved to the right. Hamid and Saeed, with obvious reluctance, joined them.

"I'll make this quick since I want this mission under way ASAP," Foster said. "First, Colonel Roberts will bring us up to date on the current status at Brevig."

Zack rattled off a concise bullet list, painting a stark picture of the horrors they would face when they reached the facility. He ended by quoting Sergeant Garcia's final e-mail—the last communications to make it out.

"I have just two more things to tell you. One, you'll have two UH-60 Blackhawks and two CH-47 Chinooks waiting for you at Nome." He glanced at Secretary Foster. "The commanding officer at Fort Wainwright was most cooperative when I made my request."

"My office is usually on the ball," Foster said.

"Yes, sir, they sure are. Now Colonel Young has a few words to say."

Nate looked all around, and his eyes stopped on Hamid. "Since I'll be in charge of safety and logistics, I wanted to give you a preview on how we're going to protect you once you're inside the hot zone. Listen carefully because what I have to say could save your life.

"All those entering the contaminated area will be wearing Racal field biological suits." Nate's gaze drifted over to Gary. "For those unfamiliar with them, they perform the same function as the Chemturion suits we use at the Institute, except these are designed to function without attached air hoses. A Racal is inflated by using a battery-powered pump to pull outside air through a virus-proof filter. This positive pressure prevents hot agent infiltration.

"All these suits are new, and each one has been inspected by qualified personnel. Once you're suited up, the only things you need to be careful of are suit tears and the battery running down. Any questions?"

"Will we have assistance?" Ann asked.

Nate's eyes made a circuit of the SecurityCheck team. "Yes. Institute personnel will assist all the observers. We'll check you over before you enter and make sure you're properly decontaminated on the way out. You'll be given more details during the flight and before we suit up for our initial insertion. This is just the preliminary indoctrination.

"Anything else?"

He waited a few moments then turned to Zack. "Colonel, that's all I have," Nate said.

"Thank you," Zack said. "Finally, I've asked Major Judson to say a few words." He turned to her. "Doctor. . ."

Her eyes went right to Gary. "This is primarily for our observers. There's no way I can adequately prepare you for what you'll see at Brevig Mission *and* what you'll smell. Trust me. It will be *far* worse than you can possibly imagine. One: If you're not sure you can handle it, let me know. Two: If you *do* decide to come with us inside the hot zone, I can administer meds to combat nausea. Don't take a chance; if you're not sure, see me. Throwing up inside a Racal suit helmet is extremely serious. Understand?"

Gary nodded. "Yes."

"You don't have to decide now. We'll be going over all the procedures again after we get there." She turned to Zack. "Colonel."

"I think that's it, Mr. Secretary," Zack said. "It's time we got these people airborne."

"I agree," Foster said. His eyes lingered on Kathy Judson. "Ladies and gentlemen, your first priority is to provide aid and comfort for any survivors. Next, and perhaps more important to the country, is bringing back the virus and vaccine samples. If you need *anything*, I'll see that you get it." His grim expression took in the entire group. "Good luck. America is depending on you."

With that, he turned and left the aircraft. Zack lingered a

moment, and Gary thought he saw a look of sadness in his eyes. Then he, too, was gone. Gary reflected on the secretary's patriotic benediction and saw something missing. In the not too distant past, before tolerance had become the national watchword, the phrase "Godspeed" had often accompanied such send-offs.

Gary snapped out of his reverie when he heard the forward cabin door shut. One of the fanjet engines began whining, followed moments later by its mate. Two air force passenger service specialists approached Nate Young.

"Sir, the aircraft commander says he's ready to depart whenever you're ready," one of the men said.

"Tell him we're all set. Where do you want us?"

"You have the run of the aircraft, sir, except for the VIP quarters. We have ten seats forward, these eight back here, and thirty-two more in the aft cabin. We're kind of loose on these flights, but the aircraft commander requests that all personnel be buckled in for takeoff."

"Very well. I'll take care of it."

The two men turned and went forward.

Nate looked at Ken, Carol, and Kathy then turned to the others. "You heard the man. Pick out a seat and buckle up."

Hamid stood up. "I'm going forward, Colonel," he said. "I must have access to the communications center."

Nate frowned. "As you wish."

Hamid and Saeed left.

Dan looked at Gary. "Think I'll go up there, also. I'd like to watch their comm honcho."

"Okay," Gary said. He had been expecting that.

Dan got up and went forward. That left three seats in the conference area.

"I'm going up front," Nate said to Ken. "I want to be near the flight deck."

Gary watched him go. He suspected Nate also wanted to keep an eye on Hamid.

The aircraft started to move. Ken, Carol, and Kathy joined Sully around his table.

"Welcome aboard, dudes," Sully said.

"Thanks," Ken said. "What do you think about all this?"

"This is some strange gig," the young man replied.

"That it is."

Gary suspected there would not be any delays leaving the Washington area. There weren't any.

The C-32A VIP aircraft had touched down at Nome at 11:04 a.m., a half hour ahead of the C-130 cargo plane, which had given Nate time to coordinate logistics with the helicopter pilots. The first order of business had been to make an initial trip to a site two miles west of the Brevig Mission facility, a safe distance upwind of the hot zone. Nate had gone out with this run, utilizing both CH-47 Chinooks hauling part of the C-32's cargo and the field tents and supplies provided by Fort Wainwright. Hamid had wanted to go along, but Nate had refused, saying that he would be too busy establishing the camp to allow for distractions.

Gary smiled at the memory of the altercation, partly because Hamid's personality grated on him, but also because of pent-up tension. It was a very dangerous thing the SecurityCheck team had agreed to do, but he had no doubt they were needed, since each member excelled in observation and investigation, amply demonstrated by the problems they had uncovered at the Institute. Secretary Foster certainly recognized talent when he saw it.

They were waiting inside a Nome Aviation Services hanger, the same one he and Ann had used to evade Colonel Edwards. The hanger doors were closed to keep out the cold, but unpleasant drafts still made it through the various cracks and openings, putting a chill in the air despite the powerful heaters mounted on the walls.

Outside it was a beautiful day. High, wispy clouds punctuated the deep blue sky. Gary found it hard to believe the revised weather forecast: clouds moving in before nightfall. To the south, the deeper blue of Norton Sound drew the eye to the horizon's distant line. A heavy blanket of snow covered everything, still a pristine white except for the roads and runways that had been plowed and sullied by traffic. The C-32 sat out on the tarmac, partially unloaded.

Gary looked toward the hanger doors where Hamid and Saeed stood looking out a window and drinking coffee. Hamid's eyes were fixed on the helipad. Saeed said something, but Gary couldn't hear him over the sound of the heaters. Hamid turned his head. His reply was masked, as well; however, the sour expression on his face left no doubt as to his disposition.

"If looks could kill," Ken whispered.

Gary looked around. "Yeah. Hamid does seem a little tightly wound."

"You don't know the half of it," Carol said softly.

"That dude needs a time-out big-time," Sully said.

Gary smiled. "I'm sure Nate would agree with you. But since he has friends in high places, that's not likely to happen."

"Bummer."

"Your objection is noted."

"What are we going to do when we get there?" Ann asked Gary.

He hesitated then realized his expression must have shown it. The SecurityCheck team rarely discussed current operations with client personnel present.

"We'll leave you to your planning," Ken said as he motioned for Carol and Kathy to come with him.

"No, stay," Gary said quickly. He smiled. "Old habits die hard, but we're not operating in spook mode right now. We're only extra eyes and ears."

Ken's eyes grew round. "Yeah, and those are *some* eyes and *some* ears."

Gary shrugged. "Thank you. The first order of business is taking care of survivors, right, Doctor?"

She smiled. "Please call me Kathy. To answer your question, yes, that's top priority. After the site is decontaminated, Colonel Young will give us our orders."

"Correct," Ken said. "Then comes recovery of the virus and vaccine—that's Hamid's thing—and tackling the hard part: How did the virus get out?"

"And that's where we come in," Gary said. "Well, for starters, we'll download all the computers and check out the electronic systems." Gary's gaze took in Ann and Dan. "You two will be in charge of that."

"Okay," Ann said.

"What about me?" John asked.

"You and Dan brought along your usual gadgets, right?" Gary asked.

"As much as Nate would allow."

"Good. Did you bring Sherlock?"

"Does DreamWorks make movies?"

"Okay, then there might be something for you to do, or at least Sherlock."

"Is the kid gonna get any action?" Sully asked. "Like, I'm not hearing about anything that needs driving."

"We'll have to see how it shakes out," Gary said. "You *may* end up snooping around like John and me."

The sound of a turbine engine spooling up cut through the mournful moaning of the wind. Curious, Gary walked to the front of the hanger and looked out a window. One of the UH-60 Blackhawks was preparing for takeoff, its massive four-bladed rotor already a blur. Ken and Carol joined him. The helicopter lifted off in a swirl of snow, turned, and flew off toward the west, leaving the other Blackhawk sitting on the helipad.

"Wonder where they're going," Gary said. "I didn't see anyone load that chopper."

"Nate said he'd be using one of the UH-60s to decon the facility," Carol said.

"How are they going to do that?" Gary asked.

"The army has aerial spraying rigs. I imagine they'll be using one of those with modified nozzles."

"What do you spray?"

"A strong solution of laundry bleach."

Gary looked at her in surprise. "You're kidding. Clorox?"

Carol smiled. "I kid you not. Bleach is one of the best viricides there is."

"Sounds like the price is right, too."

"Yeah. It's nice to get a bargain on something."

"How long before we go out?" Gary asked.

"After they finish spraying," Ken said. "Say an hour or two. Nate's anxious to go looking for survivors, but he's not going to risk our lives doing it."

"I'm in favor of that," Gary said.

A faint turbine whine drifted in from somewhere outside and grew louder rapidly. Gary turned toward runway 27 and saw a C-130 coming in from the east. The silver cargo plane made a tight approach and touched down, throwing up a billowing snow cloud as the pilot reversed the props. The low-slung transport turned onto a taxiway and began its approach to Nome Aviation Services. The turboprop roar increased steadily. The C-130 trundled past the parked C-32 and performed an ungainly pirouette to position the cargo ramp toward the helipad. The blast from the propellers shook the hanger doors and rattled the windows. The rear cargo ramp dropped, and as soon as it reached the tarmac, the engines began spooling down.

First off were the troops who would be doing the grunt work and guarding the Brevig Mission lab once the rescue team had things stabilized. Next a forklift began unloading pallets of gray steel caskets, forming a somber wall near the helipad.

The Chinooks had made multiple trips hauling the soldiers and supplies out, but so far the pilots had not come for Secretary Foster's special team. Evidently this fact had not set well with Hamid. Gary had observed him having an animated argument with Ken Underwood, after which the CIA operative had retreated to a corner to wait with Saeed. Later the second Blackhawk had flown out with a load of medical supplies.

Gary glanced at his watch and saw that three hours had elapsed since Nate had left and a half hour since the last Chinook flight, the one that had carried away all the caskets. A distant whine made Gary's ears perk up. He returned to the same window he had used before, looked toward the west, and saw a dense gray cloud bank on the horizon. An irritating whine accompanied by a heavy thumping sound penetrated the hanger and rattled the windows. It was an inbound ski-equipped CH-47.

"It's about time," Gary said.

Ken, who was standing beside him, leaned close. "Careful. You're beginning to sound like Hamid," he whispered.

"Perish the thought."

The Chinook landed, but the pilot did not shut down the engines. The aft ramp lowered slowly, and the loadmaster ran down it and over to the hanger. The man came through the door and looked around. Hamid started toward him, but the sergeant ignored him and approached Ken Underwood. The two exchanged salutes.

"Colonel Young says he's ready for the rest of the personnel, sir," the loadmaster said. "Said he wants everyone on the ground immediately."

"Very well, Sergeant," Ken said. "I'll round everyone up."

"Yes, sir," the man said. He saluted and ran back out to the helicopter.

Ken turned and raised his voice. "Let's go people. Colonel Young is ready for us."

Gary grabbed his bag and followed Ken, Carol, and Kathy out onto the tarmac. Up ahead he could see the loadmaster standing at the top of the Chinook's ramp, motioning for them to hurry. Gary instinctively lowered his head as he passed beneath the rear rotor and tramped up the ramp and into the helicopter's generous cargo bay. Nylon web seats lined each side. Ken, Carol, and Kathy dropped their bags, angled to the right side, and took the first three seats. Gary and Thomas came next, followed by John, Ann, Sully, and Dan. Hamid and Saeed stopped at the top of the ramp.

"Seats, gentlemen," the loadmaster said to them. He activated the winch to close the ramp.

Hamid and Saeed dropped their bags and sat in the first two seats on the other side. The ramp clumped shut with a clatter. Immediately the powerful helicopter leapt upward and arced in a ponderous turn to the west.

Gary looked out the round windows. Up ahead he saw a thick layer of gray on the horizon; the promised overcast was approaching. The helicopter's twin turbines whined away overhead, driving the tandem rotors. A loud thumping sound and a persistent vibration made the ride considerably less enjoyable than the quiet-riding C-32, and the pilots were obviously not dawdling. Gary ignored the uncomfortable web seat and the distracting whine of the engines as he wondered how they might help in investigating the disaster. In the abstract, it seemed an impossible task; however, he knew the team's track record, and that gave him hope.

Gary was still deep in thought when the turbines finally began to slow. He looked out a window and saw the gray clouds brooding over the blanket of new snow. Gary caught a glimpse of the Brevig facility off to the south, dark blotches against a gray and white background. The pilot was giving the site a wide berth indeed. The

CH-47 began a rapid descent. Slowing almost to a standstill, the helicopter entered a hover and settled heavily beside the other Chinook. The blast from the rotor blades whipped up the snow, temporarily obscuring everything.

The turbine whine dropped off rapidly as the loadmaster lowered the ramp. An icy blast whipped inside, turning the already cool interior frigid. Gary unstrapped, stood up, and grabbed his bag. Hamid and Saeed hurried out ahead of the others, leaving their bags behind. Gary started down the ramp and into the dull gray afternoon that seemed almost like dusk. His eyes scanned across the orderly ranks of cargo pallets until he spotted the stacked caskets. He felt an adrenaline jolt, a reminder of what the team was about to do. He looked up at the low, scudding clouds.

"You think we're far enough away?" Ann asked.

"I sure hope so," Gary said.

"We're safe," Carol said. "We're upwind, and besides, the virus couldn't live long enough to travel this far."

Gary thought that sounded like wishful thinking, but he said nothing.

Ken, Carol, and Kathy led the way toward an orderly cluster of tents. Several groups of soldiers were stacking supplies while others finished setting up the camp. Off to the right, both Blackhawks sat on the snow with their heavy rotor blades rocking in the wind. Gary noted the spray rig mounted on one of them and hoped the crew had done a thorough job of decontaminating the site. Ken caught up with the CIA operatives while Hamid was in the middle of a heated argument with Nate Young.

"You can enter the hot zone when I say so," the officer said.

"But this is *my* lab!" Hamid said.

"And *I'm* in charge of the rescue mission, and that includes the safety of all personnel."

"Afternoon, Nate," Ken said. "How is the operation going?"

Nate took his eyes off Hamid and looked at Ken, Carol, and Kathy. "We're finished with the external decon." He nodded toward the Blackhawk. "Next step is for us to plan the insertion."

"How long is this going to take?" Hamid interrupted. "I *must* get the virus and vaccine samples back to Fort Detrick."

Nate glared at him. "You'll be going in as soon as I go over the safety procedures with Dr. Judson and the Underwoods." He turned back to his officers. "Let's find someplace quiet." He motioned toward the nearest tent.

"Nate, will you be needing us?" Gary asked.

"What for?"

"To provide information of the equipment we brought."

The officer hesitated. "Very well," he said finally. "You and Mr. Mason."

"And Ms. O'Brien," Gary added.

"Okay, okay. *And* Ms. O'Brien. Now, let's go."

Hamid started forward.

"Please stay here, Mr. Momeni," Nate said. "These plans don't involve you."

Gary caught the acid glare Hamid shot the officer and wondered if Nate would be paying a price later. But for now all he could think about was entering the hot zone.

CHAPTER 22

Gary pulled on a pair of yellow rubber boots over his running shoes and stood up. He exhaled, and his breath fogged up the soft plastic bubble of the Racal helmet. The moisture slowly evaporated, but something else remained—anxiety brought on by being confined in a tight space. Gary's claustrophobia, although mostly under control, still popped up occasionally. This time had been a surprise, since he hadn't thought of the biosafety suit as being confining until Carol Underwood had slipped the helmet over his head. He took a deep breath and shook off the feeling.

Disturbing thoughts still reverberated inside Gary's skull from the pointed lecture Dr. Kathy Judson had given the Security-Check team. She had explained in graphic detail what they would see inside the buildings and, more important, the almost unbearable smells that would assault them. Again she had given them one last chance to back out. Gary had been pleased with the team's unanimous decision to see it through. When Kathy had offered them anti-nausea medication, no one had accepted. Now they were committed.

Carol pulled off two strips of brown sticky tape and sealed his boots to the legs of his suit.

"Hold out your arms," she said.

She applied two more bands to seal his sleeves to two layers of surgical gloves. Gary looked over at John, who was getting the same treatment from Ken. The brilliant orange Racal suits were certainly not designed with stealth in mind. Gary was beginning to sweat from the combined effect of the sealed suit, surgical scrubs, and thermal underwear, but he knew this would change once he went outside.

"Switch on the blower here," Carol said, pointing.

Gary turned it on. Immediately the suit puffed out, and the roaring of the air made it hard to hear. He sniffed strange odors and hoped that the virus filters would be up to the deadly environment that awaited him.

"Here's extra batteries," Carol said, almost shouting to make herself heard. "Be sure you know where they are. Change them when you hear the blower begin to slow down."

"Roger," Gary said. He stuffed them into the nylon bag containing the assorted electronic gear he would be carrying for John and Dan.

Ken finished helping John and checked over his work. Ann, Sully, and Dan were already done and waiting near the tent's exit. Dr. Judson was suited up, and Hamid and Saeed were almost done. Ken examined their suits, then he and Carol pulled on theirs, rapidly but also with great care. They checked each other over before turning to Nate.

"We're ready to go," Ken said, raising his voice.

Thomas stood off to the side, obviously relieved he would not be joining those entering the facility.

Nate looked around at the rescue team. "Okay. Now be careful, and make sure your decon is thorough."

"You know we will," Ken said.

"Got your radio?"

Ken pointed to the bag at his side. "It's in there."

"Very well. Keep in contact."

Ken turned to the others. "Okay, let's get a move on."

Gary followed Kathy and the Underwoods out under the gray, sullen skies. All four helicopters squatted on the snow, the Blackhawks looking like giant dragonflies. The rotor blasts from one of the Chinooks stirred up swirling white curtains. Gary caught a glimpse of soldiers clad in orange Racal suits before the cargo ramp closed. The CH-47 lifted off and clattered away toward the east.

"Where are they going?" Gary asked, raising his voice to make himself heard over his air blower.

"That's the decon team," Ken said. "They'll also prepare our paths inside the lab compound."

"Why? The snow's deep, but it's not *that* deep."

"You'll see when we get there."

An orange-suited crewman opened the side door on one of the Blackhawks. The turbines began to whine, and the rotor blades started turning. The SecurityCheck team followed Ken, Carol, and Kathy up into the cabin. Hamid and Saeed came next. The crewman climbed in and shut the door. Gary set his bag down beside all the others and took a seat.

The UH-60 leaped into the air and turned to the east. The dark splotches that marked the research facility grew rapidly in the windows; and even though Ken had assured him they would be safe, the approaching death compound made Gary uneasy. The pilot landed one hundred yards west of the facility, and the crewman opened the door. Gary waited for Hamid and Saeed to step down then followed them out beyond the rotor blast. He turned around and waited for his team, the Underwoods, and Dr. Judson. The Blackhawk lifted off and made a sharp turn to the west.

To the south, the Chinook sat hunkered down in the snow, its loading ramp facing the lab compound. Most of the soldiers were hauling out boxes and equipment and loading a series of sleds. One soldier mounted a snowmobile and brought it around to tow the first load. Another soldier climbed on behind the driver, and a third stepped up on the sled. The snowmobile driver pulled away slowly and angled slightly to the north.

"They'll start setting up the decon equipment," Ken said. "Follow me, and watch out for ice. The ground around the lab is a solid sheet from the decon runs. The water and bleach melted the top layer of snow."

He led them toward the compound's northwest corner until he reached the edge of the ice. Up ahead, the soldiers had finished unloading the sled, and the driver was on his way back. Ken circled around to the north until the rescue team reached the two soldiers. A light sprinkling of gray granules covered the ice in the immediate vicinity. Two serious faces looked out from their Racal helmets.

"Ready to lay down the paths, Sergeant?" Ken asked the nearest soldier, a young woman.

"Yes, sir," she said.

She held the handles of a bright green fertilizer spreader. Gary looked at the gray granules inside the hopper.

"What is that stuff?" he asked.

"Cat litter," the woman said. "Works great on ice."

Gary looked down and tested the surface with his boots. "Yeah, sure does."

"Do you have the bolt cutter?" Ken asked the sergeant.

"Yes, sir. It's over there." She released the spreader's handles and picked up the heavy orange tool.

"Let me take that," Sully said.

She hesitated then handed it to him. "Thanks."

"Okay, Sergeant," Ken said. "Let's get a move on."

The other soldier picked up an open bag and filled the hopper then picked up two more bags and fell in behind. The sergeant started out cautiously. A disc under the spreader scattered an even dusting of litter, making a wide path over the ice.

The rescue team followed the two soldiers single file over the gritty, gray surface until they reached the compound's gate. Ken turned around.

"Open it up," he said.

Sully took the heavy-duty bolt cutter and turned so he could see Gary.

Gary waved toward the high fence topped with razor wire. "Be careful."

"The kid always is."

Sully approached the gate, and with two snips of the powerful jaws, the heavy chain fell away. Gary and Ken grabbed the gate's frame and pushed it open. The overhead rollers squealed as they rolled over the icy metal track. Ken pulled his radio out of his bag and held it up close to his helmet.

"Quarterback, this is Referee," he said in a loud voice. "How do you read? Over."

"This is Quarterback, read you five-by-five."

"Roger. We are entering the hot zone."

"Copy that. Keep me informed, Referee."

"Roger, Quarterback. Referee out."

Ken returned the radio to his bag.

"You know where we want the paths?" he asked the sergeant.

"Yes, sir."

"Very well. We'll wait here."

The other soldier opened one of the bags and filled the hopper. The sergeant pushed the spreader through the gate, driving a path that led first to the lab building then to the dormitory. After another refill, the team made paths from the guardhouse to the dormitory and the lab. Then they came back to the gate.

"I think that's it, sir," the sergeant said. "Call me if you need anything."

"Will do."

"We'll be waiting for you when you come out."

"Thank you, Sergeant."

She and her assistant headed for their supply cache, laying down another layer of grit. In the distance, soldiers were unloading another sled.

Ken turned back to the compound. "Okay, let's go."

The rescuers trudged through the gate, past the facility's ice-covered Blackhawk, and into the courtyard. Off to the right, Gary could hear the diesel generators running. Up ahead, the Grand Cherokee and Humvees were as he remembered them, except for their glaze of ice.

"Okay, we divide up now," Ken said. "Remember, if you get a suit tear, tape it immediately and come see either Carol or me. Also, when your air blower starts slowing down, change out the battery. All clear?"

"Clear," Gary said. The other replies were indistinct, but he saw Ken make eye contact with each person.

Hamid and Saeed turned and began walking cautiously over the gray path toward the dormitory building. Carol led Ann, Sully, and Dan in the direction of the guardhouse.

"You ready, Doc?" Ken asked.

Kathy hesitated a moment. "Yes," she said finally.

Gary and John followed them over to the lab building. A body blocked the steps, almost buried in an ice-covered snowdrift. Gary and Ken broke through the ice, moved the rigid corpse aside, and set it down. Gary swallowed hard, trying to prepare himself for what he was about to see and smell.

Ken opened the door and went inside with Dr. Judson right behind him. Gary stepped up and crossed the threshold. An ocean of warm air washed over his frozen suit, causing condensation to momentarily blind him. With the air, delayed only a fraction of a second, came the stench, far beyond what he had imagined. The reek seemed to physically attack every breathing passage, and with the assault came an almost overpowering urge to vomit. Gary forced down the involuntary upwelling by sheer will. Slowly the vapor on his helmet evaporated, giving him his first look at the virus's grisly aftermath.

For several moments, he couldn't move. He looked all around and swallowed. Seeing the real thing was far worse than viewing the security videos, he realized. Corpses littered the white tile floor, their faces squeezed into masks of agony by a plague dormant for over eighty years. Some bodies had been placed there and covered with blankets; other victims had crawled to their final resting places because no one had been there to help them. Bloody vomit, now dark shades of brownish black, stained the bodies and splashed across much of the floor. And wrapped around it all was the horrible stench of death and decay.

Ann plodded along over the gritty path, following Carol. Her breath fogged the plastic bubble of her Racal helmet, making it difficult to see. Carol stopped at the guardhouse and opened the door. Ann looked past and saw a man sprawled on the floor face up. It was Sergeant Garcia. After a brief hesitation, Carol went inside with Ann, Sully, and Dan right behind her. Carol kneeled down and checked for a pulse. She turned and looked up at Ann.

"He's alive," Carol said. "Someone go tell Dr. Judson."

"I'm gone," Sully said. He turned and opened the door.

Gary edged into the clinic, stepping cautiously around the bodies that covered much of the floor. John stooped down and began checking the ones in the corridor. Ken stepped over and around the corpses on his way back to Slammer Junior. Gary and Kathy kneeled and began examining the four bodies sprawled across the clinic floor: three men and a woman. One of the men Gary recognized: Colonel Dick Edwards, the officer he had impersonated less than two weeks ago. Although Gary was sure they were all dead, he felt the woman's carotid arteries anyway. Nothing. He tried to move her head, but the neck was stiff.

Kathy finished her three and looked over at him. She shook her head and pointed to the ward. Gary got up and followed her in. He recognized Sergeant Davis and Captain Pratt, the helicopter pilot. Davis was obviously dead, and the other appeared to be, as well. Would they find *anyone* alive? he wondered. His suit blower droned away, making it hard to think.

"Help me!" Kathy said.

Gary looked around and saw she was examining Bob Pratt, holding one of his eyelids open. The man made a feeble move.

"He's still alive," the doctor said. "Hand me a glucose bag and an IV kit."

"What?"

She pointed. "Over there. Up on that shelf."

Gary stepped around a body. He grabbed a clear plastic bag then spotted a stack of flat plastic envelopes, each containing a coiled plastic tube and IV needle. He brought them over and waited while Kathy mounted a chrome pole on the pilot's bed. When she was ready, Gary handed the doctor the glucose bag. She hooked it on the support, inserted the needle, and started the IV.

"Is he going to make it?" Gary asked.

"Don't know," she replied. "He's very weak, but he doesn't show signs of massive edema—bleeding out."

Gary heard a shuffling sound behind him, barely audible over the racket of his air blower. He turned in time to see Ken rush in, his faceplate fogged up from exertion. "Come with me," he said. "Helen Baker's alive."

"Be right there," Kathy said.

"Who's that?" Ken asked.

"Bob Pratt, the helicopter pilot," Gary said.

"Grab another glucose and IV kit," Kathy ordered.

A noise out in the corridor attracted Gary's attention. The outside door opened, and Sully came in, tracking ice and grit with his yellow boots. He entered the clinic.

"Hey, Doc!" he said. "Sergeant Garcia's alive."

"I'll come as soon I can," Kathy said.

"Gotcha. I'll wait here."

Ken left the clinic. Gary grabbed the supplies and followed the doctor, passing John, who was on his knees checking bodies. Ken and Kathy went through the air lock entry into Slammer Junior. The nurse was on the floor with a blanket pulled up to her chin and a wadded-up coat under her head. Gary saw her bloodshot eyes fasten on the doctor.

"Thank *God* you're here," Helen managed to croak. Tears filled her eyes.

"Rest easy," Kathy said. "We're here to help you." The doctor turned to Ken. "Did you check the others?"

"Yes. She's the only one."

Kathy pointed. "Clear that bed," she said. "I need clean sheets, a pillow, and a blanket."

Ken grabbed the corpse under its armpits while Gary gripped the ankles.

"Be careful of your suit," Ken said.

"Don't you worry," Gary said with feeling.

They picked up the body and set it against the wall near the door.

"I'll strip the bed," Gary said.

He pulled off the top sheet easily enough, but the bottom one was stiff and stuck to the gurney's plastic-covered cushion. He held the cushion with one hand and peeled the sheet off. Dried chunks of bloody vomit fell to the floor. Gary gathered both sheets and the pillow and looked around.

"Toss that in the corridor," Ken said.

Gary stepped out and dropped the linen.

Ken opened a closet and grabbed clean sheets and a pillow. Gary covered the gurney's cushion then helped Ken lift Helen up. Gary covered her with the top sheet and eased the pillow under her head. Ken tucked a blanket around her while Kathy rigged the IV pole. Soon the doctor had the glucose drip going.

"What about Garcia?" Ken asked.

"I'll be ready in just a minute," Kathy said. She bent over Helen and checked her pulse. She turned to Ken. "Okay, let's go."

"I'll stay and help John. You go with Gary and Sully."

"All right." She looked over at Gary. "Let's see, we'll need glucose and an IV kit; oh, and a blanket and pillow."

Gary opened the closet and grabbed a blanket and pillow. He followed the doctor down the corridor, stepping over and around the bodies. Sully peered out at them from the clinic.

"Here, take these," Gary said.

Sully came out in the corridor and took the bundle while Gary picked up a glucose bag and IV kit. Sully opened the door and stepped outside with Kathy right behind him. As soon as Gary crossed the threshold, crisp, cold air began working its way through the filters and into his Racal helmet, diluting the stench of death, which he had largely repressed. He followed the others across the courtyard, grateful for this reprieve. On reaching the guardhouse, Sully held the door for them.

Ann crouched beside Garcia while Carol and Dan stood to the side. She looked around at Kathy.

"I think he's gone," Ann said.

Kathy kneeled down and checked carefully for a carotid pulse. She opened an eyelid with her thumb and shook her head.

"He's dead," she said.

"What should we do with him?" Sully asked.

Kathy looked at him. "Leave him here." She looked up at Carol. "Meanwhile, I have to get back to the lab."

"I'll go with you," Carol said.

"What about us?" Ann asked Gary.

"You and Dan start downloading the computer systems," he said. "Keep your eyes peeled for clues. Sully, come get me if you find anything."

"Right, boss."

Gary followed Carol and Kathy out into the courtyard. Off to the left, Gary heard a sound, barely audible over the noise of his air blower. He turned his head and saw Saeed shuffling across the ice waving his arms.

"Wait," he said, shouting to make himself heard.

Carol and Kathy stopped and turned.

"Something wrong?" Carol asked.

"Hamid wants to know when he can come for the virus and vaccine."

Gary saw Carol's expression harden. "When Colonel Young authorizes it and not one second sooner. Now, have you two finished checking for survivors?"

"Almost."

"Well, go back and help. Dr. Judson will be over as soon as we finish in the lab."

"I understand. I will give Hamid your reply." He turned and followed his tracks back to the dormitory building.

"We seem to be having some trouble with our priorities," Gary said.

"Don't get me started," Carol grumbled as they continued toward the lab building.

She reached the door and went inside with Kathy right behind her. Gary entered, and even though he had been expecting it, the nauseating stink almost overpowered him. He forced himself to take shallow breaths. When he felt his control returning, he stepped into the clinic and peered through the ward windows at Bob Pratt. With only two people still alive, that put the mortality rate at over 90 percent, so far. Not good. Gary returned to the corridor. John and Ken walked out of Slammer Junior.

"Are you done?" Kathy asked them.

"Yes," Ken said. "No more survivors. What about Garcia?"

"He didn't make it."

"Heard anything from Hamid or Saeed?"

"Saeed stopped us on our way back," Carol said. "No survivors over there, although they're not done. Hamid wanted to know when he could come for his samples."

Ken put his hands on his hips. "What did you say?"

"That it was up to Colonel Young and for them to finish what they were told to do."

"Good. I might have put it stronger than that." He turned to Kathy. "What's next?"

Kathy looked past him down the hall. "Clear the bodies out of Slammer Junior. Then clean up the place and move Bob Pratt in with Helen Baker. After I get them stable, I'll want to reexamine the bodies just to be sure."

"Okay. I'm due for a status check with Colonel Young. After that we'll get busy on the Slammer."

He picked up his radio but stopped when the outside door opened and Saeed entered.

"We need help," Saeed said. "The lights went off."

"What? The entire building?"

"No, just in the dormitory."

"I'll go check it out," John said.

Ken turned to him. "Okay. Thanks."

John followed Saeed out of the lab building.

Ken picked up his radio and walked away.

Gary stood in the corridor with growing impatience. Ken was still on the radio. Apparently it was taking awhile to bring Nate up to speed, but Gary was more concerned about John's absence. Kathy was still examining corpses in between checks on her two patients. The outside door opened, and John entered.

"What was it?" Gary asked.

"Circuit breaker popped," he said. "Took me awhile because the electrical panel was locked. Couldn't find the key, so I had to break it open."

"I hope you were careful. It wouldn't take much to rip these suits."

"Believe me, I was careful. Anyhow, I spotted the breaker right off, reset it, and flipped it back on. Problem solved."

"What caused it to trip?"

"Don't know. It's a GFI breaker because it also powers the bathroom circuits. They tend to be kinda squirrelly."

"Translation, please."

" 'Ground fault interrupter.' They prevent electrocutions when using appliances around water, like in bathrooms and kitchens. Only problem is they're sensitive and prone to trip even when no grounding fault exists. Anyhow, power's back on now, and Hamid and Saeed are finishing up."

Ken set his radio down and came over. Gary told him what John had found.

"Yeah, it's happened before," Ken said. "Dick asked me about it once. I checked with our maintenance people, and they said, 'Live with it.' "

"That's about all you can do," John said, "unless you want to take a chance on frying someone."

"Any change in our orders?" Gary asked Ken.

"Not yet. Nate wants us to finish our preliminary work: Take care of the survivors and keep looking for what caused the containment breach. After that we'll bring in teams to take care of the bodies."

Kathy approached Ken. "I need Slammer Junior made ready for my patients."

"Okay," Ken said. "We'll get right on it, but first we need to change out our suit batteries." He turned to Gary. "How about you and John tell the others."

"Will do," Gary said.

CHAPTER 23

The rescue team had been hard at work for several hours now. Kathy Judson had checked all the bodies; Helen Baker and Bob Pratt were the only survivors. Gary stood in the corridor near Slammer Junior and stepped aside to allow two Racal-clad soldiers past. The men picked up a corpse from the corridor and carried it away. On a recent break outside, Gary had seen the growing number of gray caskets arrayed along the fence opposite the lab building. Ken had told him that each body would be decontaminated, slipped inside a body bag, decontaminated again, and placed in a hermetically sealed casket. The caskets would remain in the courtyard until the army was absolutely sure there was no chance of the virus hitching a ride back to the nation's capital.

Clearing out the bodies would allow Ken and Carol to set up Slammer Junior for the two survivors; Bob Pratt had joined Helen Baker inside it in the last hour. It also brought Hamid a step closer to retrieving the virus and vaccine samples. Both he and Saeed were waiting in the dormitory building, which was also being evacuated of the dead.

"Hey, Gary," Ken said.

Gary turned. "Yes?"

"Do you have anything we can use to examine the lab's ductwork?"

"You think there might be a leak?"

Ken frowned. "Actually, no, but I still have to rule it out."

"I see. Sherlock might be able to help us out. Let's check with John."

John had been helping Carol and Sully clean Slammer Junior so it could be reestablished as a biosafety level-four suite. Once that happened, the two patients would not be coming out until they posed no danger. That also meant that medical personnel entering the Slammer would have to follow strict biosafety level-four procedures, the same as if they were back at the Institute.

Gary stuck his head inside the Slammer. "John, can you spare a minute? Ken and I need your help."

"Sure, we're almost done," John said. He came out into the corridor. "What's up?"

"Ken needs an up-close-and-personal check of the lab's ductwork."

"Using Sherlock?"

"Yeah. I know Sherlock can give us a good visual scan, but what we need is sound."

"I had to leave most of my gear behind, but there is one module that might help. I made him a microphone sensor that can hear a gnat blink."

"That might help. How long will it take to set up?"

"My bag's in the clinic. Give me fifteen minutes, and we'll be ready to go."

Gary stood in the corridor holding the stepladder while John clumped his way up and moved an acoustic ceiling tile to the side. John turned and held out his hand. Gary picked up Sherlock and gave it to him. The diminutive robot was about the size of a DVD player; and although it normally operated on wheels, for this mission it had been fitted with caterpillar treads. John lifted it through the hole and set it down.

"All yours," he said after he descended.

Gary picked up the controller and turned it on. Ken and John hovered on either side as the bright LCD display came to life.

"Where to?" Gary asked.

"The lab has two pairs of parallel ducts on either side of the corridor," Ken said. "They provide air supply and exhaust for the lab suites and Slammer Junior."

"Okay, let's check out the left side first."

Gary spun Sherlock on its treads and panned the camera back and forth. Several feet away a solid barrier about five inches high ran from the clinic all the way to the back of the building.

"What's that?" Gary asked.

"It's the ceiling for the left side biosafety level-four suites and Slammer Junior. It's double-walled and hermetically sealed, as are all the walls and the floor."

"No bugs in or out."

"Yes, but especially no bugs out."

Gary advanced Sherlock's throttle. The robot climbed the barrier with its treads and thumped down on top. Up ahead another barrier appeared, one of the sheet metal ducts.

"That's the air supply duct," Ken said. "The one for exhaust is on the other side."

Gary turned Sherlock parallel to the duct, pivoted the camera, and zoomed in. He stopped the robot and cautiously raised the gain on the sound amplifier. A sibilant sound came from the controller's speaker overlaid by a deep electrical hum.

Ken looked alarmed. "That isn't an air leak, is it?"

"Can't be," John said. "A leak would sound like Niagara Falls. That's coming from the air inside the duct."

"Would you mind looking closer, just to be sure?"

Gary moved Sherlock forward, and using the camera's telescoping mast, he examined the duct's top, side, and bottom. Then he returned the robot to its original position and settled it on course for the back of the building.

"See, the sound remains constant," John said. "There's no leak, at least not there."

"Let's hope it stays that way."

"Actually, if you had a serious leak, I think Sherlock would have already detected it."

It took a half hour for Sherlock to make the complete circuit. Gary parked the robot near where it went in and turned off the controller. Since Slammer Junior's air locks were operational again, Ken went and checked the containment sensor gauges. He was shaking his head when he returned.

"Everything's as it should be," he said. "We have negative pressure in all the biosafety level-four areas, and Sherlock shows no sign of air leaks in the ducts or filter units. There's no way that virus could get out."

"Maybe it came out on one of the scientists," Gary said.

"Unlikely in the extreme. Nothing could live through our decon procedures. Look, man, our people are professionals, and they *know* what they're dealing with."

"Hey, I'm on your side."

Ken's frustration was clearly evident. "Yeah, I know. There has to be a reason for this, and we *better* find it."

The outside door opened. A soldier came in and approached Ken. "Sir, we're ready to decon the vehicles."

"Very well," Ken said. "We'll get them out to you as soon as we can. Are the decon stations ready for when we come out?"

"Yes, sir. Do you know when that will be?"

"In an hour or so."

"We'll be waiting." He turned and left.

"Sully and I could drive the vehicles out," Gary said.

"Okay," Ken said. "That would be a big help. The keys are over in the guardhouse."

"What about Sherlock?" John asked.

"Don't worry, we're not going to forget your buddy," Gary said. "Hold the ladder."

John moved the ladder into position. Gary climbed the steps and poked his head through the hole in the ceiling. He reached over, lifted the robot, and moved down a step. He almost had Sherlock out when he felt his left sleeve snag something. A ripping sound accompanied by faint hissing shot an electric tingle down his spine. He glanced at his Racal sleeve and saw a one-inch gash.

"My suit's torn!" Gary shouted.

He stumbled down the ladder and handed Sherlock to John. Ken dashed to Gary's side and stripped off a piece of brown sticky tape.

"Hold out your arm!" Ken ordered.

He did so. The suit's torn fibers fluttered in the air stream provided by the Racal's air blower. Gary struggled to fight back both his fear of the virus plus a fresh bout of claustrophobia. After the tape sealed the gap, his suit puffed out again. Ken applied several more layers.

"Did you get it in time?" Gary asked.

"Don't worry, you're okay."

Gary saw the look of concern on Ken's face. "You're sure?"

Ken looked him in the eye. "About 99.99 percent. Look, what we're messing with is deadly, but I'm confident you weren't exposed. The tear wasn't close to your helmet, and we sealed it quickly. Besides, the air rushing out should have kept the pathogens outside the suit."

Gary felt some reassurance. "I hope you're right."

"Racal suit tears are fairly common, but I've never heard of anyone catching a bug because of one." He nodded toward the outside door. "Remember the vehicles?"

"Oh, yeah." Gary turned and went through the air lock doors into Slammer Junior. He raised his voice. "Hey, Sully."

The young Hispanic looked around. "Yes, boss?"

"Ken has something he wants you to drive."

Sully turned to Carol.

"Go ahead," she said. "We're almost done."

Gary led the way outside. Once again he felt relief as the cold, clean air infiltrated his suit, clearing the lingering stench of rotted flesh. He followed the gray, crunchy trail to the guardhouse and stepped inside. Ann looked around but kept working at her laptop computer.

"Where's Dan?" Gary asked.

"He's looking around the equipment room," Ann said.

"How's it going?"

"We're burning the last DVD now. Less than a half hour, unless we find something."

"Let me know if you do. Meanwhile, Sully and I have to drive the vehicles out. Ken said the keys were in here."

"Yes, they're in that cabinet by the door."

"Thanks."

Gary opened the cabinet and found three sets of keys, clearly marked. He handed Sully the keys to the two Humvees while he took the ones for the Jeep Grand Cherokee. They left the guardhouse and took the path that led to the vehicles. Beyond the far Hummer, tight rows and columns of gray caskets rested on the ice. Gary stopped beside the Jeep and found it covered by thick ice. Since the door was unlocked, he began yanking on the handle. After the third determined tug, the ice shattered, and the driver's door flew open with a shower of ice chips.

The nearest Humvee started, and the engine settled into a powerful rumble.

Sully jumped out. "Need some help, dude?"

Gary turned and saw he was brandishing an ice scraper. "No thanks, I can manage."

Sully started the other truck then began chipping away at the first vehicle's icy windshield.

Gary eased himself into the driver's seat, started the car, and set the defroster on high. He spotted an ice scraper on the floor. He grabbed it, climbed out, and began working on the ice. It took several minutes to clear a patch large enough to see through. He looked over at Sully.

"You ready?" Gary asked.

"Let's do it."

Sully hopped into the Hummer, backed it in a tight arc, and headed for the gate. Gary threw the Jeep into reverse, backed up, and almost spun out on the slick ice. He selected drive but, despite four-wheel drive, had a hard time controlling the vehicle. Up ahead, Sully had almost reached the orange-clad soldier waving him in. When he failed to slow down, the man turned and ran behind a tent. The Humvee entered a right turn, locked wheels, and spun around 180 degrees. Sully released the brakes and backed precisely into the decon station. Gary shook his head as he cautiously approached the heavy, squat truck. Sully jumped out and came around to the Jeep's passenger side. After a few yanks, he managed to force the door open.

"Awesome parking job," Gary said.

"Totally. Kinda freaked out that dude, though."

"He'll get over it."

Gary saw the Racal-clad soldier return with his decon sprayer. The man gave a tentative wave, which Sully returned with enthusiasm.

Gary drove back to the compound. Sully cleared the Hummer's windshield quickly, the ice softened by the defroster. His second delivery was just as precise as the first. Gary parked the Jeep short of the decon station, and he and Sully walked back to the compound. When they entered the lab building, Gary noted that the dreaded reek was less now but still quite strong. John and Ken were standing in the corridor near the Slammer. Kathy and Carol came out.

"My patients are stable," Kathy said. "The air lock, decon, and staging areas are set up. I'm ready for you to reestablish Slammer Junior at biosafety level four."

"Consider it done," Ken said. "From now on, you have to decon going in and coming out."

"I understand."

"Are we ready to retrieve the virus and vaccine samples?" Carol asked.

Ken turned to Gary. "What's the status on your team?"

"We'll be done with the downloads any time now."

"Find anything in the guardhouse?"

"Not so far, but we need to take a look inside the dormitory building."

"Okay, but be quick about it. We'll have to leave after we box up the samples."

"I'm on it, boss," Sully said.

"How about telling Hamid we're ready for him," Ken said.

"Will do."

"I'll go with you," John said.

They left the building, and several minutes later, Hamid and Saeed came in, each toting a large stainless steel box. They didn't say anything but went right into the staging room and continued through the decon and air lock rooms and finally into the biosafety level-four lab, which was home to the revived 1918 virus. Hamid came around the worktable in the center of the room and set the box down on it. Saeed placed his next to it. Hamid opened both boxes, pulled out two thin metal containers, and handed one to his assistant.

He looked up then, and his eyes met Gary's for a moment before he turned to Saeed. Hamid said something, but Gary couldn't hear what it was. Saeed opened the container and began inserting vial after vial into the fitted interior.

The building's outside door opened. Gary turned his head and saw Ann come in toting her laptop and a nylon bag. Dan followed a few moments later. They set down their burdens and joined the group watching at the lab window.

"Did you find anything?" Gary asked.

"I was busy burning DVDs," Ann said. "Dan did the looking around."

Gary looked at him.

"Not a thing," Dan said. "All communications and monitoring equipment is operating normally."

"Where are John and Sully?" Ann asked.

"Checking out the dormitory building."

Gary turned back to the lab window. Hamid took the first container from Saeed, sealed its seam with tape, and placed it inside one of the boxes. He lowered the top and latched it.

"Those are the virus samples," Ken said.

"Why such large boxes?" Gary asked.

"To allow plenty of room for padding. Remember, those boxes are coming back with us."

Hamid handed his assistant the second container. Saeed filled it as carefully as he had the virus samples and returned to the table. Hamid took the container and, after sealing it, placed it inside the remaining box. He closed and latched it.

"And that's the vaccine," Ken said.

"Too bad it wasn't ready sooner," Gary said.

"Yeah."

Saeed and Hamid each picked up a box. They walked around the table and through the air lock, stopping inside the decon shower.

Hamid grasped a chrome handle hanging from a chain and pulled. A disinfecting spray enveloped both men. They turned around in it and held the boxes up to make sure they were covered, as well. After several minutes, Hamid turned the shower off and exited the lab suite through the staging area. The two scientists came into the corridor still dripping.

"I'm ready to leave," Hamid said.

"Set the boxes down," Ken said. "I have to radio Colonel Young first."

Hamid hesitated; then he and Saeed complied.

Ken turned to Gary. "Go get John and Sully."

"I doubt they're done."

"Can't be helped. We have to egress ASAP once we have the samples. Besides, they're not going to find anything over there. The problem is in the lab—somewhere."

It went against the grain for Gary to leave anything undone, but Ken and Nate were in charge. He left the lab building and followed the gritty, gray path over to the dormitory. He stepped inside and saw Sully going through the storage cabinets in the dining hall. He looked around.

"Time to go," Gary said, raising his voice.

"I'm not done," Sully said.

"Doesn't matter. I'll meet you outside."

"Right, boss." He turned and headed for the door.

Gary walked into the dormitory but didn't immediately see John. He looked all around as he made his way back and finally spotted an open door off to the right. He went in and found John examining papers on a desk.

"Find anything?" Gary asked.

John jerked around. "Hey, man," he said. "How about letting me know you're there?"

"Sorry."

"To answer your question, no. This was Colonel Edwards's room; thought there might be some clue in here, but no such luck."

"I'm not surprised. Ken says it's time to go."

"Okay."

Gary could tell he also was dissatisfied with the rushed investigation, but they weren't in charge. By the time they got outside, the others were coming out of the lab building, dropping their bags and equipment as they went. Ken angled toward Gary.

"Nate says for us to hustle," Ken said. "Leave anything you brought with you in that pile over there."

"All our stuff is in the lab building," Gary said.

"We've already cleared all that out."

"What about Sherlock?" John asked, his voice rising.

"The samples and DVDs come out," Ken said. "Everything else stays here."

"I'm not leaving without my buddy."

"You don't have any choice," Ken said evenly. "Nate's orders; everything that comes out has to be deconned. We can't take any chance of the virus hitching a ride."

"Okay, so decon Sherlock."

"But the water and bleach will ruin it."

"Let me worry about that."

"Have it your way."

Ken waved his arm and pointed toward the open gate. "Let's move it, people," he said, raising his voice.

John grabbed Sherlock and its controller and fell in beside Gary and Sully. Ann dropped back and joined them; Dan came next.

"I sure hope they're thorough with this decon business," Dan said.

Ken had them all spread out single file before they reached the waiting Racal-clad soldiers standing in front of a rectangular box-shaped assembly of pipes and spray nozzles. Hamid and Saeed went first. One soldier took the boxes, sprayed the exterior of each one with a hand wand, then opened them, sprayed the insides, and dunked the samples in a large basin. The soldier then returned the containers to their boxes. Another soldier conducted the two scientists through the decon shower, which sprayed them from every conceivable angle. A strong bleach smell made it through Gary's helmet filters and made his eyes water.

The process was very thorough, which raised Gary's confidence level a few notches. John helped a soldier disassemble Sherlock and its controller and watched as each part disappeared into the bleach solution. He held out his hand for the parts, but the soldier pointed him toward the shower. After John endured this, he returned and reassembled his soggy robot. Gary walked into the shower and held his arms out as he had seen the others do. The spray hit him with surprising force and completely obscured his vision. After the spray cut off, he shuffled out of the way to make room for Ken.

Off to the west, Gary heard a heavy thumping sound. He turned and saw a Blackhawk approaching low. Even though it was only a little after four, the sun was low in the western sky. Soon they would be flying back to Washington, D.C., with the 1918 virus but without any idea how it had decimated the Brevig Mission lab.

At 6:05 p.m., under an overcast evening sky, the Chinook touched down at Nome Aviation Services, and the loadmaster lowered the ramp. Hamid and Saeed got to their feet, picked up the sample boxes, and were first off the helicopter. Ken jumped up and hurried after them. Gary and Thomas, caught by surprise, had to hustle to catch up.

Gary walked out from under the rotor blades. "What will happen to the lab?" he asked Ken.

"I'm not sure, but my guess is we'll keep it open until we can bring the survivors and the remains home," Ken said. "Then we'll probably nuke it."

"Will Nate have to stay until then?"

"That's up to Colonel Roberts and Secretary Foster, but he'll certainly be heading up our base camp for the short term."

"Not a very pleasant job."

"Got that right." Ken looked ahead at the soldiers waiting near the C-32 transport. "Excuse me. I have to take charge of our logistics."

John and Ann caught up. He held Sherlock while she carried the controller.

"Sure you can fix your gadget?" Gary asked.

"No problem," John said. "He's tougher than you think."

Sully and Dan joined them.

"Man, that dude only knows one tune," Sully said.

Gary followed Sully's gaze and saw Hamid arguing with Ken, although he couldn't hear what they were saying. Ken finally swung his arm in an exaggerated invitation to proceed. Hamid and Saeed, each carrying a box, followed an airman up a ramp and into the C-32's cargo hold.

"Doesn't trust *anyone* with that virus," Ann said.

Gary turned to her. "If that makes us safer, I'm all for it."

After the two scientists emerged, Ken supervised the loading of what remained of the rescue team's baggage. He then came over and took Carol by the arm. "Go find the aircraft commander," he said. "Tell him we're almost ready to go."

Carol nodded, went up the portable stairs, and entered the plane. A few minutes later, she came back down and waved for the team to approach.

"The flight crew is ready for us," she said. Behind her, the cargo hatch closed with a loud thump. "Please hurry. Take the same seats."

Hamid and Saeed turned and started up the ladder.

Carol pulled her husband aside. "Secretary Foster's on the secure phone for you," she said.

He looked distracted. "Did he say what for?"

"He wants a status report."

"Okay. You get everyone situated."

He turned and started up the stairs. Carol and Thomas fell into step and led the rest of the passengers onto the airplane. They went through the door and turned right. Gary followed them past the VIP quarters and into the conference area, where he and the others selected their former seats. The sound of the cabin door closing drifted back. One of the engines started whining, and the other quickly joined it.

Exhaustion rolled over Gary as the horrors of the long day receded just a little. He had been up since early Monday morning, eastern standard time, and after a seven-hour flight, had endured seven hours cooped up in a Racal suit, his senses of smell and sight assaulted by death and decay all around him. Now he faced a five- or six-hour flight followed by whatever debriefing Secretary Foster decided to put them through.

The plane began to move. Gary closed his eyes in hopes he would be able to sleep but, even as he did, knew it was impossible. The memories were still too fresh, too disturbing. And underneath it all was the nagging question: What would happen if terrorists managed to revive the 1918 virus?

CHAPTER 24

W ake up," a voice said, thin and far away. Gary ignored it and returned to his interrupted quest. He was about to find out how the virus
had escaped; he was sure of it. Now that he had finally gotten his legs
to work, all he had to do was burst into the lab building and. . .

"Wake up," the voice said again, this time much louder.

Gary awoke with a start and slowly came to realize where he
was. Despite his earlier belief that he would not be able to sleep, he
had drifted off shortly after takeoff from Nome. He saw John looking down at him.

"Are you all right?" John asked.

Gary blinked in the subdued lighting. "Yeah. I was dreaming
about how the virus got out."

"And?"

"You woke me up before I found out. What's up?"

"We're on final approach to Andrews. Ken said we have to hit
the ground running."

"Why?"

"Two words: Secretary Foster."

Gary managed a feeble smile. "Spill it."

"They're flying us to Fort Detrick by air force helicopter. Then, after Hamid and his buddy lock up the virus, the secretary and Zack Roberts are going to debrief us."

"Cool. Then we stand down until sometime Wednesday."

"Sounds good to me." John retreated to his seat, sat down, and buckled up.

The C-32 swept over the Potomac. Gary looked out his window at the vast grid of light that outlined the Washington, D.C., area, covering it like a luminous blanket. He looked to the north and saw the Capitol's dome and the Washington Monument. The landing gear deployed with a solid thump, and the engine whine increased. The plane flew over I-495, which was already heavy with traffic. The plane made a sharp turn onto final approach, dropping ever lower until two loud chirps announced touchdown. The rescue team was back where they started from. The preceding twenty-four hours seemed like a month to Gary; and although he was glad the ordeal was over, lingering doubts clouded his mind.

The aircraft taxied to their earlier departure point, only this time *Air Force One's* hanger doors were closed. There on the tarmac squatted a huge helicopter.

"Look at the size of that thing," John said.

Gary's eyes traced the bulky fuselage and the immense spread of its rotor blades. "That's an air force MH-53 Pave Low."

"What do they use it for?"

"Insertion of special forces personnel into hostile environments. It has terrain-following and avoidance equipment."

"Looks like Secretary Foster doesn't want to take any chances on getting the virus to Fort Detrick safely."

"Yeah, speed, safety, and security."

The plane came to a stop, and the ground crew rolled stairs up to the forward door. Gary released his seat belt and stood up. Ken appeared in the aisle.

"Get a move on, everyone," he said. "Go straight to the helicopter. The crew will take care of your baggage." He turned and left.

Gary followed Thomas out. Up ahead he saw Hamid and Saeed hustle out the forward door followed by Dan. Ken and Carol stood to the side, anxious expressions on their faces. Gary stepped through the door and went down the steps. At the bottom, he glanced back at the open cargo hold and saw Saeed standing there; Hamid, he guessed, was inside taking charge of the all-important virus and vaccine.

Gary hustled across the tarmac to the helicopter, went up the loading ramp, and took the seat next to Dan. John, Ann, and Sully came next, while Thomas waited near the loadmaster. A few minutes later, Hamid and Saeed struggled up the ramp with the heavy steel boxes and set them down. The loadmaster carried them forward and lashed them to the deck. Finally Ken and Carol boarded.

"Tell the pilot we're ready to go," Ken said.

"Yes, sir," the loadmaster said. He returned to his station and hit the switch to raise the ramp. "Ready for takeoff, sir," he said into his intercom mike.

A high-pitched whine came from one of the Pave Low's turboshaft engines, followed soon by the other. Moments later the lightly loaded helicopter leaped into the air and turned northwest toward Frederick.

Gary stared through a window as two figures in bulky Chemturion space suits entered the biosafety level-four lab. In addition to the SecurityCheck team, the witnesses included Thomas, Ken, Carol, and Zack Roberts. The two shipping boxes sat on a table near a lab bench. Hamid opened one, reached inside, and brought out a container. He handed it to Saeed, who removed the tape and carefully transferred the vials to a test tube holder. Then the men started on the second box.

"Which box is which?" Gary asked.

"The virus was in the first box," Ken said.

"I sure am glad this part is over."

"Don't you know it."

After Hamid and Saeed finished, they picked up the boxes and lugged them through the lab to the decon showers. Hamid pulled a chain to start the process.

Ken turned to Zack. "Is Secretary Foster here yet?" he asked in a low voice.

"He's waiting for us in the conference room."

Gary could tell from his tone that the USAMRIID commander was not looking forward to the debrief. Gary didn't know how he felt about it, except he was uncomfortable. Discovering how the virus had gotten out had been a long shot, but he still couldn't shake a vague sense of failure. But they had done their best, and that's all anyone could ask.

Several minutes later, Hamid and Saeed came out. Colonel Roberts led the way to the elevator lobby. Gary reviewed the mission one last time on the short trip up to the conference room near Zack's office.

Secretary Foster stood at the head of the table and watched them enter. He seemed fresh and alert in his neatly pressed gray suit and gleaming black shoes. The man was obviously ready to do business.

"Seats, people," he said.

Zack, Ken, and Carol followed Hamid and Saeed around to the far side of the table. Thomas took the first seat on the near side, while Gary and the SecurityCheck team flanked him on the right. When they were all in place, the secretary sat down and turned to Zack.

"Are the virus and vaccine secure?" Foster asked.

"Yes, Mr. Secretary. I witnessed it myself."

"Good. Proceed with the debrief, Colonel."

Zack turned the first part over to Ken, who quickly reviewed all they had found at the Brevig Mission lab: how the two survivors had been found and what was being done for them. Then he described the temporary disposition of the bodies and ended by saying they still didn't know how the virus had gotten out.

"Thank you, Ken," Zack said. Then he turned to Foster. "Mr. Secretary, there's something I'd like to ask."

"Go ahead, Colonel."

"What do we say to the next of kin? Per your orders, I've kept a tight lid on this whole situation."

Foster took his time in answering. "I know," he said finally, "and the lid *stays* in place, at least for now. This incident is classified *beyond* top secret until such time as the president says otherwise. We have *two* problems: We don't know how that virus got out, and we don't know what that Saudi sleeper cell is up to. What happened at Brevig does not get released until *I'm* satisfied America is protected against the 1918 virus."

"Until we start large-scale vaccine production."

"Exactly."

"But what about the relatives?"

"They understand their loved ones are involved in secret research, don't they?"

"Yes, sir, of course they do. But secret work or not, the Brevig personnel still had limited access to phones and e-mail. My office is receiving concerned calls."

"Handle it, Colonel. Say the work is entering a critical phase or something, and the personnel will be out of touch for a month or so."

"Yes, Mr. Secretary," Zack said, clearly unhappy about it.

Secretary Foster's eyes drifted over to Hamid Momeni. "When will you and Mr. Alsaadoun start work on the vaccine?"

"Tomorrow, Mr. Secretary."

"What are your plans?"

Hamid glanced at Gary before turning back to the secretary. "I cannot go into details, but basically we have to culture the vaccine samples to the point where a commercial lab can take over."

Foster nodded. "Very good. Let me know if you run into any snags. This work ranks near the top of national priorities."

"Thank you, Mr. Secretary. I will do my best."

Secretary Foster turned to Gary. "Does SecurityCheck have anything to add?"

"Colonel Underwood covered most of our involvement. We downloaded all the facility's data onto DVDs; we looked around for anything that could explain the outbreak. We even had one of our robots check out the lab's ductwork. We didn't find a thing."

"Do you have *any* theory on how the bug got out?"

"No, Mr. Secretary. I do have one question, however."

"What's that?"

"Will you be needing our services any longer on this incident?"

Foster took his time answering. "No, I don't think so," he said finally. He glanced at Thomas. "Get with Mr. Brooks, and plan out how you'll finish the security audit."

"Yes, sir." That was the answer Gary expected, and in a way he was relieved. At the moment, all he wanted to do was crash then, starting tomorrow, get to work on finishing the report.

Ken walked down the corridor with Carol at his side. It was nearly eight in the morning and time for their conference with Zack. Yesterday the colonel had informed them they would be meeting with him daily until the work was finished at Brevig. Then they had discussed the Institute's involvement with Hamid as the CIA agent's lab entered initial vaccine production. After that would come the research on the virus itself.

Ken knocked on the door.

"Come," a voice inside said.

Ken opened the door, and he and Carol entered.

Zack got up from his desk and headed for his conference table. "Ken, Carol; good morning. Please sit down. Care for some coffee?"

"Yes, thanks," Ken answered for them. He and his wife sat down while Zack filled three mugs from an insulated pitcher.

"Rested up from your trip?" Zack asked.

Ken picked up his mug and took a sip. "Getting there," he said. "But I'm going to be a long time getting over what I saw up at Brevig."

"I know," Zack said. "But we have to stay focused. I wanted to expand a little on what we discussed yesterday. I know you're aware of the awkward relationship the Institute has with Hamid and Saeed."

"Yes, sir."

"The way *they* see it, they're working for the CIA and ultimately homeland security. But the army holds *me* responsible for the lab: how it's used, accidents, and so on. Needless to say, it's a sticky situation. Nate is normally my liaison between Hamid and the CIA, but with him up in Alaska, I need you two to fill in."

"We understand," Ken said.

"I'm sure you do, but this job is doubly important now. We have the ongoing work at Brevig Mission, including your knowledge of how that lab was built, plus the research and vaccine production going on in Hamid's lab. Both of you are to set aside your current work so you can help me out here."

Ken nodded because he had been expecting this. "Yes, sir. What are your orders?"

"First, I want Carol to help Nate with his tasks at Brevig."

"Will I be going up there?" Carol asked.

"Not for now. You'll be more valuable to him working here."

"What do you have for me?" Ken asked.

Zack's look of concern changed to a frown. "You get the fun job, riding herd on our good friend Hamid Momeni. You're my eyes and ears, Ken. Keep me informed on what he and his sidekick are doing."

"He's not going to like it."

"Tough. That lab is *still* my responsibility." Zack paused. "This will, of course, require diplomacy on your part. If you come down too hard on him, I'll get flack from above, and I don't need that. So tread lightly."

"I'll do my best."

Zack's gaze took them both in. "I know you will. I count myself fortunate to have the Underwoods in my command."

"Thank you, sir. We feel fortunate being assigned here. Any news from Nate?"

"Routine stuff. His troops are proceeding with decontamination of the interior spaces. Kathy Judson is looking after Helen Baker and Bob Pratt. They're both doing quite well, but it'll be awhile before we can bring them home."

"Any idea how long that will be?" Carol asked.

"Not yet. That'll be something you two will be helping us determine. We have to be sure they're not contagious and that the virus isn't hitching a ride out on them."

"Talk about a bunch of unknowns," Ken said.

"That's why we're going to be extra careful," Zack said. "Any more questions?"

"Just one. Can we ask Gary and his team for help?"

"No. They are to finish the security audit and pack up and leave."

Gary looked up from his review of the audit report draft. This was the part of their work he liked least, but it had to be done and done right. He pushed his laptop away and sat back in his chair. It was then that he saw Ann's quizzical expression.

"What's up?" he asked.

"I'm not sure," Ann said. "I'd like you and John to look at this."

John looked around. "See what?" he asked.

"Videos from the dorm security camera."

John set down the circuit board he had been working on. Sherlock lay disassembled before him on the workbench. He came over and stood behind Gary.

Ann transferred the image on her laptop to one of Dan's monitors.

"Secretary Foster said we were done with Brevig Mission," Gary said.

"I know, but the DVDs we burned contained these image files. I was cataloging the files before turning the discs over to Zack's people when I happened to see this."

"Roll it."

Ann clicked the PLAY button. A few seconds later, Hamid Momeni walked into the dorm from the dining hall and entered a room on the right.

"Checking for survivors," Gary said.

"Right." Ann clicked the FAST-FORWARD button.

Saeed entered at quick-time and began checking the rooms on the left while Hamid continued down the right side until he reached the last room. Ann clicked the PLAY button. A few seconds later, the video blanked out.

"That's where the circuit breaker tripped, right?" Gary asked.

Ann clicked the PAUSE button. "Yes." She looked back at John. "What's in that last room?"

"It's a four-person room, the one next to Dick Edwards's room," John said. He paused. "It's also where the circuit breaker panel is located, as if you didn't know."

Ann clicked the PLAY button. The video flickered then steadied. A few moments later, John came out of the far room, walked under the camera, and disappeared. Ann fast-forwarded again. Hamid and Saeed entered the dorm and continued their work. The video ended.

"Don't you think it's a little strange?" Ann said. "Hamid enters the room where the breaker box is, and a few moments later, the breaker pops."

"Okay, I'll play your game," Gary said. "The breaker box was locked."

"Maybe Hamid had a key."

"That's a stretch. He's never stayed at Brevig, except as a visitor. Where would he get a key?"

"It was his lab, just like the one at the Institute. If he wanted a key, I'm sure he could have found a way."

"Okay, let's say he *did* have a key *and* turned off the power. Why?"

"I'm not sure, but it seems odd that it happened while we were busy looking for how the virus broke out."

"Whoa, hold on there," John said. "Are you suggesting Hamid let the virus loose on purpose? That it wasn't an accident?"

"The lab did *not* have a containment failure."

"That we found," Gary said.

"Think of how many experts signed off on this, plus the up-close-and-personal inspection by Sherlock."

"I'm sorry, but that doesn't prove a thing. Containment is extremely difficult, and we may *never* know the cause. In all likelihood this is a rabbit trail."

Ann looked at John. "Do you really think that breaker tripped accidentally?"

He hesitated, and a look of concern came to his face. "I have to admit, that *does* bother me. I don't understand why it tripped, especially since the circuit was stable. But who knows? GFI breakers are goofy; they're known to be sensitive."

"Is that a 'yes' or 'no'?" Gary asked.

"It's 'I don't know,'" John replied firmly.

"As intriguing as all this is, we're overlooking one *very* important fact," Gary said.

"What's that?" Ann asked.

"Hamid Momeni is a CIA spook, and as such he's been vetted like you wouldn't believe. The dudes that do security background checks do *not* mess around. Look, sometimes strange things happen, and we *never* find out why."

"Are you suggesting I'm working on a conspiracy theory?"

Gary saw her determined expression and recalled the results of Ann's past work for SecurityCheck. "No, I'm not," he said slowly. "I take what you say *quite* seriously. But I don't know what to make of your observations *this* time around."

Ann looked at the blank monitor. "At this point, I don't, either. But it bothers me. Should we call Thomas?"

Gary considered it. "I think we might be seeing things that aren't there. But, yes, we better give him a heads-up. Dan, put me through—on speaker."

"Coming up," Dan said.

The phone clicked after the first ring. "This is Thomas Brooks."

"Thomas, this is Gary. We've come across something we thought you should hear."

"What is it?"

Gary quickly reviewed what Ann had found and the team's concerns. When he finished, the speaker remained silent.

"Thomas, are you there?" Gary said finally.

"Yeah, I'm here. I don't buy it. You said yourself it could be coincidence, and I think that's *exactly* what it is. Listen. I know how thorough the CIA background checks are. Hamid Momeni is squeaky clean; believe it."

"Okay, it's your call. If anything else turns up, I'll call you."

"Thanks. Bye."

The connection went dead.

Ken went through the careful process of checking out his Chemturion space suit, and only then did he proceed through the air lock and into the biosafety level-four lab. He attached to a coiled air hose and approached the workbench where Saeed stood. Ken could tell that the man didn't want company.

Ken stepped close and raised his voice to be heard over the roar of air in his suit. "Have you started work on the vaccine?" he asked.

"No. I am waiting for Hamid."

Ken saw there were two sets of vials on the workbench. "You checked out both the vaccine *and* the virus?"

"Yes."

"What does he plan on doing with the virus? We're supposed to be getting the vaccine ready for production."

"Hamid said he wants electron microscope pictures for reference and documentation."

"What else did he say?"

"Only that I was to check out the samples and wait for him."

"I see. When is he supposed to get here?"

"He was due an hour ago."

"Did he say he might be late?"

"No."

Ken looked at the man's face, framed by his space suit's faceplate. Was it irritation he saw, or anxiety, or something else? "Well, I'll leave you to your work," he said finally. "Tell Hamid I need to see him."

"I will."

Ken disconnected his air hose and hurried toward the air lock.

Carol waited until 1:00 p.m. to call Nate, to give him time to get his day started. The Institute's comm center patched her through using

308

the automatic radio repeater recently installed in the Brevig lab guardhouse.

"Colonel Young," Nate said. His voice had a slight electronic twang left over from the voice encryption electronics. In spite of that, he sounded worried, but then he usually did.

"Good morning, Nate," Carol said. "This is Carol. Colonel Roberts wanted me to check and see how things were going. He's assigned me to be your expediter here at the Institute."

"Yes, I know. I just got off the phone with him a few minutes ago."

"How are things progressing?"

"Slowly. We're continuing our decon work inside the buildings, but there's no hurry since it will be awhile before the survivors can leave."

"How are they doing?"

"Kathy says they're in surprisingly good shape, although still quite weak."

"Any new theories on how the virus got out?"

"Not a thing, but we're still looking. I'm convinced it wasn't a defect in the lab. Maybe it got out on one of the lab workers."

"Surviving the decon shower? I don't think so."

"I hear you, but how else do we explain it?"

"I don't know. Listen, call if you need anything. Meanwhile, I'll be in touch."

"I will. Thanks."

The line clicked dead.

CHAPTER 25

hat's going on?" Zack demanded, an angry scowl on his face.

"I have no idea," Ken said.

Hamid Momeni had not shown up for work on Wednesday; of that Ken was quite sure. It was now almost 8:00 a.m. on Thursday, October 14, and Zack was beginning to show the strain.

"Let me see if I have this right. Saeed checks out the virus and vaccine, says he's waiting on Hamid, only Hamid never shows up, so Saeed finally checks the samples *back* in and goes home."

"Yes, sir."

"What time did he leave the building?"

"According to security, he swiped his badge out at 1404 hours— 2:04 p.m. I guess he didn't have anything else to do, so he went home."

"Have you tried to reach Hamid?"

"Yes, sir. I called his apartment yesterday. After I deconned out of the lab, I checked with security to see if he was in the building. Then I called him at home and left a message on his answering machine. I called again near quitting time and also tried his mobile number but got his voice mail. I did the same that evening; same results."

"This is absurd. Listen. I want you to grab Hamid the moment he enters the building. I want to know *what's* going on, and don't let him put you off with any CIA baloney."

"I understand. I told security to notify me as soon as either he or Saeed comes in."

"Good."

"Anything new from Nate?"

"No. It's going to be months before we're done up there."

"How are we going to decide when it's safe to bring the survivors home?"

Zack's face slid into a weary smile. "You and Carol get to figure that out."

The phone rang. Zack picked up the handset. "Colonel Roberts," he said. His eyes bored into Ken's. "I see. Yes, I'll tell him." He hung up the phone. "Hamid just came in through the rear entrance."

Ken jumped to his feet. "I'll call you later."

The elevator doors opened. Ken stepped out and proceeded down the corridor as fast as he could without attracting attention. Up ahead he saw Hamid disappear through the door leading into his lab suite. Ken reached the door, swiped his badge, and entered. The CIA agent had his briefcase open and was looking at a paper.

"We have to talk," Ken said, aware that his tone was preemptory.

Hamid looked up and frowned. "Is that so?" he said. "I report to the CIA, not Colonel Roberts."

"Yes, but you are *still* subject to USAMRIID security regulations and procedures."

"I am well aware of that. I abide by your rules."

"We'll see. Where were you yesterday? Our lab report had you down for initial research on the virus and vaccine."

"I was away on CIA business. I phoned Saeed and told him to

311

cancel Wednesday's schedule and said we would start on Thursday."

Ken felt heat rising in his face. "Not according to Saeed! He checked out the virus and vaccine and said he was expecting you in later."

"That can't be!" Hamid said, almost in a shout. For the first time in Ken's memory, the agent appeared unsure of himself. "You are sure of this?" he asked.

"Absolutely! I talked to him myself in this lab."

"This makes no sense." Hamid grabbed his mobile phone off his belt and punched in a number. He held the phone to his ear and listened as his scowl deepened. "This is Hamid," he said finally. "Call me." He looked at Ken. "His voice mail picked up." He tried another number. After what seemed like a long time, he punched the phone off. "He's not in his apartment, either." Hamid returned the phone to its holder. "This is very serious."

For a few moments, Ken could not come up with a reply. He felt a sudden chill as he thought about Saeed acting without the consent of his boss, having access to a lab containing the world's deadliest virus, and now the man couldn't be reached. "Serious? We're talking national emergency here!"

"Don't jump to conclusions. There must be a logical explanation."

"You better *hope* there is."

"I must consult with my boss at Langley."

"You do that. In the meantime, this lab is closed."

"You can't do that."

"You just watch me. Gather your personal effects and clear out."

"What about my technicians?"

"I'll take care of them." Ken motioned toward the corridor door. "Hurry up. I have a lot to do."

It took until after four for Ken to gather enough information to give

Zack an acceptable status report and for him to find out the full extent of the newest disaster, one potentially far worse than the outbreak at Brevig. Although he had access to all the Institute's resources, he had to do many of the tasks himself, and that took time. He knocked on Zack's door and, after receiving a reply, entered. His boss turned away from the window. He looked worried.

"I hope you have good news," Zack said.

Ken braced himself for what he had to say. "No, sir. In fact, it couldn't be worse." He waved a file folder. "I had virus and vaccine samples from Hamid's lab photographed by an electronic microscope. It's ordinary swine flu. The 1918 samples are missing."

Zack shook his head. "No! There *must* be some mistake."

"I wish there were. I had the samples run twice, and the results are conclusive."

Zack's hands were trembling slightly. Ken had never seen him do that before.

"How? How could that *possibly* happen?"

Ken shook his head. "No idea, except it *had* to be Saeed."

"Have you notified any of the homeland security people?"

"I notified Hamid's boss right after I posted guards on the lab. I called again after I got the electron microscope results."

"What did he have to say?"

"Just that the agency would be taking over the case, including notifying law enforcement. I asked if they would be giving us status reports, and he said no. But we're to keep *him* informed of whatever we discover."

"That figures." Zack paused, and he seemed unsure what to say. "Secretary Foster called me about an hour ago. He wants to know what's going on. I told him I'd call back after I talked to you." Again he paused. "What in the world am I going to tell him? He's going to go *ballistic* when he hears about the missing virus."

"Yes, sir, I'm sure he will," Ken replied

"And he's not the only one. This will leave burn marks clear up to the army chief of staff and beyond. Which reminds me, we better make sure *we're* covered. Our security procedures had better be perfect."

"I've already checked that out. We're clear. All security systems are working properly, and the log entries are complete for the time in question. We logged all personnel into and out of that lab."

"Who all had access?"

"Yesterday, it was Saeed and one of our technicians and me when I went inside to ask where Hamid was."

"Saeed and the technician were the only ones handling the samples?"

"Correct."

"And Saeed checked them back in?"

"That he did. And I caught Hamid before he entered the lab, so the theft had to be sometime yesterday."

"But how?"

"Don't know that."

"Did you check out Hamid's claim that he called Saeed?"

"Yes, sir. A friend of mine over at the judge advocate general made inquiries for me. Took some digging, but he finally located the right mobile phone company. Hamid did in fact call Saeed yesterday and talked for a little over four minutes."

"Anything else?"

"Yes, sir. The virus and vaccine we brought back are the only samples in existence. I knew that was our plan, but I checked with Nate to be absolutely certain. To get back to where we were, we'll have to reopen the Brevig lab, culture the virus, and re-create the vaccine."

Zack groaned. "How long will that take?"

"I don't know. Carol could give us an estimate since she helped establish the original protocols."

"Do it. When Secretary Foster calls, we better have some answers."

"What did Nate have to say?" Ken whispered to Carol as they struggled to keep up with Zack.

"After his initial shock and blowup, he went on a long rant about Hamid," Carol replied. "After he calmed down, he gave me the status report. Then he asked if we were planning to restart the lab up there."

"Guess we'll find out shortly."

They entered the conference room. Secretary Foster stood at the head and looked around at the newcomers. He looked grim and drawn. Hamid sat on the far side of the table. Ken was surprised to see Thomas sitting opposite Hamid but figured he must be representing SecurityCheck. Zack sat next to Thomas. Ken and Carol took the seats to the right of their boss.

The secretary sat down, and his earlier frown grew even deeper. "People, I've called you here for one thing: I want answers—not alibis, not excuses, *answers*. I *demand* to know what went wrong and what we're going to do about it!" He stopped, and his eyes fell on each one there. Then he waved toward the center of the table. "I have Colonel Young on the speakerphone. Can you hear us, Colonel?"

"Yes, Mr. Secretary."

"Good." Secretary Foster looked at Thomas. "Mr. Brooks, *you're* here to take care of some unfinished business. As you recall, I decided the SecurityCheck team would no longer be involved in the situation at Brevig. It's my understanding that they're done once they turn in the report, is that correct?"

"Yes, Mr. Secretary," Thomas said.

"For reasons that will become apparent, you are to get with Mr. Nesbitt and set a definite date for them to turn in their report. Tell him they are *forbidden* to contact any of the personnel they've worked with. Also remind him that what they have seen and heard is classified *beyond* top secret, and if they divulge *any* of it, they'll be looking at a long stay in a federal pen. Any questions?"

"No, Mr. Secretary. I'll take care of it."

"See that you do." Secretary Foster paused, and his piercing brown eyes passed over the army personnel. "To say this is a national emergency doesn't *begin* to cover how bad off we are. What you people don't know, because you had no need to, is that the agency has fresh intelligence on the Saudi sleeper cell. They've been expecting a breakthrough for some time in obtaining the 1918 virus. Unfortunately, we now know their source."

Zack's mouth fell open. "What?"

"If you'll allow me to finish, Colonel. It's obvious that Saeed Alsaadoun took the virus and vaccine; the only question is how. It seems there's a security loophole in how USAMRIID handles these things."

"With all due respect, Mr. Secretary, no there's not," Zack said.

"Then how did Saeed get his hands on the samples?"

"We don't know that yet, but I've gone over our procedures with Colonel Underwood. They're airtight."

"No, Colonel," Foster snapped. "It's obvious they're not."

"What about Saeed? How did he slip past CIA vetting?"

Foster's eyes flicked over to Hamid.

"We are checking into that, Colonel," the agent said. "But right now, I think the secretary is more interested in finding the security loophole and then discussing how we go about re-creating the virus and vaccine."

"I think that sums it up pretty well," Foster said.

"Okay, let's start with USAMRIID procedures," Zack said. "Yesterday, the virus and vaccine were checked out to Saeed, who was never alone with the samples."

"Who was with him?"

"One of our technicians and for a short time Colonel Underwood. In the afternoon, Saeed checked the samples back in."

"Did you have complete accountability on the trip from Brevig?" Zack looked to Ken.

"Yes, Mr. Secretary," Ken said. "There were multiple witnesses every step of the way. We watched Hamid and Saeed load the vials into the shipping containers; we were with them when they carried the boxes out and went through decontamination and on the trip back."

"Then you're saying at least one of your personnel observed each and every step."

"Yes, with only one minor exception."

"What was that?"

"Hamid insisted on loading and unloading the boxes on the C-32. During those times, he was assisted by the airman responsible for the cargo. I talked to the man at length, and he's *positive* the boxes were not tampered with in any way."

"Colonel Young," the secretary said. "Are you *sure* they loaded the correct virus? Is it possible they picked up the wrong stuff?"

"They had the correct vials, Mr. Secretary, no doubt about it. There weren't any other samples in that lab. I checked carefully after the rescue team left to make sure it was clean."

Secretary Foster frowned. "Well *someone* messed up, and we *will* find out who before we're done. But right now we have to head off this crisis. If that Saudi cell has the virus, we *have* to come up with new vaccine. Are you sure there's none at Brevig?"

"Absolutely positive," Nate said. "It was the plan all along to leave nothing behind because of security concerns."

"What will it take to crank up production again?"

"Carol is the best qualified to answer that since she designed the original culturing process," Zack said.

"Well, first we would have to make Brevig functional again," Carol said. "We'd have to recertify the containment structures then train replacement scientists, technicians, and support personnel. And at some point, we'd have to bring Major Baker and Captain Pratt home. . .and the bodies."

Foster waved impatiently. "How long?"

"I'd say a month to six weeks."

"We may not *have* that long if the terrorists get cranking on that virus."

"It can't be done any quicker, Mr. Secretary."

Secretary Foster looked at Zack. "Get moving on this, Colonel. I want that lab back up ASAP." He paused and his face lost its color. "People, unless we find these terrorists *and* stop them, we're looking at the end of America; I don't know how else to put it. If over half of our citizens are wiped out. . ." He stopped and cleared his throat. "Law enforcement agencies are being mobilized as I speak, but I *have* to know how long we have."

Ken saw his wife look toward Zack. Their commanding officer gave a barely perceptible nod.

She turned to Secretary Foster. "Worst case, two weeks."

Gary took his time walking across the Institute's brightly lit parking lot, his mood matching the nighttime gloom that hovered just beyond the security lights. He had a lot to think about—even more after his emergency meeting with Thomas. They had concluded their business quickly, and what Thomas had said didn't make sense and still rankled. Gary opened the truck's rear doors and climbed inside. All eyes were on him.

"So what did he want?" John asked.

"It's more what he *didn't* want," Gary said in irritation.

"What?" Ann said.

"We are to cease and desist. We are not to contact anyone even remotely associated with what we've been working on; USAMRIID, homeland security, CIA, what have you. He reminded me—actually it was more like a threat—we are not to disclose *any* of what we've seen or heard on penalty of a long stretch in a federal slammer. 'This never happened,' was one of the things he said."

"What in the world is going on?" John asked.

"Thomas wouldn't say, but obviously something's up. I've never *seen* anyone that worried."

"Something related to the virus?" Ann asked.

"Yeah, has to be, but what?"

"You don't suppose there's been another outbreak?"

Gary felt a sudden chill. "You mean here? I sure hope not. But whatever it is, it's obviously a full-blown national emergency, and we're just in the way, according to Thomas."

"Hey, they need us, man," Sully said.

"Big-time," Ann added.

"I hear you, but those are our orders," Gary said.

"So what do we do now?" John asked.

"Thomas says to wrap up the report, and I agreed to deliver it to him next Friday. Then he'll give us our final check, and we'll be on our way back to sunny California."

"I hope they know what they're doing," Ann said. "What about our link into the Institute's intranet? Want me to nuke it?"

Gary hated to give it up but knew it was the right thing to do. "Yeah. Be sure and cover your tracks."

"They'll never know I was there." She turned to her laptop and began keying furiously.

CHAPTER 26

At precisely 8:00 a.m., on October 22, Gary and John sat waiting inside the truck's command center, the meeting time and place Thomas had specified. But the truck was parked outside the team's motel rather than in the Institute's parking lot. The missive banning them from Fort Detrick had come with Thomas's earlier order to cease and desist.

"This is a bunch of claptrap," John grumbled.

"I agree entirely," Gary said. He looked up at a monitor. "Well, there he is, right on time."

Thomas turned in, parked, and got out of his car. He was dressed in a dark suit for the occasion. The outside mikes picked up the crunch of his footsteps as he approached. He reached the back doors and, after a brief hesitation, knocked.

Gary stood, walked to the doors, and opened them. Thomas scrambled up inside and waited until Gary closed the doors.

"Shall we get to it?" he asked, avoiding Gary's eyes.

Gary motioned to the chair Dan usually occupied. "There's the report," he said.

Thomas sat down. Gary and John took the chairs flanking him. Thomas eyed the thick document, riffled the pages without enthusiasm, then pushed it aside. He reached into his suit coat, pulled out an envelope, and gave it to Gary.

"Your final check," he said.

Gary opened the envelope, unfolded the check to verify the amount, then looked at Thomas. "So is that it? Thank you, good-bye, and keep your traps shut? What's going on, Thomas?"

Thomas looked Gary in the eye and shook his head. "No comment. But remember what I said. Secretary Foster is deadly serious."

"Please tell the secretary not to worry. We wouldn't survive in this business if we were blabbermouths."

"Okay."

"And one more thing. You better also tell him he *needs* us. Digging up secrets is what we do best."

"I *know* that, Gary, but there's nothing I can do."

"Okay, I've had my say." Gary paused. "Good luck."

Thomas picked up the report and stood up. "Yeah. We're sure going to need it."

Gary and John stood. John let Thomas out then turned back to Gary. Worry lines creased his forehead. "Am I reading this right? Has something else gone wrong, or are they still flailing around about the virus outbreak?"

"Don't know, but I sure have a bad feeling about it."

"I think this calls for some serious prayer."

"Let's do it."

After Gary had briefed the others on Thomas's final words, he had expected to pack up and head for home. But somehow he hadn't been able to decide that. They all believed that leaving would be a dereliction of duty, despite Secretary Foster's orders delivered through

Thomas. So they had spent a long and largely unproductive weekend hunkered down in the truck's command center trying to figure out what had happened. Although Ann had spent a lot of time prowling the Internet and sifting through the mountain of files left over from the security audit, she had come up with nothing. It wasn't until midmorning on Monday that this changed.

"Gary, come look at this," Ann said.

He came over and sat down beside her.

She transferred the laptop window to an overhead monitor and clicked the PLAY button. It was a familiar image: The Brevig dormitory corridor, but it seemed to have an odd flicker.

"Is there something wrong with the video file?" Gary asked.

"No." Ann selected freeze-frame. "I alternated one-second shots from recordings taken roughly thirty minutes apart. "Here's a blowup."

An enlarged shot of the bathroom door at the end of the corridor appeared; then over it, she merged another shot. The outlines of the door did not quite match up.

"The camera seems to have shifted slightly," Gary said. "When were those recorded?"

"Before and after the power went out in the dormitory."

Gary hesitated. "What are you suggesting?" he asked.

Ann looked around at John. "Did anyone touch that camera after you reset that breaker?"

John shook his head. "No, at least not while I was there."

"The second image was recorded *immediately* after the power came back on."

"You're suggesting someone tampered with the camera while the power was off," Gary said.

"Not exactly. What if someone *replaced* the camera, using the power outage as the opportunity to do it without being detected?"

"Whoa, heavy-duty," Sully said.

Gary closed his eyes as he thought about the implications. A chill settled over him. "I assume you're connecting this to the cause of the virus outbreak."

"I am," Ann said.

Gary turned to John. "What do you think?"

"According to our research, that camera would be an ideal place to hide an aerosol device," John said. "It's up high, and everyone has to pass underneath it."

"Yeah, all you need is an opportunity to install it and then some way to dispose of it later."

"And there are only two possible culprits: Hamid and Saeed."

"Correct. They took the cameras to Brevig, and they were the only ones in the dorm when the power went off." Gary snapped his fingers and turned to Ann. "Did you check the outside cameras?"

"Yes," Ann said. "The north-facing camera is too close to the dormitory building to show the entrance."

"Rats. That sure would have helped."

"So is it Hamid or Saeed?" John asked. "Or could it be both?"

"Good question," Gary said. "We know that a Saudi sleeper cell is supposed to be trying to revive the 1918 virus, and Saeed is of Saudi extraction."

"Slow down," Ann said. "It was Hamid who arranged the trip when the cameras were installed."

"Saeed could have been looking for an opportunity, which the trip conveniently provided," Gary said.

"Yeah, good point."

Dan turned away from his communications gear. "You're all overlooking something."

"What's that?" Gary asked.

"This is *all* circumstantial. One, we don't know *what* Secretary Foster is upset about, if anything. We were at the end of our job, and Thomas could just be making it clear we're not to divulge sensitive information."

"Man, if that's the scene, that Foster dude needs an attitude transplant," Sully said.

Dan held up his hand. "And two, the outbreak at Brevig could be what the army thinks it is: an unexplained containment breach, end of story."

"Those are good points," Gary said slowly. "It *is* all circumstantial evidence, but I'm convinced that something else has gone wrong. And if the outbreak at Brevig *was* deliberate. . ."

"It sure would be nice if we could check it out," John said.

"I agree, but that's kinda difficult with us being on the outside." He turned to Dan. "Put me through to Thomas's mobile phone."

After the third ring, "Thomas Brooks."

"Thomas, this is Gary. We—"

The line clicked dead.

"Want me to try again?" Dan asked.

Gary shook his head. "No, get me Colonel Roberts."

Gary waited while the phone rang.

"Colonel Roberts's office, may I help you?" an unfamiliar voice said.

"Put me through to Colonel Roberts," Gary demanded.

"Whom shall I say is calling?"

Gary hesitated then said, "Gary Nesbitt of SecurityCheck."

"Mr. Nesbitt, I have standing orders not to receive your calls. Do not call this number again."

The line clicked dead.

Gary turned to John. "This isn't getting us anywhere. We need proof, and there's only one way we're going to get it."

John's eyes grew very round. "You're not suggesting we go up to Brevig, are you?"

"You got any other suggestion?"

"Man, I don't know about that. Sneaking into a heavily guarded compound to look for a smoking gun that might or might not be there?"

"We've done harder things," Gary said. "Listen, I want everyone to turn to and start digging. If we strike out, fine, we've given it our best shot. But if Ann is right, we *have* to act."

Ken waited until 1:00 p.m. to call Nate. He had the comm center place the call then waited.

"Colonel Young," Nate replied.

"Morning, Nate, this is Ken. How's it going?"

"As well as can be expected. I know this is something we have to do, but cleaning up the site and preparing for reactivation at the same time. . . It's a zoo."

"I know. So what's the status?"

"We've deconned the insides of all the buildings except for Slammer Junior. Everything is clean, and we *still* haven't found out what caused the outbreak."

"We may never know."

"Don't say that. Listen, does anyone know what we're going to do with the survivors?"

"Not yet. Training the replacement crew currently takes precedence."

"When can we expect them?"

"Carol told Secretary Foster it would take at least a month to have everything up and running. The secretary is pressing Zack pretty hard, so we're aiming for two weeks from today. Carol is heading up the recruiting and training as we speak."

"What about Major Baker and Captain Pratt? Can we bring them home that soon?"

"We'll have to see. If not, they'll have to stay in Slammer Junior while we crank up the lab around them."

"Man, I don't like the sound of that."

"Hey, we follow orders. You need anything from us?"

"No." The line went silent for a few moments. "Are we *sure* Saeed was the one who snatched the virus?"

"It certainly looks that way. Gotta run. Call me if you need anything."

"Will do."

By late afternoon, Gary was bleary-eyed from staring at his laptop's screen. He was viewing the Brevig facility's security videos made during Hamid's visit to install the new cameras. As he had expected, he saw nothing out of the ordinary. He shut down the player and sat back in his chair.

"Gary?" Ann said.

He scooted his chair back so he could see around Dan. "Yes?" He noted the look of concern on her face.

"Take a look at this."

He moved his chair around Dan and sat down. The top window seemed to be a spreadsheet, but one look at the title bar and buttons told him it wasn't Excel. "What's that?" he asked.

"Security log records," Ann said. "I decided to poke around in the files we saved on disk. The top record shows Saeed Alsaadoun entering the Institute through the back entrance. He swiped his badge at 7:54 a.m. on Wednesday, October 13. The next record logs him out at 2:04 p.m."

"Mighty short day."

"Yeah, but the kicker is that Saeed hasn't been back to the Institute since then."

"What? He's supposed to be working on the vaccine."

"Wait, there's more. This other window shows log records for Hamid's lab." Ann pointed to the first two lines. "There's Saeed and another person entering the lab together at 8:21."

"Who's the other one?" Gary asked.

"I don't recognize that ID, but it has to be one of Hamid's technicians. I can probably find out if you want."

"No. Keep going."

"This next record is for Ken Underwood. He came in at 11:36 and left at 11:42. Then Saeed and the other person left at 1:41, and that's it for Wednesday."

"The lab wasn't used the rest of the day?"

"That's correct. Now here's Thursday. Hamid entered his lab at 8:09 a.m. and Ken right after him. Then at 8:18, they both leave, and that's it. From then until we shut down the link, that lab has been empty."

"What? And the Institute is *supposed* to be cranking out vaccine? That doesn't compute."

John came over and stood behind them. "I'll say it doesn't," he said. "What's going on?"

"Good question," Gary said. He stood up, walked to the front of the command center, and turned around. "We've seen a lot of strange things over the past two weeks. Talk to me. What's going on?"

"Those CIA dudes released the virus with that camera," Sully said.

"Quite likely, but let's work backward from current events. The Institute is supposed to be going all out on vaccine production, and yet Hamid's lab is lying idle. Why?"

"Either they can't produce the vaccine, or they've hit a snag," John said.

"Maybe," Gary said. "Is there anything else that could account for it?"

"They could have moved the production to another lab," Ann said.

Gary thought for a moment then nodded. "Good point. That's possible, I guess, but unfortunately there's no way we can check it out."

"They never said anything about another lab," Sully said. "It was always Hamid and his best bud, Saeed."

"Also a good point," Gary said. "If they didn't change labs, what could keep them from producing the vaccine?"

"Maybe the vaccine is dead," John said.

"That's a possibility, I guess, but why not start work on culturing a new vaccine from the virus they brought back? If they did it in Brevig, they can do it here."

"What if neither the virus nor the vaccine made it back?" Ann asked.

"As opposed to being sterile?" Gary saw the answer in Ann's eyes before she could answer.

"Yes," she said.

"Dudes, this is freaky," Sully said.

"Correct. That is the scariest thought of all," Gary said. He looked at each team member. "Can anyone find a hole in that argument?"

"No, but it's sheer guesswork," Dan said.

"I know that. Unfortunately important decisions often rest on circumstantial evidence, and if we sit here and do nothing, a lot of people could die."

"But we *saw* the samples come back, from the time Hamid and Saeed packed them until they were safely inside Hamid's lab," John said.

"Let's get an unreality check from Sully," Gary said. "Could someone have made off with the virus and vaccine?"

"You mean like Hamid or Saeed took it?"

"Just in general."

Sully thought for a moment. "I'm not sure either of those dudes has the skills, but, yeah, I think it's possible. There're lots of ways, but which one?"

"Hold that thought."

"Now we're back to the virus outbreak," John said.

"Right," Gary said. "That happened right after they cultured the vaccine."

"Isn't *that* convenient? So did the culprit remove the aerosol device or swap out the entire camera?"

"Could be either. The next question is: Where did he hide it?"

"Inside the dorm somewhere?" Ann asked.

Gary shook his head. "Too likely to be found. I'd say outside in the snow. The northern security camera doesn't cover the front of the dorm or the sides until near the back."

"So who's the bad dude?" Sully asked.

"Could be either Hamid or Saeed or both," Gary said. "But since Saeed hasn't been back to the Institute, he seems the likely one."

"Assuming this is all true, what do we do about it?" Dan asked.

"Call Thomas. Tell him we *have* to see either Zack or Secretary Foster."

"He won't talk to you."

"Hey, it's the only chance we have." Gary's eyes took in all the team members. "But first, are we all in agreement? We're sticking our necks out here."

"I don't see any other way," Ann said.

"I agree," John said.

"Me, too," Sully said.

Dan hesitated, his eyes seeming very large behind his thick glasses. "I'm convinced."

"Can you fix me up with a nontraceable call?" Gary asked.

"Surely you jest," Dan said. "You want his mobile number?"

"Please."

Dan brought up a communication application on his laptop and selected a number. Gary picked up the handset and listened to the electronic trilling.

"Hello," a voice said.

"Thomas, this is Gary. We have to talk."

"Gary! No, we don't. Bye."

"Wait! We know what happened—about the missing vaccine."

"What? That's impossible."

"Then *why* am I calling? You *have* to set up a meeting with either Zack or Secretary Foster."

"Listen, Gary. I don't know *what* you've found, but you better forget it. You're out of the loop."

"No, we're not."

"Yes, you are. You guys don't know who you're messing with. If the CIA *or* the FBI catches even a *whiff* of you guys snooping around, I guarantee you'll be behind bars before you can hang up the phone."

"But Thomas, we can help."

"Hey, this isn't up to me." He paused. "Look, I could get in trouble for this, but I will tell you one thing. We're in deep trouble over here, and federal law enforcement is going ballistic. They don't know *who* did it, but *everyone* who was up at Brevig is under suspicion. Understand what I'm saying?"

"Yes, I guess I do."

"I hope so. Good-bye."

Gary set the handset down and looked all around. "Essentially, we're on our own. Thomas can't help us."

"Why does that not surprise me?" Dan grumbled.

"Hold it, we're not done here," Gary said. "If we give up, think of what might happen. Remember Brevig. What if that virus sweeps across America; goes around the world?"

"Yeah, dude, but what can we do about it?" Sully asked.

"We have to come up with proof, or the Feds won't listen to us," John said.

"I agree," Gary said. "Okay, we've done hard stuff before; we can do it again. We *have* to find out if that smoking gun is really up there. Show me how."

"Man, that place is crawling with mean dudes carrying big sticks," Sully said. "What can we do about that?"

Gary smiled in spite of the situation. "Thanks for the insight, Mr. Sullivan. You go first. Talk to me, dude."

CHAPTER 27

Only one way in that I see, dude," Sully said. "You and John strap on the hang gliders and make like birds."

"That's what I was afraid you'd say," Gary said. "I was hoping you might have some stuntman trick up your sleeve."

"Naw, man. Those dudes have that place covered, and then there's that way-ugly fence."

"Okay, then we'll have to go in by air." Gary's gaze took in each team member. "This will require two teams."

"We're not all going?" Dan asked.

"No. I want you to run our communications network from here," Gary said. His eyes flicked over to Ann. "And someone has to start digging up dirt on Hamid and Saeed. Can you two handle that?"

"Sure, no problem," Ann said.

"Yeah, I'd feel lost without all my gear," Dan said.

"Good," Gary said. "Now, how do we make this work? What does the away team need to do the job?"

"Obviously we need the hang gliders," John said. "Then some way to find and document the camera. I think I can modify Sherlock to do that. A metal detector, miniature excavator, and a low-light video camera."

"Sounds good. I'll leave the details to you."

"Guys, what if they see you?" Ann asked.

"We'll definitely have to fly in at night," Gary said. "We'll be wearing dark clothing, and the hang gliders are gray. Should be hard to see."

"But you could be silhouetted. We're coming up on a full moon."

"You dudes need a diversion," Sully said.

"That would be nice, but how?" Gary asked. "Sherlock is spoken for."

"How about the kid on a bike plus some light and sound from Dan-the-man?"

"Remember, they have helicopters. They'd catch you for sure."

"Oh, yeah, forgot about that."

"Otherwise, nice idea." Gary turned to John. "What about the UAV? Wouldn't that work?"

"I guess, but can you operate it and fly a hang glider at the same time?"

"Hey, man, let me do it," Sully said.

"You've never flown it," John said.

"I can drive anything, dude. Gary can check me out."

"I think we can make that work." Gary looked around at Dan. "What about communications?"

"No problem. I can fix you up with satellite comm gear," Dan said.

"Hold on, how are we going to get up there with all that stuff?" John asked. "We have hang gliders, the UAV, Sherlock, comm gear, and who knows what all."

"Pack everything up and airfreight it." Gary turned to Ann. "Better get started checking the airlines."

"Guys, we're looking at days here, minimum," Ann said. "We probably don't have that much time."

"Yeah, and our freight might be delayed," John said. "*Then* where would we be?"

Gary frowned. "I *know* all that," he said. "We'll just have to do the best we can."

"Assuming we *can* make this work," John said. "If we find the camera, why not give it to Nate? It would sure save time."

Gary shook his head. "Nope, too risky. He'd turn us over to the feds, and they'd slap us behind bars and fiddle around until it was too late. No, we *have* to bring the evidence back to D.C., or we'll end up as a footnote to history, assuming anyone's left to write it."

"Am I hearing a need for speed?" Sully asked.

"Yes, it would help," Gary said.

"The kid might have the answer."

"What do you have in mind?"

"How about I call Paul Wilson?"

Gary snapped his fingers. "Your producer friend; his contract with GalaxyBizJet."

"Jackpot. I'm in pretty tight with him. Maybe he can arrange a trip for us."

"That would solve a lot of problems. We'd be glad to reimburse him."

"Comm boss," Sully said.

"Yes?" Dan replied.

Sully scrawled a number on a pad. "Here. That's his mobile number."

Dan gave him a handset.

Gary sent up an arrow prayer. If Sully could manage it, with help, it would certainly simplify things.

Sully's face grew animated. "Paul, this is the kid. What's up, dude?" His face nodded in time to the other's reply. "Cool. You're keeping me in mind for future shoots, right?" Sully's smile remained in place. "Cool. You know I'd rather work for you than anyone else in

Hollywood." Sully nodded at Gary. "Listen, dude. I have a heavy favor to ask."

Sully rattled off the request in his typical offbeat way, but he covered the essentials. He placed a hand over the mouthpiece. "He's cool. When and where?"

Gary looked at John. "We'll have to leave in the evening to arrive in Brevig around midnight. Prepare tonight and tomorrow and leave Tuesday night?"

John took a deep breath and nodded. "Yeah, we can do it."

"Clock's running, dudes," Sully said.

"Hold on a sec," Gary said. He thought about the range and speed of a Learjet 45XR, the time he wanted to be at Brevig Mission, and factored in the four-hour time difference. "Okay, tell him 7:00 p.m. tomorrow at Frederick Municipal. The flight is to Nome, Alaska, and then back to Frederick."

Sully relayed the information, nodded a few times, and punched off the handset. "He'll call me back on my mobile with the confirmation."

"Thanks, Sully," Gary said.

"Yeah, glad I could help."

"Okay, everyone. We have a lot to do."

At 6:40 p.m., a little more than twenty-four hours later, Sully drove the SecurityCheck command center truck to Frederick Municipal Airport and parked outside Antietam Aviation. Gary stood, walked to the back of the truck, and let Sully in. Arrayed on the floor behind Dan's workstation was an orderly mound of equipment and supplies. John stepped slowly around it.

"Do we have everything?" Gary asked.

"Yeah," John said. "Just double-checking to make sure. I'd hate to get up there and find out we're missing something."

"You and me both."

The two powered hang gliders made up most of the bulk, followed by the UAV, Sherlock, and the satellite communications gear Dan had provided. John packed up the smaller pieces of equipment in two large nylon bags.

"Here's your ride," Dan said.

He pointed to an overhead monitor and zoomed in with an exterior low-light camera. In the dwindling glow of sunset, a sleek Learjet 45XR entered Frederick Municipal's traffic pattern for runway 23. Gary's eyes followed the pilot's precise turns. The plane's landing gear came down, and the flaps extended. It came around on base leg then turned on final approach. Moments later, the twinjet crossed the runway threshold and touched down.

"Nice," Gary said. "Are we clear?" he asked Ann.

She checked through the applications running on her laptop. "Looks okay to me," she said. "Dan?"

Dan's eyes roved over the instruments arrayed all around him. "All I'm picking up is normal communications. No unusual radio traffic. I don't think anyone's looking at us."

"Good. Keep a close watch," Gary said.

He picked up one of the hang gliders. The tightly bundled aluminum rods and Dacron, plus the compact engine and propeller, made a heavy and unwieldy package. Ann opened the rear doors. Gary stepped down with his load. Up ahead a fence separated the parking lot from the flight line. Gary hurried along a row of parked cars, squeezed between a Mustang and a Lincoln Aviator, and on through the gate in the fence. The business jet turned off the taxiway and pulled up to the aircraft ramp. The floodlights mounted high on Antietam Aviation's passenger lounge illuminated the gleaming white fuselage with cobalt blue trim. The high-pitched whine tapered off rapidly as the engines spooled down.

Gary looked through the aircraft's wraparound windshield and recognized Mike Jacobs and Chuck Allen. He smiled in relief, since the mission required Gary to convince the pilot to alter his flight plan. His long friendship with Mike would make that task easier, he hoped. He angled around the jet's nose and set the hang glider down. John and Sully lowered their burdens.

Gary led the way to the cabin door, just aft of the cockpit. The upper door opened smoothly, aided by the gas struts. Mike looked out at them as he unlatched the lower door and lowered the air stair by its cable. Once it was down, he extended the flip-down step and came down to the pavement. It was then that Gary noticed his grim expression.

"Hi, Mike," Gary said, shaking his hand.

"Gary," Mike said, with a nod to the others. "I'm afraid we have a problem."

"What's wrong?"

"Chuck's sick as a dog; he picked up some kind of bug in New York. Anyhow, company regs say I have to call in a relief copilot."

Gary felt momentary panic at what might happen if they were delayed. Then he remembered who was really in charge. "I'm sorry to hear that. Can we help?"

"No. I don't think it's all that serious or I would have radioed for an ambulance. He just needs to get over it. If you'll excuse me, I have to call GalaxyBizJet. Then I'll take Chuck into town and get him a motel room."

"Anything we can do?" Gary said.

"No, no. You're the client, even if Mr. Wilson did the arranging."

"Please, I insist. We have a cot in our truck. The motel where we're staying is nice, and I think they have vacancies."

The anxious look on Mike's face eased a little. "That's very nice of you." Then he laughed. "Most of the rich dudes we fly around treat us like hired help." He paused. "Which is what we are, so why am I complaining?"

"Does he need any help?" Gary asked.

"No. I told him to sit tight until I arranged us a ride." Mike approached the door from the side and leaned in. "Hey, Chuck, our ride's here."

"That was quick," came the faint reply.

Chuck appeared in the door and took his time easing down the steps. His face looked drawn and ashen.

"You remember Gary and John," Mike said.

"Yeah," Chuck mumbled. "Sorry about this."

"Don't be," Gary said. "I'm sorry you're feeling so bad."

Mike rotated the flip-down step and closed and latched the lower door. Then he pulled down the upper door, pushed it shut, and rotated the locking handle.

Gary led the way across the tarmac. They walked through the gate and across the parking lot to the truck. Ann opened the rear doors and looked down in concern.

"Come on in," she said. "I have the cot ready."

Mike looked at Gary. "How did she know?"

"Step inside, and I'll tell you."

After introducing Mike and Chuck to Sully and Dan, Gary took only a few minutes to bring them up to the critical point, after letting them in on the bare bones of their audit work for the army. Then he delivered the bombshell and spent the next twenty minutes explaining why they had to make the trip. Then he stopped and waited.

"Gary, if I didn't know you, I'd say you were wacko," Mike said finally. "Terrorists spreading a virus that could decimate America?"

"The world actually."

"I had no idea; I mean, I've *heard* about bioterrorism, but I didn't realize we were in imminent danger."

"Until homeland security hired us, we didn't, either. But believe me. This is for real. We've seen firsthand what that virus can do, and if we *don't* stop these terrorists, it means the end of civilization as we know it. That's why it's *imperative* we get to Brevig Mission immediately. Every hour brings us closer to disaster."

"I understand. I'm pretty sure our company can have a relief pilot here by sometime tomorrow."

"No good. We can't risk a day's delay."

"Nothing I can do about it. Per FAA regs, the Learjet is a two-pilot plane."

"Why can't *I* be the second pilot?" Gary watched as his friend thought the problem through.

"Under normal circumstances, you know very well why not: You're not rated, my company's regs, the FAA. You're talking about throwing the rule book away."

Gary shrugged. "Yeah, I guess I am. So are we going to do this or not?"

Mike shook his head slowly. "I don't see as I have a choice. Are we ready to go?"

"Let's do it," Gary said.

"We'll take good care of Chuck," Ann said.

Gary glanced at the young man stretched out on the cot. Even as sick as he was, he looked even more distressed now, but apparently he had decided not to try to influence Mike's decision.

Ann moved to the doors and opened them. Gary, John, and Sully followed Mike out into the chill October evening.

CHAPTER 28

After a short delay to fill the tanks with jet-A, they were ready to go. Mike closed the lower door, then pulled the upper clamshell door down into its seal, and rotated the locking handle. Gary glanced back into the cabin. John and Sully were sitting in the first two forward-facing club seats and working on their seat belts.

"Come on forward," Mike said.

Gary followed him into the cockpit, slipped past the center pedestal, sat down in the right-hand seat, and fastened his harness. Mike began bringing up the avionics. Gary's eyes fell on the four large displays of the Honeywell Primus 1000 Electronic Flight Instrument Systems, which provided a primary flight display for both pilots plus navigational, communications, and engine instrumentation. The information overload, intense at first, slowly dissipated as he began picking out the various instruments.

"Your headphones," Mike said, pointing.

Gary slipped them on and adjusted the boom mike.

Mike handed him a card. "Read off the checklist for me."

As soon as Mike had both engines running, he advanced the

power levers and turned onto the taxiway. Gary read the checklist while the Learjet trundled toward the end of runway 23. Less than a minute later, Mike brought the aircraft to a stop.

"Potomac Clearance Delivery, this is Learjet one-seven-four-niner Golf Bravo, on IFR flight plan to Flying Cloud Airport, Minneapolis," Mike said into his boom mike.

"Four-niner Golf Bravo, clearance delivered as filed," the controller said in Gary's headphones. "Contact Potomac Departure on entering controlled airspace."

"Four-niner Golf Bravo, roger."

Mike released the brakes and advanced the power levers slightly. He turned onto the runway and pushed the power levers forward in one smooth motion. The aircraft surged forward driven by seven thousand pounds of combined thrust delivered by the Honeywell turbofan engines. The colored runway lights punctuated the gathering darkness and seemed to merge in the distance. They slipped past slowly at first but soon became blurred streaks.

Mike pulled back on the yoke. The aircraft promptly rotated and sprang into the air without the slightest hesitation. Moments later the landing gear retracted with a solid thump. Mike brought the power back slightly and retracted the flaps. A few minutes later, he engaged the autopilot to handle the mundane tasks of flight control. They gradually worked their way up to flight level 310.

"I see our first stop is Minneapolis," Gary said. "We're making two fuel stops?"

"Got to," Mike said. "We have 110-knot headwind currently. It'll drop to 60 farther west then back up to 90 for the final leg. The Learjet 45 has long legs but not that long. Coming back we can make it with one stop."

"I see."

"But we'll still beat commercial air by a long margin."

"Oh, I'm well aware of that. I'm praying this will give us the edge we need."

Mike looked over with a self-conscious grin on his face. "If that works for you, I'm glad. I hope you guys find the proof you need."

Whether God would honor Gary's prayers or not, he didn't know. But the team had come through tough situations before when it had seemed all hope was lost.

"Anything particular you want me to do?" Gary asked.

"Mainly navigation and radio work. On takeoffs and landings, you'll monitor airspeed and read checklists."

"Roger that."

Mike pointed to one of the large displays. "There's the GPS moving map display for the leg to Flying Cloud Airport."

"Any bad weather up ahead?"

"Nothing worse than clouds until we get close to Nome. It's overcast right now, but they're expecting light snow later on."

"I hope that won't affect us."

"Probably won't. Accumulation should be light, and Nome has a pretty decent airport."

Gary yawned. It was 10:58 p.m. Alaska daylight savings time, and they were about 557 nautical miles from Nome, a little over an hour away. Gary felt he had performed his first officer duties quite well. The stops at Flying Cloud and Skagit Regional Airport outside Seattle had both gone smoothly. The FBOs (fixed base operators) had been efficient and friendly, filling the plane's tanks with jet-A and the cabin dispensers with hot coffee. Leaving Skagit, they had overflown British Columbia until reaching Alaska's southern border, where their track had taken them over the Gulf of Alaska.

"Mike," Gary said. "We need to revise our destination."

"What? My instructions said Frederick to Nome."

"I know, but we have to get closer to that army lab. Remember, we're flying hang gliders in there."

Mike shook his head. "I thought you'd be driving to your launch point."

"We don't have time."

Mike frowned. "Okay, so where do you want to land?"

"Brevig Mission Airport, about sixty nautical miles from Nome."

"What kind of strip?"

Gary took a deep breath. "Three thousand feet; gravel."

"No can do. That's *way* too short, and company regs forbid me landing on gravel."

"Bush pilots fly in there all the time."

"Does this look like a bush plane?"

"No, but I know you can do it. You're an excellent pilot, and we're light on fuel. You don't really think we'd pick up gravel damage, do you?"

Mike was silent for a moment. "No, probably not, especially frozen over like it is."

"And remember the mission."

"I know, I know."

"Then you'll do it?"

"Yeah."

"That's a relief," a deep voice behind them said.

Gary turned and saw John looking in with Sully right behind him.

"How long have you guys been standing there?" Gary asked.

"Not long," John said. "I was just wondering how things were going."

Gary thought that over. "In light of eternity, couldn't be better," he said.

"I hear that," John said.

Gary glanced back at Sully. The kid seemed lost in his own thoughts.

Mike pointed to the keys and cursor controls on the center pedestal. "I presume you have the coordinates for the Brevig Mission

Airport, so how about punching them in."

"Roger," Gary said.

He deleted Nome as the destination and keyed in the mission airport's coordinates instead. The autopilot obediently turned to the new course. The Learjet arrowed its way over the Alaskan wilderness far below them, hidden by a heavy overcast. Ahead lay Norton Sound. Mike took the plane off autopilot and began the descent.

"Gary, contact Anchorage Center and tell them to cancel our flight plan," Mike said.

Gary selected the correct frequency. "Anchorage Center, this is Learjet four-niner Golf Bravo. Request cancellation of our IFR flight plan to Nome."

"Four-niner Golf Bravo, this is Anchorage Center. Roger. Your flight plan is closed."

"Four-niner Golf Bravo, roger."

Several minutes later, the aircraft sliced into the heavy overcast, and the moon and stars winked out as if some celestial plug had been yanked.

"I hope this doesn't go all the way to the ground," John said, still standing behind the flight deck.

"It's not supposed to," Gary said.

The altimeter continued its relentless countdown. They dropped below the cloud base at 950 feet.

"Man, that is *way* dark," Sully said.

"It should be," Gary said. "No moon or stars."

"I have the runway lights," Mike said. "Man that looks tiny. I presume this is an unattended strip."

"That's a roger."

Mike pulled back on the power levers. "Okay, I'm gonna need your help." He made a gentle turn and centered the aircraft on a long, straight-in approach. "Full flaps." Gary moved the lever to the full-down position. The wind noise increased, and there was a slight vibration. Mike pulled the power back a little more.

"Okay, when I tell you, I want full thrust reverse," Mike said. "Got it?"

"Roger."

The landing strip's narrow lighted rectangle seemed to come up to meet them. Gary swallowed. They were *very* low. Mike brought the power up, held it a few moments, then pulled the power levers all the way back and pulled back on the yoke. The airspeed bled off. Gary watched with wide eyes as the runway lights rushed toward them. The main landing gear wheels chirped loudly.

"Now!" Mike shouted as he operated the yoke and clamped his feet on the brake pedals. The antiskid brakes gripped and released rapidly, giving maximum stopping power.

Gary actuated the clamshell thrust reversers and ran the power levers full forward. The engines roared, and the hot engine exhaust buffeted the airframe. The runway's end lights flew toward them: a thousand feet, five hundred, two hundred.

"Thrust reversers off," Mike ordered.

Gary pulled the power levers back and reset the thrust reversers.

"Man, that was something," John said.

Gary looked back and saw John and Sully still standing behind the flight deck.

"Hey, you guys were supposed to be strapped in," Gary said.

"I know, but I *had* to see that."

"Me, too," Sully said. "That was *way* cool."

"Glad you enjoyed it," Mike said. The wedge of illumination provided by the landing lights picked out a parking apron off the main runway. Fine snowflakes winked in the brilliant lights. Mike stopped on the deserted apron, turned, and looked at Gary. "Okay, the rest is up to you guys."

Gary got up and worked his way past the pedestal and back to where they had placed their coats and boots. He shrugged into his navy blue parka, sat down, slipped off his shoes, and pulled on his boots. Mike stood by the cabin door, waiting for them to finish. Then he opened the cabin door and stepped down on the frozen surface. Gary, John, and Sully followed. The moaning wind swirled the light snowfall about them. The men shuffled over the frozen gravel, past the wing-tip, and back under the left engine nacelle. Mike opened the baggage door in the feeble light filtering down through the door. He stood back and wrapped his arms around his lightweight uniform coat.

"Go back inside," Gary said.

Mike nodded and ran around and up the steps. The cabin door closed. Gary slipped on his night-vision goggles and pulled out his hang glider. He moved a short distance away and began assembling the tubes, rods, cables, and the all-important engine. The Dacron wing fluttered in the wind as Gary checked over his work. He looked over and saw that John was almost finished.

Sully had the UAV out and sheltered under the Learjet's wing. After he checked out the control unit, he examined the flash and bullhorn. Then he started working on Dan's satellite communications unit. After he finished, he placed it clear of the aircraft and pressed a button. The parabolic antenna homed in on the satellite.

"It's ready," Sully said.

Gary closed the baggage compartment and led the way around to the cabin door. He rapped lightly. The upper door swung open followed by the lower one. They hurried inside and removed their low-light goggles while Mike closed the door.

"Here," Gary said, handing the pilot a spare earphone radio. "You'll be able to hear us and talk to our command center." He cut his eyes over at Sully. "Assuming Dan's fancy comm box works."

"Hey, man," Sully said. "I set it up like he said."

"Turn it on here," Gary said, pointing. He slipped his own radio in and turned it on. Mike, John, and Sully did the same.

"Star Chamber, this is Gooney Bird One, radio check."

"Gooney Bird One, this is Star Chamber. Read you five-by-five."

"Cool," Sully said.

"That was Stuntman," Gary said.

"Oh, yeah, sorry, dudes."

Gary looked at Mike. "Your call sign is 'Captain,' " he whispered.

"This is Captain. How are things there?"

"This is Star Chamber," Ann said. "It's quiet. Be advised that your assistant is feeling better. We're taking good care of him."

"This is Captain. Thanks."

"This is Gooney Bird One. Stand by. We launch in approximately five minutes."

"Star Chamber standing by," Dan replied.

Gary turned to Sully. "Are you clear on the mission?" he asked.

"Yeah. Fly the UAV bird to the GPS coordinates north of the bug farm and make like the Pied Piper."

"Right. Draw the guards toward you, but don't forget the helicopters. If you see one getting close, get out of there."

"Don't worry, man."

"You ready?" Gary asked John.

His broad face was serious. "Let's do it."

"Okay, I'll help Sully."

When Mike opened the cabin door, a cruel wind whipped inside. The three men hurried down the steps and out onto the ice. Gary slipped on his night-vision goggles. The cabin door closed, cutting off the brilliant green light source.

Sully retrieved the UAV. Gary took it, got down on his knees, and checked the engine. He looked up at Sully. "Check the controls," he said. The servos whirred, and the tiny control surfaces moved all about. "Looks good," Gary said. He turned on the ignition and set the choke. He picked up the electric drill, pressed the rubber cup in its chuck against the engine's spinner, and pressed the trigger. The engine, still warm from the heated baggage compartment, caught after a few turns.

Gary turned his head but could barely hear the engine's exhaust. He picked up the UAV, ran out onto the runway, and set the plane down.

Gary stood up. "You're good to go."

"Roger that, dude," Sully said.

The UAV shot down the runway a few feet, leaped into the air, and was gone.

"Come on," John said.

Gary slipped under his hang glider, worked his way into the harness, and snapped it to the frame. He lifted his nylon backpack and hooked it to the ring under the engine. Gary set the choke on his engine and engaged the starter. He felt the insistent push from the propeller but couldn't hear the engine. He waited a few moments then turned off the choke. He checked his instruments then looked over at John and pointed.

Gary turned into the blowing snow and began running. Wind filled the Dacron wing, lifting the deadweight off his shoulders. After a few more steps, the harness straps jerked him into the air. A few seconds later, he began a sharp turn to the right to their initial heading of 10 degrees true, which was 353 degrees on his magnetic compass because of 17 degrees of east variation. They would hold this course to take them clear of the native Alaskan village of Brevig Mission.

"Star Chamber, this is Gooney Bird One. We are airborne."

"Roger, Gooney Bird One," came Dan's clear reply.

A few minutes later, Gary turned left and settled on a course of 283 magnetic. The light snow looked like slanting sparks of green light in Gary's low-light goggles. He looked up at the cloud base, quite close now. Gary watched the GPS coordinates counting up slowly. Fourteen minutes later, they were nearing the army's perimeter guards.

"Stand by, Gooney Bird Two," Gary said. "Watch your instruments."

"Roger that," John said.

"Execute."

Gary began a gentle turn to the right while John continued straight, climbing up into the clouds. Gary came around in a full turn, putting him about a half minute behind. When his compass reached 283 degrees again, he pushed forward on the control bar. Moments later the icy mist enveloped him. He focused on his instruments, watching the GPS coordinates slowly count up to 65 degrees, 28.231 minutes north latitude, 166 degrees, 45.540 minutes west longitude.

"Gooney Bird Two, what do your instruments read?" Gary said.

"Straight and level, heading 283. Position is 66 degrees, 27.891 minutes north, 166 degrees, 44.384 minutes west."

"Looking good, Gooney Bird Two. Just report the minutes."

"Roger that."

"This is Stuntman," Sully said. "Skyhook is on station."

"Roger, Stuntman," Gary said. "Execute."

Sully stood clear of the Learjet to avoid any possible radio interference, his face bathed in an eerie blue glow from the controller's LCD display. He aimed the powerful light strobe and bullhorn and pressed a button. The brilliant flash temporarily washed out his display, and the onboard mike transmitted a muted boom through the controller's speakers.

"Bomb's away," Sully said.

"Roger, Stuntman," Gary said.

Sully zoomed in a camera on the soldiers below. "Whoa, they're coming after me, dudes."

Sully pulled back on the joystick. The display banked out as the UAV disappeared into the scud.

Gary checked his hang glider for ice but didn't see any. A glance at his GPS readout told him they were less than a minute away.

Hopefully the perimeter guards would be fully engaged with the phantom threat by the time he and John arrived. If not, things would become dicey in short order.

"This is Gooney Bird Two," John said. "28.231 north, 45.540 west."

"Execute landing; Gooney Bird One is right behind you."

"Roger that."

Gary reached the same coordinates, pulled his throttle back to idle, and pulled back on the control bar. A few seconds later, the hang glider swooped out of the clouds. Gary looked all around. The soldiers were all running to the north. Several hundred feet below, John was executing a series of tight figure-eight turns over the dormitory building. Gary did likewise, descending rapidly. Off to the west, a dark dragonfly shape shot into the air and turned north.

"Stuntman, there's a Blackhawk headed your way," Gary said.

"Roger that," Sully said. "Skyhook is heading for home."

Gary looked down. A hundred feet below, John made a final turn and began his approach to the dormitory's flat roof, clearing the north fence by less than ten feet. The hang glider slowed and finally stalled. John was down. Gary looked all around. The soldiers were still running north across the frozen tundra.

Gary pulled his control bar farther back, increasing his descent and also his speed. He swept across the north fence heading away, leveled out, made a 180 turn, and lined up. He came back low over the fence and crossed the roof. He pushed the control bar forward, stalled the hang glider, and ran the landing out.

"Gooney Birds One and Two are down," Gary said.

"Star Chamber copies," Dan said.

Gary removed his harness and stepped out from under the flapping wing. He unhooked his backpack and hurried over to where John was waiting. They were standing on the western edge of the roof, next to the perimeter fence. On Gary's left, the lab building ran parallel to the dorm, and straight ahead he could barely see the roof of the guardhouse. He kneeled down, pulled Sherlock's controller out of his backpack, and flipped it on. All systems were functional.

"Ready?" Gary whispered.

"Yeah," John said. He held Sherlock out over the roof's edge and pressed a button on Sherlock's deck. The robot lowered itself with its tiny winch. As soon as it reached the ground, John threw the line down for it to retrieve.

Gary started Sherlock inching along on its caterpillar treads.

"You really think the camera's on this side?" John whispered.

"It's less likely to be found next to the fence," Gary said.

"Assuming it's there at all."

"Let's keep a positive attitude." Then Gary thought about how deadly the camera was and hoped the virus couldn't reach them where they were. He swallowed and forced himself to concentrate. Sherlock started up a gentle ice slope, and the metal detector indicator jumped.

"Looks like we've found something," Gary said.

After Sherlock crawled another foot, the readout dropped. Gary pivoted the robot, approached the anomaly, and stopped. He switched the joystick control to the excavator and started scraping away the encrusted ice. It took ten long minutes to reveal an oblong object lying on its side.

"There's the smoking gun," John said.

"It's a camera, all right. But what's inside?"

Gary retracted the excavator and extended a miniature electric screwdriver. He positioned the tool and removed four screws. Then, using the driver head along with considerable body English, he levered the cover up. There, under the glare of Sherlock's work light, was the camera's electronics, plus something else. A canister took up most of the free space. Next came a tiny cylindrical object attached to a clear plastic hose that ran to a miniature fan.

"Very sophisticated," John said. "See those wires on the cylinder? Bet that's a solenoid valve to release the virus at a preset time."

"I'll take your word for it. Any question in your mind what that is?"

"Nope."

"Star Chamber, this is Gooney Bird One," Gary said. "Did you get all that on disk?"

"Roger that," Dan said.

Gary turned off the controller. He and John crawled upwind, staying low so their silhouettes would blend in with the roof. When they reached their hang gliders, Gary pulled out a pair of low-light binoculars and, substituting them for his goggles, swept the western expanse of tundra.

"Not good," he said, lowering the glasses. "They've reformed the perimeter. Sully's diversion didn't fool them for long, and you can just bet they're on their guard now."

"What are we going to do?" John asked. "If they see us take off—"

"I know," Gary interrupted. He raised the binoculars again and started a slow sweep of the entire horizon. "What we could really use right now is. . ." He stopped turning. Gary felt an inward hope that shifted into gratitude. "There. That's *exactly* what we need." He lowered the glasses. "Get ready. There's a snow squall moving toward us."

Gary packed Sherlock's controller in his backpack and snapped it to the ring below the engine. John zipped up his largely empty pack and stowed it. Then they strapped themselves back into their harnesses and waited. The heavy snow scudding toward them looked like a green, moving wall. The storm swept over the guards to the west, obscuring them.

"Start your engine," Gary said.

Gary started his and after a few moments turned off the choke. He watched the cloud approach. Finally the snow enveloped them, dropping visibility to ten or twenty feet.

"Launch," Gary said.

He waited until he saw John running down the roof then fell in behind him, sprinting to keep him in sight. John's hang glider staggered into the air just short of the roof's western edge. Gary's harness yanked him into the air.

"Come left to 183," Gary ordered.

"Roger," John replied.

Gary left the throttle at full power until he passed John, held his southerly course for several more seconds, then turned to the southeast toward Brevig Mission Airport. He kept climbing until he reached five hundred feet then leveled off. About a minute later, they flew out of the storm. Gary looked down and saw they were past the eastern guards.

"Stuntman, this is Gooney Bird One," Gary said.

"This is Stuntman, go, dude."

"Tell Captain a snow squall is coming in from the west. We're going to have to hustle."

"Roger that."

CHAPTER 29

Gary left his throttle wide open all the way back, arriving at Brevig Mission Airport barely ahead of the snow. He looked back. The line of clouds had almost reached the village, less than a mile away. He looked down and saw that Sully had already packed up the UAV and the comm gear.

"Man, this is going to be tight," John said.

"Follow me in," Gary said.

He chopped the throttle, swooped down to ten feet, and leveled off going downwind parallel to the runway. He brought the hang glider around in a tight right turn, waited until his speed dropped off, then pushed the control bar full forward. Gary landed on his feet and cut the engine. John swept past him, touched down, and almost fell on the slick ice.

"Whoa, dude," Sully said.

He came out and began helping John. Gary slipped free of his harness and out from under the hang glider.

"Leave them," Gary shouted. "The storm is right on us."

John and Sully dashed up the steps and into the cabin. Gary

came next and ducked into the flight deck, pulling off his low-light goggles and removing his earphone radio as he went. He sat down in the right seat and buckled in. Behind him he heard the cabin door clump shut. Mike scrambled into his seat and fastened his harness. His hands flew over the controls as he started both engines. He turned the aircraft around and taxied onto the runway. They bounced and skidded along, going downwind on the icy gravel.

"Give me full flaps," Mike ordered.

Gary moved the lever, and the indicator moved to the full-down position. Finally they reached the end, and Mike brought the aircraft around. The lights at the end of the runway winked out.

"The storm's here," Gary said.

Mike pushed the power levers forward and released the brakes. The fanjets roared as the aircraft surged down the icy runway. Mike worked the yoke and rudders to maintain control. The plane hurdled toward the encroaching darkness. The runway lights disappeared. Mike pulled back on the yoke, and the lightly loaded jet leaped into the air.

Gary swallowed. "That was close," he managed to say.

"I've lost track of how many rules I've broken," Mike said. "How about calling Anchorage Center and tell them our destination is Nome Airport."

"Roger. You think we'll beat the storm?"

"Probably. It's not moving all that fast."

Gary hoped so. He thought of the long trip ahead and all the team had to do. He checked the radio frequency and keyed the mike. "Anchorage Center, this is Learjet one-seven-four-niner Golf Bravo."

Ann jumped at the ringing sound even though she had been expecting the call.

"That's Gary's mobile," Dan said. He pushed a button to put the call on speakerphone. "Hello, Gary."

"Hi, gotta make this quick," Gary said. "We're in Nome, and we'll be leaving as soon as we refuel. ETA at Frederick is somewhere around twelve thirty your time. Listen, Ann?"

"Yes, Gary?"

"We *have* to be ready to roll as soon as we get in. How about giving Ken a heads-up on what's coming. We can't afford any delays on bringing Zack up to speed on what we've found."

"Okay, but do you think Ken will listen?"

"I'm sure you can find a way."

"How much should I say about what we've found?"

"Try to keep it general. I want their full attention when we show them the video."

"I'll do my best."

"Couldn't ask for more. Find anything yet on Saeed or Hamid?"

"Maybe. I hope to know more shortly."

"Okay, see you later. Mike's ready to roll."

"Right. Bye."

Dan disconnected the call and turned to Ann. "You found something?"

"Maybe. Both Saeed and Hamid have squeaky-clean backgrounds, which they should, since they work for the CIA. But what if we're dealing with an imposter?"

"What? Which one?"

"Hamid, but it's just a theory so far."

Ann turned back to her laptop and again went over the two documents she had found. One was an employee profile the army had required of Hamid as a condition for using the Institute's lab. The other was a student information form obtained by hacking into Cambridge University's computer network. The two documents were fairly congruent except for one thing: Hamid Momeni was an inch shorter according to the Cambridge data. But was that really significant? Ann wondered. There were many possible explanations for such a difference.

On a hunch, Ann retrieved the rest of the student records for the same academic year, imported them into an SQL Server database and began massaging. The first thing that popped up was that there had been eleven other Iranians enrolled in Cambridge, three of them in biological medical and veterinary sciences, same as Hamid. One was female, and of the men, one was five foot nine while the other was six foot even. Ann pulled up the latter record and saw that Ebrahim Hosseini was the exact same height as the army had for Hamid Momeni.

Ann did a power search on Hossein, including the archives of local newspapers. An article in a student newspaper gave a brief bio, noting he was from Iran and that his father was a Shiite cleric and a friend of Ayatollah Ruhollah Khomeini, apparently the reason for the article. Next she read an archived article from the April 22, 1982, issue of the *Cambridge Evening News*. It reported Ebrahim Hosseini missing. The police report stated that he had been last seen in classes the previous week, and there was no evidence in his apartment suggesting foul play. Ann tried several more searches and couldn't find any later references to the man. He had simply disappeared.

Ann pushed her laptop away and reined in her imagination. Was she seeing connections where there weren't any or because she *wanted* to see them? But *someone* had deliberately unleashed the world's most lethal virus and then stolen the only live samples *and* the only vaccine. Hamid Momeni might have a background the CIA would love, but what about a Shiite Muslim in tight with Khomeini? The more Ann thought about her suspicions, the more sure she became. For the first time in this crazy project, the clues were fitting together. She leaned forward and began printing off her research.

She turned her head. "Dan, what numbers do you have for the Underwoods?"

"Office, home, mobiles, and pagers."

"How about ringing their home number?"

"Coming up," he said. He pushed a handset over to her.

Ann picked it up. After two rings she heard a female voice answer, "Underwoods."

"Carol, this is Ann O'Brien."

There was a sharp intake of breath. "You're not supposed to call us. If homeland security hears—"

"Listen, we've found out something," Ann interrupted. "The virus outbreak was deliberate."

"What? How?"

"We'll show you, but you and Ken have to get us in to see Zack. Can you do that?"

"I don't know."

"You *have* to. We've got the proof, plus I think I know who stole the virus."

"Who?"

"We'll go over everything at the meeting."

"Okay, what time?"

"Let's say one o'clock."

"I'll see what I can do."

"Thanks. Bye."

Ann got up, picked up her printout, and slid it in front of Dan. "Take a look at this." She explained her theory as he looked over the pages. "What do you think?" she asked when he looked up.

"It sure answers a lot of questions."

"How about we drive over to Hamid's—I mean Hosseini's—apartment and do some snooping?"

Ann turned left on Buckystown Pike out of the Days Inn parking lot and merged with Urbana Pike just south of I-70.

"I'm picking up his mobile phone," Dan said over Ann's earphone radio.

"Great. Where is he?"

"I have line-of-bearing only, but it passes close to his apartment, so I guess he's home."

Ann drove under I-70 where the road changed to Market Street. She looked down at the GPS map on her laptop and decided to cut across on South Street to Patrick.

"Hold on, he's moving," Dan said suddenly.

"Where's he going?"

"Don't know yet."

Ann turned left on South Street while she waited. Two blocks later she said, "Dan, I need some directions."

"I can't triangulate with a single antenna."

"Take your best shot."

"The bearing is swinging rapidly to the south. I'd say he's on southbound 15."

Ann glanced at her PC and saw that Hosseini had plenty of options. He could go straight and take I-270 toward Washington, get on I-70 off I-270, or turn to the southwest on 340. "Okay, I'm turning left on Jefferson."

Ann slowed down as she approached the interchange.

"He's taking 340," Dan said.

Ann accelerated and drove under the bridge where the road became highway 340. Ann's eyes traced the route ahead. Since it was unlikely Hosseini would be going to West Virginia, she scanned the southbound routes. The first major one was where highway 15 turned off 340 on its way across the Potomac into Virginia.

"Is he still on 340?" Ann asked.

"Yes, and he's *really* moving. The signal strength is dropping off."

Ann held the truck to the legal limit. When Hosseini failed to turn off on 15, it surprised Ann. Where was he going?

"I just lost him, but I think he turned on state highway 180," Dan said.

"Did he switch off his phone?"

"No, it went out of range."

Ann divided her attention between driving and the roads branching off 180. The only major southbound route was highway 17, which crossed the Potomac near Brunswick, Maryland, becoming Virginia 287. Ann took the 180 exit and continued for a few miles, but Dan failed to pick up Hosseini's phone. She finally pulled over and stopped.

"Where do you think he was going?" Dan asked.

"Gotta be his secret lab."

Ann turned the truck around and started back to Frederick.

"Man, you really freaked out that Foster dude," Sully said. He and John were standing behind the Learjet's flight deck, crouching so they could see through the windshield. There, hunkered down on the Antietam Aviation tarmac, waited an air force MH-53 Pave Low, its long rotor blades moving slightly in the wind. Washington Center had notified them of their reception, so it wasn't a complete surprise.

"Good," Gary said. "We need some action."

Dan stood with Thomas and the Underwoods. Ann held her laptop and was saying something to Zack. Gary turned to Mike.

"We're gonna have to scoot," Gary said.

"I'll see your stuff gets to the motel," Mike said.

"Thanks."

Mike brought the aircraft to a swift stop and shut down the engines. He hurried past Sully and John, opened the cabin door, and waited for them to deplane. Gary rushed down the steps and over to Ann.

"What happened?" he asked.

"After I called the Underwoods, Ken called Zack to set up a meeting. Zack had Nate verify the camera then decided to call Secretary Foster's office. And here we are."

"Good." He glanced at her laptop. "Is that the video?"

"Yes."

"Come on, people," Zack said, raising his voice. "The secretary's waiting."

Secretary Foster watched them enter. Thomas and the Security-Check team filed along the near side of the conference table while Zack and the Underwoods went around to the other.

"Seats, ladies and gentlemen," Foster said. He waited then sat down himself. He raised his voice. "Colonel Young, can you hear me?"

"Yes, Mr. Secretary."

"Good. Would you repeat what you told me earlier?"

"Yes, sir. After Colonel Roberts called, I took a team into the compound and found the camera. We deconned it and the surrounding area then took it out, disassembled it, and dunked it." He paused.

"Go on, Colonel."

"I examined the parts. I concur with what the SecurityCheck people say. It's an aerosol dispensing device controlled by a micro-circuit-actuated solenoid valve."

The secretary turned to Ann. "Please show us the video."

"Yes, Mr. Secretary."

She stood and ran a cable from her laptop to the large-screen monitor at the end of the table. She returned, sat down, and brought up a media player. An image popped up on the monitor. Ann fast-forwarded to where Sherlock revealed the aerosol device then clicked the PLAY button, ending on a freeze-frame close-up.

Secretary Foster looked all around. "I'm convinced," he said. "I think it's obvious Saeed did it, but since he's disappeared—"

"Excuse me, Mr. Secretary," Ann said. "It wasn't Saeed; it was Hamid Momeni, or actually, Ebrahim Hosseini."

"What? Who's that?"

Ann switched to a PowerPoint presentation and gave him a summary of her findings, including images of the records she had found and the article from *Cambridge Evening News*.

Foster turned his gaze on her after she finished. "How can this *be*?" he asked. "*Surely* if he did this, he'd be on the run by now."

"I think you'll find he is," Ann said. She told him about the chase earlier that day.

"I'll check that out." He paused. "But answer me this: How did he make off with the virus?"

Ann shrugged.

"Mr. Secretary, I've been thinking about that for quite some time," Gary said. "It *seems* we can track the virus and vaccine from Brevig *to* the Institute with full accountability."

"You *bet* we can," Nate interjected.

"So it would appear," Gary continued. "And yet the samples turn out to be ordinary swine flu."

"I'm well aware of that, Mr. Nesbitt," Foster said. "What are you getting at?"

"I saw those shipping boxes: heavy-duty steel with lots of padding inside." Gary turned to Ken. "That padding is loose, isn't it?"

"Yes," Ken said. "It's foam plastic chunks you can arrange to fit whatever you're shipping."

"I thought so. I believe Hosseini inserted the swine flu virus and vaccine underneath the padding while he was getting ready for the trip. Then at Brevig he opened the boxes, pulled out the fakes, and slipped the real samples under the padding."

"Wasn't he observed from the window?" Foster asked.

"We couldn't see the sample containers after they entered the shipping box. I saw his hands moving around, but I assumed he was arranging the packing material."

"What about Saeed?" Zack asked. "He was inside the lab."

Gary shook his head. "Saeed was on the other side of the table, so he saw even less than we did. To continue, when we got to the Institute, the swine flu samples got checked into the lab while the 1918 virus remained hidden inside the shipping boxes." Gary looked at Ken. "What happened to those boxes?"

"They got deconned, which you saw, then taken to a storeroom," Ken said.

"How hard would it be to get to them?"

"Unfortunately, not hard at all. That storeroom isn't a secure area."

"Comments, Colonel?" Secretary Foster asked Zack.

"I'd like Colonels Underwood and Young to respond," Zack said. "They're more familiar with our procedures."

Ken glanced at Gary then focused on the secretary. "I think Gary's right. It explains everything."

Silence fell for a few moments. "I agree, I'm sorry to say," Nate said finally. "There's *another* loophole we have to address."

"Later, Colonel," Foster said. "Okay, now where do we stand?"

"Mr. Secretary, I discussed this with my team on the way here," Gary said. "We're looking down the gun barrel. From what I've heard, the terrorist cell has already had enough time to manufacture the virus, and the fact that Hosseini has bugged out seems to confirm it."

"Any chance he knows you're on to him?"

"I don't think so. He was probably making a routine trip to the lab when Dan lost him."

"I see. Of course homeland security will be launching an all-out search, but is there any way *your* team could help?"

"Yes, Mr. Secretary. Dan has Hosseini's mobile phone ID. We could search for it using our command center truck and our UAV."

Secretary Foster nodded. "Do it."

It was almost midnight, and Gary was running on caffeine and adrenaline. Even though he had catnapped on the flight back to Frederick, he was still running a considerable sleep deficit. He had the UAV's controller propped up on the workbench between John and Ann, its transmitter connected by cable to an exterior antenna. A thousand feet overhead, Skyhook flew parallel north-south tracks over western Virginia.

Sully had driven them south on Virginia 287 to where it dead-ended into state highway 7 near Purcellville. Then they turned north and gradually began working their way westward, checking out all the meandering roads and trails.

"Hey, dudes, coin-flip dead ahead," Sully said.

Gary glanced up at the monitor above Dan's station and saw it was the T intersection where Bolington Road ran into Picnic Woods Road. Ann rotated between several GPS map views on her laptop.

"Hang a right," she said.

"Roger that, hacker dude."

Gary turned back to the UAV controller. The low-light camera provided an excellent bird's-eye view. Skyhook finally reached the Potomac, and Gary turned it around for the next southern pass. A few minutes later, a familiar sight crawled onto his LCD display.

"Skyhook is overhead," he said.

"How are you doing on fuel?" John asked.

"Getting low. I'll land on the next pass."

"You're the pilot."

It took almost fifteen minutes for the UAV to reach Harry Byrd Highway, turn, and head back north, offset a mile from its previous pass. Gary felt drowsiness beginning to steal over him.

"Any coffee left?" he asked.

John shook the thermos. "Yep." He removed the cap and filled Gary's foam cup.

"Thanks." Gary took a long sip and waited for the caffeine to do its thing.

A shrill electronic bell sounded.

Dan sat upright and scooted up close to the workbench. "Bingo! You have him."

Gary looked down at the display. "Don't see anything yet."

"Turn left ten degrees," Dan said.

Gary came to the new course and glanced at the fuel gauge. It showed empty, but surely there had to be *some* left. Several minutes later, a large house came into view. Four cars lined the gravel drive, but not a light could be seen.

"That's it," Dan said, looking around.

"Call it in," Gary said.

Dan picked up a mike. "Eagle, this is Star Chamber. We have a fix on Spook; he's in a house off Edgegrove Road. GPS coordinates are 39 degrees 11.558 minutes north, 77 degrees 45.897 minutes west."

"Roger, Star Chamber. Stay clear. I say again, stay clear. Eagle out."

Dan grabbed the mike. "Pull over, Sully."

The truck slowed and stopped.

A red light on the controller flashed, accompanied by a strident buzzer. "Out of gas," Gary said. Although Skyhook could glide quite awhile, the UAV couldn't make it back to the truck.

A heavy thumping sound came from the controller's speakers.

"Slue the camera around," John said.

Gary thumbed a switch until the camera faced north. A Black-hawk helicopter was clattering south at treetop level. Gary panned around to the south. Over a mile away, several cars were racing north on Woodgrove Road.

"They're going to spook the terrorists," Dan said.

Gary panned the camera back to the house. A dark figure dashed out the front and across the wooded fields heading south.

Gary lost him almost immediately.

"Dan, warn Eagle."

"Eagle, this is Star Chamber," Dan said. "Suspect heading south on foot. Over." There was no response. He keyed the mike again. "Eagle, this is Star Chamber, come in, Eagle. Over." After trying several more times, Dan turned to Gary. "Looks like we're out of the loop."

"That's just great," Gary said. A few minutes later, he landed Skyhook in an open field.

For the second time in twenty-four hours, Gary and the Security-Check team sat beside Thomas Brooks in the same conference room. Across from them, Zack Roberts was USAMRIID's sole representative. An unshaven Secretary Foster commanded the head of the table, this time wearing a wrinkled suit and loosened tie.

"To bring us all up to speed, joint teams under the department of homeland security raided a bioterrorism lab this morning. We have arrested five suspects, however Hosseini escaped. Colonel Roberts, how is the cleanup proceeding?"

"Mr. Secretary, my personnel, commanded by Colonel Ken Underwood, have secured the lab. I talked to Major Carol Underwood a few minutes ago, and she's quite certain we have containment. Of course, our personnel will decontaminate the house thoroughly and the surrounding area just to be on the safe side."

"You're *sure* it was a functioning lab?"

"*Absolutely*, sir, and very well designed. Hosseini really knew what he was doing; which is not surprising, given his background."

"Anything else?"

"Major Underwood believes Hosseini escaped with a vial of live virus because her team found a rack with one missing slot. Also, she found drawings of a compact aerosol device. I think we have to assume that Hosseini has the means of unleashing a pandemic."

Gary shuddered. In his mind, he saw a new terrorism: Instead of quick, violent attacks leaving scores dead, silent assaults of tiny parasites spreading deadly infection throughout America and around the world, killing millions.

"I have one more thing to add," Foster said slowly. "Less than an hour ago, a man was found murdered on Woodgrove Road. Based on tire tracks at the scene and the proximity to the lab, I think we have to assume Hosseini now has a car." He stopped and looked at Gary. "The big question, of course, is what will he do next? Your thoughts, Mr. Nesbitt."

Gary sent up an arrow prayer as chaotic thoughts swirled through his brain. Then he felt a calming influence that he recognized but no clear guidance.

"Mr. Nesbitt," Secretary Foster prompted.

"Mr. Secretary, the best way to spread a virus is to infect travelers. I think the target will be a major transportation hub, preferably one close to a center of power. Washington, D.C., would be perfect. The airports and the Metro would be prime targets."

"Okay, my people will direct law enforcement accordingly." He paused. "I want your team involved, as well. Will you do it?"

"Yes, Mr. Secretary," Gary said.

"Thank you. Where do you think he'll strike?"

Gary closed his eyes and thought. This was worse than a needle in a haystack; there were so many targets to choose from. He considered the Washington Metro; that would certainly strike into the vitals of the federal government. But then he thought about how many terrorist attacks had targeted air travel."

"I'd say one of the airports."

"Homeland security will be covering them all, of course. Which one do you want?"

Assuming he was right, Gary knew the attack could come at

Dulles, Reagan National, or Baltimore. Each one offered *thousands* of passengers—potential worldwide carriers of the deadly 1918 virus. Which would Hosseini choose? Then a very clear picture came into his mind. It was an immense glass building with an upswept roof. He opened his eyes.

"Dulles International," he said.

CHAPTER 30

Gary stood near the central ticketing counter inside the upper level of Dulles International Airport's main terminal. He wore a snug skullcap that made him bald on top with a fringe of hair around the sides. Foam appliances gave him sagging jowls, while makeup provided a substantial beard shadow. He removed the lid from a trash container, lifted out the plastic liner, and dumped it into his cleaning cart. After installing a new liner, he wiped the back of his hand across his forehead and surreptitiously scanned the terminal. Off to the right, tall glass windows sloped outward, soaring up to the lofty, curved ceiling. Traffic was light; however, he knew the volume of travelers would swell as the peak travel time approached. He turned his head to make sure no one was near.

"Star Chamber, this is Tidy Man," Gary said. "Status check."

"This is Star Chamber. Stuntman and Hacker are on patrol. All cameras and sensors are in place. Artist reports he is nearly ready."

"Roger, Star Chamber."

Gary turned his cleaning cart around and meandered toward

the west end of the terminal. Just past the escalators, an African-American man in Dockers and a sport shirt stood atop a tall ladder adjusting a sign suspended between two large models, the Montgolfier Brothers' hot-air balloon on the left and the space shuttle *Enterprise* on the right. The man had a full beard and wore a beret, and Gary recognized John only because he had helped with the disguise. The sign, ostensibly, advertised the Smithsonian National Air and Space Museum Steven F. Udvar-Hazy Center, which was adjacent to the airport.

Gary walked past without looking up. He emptied another trash container, straightened up, and continued working his way along at a leisurely pace. Near the end of the terminal, he turned around, facing the broad expanse of ticket counters and escalators. On his left, a few early passengers pushed through the doors between the panoramic windows.

Ebrahim Hosseini stepped out of the car and started walking. Dulles International had been his assigned target from the beginning, a fact not altered when the Great Satan had discovered his secret lab. The far-flung simultaneous attacks originally envisioned were now impossible, but a single outbreak from the American capital could still sweep the world. It was his fervent wish that it do so.

Hosseini entered Cub Run Stream Valley Park and, after following a trail a few hundred feet, turned aside and approached a large rock. He looked around and saw he was alone, it being a little early for hikers and bike riders. He stooped down and lifted a stone. He breathed a sigh of relief; the plastic-covered package was still there. He picked it up and again looked all around. There wasn't another person in sight.

He stepped behind some bushes off the trail, opened the bag, and removed a black burka, head scarf, and veil. He pulled the tentlike burka over his head and clothes then arranged the head scarf and attached the veil. Last he carefully placed what looked like a can of hair spray inside a shoulder bag. He ran his fingers over his face. It still felt smooth, and of course his mustache was gone. He looked down at his athletic shoes. Although they looked out of place to him, he knew that many American Muslim women wore them. *Corrupted by the American infidels*, he thought to himself.

Hosseini stepped out of his hiding place and followed the trail east out of the park. Off to his left, an American Airlines 757 growled overhead on departure from Dulles International. Soon he was out in the open, and he spotted the Hampton Inn Dulles South. He covered the short distance quickly, and as he approached, the airport shuttle bus entered the drive and stopped by the lobby entrance. Hosseini smiled. Everything was going according to plan. He rounded the back of the bus, walked straight up to the open doors, and climbed aboard.

"Tidy Man, this is Star Chamber. Stuntman and Hacker are passing the east escalators."

Gary heard a faint whining sound. A large electric cart came into view and turned toward him.

"Roger, Star Chamber. I have them."

The driver wore a black uniform, white shirt, and a hat that looked vaguely nautical. With a liberal application of makeup and a full beard and thick mustache, Sully was unrecognizable. This disguise had been a compromise, since Sully had refused to shave off his mustache. The cart continued past without any sign of recognition from either the driver or passenger. The latter appeared to be an elderly woman holding a cane.

Gary picked up his broom and dustpan and returned to his work while doubts swirled around inside his head. Were they in the right place, and if so, would they be able to spot Hosseini in time to stop him? Despite their careful preparations and the team's well-honed skills, he knew they could very well fail. Again his thoughts returned to the horrors he had seen in Alaska, and he had to force himself to concentrate on his job. They would do their best, which was all that anyone could ask.

The shuttle-bus driver was taking his time, which was fine with Hosseini since he knew that Dulles wouldn't reach peak travel time for another half hour or so. But even so, there should be ample victims to carry the deadly virus worldwide as well as deep inside the heart of the American capital. He smiled at the thought.

The driver took the airport off-ramp, which swept around in a long left-hand loop. After merging with the traffic, he followed the access road around to the south and entered Saarinen Circle. Hosseini took a deep breath; he was almost there. The bus came around the circle and stopped at the west end of the main terminal. Hosseini waited while the other passengers hurried past then got up and made his way outside. He stopped when he reached the sidewalk and looked all around. He felt inside his shoulder bag to make sure the aerosol can's nozzle was positioned against the camouflaged vent. He was ready.

"Tidy Man, this is Star Chamber, I have traffic," Dan said. "Two cabs dropped off fares near the center of the terminal: a man in a suit and a woman with two children. At the west end, a bus just drove off. Looks like business commuters; five men and two women, no, make that three women. One of the women is wearing Muslim clothing."

"This is Tidy Man," Gary said. "You mean a burka?"

"Roger, Tidy Man."

"See anything suspicious?" Gary knew he might be overreacting since he had already seen several Muslims, both men and women.

"Not sure, Tidy Man. The woman in the burka is looking around the traffic circle. Wait, now she's coming inside."

Gary felt a jolt of adrenaline. "What does she look like, Star Chamber?"

"Wait one, I'm training a door camera on her. Man, I can't tell much with that getup she has on, but she's tall."

"How tall?"

"Looks close to six feet."

"Stuntman, this is Tidy Man. Get in position."

"Roger that, Tidy Man," Sully replied.

"Artist, this is Tidy Man. Stand by."

"Roger, Tidy Man," John said. He reached up and made a minor adjustment to the hanging sign.

"Tidy Man, this is Star Chamber! It's a man! I got a real tight close-up over the top of his veil and saw whiskers. Also, the magnetometer registered an iron mass in line with her—I mean *his* bag."

"Roger. This is Tidy Man. Stand by, all."

"Artist, roger."

"Stuntman, roger."

"Hacker, roger."

Gary angled his cleaning cart to the inside of the hot-air balloon model. Up ahead, Sully drove toward him on the outside. Gary felt the hairs on the back of his neck rise as he heard footsteps overtaking him. It wouldn't be long now.

Dan held the mike close to his lips as his eyes roved over multiple monitors. Sully's cart and Gary had the target hemmed in so he had to walk right past John's ladder. The timing looked perfect. Dan hoped it really *was* Hosseini and that the plan worked. If it didn't. . .

The person in the black burka passed the ladder at the same time the electric cart whined by. An almost inaudible *ping* sounded overhead. The target's head began to tilt upward. Ann leaped off the cart and plowed into the man, pushing him under a large plastic bag streaking down from inside the balloon display. Gary leaped forward and stopped the man from falling, jerking his hands away as a heavy iron hoop enveloped the target. The ring hit the floor with a crash. Gary tackled the black figure, carrying him down.

"Shove his feet inside!" Gary shouted.

Sully appeared at his side, grabbed the man's ankles, and shoved hard. The black-clad target shot several more feet into the slick plastic envelope.

Gary wrapped his arms around the struggling man. "Seal it!" he ordered.

John brought a heavy sealing iron across the thick plastic along the bottom. "Hold on!" he said.

"I have him!" Gary said.

John ran the iron repeatedly across the end of the bag, making absolutely sure he had an airtight seal.

"Ann—decon!"

She grabbed a large garden sprayer off the electric cart and sprayed the envelope with a powerful bleach solution.

"Star Chamber, this is Tidy Man," Gary said. "Alert Eagle."

"Roger, that. Already have."

Moments later an approaching siren sounded outside.

"I'll hold him," John said.

Gary waited until John had a good grip then scrambled around to the top of the bag. There, through the clear plastic, he saw the man's face since his veil had been torn away in the fall. It was Hosseini, all right, recognizable even without his mustache. Gary looked down toward the man's waist and saw the top of a can peeking out of the bag. Hosseini's mouth was moving; he was gasping for breath.

Terminal doors crashed open and two men in orange Racal suits entered at a hobbled run, carrying a biosafety level-four bubble-stretcher. They set it down beside the captive and helped Gary and John lift him up on it. John held on until the soldiers could strap Hosseini down. After they finished, the men took their captive out.

No sooner were they out the door than more orange-suited soldiers entered, some carrying additional bubble-stretchers. Others fanned out, decontaminating the surrounding area with a disinfecting chemical fog. The passengers and airline employees needed no urging to keep their distance. One of the soldiers approached. Gary looked through the clear faceplate and recognized Carol Underwood. She waved toward the stretchers.

"Come on, Gary," she said, her voice attenuated by the Racal's blower. "It's not over yet. We have to get your team back to the Institute."

Then Gary understood. They couldn't be sure the virus hadn't escaped. And if it *had*. . . Gary turned to Ann, John, and Sully. "You heard her," he said. "Get on the stretchers."

They all looked stricken. Gary went to the nearest stretcher and sat down. Two soldiers helped him lie down then enclosed the stretcher in a clear plastic biocontainment bubble. Gary looked out at the cordon of orange-suited soldiers and beyond them to the cowering civilians as he was carried out the door to the waiting ambulance. *All I need is a lily*, he thought as he looked down at his hands clasped over his chest. Then the realization hit home: If he *had* been exposed, his next means of conveyance might indeed be a casket.

Gary looked out through the Slammer's heavy windows and saw Major Carol Underwood approaching in her crisp working uniform.

Her broad smile was everything he had hoped for.

"Good news," her voice said through the intercom. "Tests show your team *did* contain the virus: Hosseini released it, but nothing got out. So I've ordered the hospital personnel to release you."

"Great," Gary managed. Relief swept over him; they had in fact dodged the bullet. He sent up a silent prayer of thanks. Then his mind drifted back to one final question. "What happened to Hosseini?" He saw her face harden.

"He suffocated before we could get him into the Slammer," she said. "There was no way we could get him out until we had him safe inside, and by then it was too late."

"I see," Gary said, although he wasn't at all sure how accurate that statement was. What had happened to the Iranian terrorist seemed fitting—poetic justice some might say, but ultimately it was God's business.

Gary turned to John's smiling face. "I'm for getting out of here."

"I'm right behind you," John said.

CHAPTER 31

T hank you for the invitation," Gary said.

"You're welcome," Secretary Brad Foster said. "The president said he wanted to talk with you before you went back."

The receptionist opened the door. "The president will see you now," she said. After they entered, she closed it.

President Alex Vance stood in front of his Oval Office desk with a photographer.

"Come on over here," he said with a friendly smile. "We have to have our pictures made."

The president, obviously used to the drill, stood to one side while Secretary Foster took the other flank. Gary, John, and the Security-Check team formed the center. The photographer took shots from the center and each side then scooted out.

"Please be seated," the president said, motioning toward sofas and chairs arranged around the presidential seal woven into the thick carpet.

Gary and John sat on one sofa while Ann and Sully picked the other. Dan sat in one of the chairs in front of the fireplace. Alex

Vance and Brad Foster sat in chairs facing them. The president looked at Gary.

"Secretary Foster briefed me on all that you and your team did. On behalf of the American people, I *thank* you for your courage and sacrifices. Much of what happened can't be told, but please believe me when I say *I'll* never forget it." He paused and shook his head. "America really *is* in a war against terrorism, but it gives me hope when I see private citizens coming forward to meet the challenge."

"Thank you, Mr. President," Gary said. "Those are kind words, but I believe the only reason we're sitting here is because *God* answers prayers. Looking back on all that happened and how it worked out, I can't explain it any other way."

The president's smile projected understanding. "I'm glad to hear you say that. I was praying, too." After a few moments, he turned to Ann. "I've *also* been told that none of our computer systems are safe from Ms. O'Brien. I sure am glad you're on *our* side."

Ann smiled. "Just doing what homeland security hired us to do."

"I'm mighty glad you did." He looked at Sully. "I've heard that Mr. Sullivan goes by 'Sully' or 'the kid' and that he can drive just about anything."

"Uh, yeah, Mr. President."

"And you're a Hollywood stuntman to boot."

"When I'm not working with these dudes, yeah."

"Tell me, what was it like driving an Abrams tank?"

"Oh, it was *awesome*. Totally."

"I *bet* it was." The president turned to Dan. "Now, Mr. Thompson was your communications top hand, operating out of the back of a truck, is that right?"

"Yes, Mr. President."

"That's amazing. I understand some of your gadgets stirred up *quite* a ruckus among our techies."

Dan's face broke out in a rare smile. "It's really a joint effort.

John makes most of our equipment."

"I hear you." The president turned to John. "And last but definitely not least, the *amazing* Mr. Mason, co-owner of Security-Check *and* the world's foremost gadgeteer." He snapped his fingers. "Say, what was that robot thing Brad told me about?"

"You mean Sherlock, Mr. President?"

"That's it. Isn't that how you found out what caused the outbreak?"

"Yes, Mr. President. Sir, since you brought it up. . ."

"I don't think the president wants to hear about that," Gary said. "He has more important things to worry about."

Alex Vance looked from John to Gary and back. "What happened?"

"We had to leave Sherlock behind," John said. "We were told they were impounding him because of security." He sat forward. "They said we would be compensated, but I'd rather have Sherlock back, if you know what I mean."

The president leaned back in his chair. "I know *exactly* what you mean." He paused and turned to Secretary Foster. "I think we ought to do something about this."

Secretary Foster flushed. "I'll take care of it right away, Mr. President."

John's face lit up. "*Thank* you, Mr. President."

President Vance smiled. "I'm glad I could help." He looked at Gary. "Has the government met all its other obligations?"

"Yes, Mr. President."

A door opened, and the receptionist stuck her head in. "The congressional delegation is here to see you, sir."

The president and his guests stood. Gary appreciated the private visit, but he was also looking forward to getting home to California.

"Now you all have a nice trip home," President Vance said as he walked them to the door.

"I'm sure we will," Gary said. "Thank you, Mr. President."

Outside the office, Gary and John fell into step as they followed the White House staffer.

"Brother Gary?" John said.

"Yes, Brother John?"

"I sure am grateful for *all* the help we received."

Gary looked at him and saw what he meant. "So am I."

If you enjoyed

BREVIG MISSION

PLAGUE

check out Frank Simon's

The Jewel in the Crown

Gary Nesbitt and John Mason, leaders of SecurityCheck, Inc., have earned the job of a lifetime—testing the defenses of the Tower of London. The two Christians are hired to attempt a break-in to steal the Queen Mother's crown and see how well current security systems are working. With the help of computer expert Ann O'Brien, a new believer with a checkered past, they succeed in their mission—only to find themselves conned out of the priceless artifact. Now the team must steal back the crown or face long years in jail for pulling off the biggest heist in Britain's history.

Available wherever Christian books are sold.